The Fate of Kings & Queens

Joseph S. Samaniego

THE FATE
OF
KINGS AND QUEENS

A LEGEND OF THE CAROLYNGIAN AGE

JOSEPH S SAMANIEGO

Copyright © 2021 Joseph Samaniego Smith.

THE FATE OF KINGS AND QUEENS

Written by Joseph S. Samaniego.

Published by Joseph S. Samaniego, 2020

Mage's Moon Publishing

This is a work of fiction. Names, characters, businesses, places, events and incidents are either the products of the author's imagination or used in a fictitious manner. Any resemblance to actual persons, living or dead, or actual events is purely coincidental.

No part of this book may be reproduced or transmitted in any form or by any means, electronic or mechanical, including photocopying, recording, or by any information storage and retrieval system, without permission in writing from the publisher.

Maps and cover created by Joseph S. Samaniego

Also by Joseph S Samaniego

A Legend of the Carolyngian Age Series

Chronological Order:

In the Time of Standing Stones

The Far - Off Kingdom

In The Court of Dreams and Shadows

The Fate of Kings and Queens

The Queen of War

The Dead Queen's War

Separate within the Series

Heroes of the Carolyngian Age

To my inspirations, my wife and two daughters; the strong and fierce women who helped inspire the Amazons of the Carolyngian Age.

Also, thank you to my mother for being the first to show me what it means to be a true warrior.

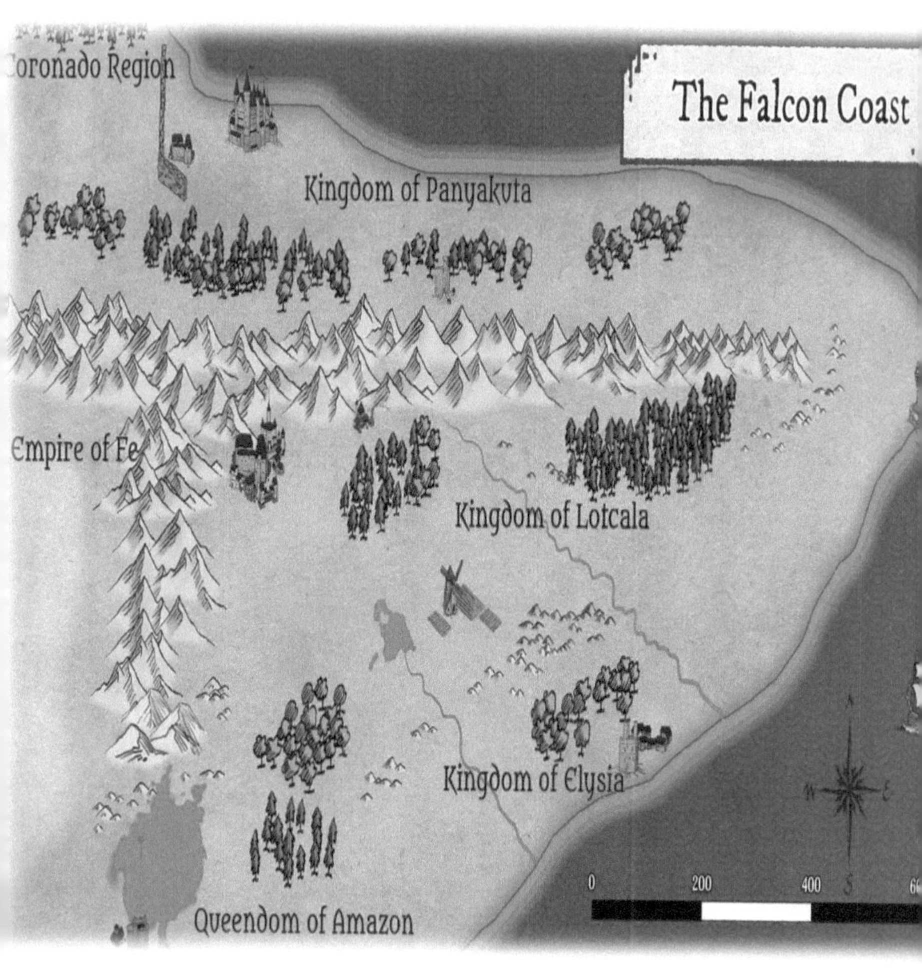
The Falcon Coast
Coronado Region
Kingdom of Panyakuta
Empire of Fe
Kingdom of Lotcala
Kingdom of Elysia
Queendom of Amazon
0
200
400
600
N
E
S
W

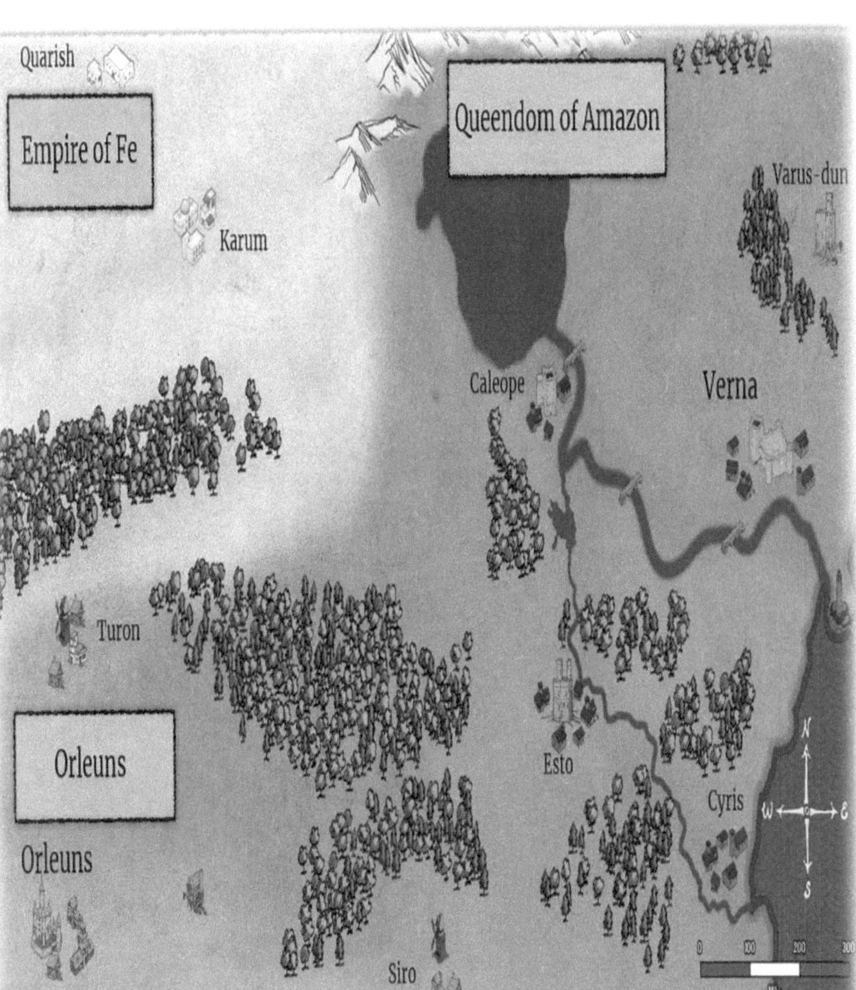

Quarish
Empire of Fe
Karum
Queendom of Amazon
Varus-dun
Caleope
Verna
Turon
Esto
Orleuns
Cyris
Orleuns
Siro
N
W
E
S
0 100 200 300
Miles

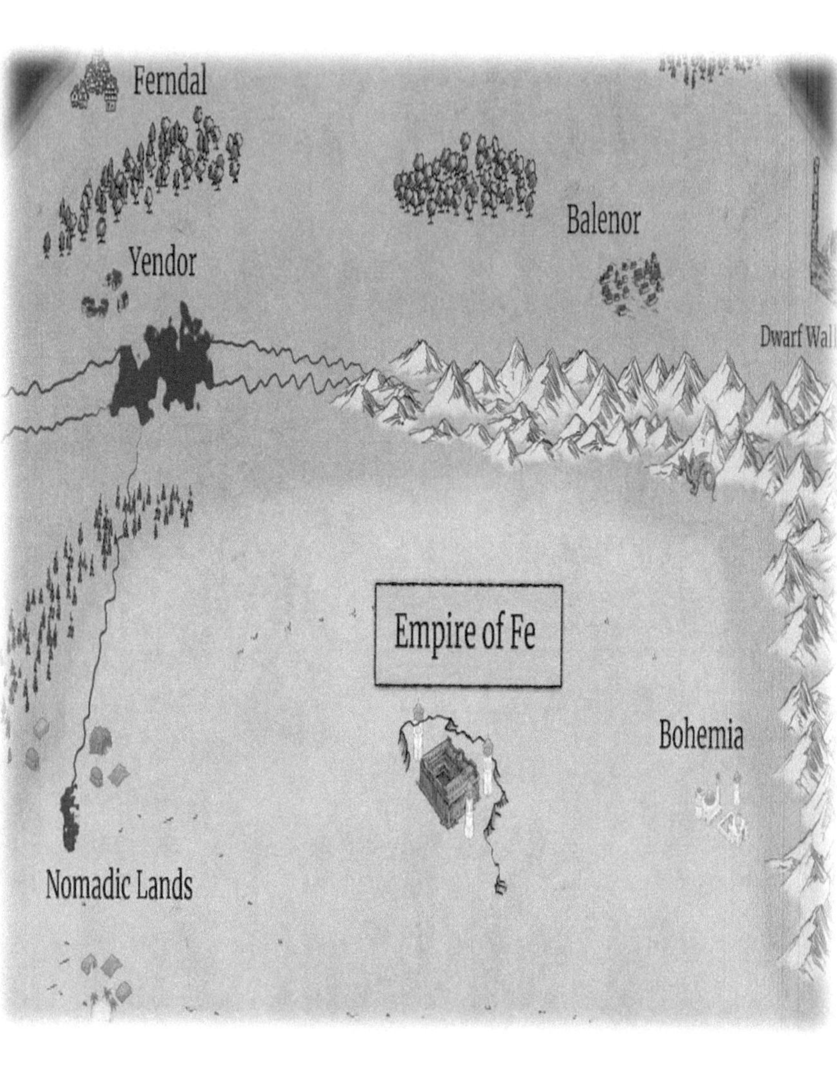

Ferndal
Balenor
Yendor
Dwarf Wall
Empire of Fe
Bohemia
Nomadic Lands

Table of Contents

The Herd

How does one of the strongest nations in the world create such strong warriors? They breed them, break them and then remold them into the Legion.

Five young girls, around the age of twelve, joined four hundred and eighty-seven other girls of the same age. They each carried a blanket and one linen woven sack with three loaves of wheat bread, a small wheel of cheese and a waterskin. These were their rations for the week. They slept on a blanket that was laid on the stone floor. Up to fifty in a bunkhouse. Throughout the entire fortress there were forty-five bunkhouses. Young girls from different families, a few nobles and many more from the labor class. These were the new grunts and this would be their home for six years. This was the Herd of the Paideia, the elite military training for all Amazonian women.

Thunder echoed across the stone floor in the dimly lit hall of the bunkhouse. A funny name considering that there were no bunks. It was an empty space with only a handful of chamber pots off to each side. The girls all walked in, eyed by the grizzled stare of an older veteran. They could see her eyes, though one was discolored from an old injury, through the corinth helm but not much else of her features. The veteran's stare, however, was as cold and unloving as any they would ever know.

Each of the girls made their way to their assigned blanket on the floor and settled in. A few had taken to getting to know one another as children do; sharing stories and exchanging pleasant greetings. However, most just sat in their new surroundings, taking it all in. Soon they would all be handed bowls of a gruel made of oats and barley but that would be it for that day.

It stunk, but it was now home so they had to make the best of it. It was also on purpose that the place felt dirty and smelled rank. This was the training center of the fiercest warriors that the Central Continent had ever known, perhaps the world. The harsh conditions, including the smell, were meant to toughen them up. Here they would learn how to be part of a military cohort, how to live and drill as a unit. It was also the place where they would learn how to fight and kill without fear.

The five girls were assigned blankets near one another. There they stayed silent for a few hours, just sitting and observing. Finally, after they had finished their gruel one spoke up.

"What families are you from?" She asked to the two girls across from her, sitting on the stone floor. "I'm Althaea of the Coalemos Family." She stated proudly.

"I'm Melantho Laskaris." One of the girls said.

The other girl looked over to Melantho, sitting on her left. "I'm Mestra Pappas." Mestra looked to another girl on her right. "What's your name?"

The girl was sitting with her legs crossed and staring into space when Mestra asked a second time.

"What's your name?" Mestra said again.

The young girl snapped out of her thoughts. "Sorry, I'm Ino."

"Ino what?" Althaea asked.

"Selinofoto." Ino answered.

Althaea smirked. "Selinofoto? That's a laborer's name. You're a laborer?"

"What of it?" Ino jumped up, her anger rising. Althaea joined her and the two were only an inch apart.

"I don't think we're supposed to fight." Melantho said, standing up and walking up to the two girls. "Besides who cares if she's a laborer?"

"I care. This filth is here with us. I'll bet her mother is a *six year*." Althaea taunted.

"Take it back!" Ino said.

"No!" Althaea replied but in a second Ino lunged at the girl and the two were throwing punches at one another, brawling on the floor.

Other girls from around the bunkhouse came around and cheered on the spectacle. It didn't take long for blood to fly as Ino landed a punch onto Althaea's nose. Althaea flipped Ino before landing on the girl and returning the blow with one of her own.

Just then another girl came over and pulled the two apart by their cotton chitons.

"That's enough!" She shouted. Others protested, but the unknown girl was undeterred. "We're here to learn how to be sisters."

"I'm not sisters with some labor whore's daughter!" Althaea shouted.

"You are now!" The mysterious girl said. "Now get in your bedrolls and shut up!"

The two girls begrudgingly obeyed, but they still whispered insults under their breath.

The next day provided little relief. A ten-mile run and carrying the gear of older recruits was now part of their lives. The week went on much like that. Melantho tried to play peace maker while Mestra attempted to get the mysterious girl to open up about who she was. Althaea and Ino stayed away from one another.

Until one day when a few older girls burst into the bunkhouse.

"Here we are, sisters! The grunts!" The leader of a group of four older girls shouted. "Such little things they are."

"What are *you* doing here?" The Mysterious girl said, standing to face the older girls. "This is our house, Cecilia!"

The room was quiet. Everyone heard the name, but many could not believe that it was her.

One of the older girls stepped up and smacked the mysterious girl across her face. "You better respect her. This is your crown princess, grunt!"

The young girl picked herself off the floor. "We don't have titles here."

The older girls laughed. "You believe that?"

"You better hope I do, because I'm Princess Syrena, second daughter of Queen Saria, you pissant idiot!" The Mysterious girl revealed.

For a moment everyone in the bunkhouse breathed in one collective gasp. The one that had been so quiet after interfering with Ino and Althaea was royal?

Princess Cecilia stepped in front of her friend. "No titles, little sister." She said before smacking Syrena across the face.

"No titles? That's great!" Ino shouted before leaping on Cecilia and landing three punches before being kicked off by Cecilia's friend. The streetwise girl has crept in unseen and now was able to strike.

Syrena jumped back into the fight, as did Melantho and Mestra. Each trading blows with an older girl. Cecilia returned to the action, but she couldn't do much damage to anyone before Althaea tackled her to the ground. The younger girls fought their best, giving the older ones bloody noses and at least one broken jaw, but eventually the older group got the upper hand.

Guards rushed in and pulled the group apart. Looking at the scene the adults seemed to be proud of the younger girls.

"You four know you can't be in here!" One guard shouted. "Stables for a week." She ordered as the punishment. The head guard looked to the younger group. "Shithouse. Tonight." She said, before cracking a smile.

The other guards grabbed Syrena, Melantho, Ino, Mestra and Althaea by their chitons and led them outside.

An hour later the five girls were scrubbing the back, exterior wall of one of the few outhouses in the fortress. It was a rank building with multiple outhouse facilities, but it all emptied below. Each was scrubbing a portion to keep the wood from rotting too soon. In reality, it was a punishment to show that you could be punished anytime and with the worst possible labor that no warrior should feel above doing.

"Sorry." Syrena said.

"What for?" Mestra asked, looking to the princess.

"Getting us punished and not telling you all who I was."

Ino laughed. "That was a great fight. I haven't had one like that since the other day with Althaea." Ino looked to the Althaea next to her and smiled. "Nice tackle on the princess by the way."

"Thanks." Althaea smiled. "That was my second fight actually."

Ino touched her jaw. "Fooled me."

Melantho smiled. "I knew you two would be friends, eventually."

"Yeah, just took us beating up on the crown princess to do it." Mestra laughed. The others joined in the joke with glee.

All the girls stopped scrubbing and looked at the work.

"I think this looks good." Syrena said.

"Definitely better now that the shit is gone." Althaea remarked.

Just then, a lever clicked in the outhouse and a door underneath the floor opened, dropping several mounds of excrement by the five girls' feet. They all jumped back and looked at it. The wall they had cleaned was now freshly covered.

"Son of a whore!" Ino cried out.

"Yep, I'm done." Mestra said, tossing her scrub brush and walking off.

Four years later in a training yard, Syrena stood alongside her four closest friends and sixty other legion recruits as sixty-five other recruits stood opposite of them. In a flash they charged and banged shields off their opposing recruits to force the others to back down. It wasn't simply to push the recruit opposite of you, but to push while your sisters pushed alongside of you. It was paced and everyone had to be of one movement. Each warrior had to step together or the whole line would crumple.

Syrena's clasis, or military group, was the best. Each could sense the others' movements just as they began to move and this allowed them to move in kind. Give up a foot so that a sister could regroup and gain two feet once she was ready. Time and again, Syrena scored a victory.

From a dais above the training field, the Legion Commander Honora watched with her cohort of officers. It was rare for the commander to be within the fort but she had to see the now famous Princess Syrena.

"She's good but aggressive to a fault." One officer said. "She leaves herself open on the left flank."

"Her stance is unorthodox. It causes her sisters to have adjust to her." Another officer commented.

"She's seeing what you two do not; an opening. Her sisters follow her lead because they trust her with their lives." Honora replied to their skepticism.

One of the officers gave an audible 'hmpf'. "She's a princess. Of course they follow her. If her clasis fails then they'll take the blame."

Honora wasn't convinced. "I've seen legionnaires following a bad leader. This isn't that. She proved that years ago when she first arrived. I've watched her with great interest and I'd say that she has earned their trust through her willingness to put herself in harm's way. Why else would she be at the point?" She looked over to a third officer. "Sara, why is she even here? She's as noble born as you can be and she didn't join the cavalry. Why?"

Sara was the captain in charge of the recruits and oversaw all of their training. Though she was the lower ranking member of the group standing on the dais, Sara was often sought for her thoughts. If anyone knew about a particular recruit's reasoning's for doing anything it would be Captain Sara.

Sara stepped up to Honora. "She chose to stay when offered a place in the cavalry. Syrena said she wouldn't leave her sisters behind."

Honora grinned. "And your take on her movements along with her sisters?"

Sara smiled. "They are one unit. She bleeds for her clasis and they bleed for her. Those beside her and behind her know no other step but hers and she rewards them with victory. Their minds are in tuned with hers and she guides them with slight nuances. When they are in the phalanx they are one person, the perfect legion."

Honora nodded. "You see, a legion cohort doesn't fight like a shieldwall in Lotcala. Though, they are strong and united. A cohort must move as the leader moves and be of one mind. That way the phalanx will be unbreakable. Syrena has drilled that into them. That unorthodox stance, the opening and the aggression are all on purpose. She pushes her sisters and drives them because every battlefield will be different. They have to adapt and it looks like they are doing that flawlessly."

"Do you think that you might be putting too much stock in this princess?" One of the officers asked.

Honora shook her head. "This one will command one day and when that day comes, our enemies will know the unstoppable might of the Amazons!"

The Siege of Varus-dun

Boulders, lit with burning oil, flew from trebuchets and mangonels, crashing against the walls of the fortress of Varus-dun. The massive, but ancient, border stronghold was the last gasp for the Elysian army. The once mighty kingdom was now a shell of its former self, ineffective rulers were often detrimental to most kingdoms. Elysia had yet to recover from some of the worst leaders in history.

King Ahab III broke a peace lasting nearly two-hundred years over a perceived insult by King Liam of Lotcala. Ahab, the Elysian king with little more than a toddler's temper, attacked the province of Antei. That act goaded Liam to retaliate. King Ahab failed to consider one of the most important factors in war: who had greater numbers. In this war, King Liam of Lotcala did.

The Empire of Fe, a loose network of horse-riding nomads and warlords answering to one leader, and the Queendom of Amazon answered Liam's call for aid. With the might of the three nations, Elysia went on the defensive. Soon a peace treaty was brokered with Fe and then several months later another treaty with Lotcala. The Queendom of Amazon, however, was left out of talks.

Elysia held little regard for the female leaders of the queendom, and this meant that their peace would have to be won. Queen Saria smiled at the thought. She led a queendom that bred some of the fiercest warriors that the world had ever known. For over a thousand years, the sole occupation of the Amazons was war!

In the year since the war began, the Amazons had been on a warpath, tearing through the southwestern territories of Elysia. Queen Saria invaded north from the capital in Verna, while Crown Princess Cecilia had taken the cavalry further northeast and flanked Elysia. Cecilia was not one to run from battle, leading her soldiers deep into Elysia before turning to the west. A path of devastation followed Cecilia. The princess left nothing behind her, including prisoners.

Princess Syrena brought her legion in through the sea, landing south of Elysia's capital of Gib and burning the countryside before moving south. Her goal was to put fear into the populace. However, she would not put innocent bystanders to the sword.

The younger princess was the commander of Amazon's famed Legion. There were similar factions in the militaries of many nations, but in Amazon there was only one. One legion for one queendom.

At the time of the invasion, Lotcala was driving south against Elysia and was close to Gib. This allowed Syrena to move the legion south to rendezvous with her mother and sister, choking Elysia into submission. King Ahab started the war, no one else had asked for it. Therefore, there was nothing to gain from it except a means to an end.

Even as warriors and knights from within the fort came out to fight, Cecilia's cavalry rode them down with a deadly effectiveness. Warriors clashed in the dark of night, the moon shrouded by the smoke of burning fires. A night lit only by the fires that burned upon the Elysian fort. The bundles of flaming wood, oil and stones lit the night sky in a yellowish haze, soaring to dizzying heights at tremendous speeds. With each pass of the Amazonian cavalry, soldiers could see Cecilia in the yellowish light, smiling with joy.

In another part of the camp, legionnaires lined up ready to march on the defenders. Once the wall was weakened, the order would go out for a larger assault, an assault that would dismantle the entire fort. Other units of legionnaires were fighting on the ground as defenders rushed to push the Amazons back. Some engagements away from the fort occupied the Amazons, but the legion was strong and ready with fresh warriors to relieve those that had been in the toughest of the fighting.

Syrena walked behind the trebuchets and made her way to the legion's command tent. She wanted a report from her second in command, Ino.

Ino, a close friend of Syrena's, commanded the siege artillery of mangonels and trebuchets as a Prefect of the Legion. Like all the queendom's warriors, Ino was a veteran of the Amazonian Herd, the corps of soldiers in training during the mandatory Paideia. For all female Amazons, and the lucky few men that would be chosen, the Paideia was the proving grounds for young warriors. Pass the Paideia, nicknamed Herd for the way the recruits were moved around like cattle, and you would be accepted into a cohort of the legion or in the cavalry for no less than six years, afterwards further military or economic opportunities opened up. Fail the Paideia and you were shunned, forced into the levy or conscripted into gleaner regiment carrying the dead off the field.

Syrena, Ino and three others, nicknamed the Furies, came out of that grueling school as bonded sisters and for the Amazons, no bond was greater save one; the bond between mother and daughter.

"The queen wants those walls broken by dawn." Syrena said, walking into the tent.

Ino was standing over maps of the fortification and the outlying areas. Her fists on the table, muscles taunt. Ino had removed her iron cuirass but keep her chiton and greaves on. Her corinth helm, with the blue plume of her rank, sat on a corner of the table.

Without looking up at the princess, the prefect shook her head. "I told your mother that the north face was the weakest. Yet, we are hitting the eastern face, the thickest section of the damned wall!"

"If we had set the siege in the north, we'd have our backs to Gib." Syrena replied with a smile. Ino looked up and eased. The princess grabbed a wine skin and two ceramic cups. "Leaving us vulnerable to attacks from the capital and their reinforcements isn't really the idea in winning a siege." She said pouring the wine and handing a cup to Ino.

Ino sneered at her friend. "Your sister could deal with them. She's been doing a hell of a job so far. Killing many dangerous warriors." She chided, referencing a recent village massacre before sipping the wine.

Syrena drank her wine, but her smile faded. "Speak lightly, Ino." She replied. "Cecilia is the crown princess and our future queen." Syrena sat at the table across from her friend. "Tell me honestly, can those walls break before the sun rises?"

"They better or the queen is likely to send me to the levy." Ino remarked, sitting in a chair.

Syrena unbuckled her cuirass and let it fall to the floor. The iron armor, molded into a muscular form, made a loud thud as it hit the ground. Syrena removed her helm, plumed with black and gold. "I have the last word on that and I'll give you two days." Syrena smiled.

Ino smirked. "Aren't you kind? I'd give my fief for a cohort of witches right now. Mestra's wizards and witches would just lift the damn earth up or send bolts of lightning crashing down on those damn walls!" The prefect sighed.

Syrena smiled. "They're not wizards or witches, they're mages. There is a difference, and that difference is their training. The queen didn't want any more than our usual compliment of healers."

Ino grunted in reply before slapping her knee and continuing with her complaints. "Damn, I miss the old days when we just patrolled. Don't get me wrong, I love battles, but this is camp life. Mel, Mestra, and you were the campers. I need to be moving."

"You realize that the duties of the Artillery Prefect of the Legion are largely completed in a siege camp, right?" Syrena asked with a laugh.

Ino rolled her eyes. "It was the only prefect position available."

Within the legion there were five prefects; artillery, infantry, archers, pikes and supply. Overseen by the Legion Commander, Syrena, each of these five prefects commanded ten cohorts. Ino and Melantho, along with Artemisia, Ino's sister, had become prefects when the previous officers had fallen during the grueling war against Nara and Tresha.

Many of the current officers were of a younger age given that older officers died or retired due to Naran-Orleuns War. The war was between two rival Quarmi nations, but the Amazons stepped in to help Orleuns, their longtime allies. The war, however, was devastating and left many grievously wounded or dead. It also allowed Syrena and the other Furies a chance to prove their worth and gain more members. Heroes and legends were made from that devastating war!

"How is Mel holding up out there?" Ino asked of their other friend from the Herd. Melantho, the Infantry Prefect.

"She's keeping the defenders busy, along with Cecilia, and keeping reinforcements away by engaging them in the north. She's further north between Varusdun and Gib, tightening our grip." Syrena responded.

"That's her calling. She was born to be a prefect and one day she'll be a stratego." Ino smiled. Mel was born into nobility and excelled as a military leader. This would allow her to join the ranks of the general class called the stratego. These warriors were the queen's own advisors. Only two existed at a time. One for the navy and one for the ground forces.

"There are many capable prefects in the legion and cavalry. She is in good company, yourself included." Syrena commented.

Ino smiled at Syrena's words. "I'm not noble born. My family now has a title, yes, but strategos must be of noble birth. I'm still shocked I wasn't made a landgrave like most low-borns with titles. I guess I knew the right women." Ino smiled and winked at Syrena. "No, the life of a stratego isn't meant for me, not by the right of birth. My daughters have that right, but not I. Though, given the honor of coat of arms is a pleasant touch."

Ino was born to an ergatis mother, a woman from the labor class. She had left the army after her six years, an unheard of action, shameful for an ergatis, and joined a mercenary company to gain wealth for her family. Though Ino and her family received some gold from their mother, the act left Ino and her siblings with a black mark, one that stayed even after her mother's death in another land. Only when Ino was accepted into the legion on her own merits from the Herd, was the mark of shame removed. In the years since, Ino worked hard and rose in the ranks, even being granted a title of Palatine, a landholder and lord under a Vicountess.

"And you make your arms a red shield and a spear?" Syrena quipped.

Ino shrugged. "Looks menacing. Besides, it's just a formality because I'm not eligible for anything else."

"Laws can change." Syrena said in a serious tone.

"Not with Cecilia as heir, not in our lifetime." Ino sighed. "Hell, we both know that Cecilia won't put anyone loyal to you near her throne, anyway."

"Shame she feels like that." Syrena replied.

"I understand the old ways and I follow most of them. Cecilia though, damn, she'd have us enslave men and put any six year ergatis into the levies." Ino huffed. "You know as well as I that the levies don't fight for shit!"

Syrena smirked. "Levies seem to work for Lotcala. They call them up whenever there is a war."

"They also have a damn good standing army. Their heavy horse is unstoppable and with that Crown Prince Liam leading them; unbeatable. If he wasn't married, I'd have thrown my name into consideration to be his wife." Ino laughed. "Maybe Cecilia should have gone after him instead of..." Ino stopped short. "Sorry."

Syrena shook her head. "It's fine." She sighed. "Cecilia would have been a terrible wife for Gabriel, anyway." Syrena thought back to her teenage years and the few months she spent as an envoy in training with her sister in Jovag, the capital of Lotcala.

Centuries old allies, Amazon and Lotcala had always had a friendly relationship, and that was because of the willingness of the royals to be welcoming to each other. The two sovereign nations considered themselves to be brother and sister realms.

Queen Saria had sent Cecilia at eighteen years old and her younger sister to the court of King Liam. There they met their distant cousin Gabriel, and Syrena was enamored. Cecilia, not so much. As the years went on, however, the talks of marriage between the Amazonian crown princess and the younger son of Liam was a foremost priority. That is until three years later when Prince Gabriel left the kingdom to join the Northland Rangers, following the footsteps of his uncle Ragnall.

"Cecilia couldn't marry Prince Liam, anyway. Amazon needs a queen on the throne, just as Lotcala needs its king. That marriage would have forced one to abdicate or be absent for far too long. That's why Gabriel was the obvious choice." Syrena continued.

"Yeah, that is a good point." Ino conceded. "It would have been interesting with Gabriel living here, though. All those times you talked about him, I've always wanted to meet the man. Very few men impress me and he seemed to be of the sort."

Syrena smiled at her friend and her memories.

Just then, a young solider burst into the tent and dropped to one knee, hitting her right fist to her armored chest.

"Commander?" The young soldier panted. "The queen is calling for you."

Syrena rose from her chair, along with Ino. She reached for her armor to fasten it back on. "Duty calls." Ino walked over to help the princess with the side buckles.

"Don't just kneel there, girl!" Ino barked. "Get her helm and take her to the queen."

The young soldier shot up and rushed to the helm and presented it to the princess.

Syrena noticed the young woman's shaking hands. "Relax young one." Syrena smiled. "What's your name?"

"Garra." The soldier replied, her head bowed.

"Did you just graduate from the Herd?" Syrena asked.

"Yes, your highness." Garra replied.

Syrena smiled and clasped Garra's shoulder. Ino huffed.

"This one has been helping with the supply train. She'll probably make a fair legionnaire one day." Ino quipped.

Syrena nodded before putting on her helm and exiting the tent with Garra in tow.

* * * *

Queen Saria flung open the flap of her tent and laughed as she threw her helm to a nearby attendant. Warriors followed her inside the tent.

"Damn! I feel like molten steel!" She exclaimed, raising her fists in the air. Her armor had streaks of blood, and there were a few bruises forming on her exposed biceps. "It's been years since I've been in a good battle." She looked to her husband and smiled.

The tall man smiled back, happy to see his wife in such a pleasant mood. "You look as beautiful as the day we wed."

"Come here!" Saria roared, a command her husband gladly obeyed. She embraced him and locked him with a deep kiss. Once they broke the kiss, he handed her a cup of wine and he unbuckled her cuirass. "A queen never deserved such a man as you." Saria smiled at him, and he winked. She then realized that the other people, fellow warriors, were still in the tent. "Well, what the hell are the rest of you waiting for? Get out!" Saria growled.

The attendants and the other warriors scrambled out of the tent, knowing their queen's temper.

"Now you may finish, Agis." The queen purred into the ear of her husband.

Agis grinned as he removed her armor and placed it on a nearby stand. He then pulled her close for another kiss as he undid the strap of her chiton and let it fall to the ground. Agis led his wife to the cot, fitted as a bed for the both of them. He laid her down and removed her greaves and sandals.

"If only I could still give the queendom strong daughters. Think of the world we'd create." Saria smiled as Agis removed his own chiton and joined her in the cot.

"Doesn't mean we can't try." He smiled before embracing his wife.

The loving couple were making love when a messenger entered the tent.

"My queen, we have news from the front lines!" She said before realizing her mistake. Her face, however, showed her embarrassment as the queen's anger rose in her reply.

"Get the hell out!" Saria roared.

The messenger did as instructed and returned to the attendants outside, who burst into laughter over the scene.

It was a while later when the messenger was permitted into the tent. There she found Saria and Agis both laying on the cot, the queen draped over her husband.

"Your majesty, the Elysians have sent an envoy to request a ceasefire and truce." The messenger said excitedly.

Saria smirked. "I figured as much. Fetch my daughters!" Several warriors rushed out, leaving the queen and husband alone. "We have ten minutes, I figure." She grinned.

A short time later, Syrena arrived and entered the tent. Once inside, she removed her helm, dropped to one knee and struck her right fist to her chest.

"My queen, I've come as you summoned." Syrena said, looking to the ground.

Saria rose from the bed and walked over to a table where some linens were laid out. "Come in, daughter." She said. She threw a linen chiton to her husband, and then she put one on for herself. "We have news of peace. The Elysians wish to treat with us."

Just as she finished, Cecilia burst in. She, too, dropped to her knee and saluted. "My queen, you called for me?" Cecilia glanced over to Syrena as the younger sister rose. Cecilia stayed kneeling, however.

"Yes, my daughter. My daughters." Saria said lovingly. She walked over to the princesses and guided Cecilia up, cupping their cheeks tenderly. "We've won."

The Heart of the Queendom

Two weeks after the siege, Syrena found herself in Verna, the capital of the queendom. This was her home from birth, but in the years since her advancement from the Herd she had been in Caleope, ruling as the Vicountess. This stopover in Verna, however, was necessary given the recent victory but also the strain on her soldiers. The Legion had been marching for days with only rests during the night. They had to stop and regroup.

"Prefects Ino and Melantho, move your soldiers to the barracks and then meet me in the morning for reports." Syrena said as she neared the northern gate of Verna with her friends. Both the women saluted by striking their right fists to their chests.

Syrena watched them ride off, along with many of their soldiers. The procession back into the queendom had taken days, with warriors filing in by the hundreds each day. The princess then turned her horse to a warrior riding behind her. "Kora." Syrena called out to the lochagos of her personal legionnaires. The armored woman rode up to Syrena and saluted. "See our sisters to my residence and let them have a rest. You all have earned it."

Kora nodded and then kicked at her horse, pulling the large animal to turn. She was a lady of very few words but strong actions. Syrena was confident in her role as lochagos, captain of the Caleope Legion and levy. Syrena kept lodgings in the capital, but she wasn't ready to go there just yet. First she wanted to report in to the queen.

Queen Saria arrived in Verna a week prior and Cecilia a few days after that. Syrena was the last to arrive since she was in charge of moving the large force of legionnaires, all on foot.

The princess walked up the steps of the Queen's Hall and pushed open the large oak doors. Immediately she was struck with the smell of lilac and lavender, favorites of the queen. Syrena enjoyed the scents as well, but Cecilia preferred roses. It was enjoyable to be in a quieter and softer setting than a legion camp for the first time in months. Syrena walked past guards, saluting as she passed, until she reached her mother's quarters.

A lone guard stood by and opened the door once Syrena neared. A grateful nod and smile, given to the guard and Syrena was soon in front of her mother's breakfast table. On her right was the queen, smiling across the table to her husband, seated at Syrena's left. Syrena dropped to one knee and saluted.

"My queen!" The princess said.

"Syrena, my dear, come and join us." Agis said to his daughter. Queen Saria looked to her daughter and smiled.

"Come now, drop the formality and sit. Eat." Saria said, still wearing her golden laurel wreath crown.

Syrena stood and smiled as she pulled the chair in front of her. She took her seat and served herself cantaloupe and blackberries. On the table was a platter of pastries, filled with a honey, almond and hazelnut mixture.

"What are you reading mother?" Syrena asked before biting a piece of ripe cantaloupe.

Saria scoffed. "Letters congratulating me on our victory over Elysia. Most of these are from landgraves and palatines. One has arrived from Fe. Emperor Hel sends his regards on the glorious victory. The frail, old coward rushed out of the damn war before he even committed one man to battle!" Saria chuckled. "Probably had some concubine to bed." She winked to Agis.

Syrena smiled. Agis was a bit more pragmatic. "If Elysia had offered us such favorable terms early on, I'm sure you would have strongly considered peace as well."

"Perhaps." Saria conceded without looking up from her papers.

Agis looked to Syrena and smiled. "My dear, your journey was well I trust?"

"Yes, father. Nothing unusual to report. I have sent the Legion back to their posts." Syrena replied in between bites. She reached over and picked up a piece of the sticky pastry.

Agis grinned and nodded. He wasn't the king, Amazon did not have kings. However, he was intelligent and respected. His mother was a stratego, and Agis learned at her side. Saria was more than happy to leave some of her administrative duties to her capable husband.

In his youth, Agis captained a cohort of male soldiers and was now highly regarded in his role as a spy master and apothecary for the queen. Many kings and queens once employed his family, one of the oldest in the queendom and throughout the world as expert apothecaries and poisoners. It was a family art that he taught Cecilia and it came natural to her. However, when Saria became queen, she outlawed much of his work, meaning his family was out of work in the queendom.

While he never visibly held a grudge, a few knew of the tension it had caused within the royal family.

Notably their daughters, each taking a side. Saria forbid the two princess from speaking of it, but that didn't stop the rumors from swirling.

Agis smiled. "The Prefect of the Archers reported in yesterday. She's moved on to her lands in the southeast. She was rather upset in the artillery barrage of the recent siege. A matter I asked her to take up with you."

"Thank you, father. I will send her a letter asking to meet. I'm sure it is nothing of great important considering we won the siege and because of Ino's tactics." Syrena said. "The two can come to terms, I'm sure. Their rivalry is well known, but I suppose that is how it is with most blood sisters."

"Nevertheless, you should not leave your prefects to think you are showing nepotism." Agis replied.

Syrena nodded. "Ino is still learning. She would rather be in the field. Artemisia has the post she really wanted. Ino does her best to learn, but artillery was never a strong suit for our people."

"I'd say it was the archers that needed to be sent back to the Herd!" A voice boomed from a nearby hallway. Everyone turned to see Cecilia walk into the room. "Good morning. My queen." She said, kneeling and saluting.

Saria rolled her eyes. "Up, up!"

Cecilia rose and grinned to her mother.

"Why must my daughters salute so much to me in my own home?" Saria fumed.

Cecilia sat across from Syrena. The sisters smiled at one another, but there was an uneasy tension in their faces. It was a common sight in the queendom.

The bond that existed between siblings was not always the strongest in the military classes. Perhaps in the ergatis, also known as the laborer class, and levy class, siblings had closer bonds. However, for those from the axio or noble class, the bonds that were strongest were those of Herd sisters. Sometimes, biological sisters might be little more than strangers when compared to the Herd. Those were the women that bled and fought together.

Agis looked to his eldest daughter. "And your cavalry? Are they having a much needed rest?"

Cecilia nodded while chewing on a piece of pork belly. "Yes father, thank you for your concern." Cecilia smiled at her father. "A rested army is a healthy army. You taught me that, father." Cecilia was a frigid woman in most regards but to her father she was a loving daughter and he a proud parent. The two exchanged wide grins. Cecilia was like her father. She was cunning and relied on her intellect to win battles.

Like many Amazons, Cecilia lived for war and she loved to charge into battle. What she did not love was the idea of a marriage. She had a sword sister, a close bond of companionship, with another officer, and that was enough for her. However, she knew that one day she'd be the queen and that meant producing an heir.

As the family enjoyed a quiet and peaceful breakfast, a messenger walked in with a sealed letter for the queen.

Saria gripped the folded letter and smiled. "Lotcala. King Liam is sending his regards." She cracked the seal and read the letter silently. She stopped and then looked up in shock. First to her husband and then to Cecilia.

"What's the matter, my love?" Agis asked. Syrena and Cecilia looked to their mother curiously.

"Liam sends his regards on the victory." Saria replied. "He plans to hold a parade in our honor."

"That's good news, mother." Cecilia said with a smirk. "They're good men, mostly. I wish King Liam had seen our victory."

"I agree, Cecilia. Saria, your expression had me a bit worried, love." Agis said to his daughter and then wife before returning to his meal.

"Liam finished the letter with news that Prince Gabriel has returned to Jovag." Saria said.

Cecilia scoffed while Agis and Syrena stopped eating.

"He has?" Syrena asked.

Cecilia looked up at her sister, her eyes narrowing.

"That's good news... right? It could be a sign that they want to renew talks of an alliance cemented in a new matrimony bond?" Syrena asked.

"No." Cecilia replied, slamming her hand onto the table. "He was too much of a coward the first time, and that's not the type of man we want in this family." Cecilia leaned back in her chair, picking her teeth with her knife. "I won't be entertaining any possibilities with him."

"I'm afraid Cecilia is right." Agis continued. "That was the plan once, but our bond is still strong even after he ran off. Why do we need a marriage to cement what is already as thick as Herd sisters?"

"Thank you, father." Cecilia smiled, looking at Syrena.

"I heard that he went to join the rangers in the north, to help the villagers there against the Huns. Even a few Amazons have traveled that way." Syrena replied. "They say that the fighting is brutal on the Northern Continent."

"Is that how you've heard of his journey?" Saria asked. "From our sisters?"

"Some of our sisters return to see family or rejoin the ranks. They have mentioned seeing him during their time there. A few fought alongside him as well." Syrena confessed.

"As honorable as his intentions might have been, your father and sister are right. The heart of the queendom is the queen and it must be a heart that beats for her people. His abandonment of the engagement showed he was unfit for our queendom. We will find a suitable man for your sister here in the queendom." Saria replied. "Now, I'd like to finish this meal without another damn piece of parchment shoved in my face!" The queen bellowed to the nearby attendants.

All of her servants stepped back except one.

Saria rolled her eyes at her steward. "What is it, Katrina?" She asked.

The queen's steward saluted. "The Queen's Guard has apprehended the usurer in River Port. He is being brought up to court and should arrive in a week."

The queen nodded and the steward left. Cecilia looked confused. "A usurer? That's something for the magistrate."

"Not this one." Agis replied. "This one was caught selling weapons and armor during the war to our queendom and to Elysia." He looked to Cecilia. "That warrants an explanation to the queen."

Cecilia grinned a sly smile. "Then let us see justice prevail."

* * * *

Later that day, Syrena went to relax by taking a short walk around the palace. Not far away, Cecilia thought of doing the same. The crown princess came from restocking her personal supply of potion and poison ingredients. That was a task that often put a smile on her face. This day was no different as she entered the garden in the large courtyard.

Seeing her younger sister, Cecilia strolled up to her. "Sister, are you enjoying your stay here in Verna?"

"I am. Glad for a chance to rest some before I return to Caleope. And you? Will you return to Esto soon?" Syrena asked, taking a seat on a nearby bench.

Cecilia smiled. "That is my plan. I've been wanting to return for some time. The capital is a bit stuffy for my tastes." She sighed. "Mother wants me to stay longer here in the capital. She wants me to be at court when the usurer arrives for trial and sentencing. I suppose that is my role." She lowered her head dejectedly. "To be free to run off to some goddess forsaken continent in the north like Gabriel did." Cecilia chuckled. "Must be nice."

Syrena winced at the reference. "It's not a perfect life sister." Syrena replied.

"Nor should it be. These imperfections strengthen us and train us to be better than we were before."

"True enough." Syrena nodded in agreement. "I see you've kept the shaven head from the battle. A recent shave?" Syrena asked.

Cecilia grinned. "I like the feel of it, to be honest. I remember the feeling of battle when I shave it and the feel of the smooth skin comforts me." It was a style worn by many during times of war to help helms fit better, and limit the chance of their hair becoming a hindrance during a fight.

Cecilia looked to her sister and strained a smile. "Forgive me, but it's getting later than I'd like and I still have to check on my horse."

"Of course." Syrena nodded as Cecilia walked away towards the stables.

She thought to the years away from the capital. They weren't perfect years, but they were much more peaceful.

From a balcony close by, Agis watched his daughters. He knew the divide between them was growing and had been for years. There wasn't much he could do, even as their father. Agis knew their personalities were so different from one another, but still he hoped that there would a reconciliation. The only problem was that he had little clue to the source of their tension.

No one did, in fact. Not even Syrena or Cecilia could say what drove them apart, but here the queendom rested on their future.

* * * *

Eight days after their meeting in the courtyard, Cecilia and Syrena joined their mother, her advisors and their father, in the queen's throne room. The usurer had arrived.

Syrena, with her attendant, the Quarmi woman Mitzudi, walked to where her father stood amongst other nobles. One such noble, Lady Theodora Orsini, was the Guild-master of Merchants. It was her role to oversee the importing and exporting of all supplies. She was the first to notice irregularities with the accused man. It was her luck that she noticed the miscalculations or she might have been standing next to him.

Syrena and her father stood at the left of her mother but on the ground level while her mother sat upon her throne, atop a raised platform. Cecilia stood to her mother's right on the platform. This was the queen's throne room, her court. She sat nearly eight feet above everyone standing below her. On the ground level were many landgraves, palatines and other officials.

The guards took the accused man into the throne room. Syrena and the others in the court could see the blood crusted to his hair and his beard. Syrena grimaced at his broken nose and bruised face. She wasn't a fan of the tactics used by the Queen's Guards.

Agis leaned over to his daughter. "They said he tried to fight back. He found out the hard way that wasn't a good idea."

Syrena looked to her father, and he smirked. "Who is he anyway?" She looked back to the man. "Why would we put our trust or gold into the faith of him?"

Agis sighed. "He told a fanciful tale. What we know is, he is the son of a Sile lord, a count. That gave him some clout."

"He is noble and offering weapons." Syrena said. "Where were our smiths?"

The woman next to Syrena spoke up. "Your highness, the guilds overworked us with supplying Fe and Orleuns during their war with Nara."

Syrena looked and nodded to the woman. "Of course, my apologies on my assumption, Lady Orsini."

"No apologies needed, your highness." Lady Orsini replied. "He spoke very well, weaving such a beautiful tale that I believe he might have a future in the theater. If he has a future."

Syrena turned from the woman, a commoner but one elevated through wealth and status. The princess refocused her attention on the scene before her. The Queen's Guard, holding the man, drug him up by the chains holding his wrists.

"This is the traitor, your majesty. His name is Domino Eolas." The guard announced.

"Can't really be a traitor if I'm not a citizen of you country." The man grinned defiantly.

"A blessing for us all, I'm sure." Saria replied coldly. "I accuse you of two crimes, sir. The first is usury and the second and much more disturbing is duplicity. How do you plead?"

Domino stood up. "Well, I suppose the second one is true."

There were murmurs throughout the court at his response.

"Silence!" Cecilia ordered. "So you admit to your crimes?"

"Cecilia, silence." The queen said, looking to her daughter.

Cecilia bowed and saluted. "Forgive me, my queen."

Saria waved her off and Cecilia stepped back. "Eolas, your father is Constantino Eolas, Lord of Talammil, is he not?"

Domino nodded. "He is, your majesty. Though I would not expect a ransom. He is a lesser lord, a count, and only a first generation count. We are a family of little land and even less money."

"Why should I care about that?" Saria asked.

"I suppose it is not my place to ask anything of you but as my father is poor and I'm not the first born waiting for an inheritance. I'm just a bit desperate."

"Then speak on your reasoning for selling arms and armor to two nations at war with one another." The queen said.

Domino lowered his head. "As I said, it was desperation. I felt compelled to act in a way to increase my standing in this world. In Aran, I could never inherit, nor would I be able to get too far in life. I came south to make my way, but I'm good with numbers, not my hands. I've made some gold in my years away from Talammil, so I like to invest it."

"You invested it? In my queendom?"

Domino smiled. "Exactly!"

Saria snarled. "And Elysia?"

"It is wise to back a winner and at the time of the investment, the war was new and I had seen no clear favorite." Domino stuttered.

Saria gripped the arms of her throne. Anger seethed in her eyes, burning with hate. She leaned forward. "Never 'invest' against Amazon." She gritted through her teeth.

Domino lowered his head and stumbled across his words. "Hmm, yes, your majesty. It was early on and I sold many more weapons to your beautiful queendom than to Elysia. Many, many more." He said.

The queen leaned back in her throne. "Lady Orsini, step forward." The Guild-master walked up and saluted the queen. "What can you say for or against this man?"

"His sob story from Aran, I can't say. However, based on the papers we found him with, he sold us more war supplies than he sold to Elysia." Lady Orsini replied. "They were of excellent quality as well."

"Thank you. Please return." Queen Saria responded. Lady Orsini saluted and then turned to Domino. She gave him a sneer before walking back to the place.

"You have no friends here, Lord Eolas. Even our guild-masters are skilled enough to kill you with ease."

"I'm not a lord. My father is. I am Domino Eolas, and I only sought to make enough gold to provide a future for myself."

Saria looked around the court and saw the faces of unconvinced nobles and masters. She was correct in saying that none would stand with Eolas.

"What of the charge of usury?" Saria asked.

"Not guilty." Domino replied.

"So you didn't give loans, charging high interests." Saria asked, raising an eyebrow.

"Well, yes. I did do that. Is that a crime?" Domino smirked.

"Yes, it is. Are you such a fool that you would joke at a time like this?" Saria was stunned at the man before her.

"Your majesty, it is a common practice. Banks do it all the time!" Domino said.

"Banks' interest rates are not so high that commoners and minor lords can't pay them!" Saria yelled. "Where is your gold? Our guards did not find our money on you when you were captured. Nor did they find anything in the area where the guards found you."

"It is safely put away."

"Where?" The queen pressed.

"It's secured where only I can retrieve it. Its location will die with me." Domino said defiantly.

"Fine. I've heard enough, anyway. You have admitted, through your own month, to both crimes. Take him to the dungeons and we will see to his fate at a later date. I fear that should we listen to him any further that we might lose our own wits and intelligence." Queen Saria said as she stood to leave the throne room.

The guards moved in and took hold of the man.

"Your majesty, the sentence for his crimes is death." Cecilia interrupted. Other nobles around the court agreed. "Many of our own had loans to this man and..."

Saria spun and sent a sharp gaze to her daughter.

Cecilia dropped to one knee in salute.

"Any loan he holds to an Amazon is now forgiven. He is to be jailed until I say otherwise." Saria responded, looking to her daughter. "That's final." The queen walked off as her daughter and the rest of the court saluted.

Cecilia stood from saluting and watched her mother walk off. She was angry, but she couldn't react. Agis walked up to his daughter and stood with her.

"She must have a good reason." He said.

"Yes, of course. No one can dispute a queen's word." Cecilia said to her father, trying to sound understanding.

Syrena watched the scene. She turned to her attendant Mitzudi. "We leave for Caleope tonight." She said before walking out of the court with the Quarmi woman.

* * * *

"My love, why let that man live?" Agis asked his wife when they had retired to their bedchambers for the evening.

"Agis, I don't really want to talk about that charlatan."

Agis looked to his wife. "Then why not sentence him to die and be rid of his memory?"

Saria sighed as she sat down on the bed. Agis sat next to her and put his arm over her shoulders, pulling her close. The queen smiled to her husband.

"Don't think I didn't want to." Saria replied. "His story wasn't that good for me to be so merciful. A lowly lord trying to make his way in the world is honorable, but not off the misfortune of others. There is nothing in that worth saving, normally." Saria stood and walked to the window. She looked out over her great city. "Mestra saw something in his life. A reason for him to live, but we would need him to be close by."

"Mestra, the Magister of Oracles? You consulted her about that Eolas man?" Agis asked, walking over to his wife.

"I felt like I needed someone to interpret a reoccurring dream. War is coming." Saria corrected.

Agis laughed. "What queen doesn't dream of war? What Amazonian, for that matter?"

Saria looked to her husband with tears welling in her eyes. "No, my love. There has been so much turmoil in my dreams of late. Mestra spoke to them, vaguely, as is the way of the oracles. Gabriel's homecoming, this man, Fe's early retreat. It all means something."

"What did you see?" Agis asked.

"Many dead on the field. I saw a dead dragon, dead stags, dead horses and dead griffins. So many dark images. Mestra couldn't help much, but she told me that this Eolas was going to play a part."

"I see. A dead dragon?" Agis asked. Saria embraced him in a hug. Tears in her eyes.

"Forgive me Agis. A queen crying over stupid dreams. An embarrassing scene for the heart of the queendom." Saria said, trying to sound light hearted.

"It's completely understandable, dear. Besides, it's just a dream, my love."

Caleope

It took Syrena and her entourage thirteen days of hard and fast riding to reach her keep in Caleope. A welcome sight once the stone building came into view. As keeps went, it was smaller than most. Two bedchambers on the highest of the three levels. The first level was for the attendants and servants. The second level was her throne room, which served as her court. As viscountess, the queen expected Syrena to hold court and now that the war was over and she had returned, she knew that there would be a long line of petitioners.

The westward approach was not as crowded as Syrena had thought it would be, but it was late in the day, nearly sunset. She led her band on and passed a local tavern. From inside she could hear raucous commotion and activity. The sounds of laughter lifted Syrena's spirits. A little further up the way she saw guards on patrol. They kneeled and saluted as she rode past.

Syrena looked up at the stone keep, sitting atop a large motte. That hill was the impressive feature of her home. Steep and high, it would be a very difficult task for invaders to reach the keep. Syrena's great-grandmother had commissioned it for the town.

Entering the lower bailey of her fortification, Palatine Honora greeted Syrena.

"Welcome home, princess." She saluted the princess.

Syrena smiled and touched the older woman's shoulder, indicating for her to stand. Honora stood and, cane in hand, walked along with Syrena, though at a slower pace.

"We've kept the town just as you left it." Honora joked. Syrena smiled. Syrena grew up close to the elder veteran and enjoyed her warm nature.

Contrary to her warm nature, however, Honora's exploits in the Legion were legendary. As a former Commander of the Legion, she led the famed warriors in many battles against Tresha and Nara. However, her military carrier ended with a near mortal wound to her left leg. It took all the skills of no less than three healers to save her leg and her life. After that battle, Honora relinquished her post and adapted to life as a palatine.

"Your village must miss you, Lady Honora." Syrena smiled as she sat down at the table where a servant had laid out plates for her and her party.

Honora sat across from Syrena. "It's a small village that never needed a palatine. My grandmother must have done something truly terrible to receive such a title." She laughed.

Syrena tore a piece of bread and dipped it in the beef stew. "Some women are lucky to receive such a post."

"Ino deserves more than a palatine title." Honora replied, catching Syrena's meaning. "Her mother was an outstanding warrior and a fine Herd sister, but she would never have made much of a name for herself in the queendom. It was a time of peace and she saw that." Honora scoffed. "Ino's mother was in the wrong Herd. She was an excellent warrior in a Herd of excellent warriors. If she had been born anything but an ergatis, then she would have had a better life and she would have been able to provide something more for Ino and her siblings. The queendom's class system holds down the commoners."

"You are aware that you are speaking to the princess?" A warrior to Honora's right interjected.

"Aye. I can see her. I lost my ability to walk, not my sight!" Honora quipped. "Let her flog an old, feeble woman if she doesn't like my words."

"Only a fool would believe you to be feeble." Syrena smirked. The rest of the table laughed at the truth of the statement.

"Perhaps. How is Ino anyway?" Honora continued.

Syrena wiped her mouth on her cloak. "She's good and stressed." Syrena chuckled. She put her spoon down. "Ino led the artillery with honor and skill. Her mother would have been proud."

"She is. The ancestors smile upon us in victory and wipe away our shame in defeat." Honora stood from the table "I must rest before my ride back to Philippi tomorrow. I'm sure they lament my absence with daily festivals."

Syrena stood. "You have my thanks Lady Honora for your care of Caleope." She said, clasping wrists with Honora.

"It was an honor, princess." Honora said before retiring to her quarters.

"Are the stories they say about Lady Honora true, Lady Syrena?" Asked the woman seated next to the chair Honora once occupied.

Syrena raised her eyebrow. "Why not ask her yourself?"

The other warriors at the table laughed.

Another woman further down the table spoke up. "Just before this recent war started, I saw Lady Honora kill three bandits on her own! With that cane of hers. I'd say she is more deadly now than she's ever been!"

The other warriors cheered and toasted their compatriot. Syrena smiled to the others at the table. She felt happy to be home.

The next morning was sunny and warm as the princess made her way down to the great hall. She had her first hot bath in nearly two weeks and she felt refreshed. Syrena walked down the steps of the keep, her leather sandals treading lightly with each step. Many Amazonian warriors went to great lengths to practice walking silently, the soft leather sandals helped. Syrena's linen chiton, trimmed with blue fabric, flowed around her thighs when she entered the hall.

"We're leaving the doors open now?" Syrena grinned.

A servant nearby bowed and saluted. "No, my lady, but there are many deliveries today. We thought it more efficient. I can close it if you wish."

Syrena held her hand up to stop the servant. "The warm air is pleasant, and the light is welcoming. Leave it for now." She said, taking her seat at the head table of the hall.

Mitzudi came over and placed a wooden bowl of vegetable and mussel soup in front of Syrena. "It's nearly midday."

Syrena grinned, pulling the bowl closer and grabbing a spoon. "Worth your scorn to have this for a midday meal."

The stew was Syrena's favorite. A special recipe from the chef. A hearty stew made of mussels, white wine, leeks and scallions. To top it off, the chef mixed in a combination of wild herbs.

Syrena smiled at Mitzudi as the older Quarmi woman gazed at the princess.

"Sleep until midday if you must, but any longer and the ostrea stew would have cooled." Mitzudi replied with a sigh.

"Since when do you get to scold the princess and lady of the keep?" Syrena asked, raising an eyebrow.

"Ever since I used to pick you up when you fell as a babe." Mitzudi replied, laughing.

The stew was delicious and Syrena poured herself a second helping, but she had to finish it quickly. Syrena was expected to begin her court.

As was customary, the ruling archon would preside over the local court. It was a time for lords and commoners to bring their problems to their sworn lords. Syrena was viscountess, one of four, and her title was second only to the queen, when one did not count the crown princess. This meant that the palatines and the landgraves would answer to the viscountess.

Syrena walked into the hall that served as her court and greeted those standing in attendance, waiting for her to arrive. She took a seat on her throne and signaled the first to step forward.

Mitzudi walked up and called the first name. "Palatine Orestilla pleads her case of rents due from those serving in the recent war."

Palatine Orestilla walked up and saluted Syrena. She was an older woman, and like Honora, she used a cane to walk. In Orestilla's case, the rumor told of an old war wound had damaged her leg. Others thought in more accurately as a simple infection that damaged her nerves. As always, she dressed in fine silks and linens. Her blond hair pulled back in a braid.

"Viscountess, praise the goddesses that our sisters saw victory. Forgive me for asking, but with the Legion gone to war and our tithes due, rents were not given in due time as they should have been. We were lenient, because of the war of course, but we have our own mouths to feed and seed crops to buy for the land." Orestilla sighed. "I'm sure I'm asking for my sisters here, but when might we see a return to regular rents?"

Syrena leaned forward. "How many of you are here for rents?" No less than eighteen of the twenty four archons in attendance raised their hands. "That will have to come when the legionnaires, riders and levy return and settle back home." Syrena noticed a collective look of disappointment on the faces of her lords.

"Until such time." Syrena rose from her throne. "Let the spoils of our victory hold your lands over. We expect the supply wagons in a few days and they will have gold, silver and copper. That should help with the purchasing of crops."

"That is generous my lady, but we will need to raise taxes to recoup this loss." Orestilla replied.

"See first what your lands can claim from the spoils. Your sisters fought valiantly and showed in large number." Syrena responded. "I'm happy to share the spoils with such brave warriors. It will also help those whose mothers and sisters won't be returning." Syrena turned back to her throne but stopped when Orestilla spoke up.

"That is honorable, your highness, but I support this realm far more than Palatine Honora, whom I do not see here today."

"Palatine Honora has returned home after caring for this land in the princess' absence while away at war." Mitzudi replied.

"Honora was vital to Caleope's success and the success of the surrounding realms." Syrena added.

Orestilla was not content with Syrena's reply. "Of that I have no doubt, but I have a wide berth of land that needs seed for the coming months. I send my grain and barley to the capital, while Honora's crops remain with her lands. Your mother's taxes for the war against Elysia bled us. Without the crops, then my land will suffer after we pay our tithes. How often did the palatines yell for peace while the landgraves and the levies suffered? Did your mother ever listen to us?"

"Tread carefully." Mitzudi replied.

"I speak the truth that the palatines and landgraves all know to be honorable." Orestilla replied.

"Perhaps in your ears, but the queen is above the opinions of the lambs. She does what is right for the queendom not a cavalry rider that can't hang up her bridle." Mitzudi continued.

"Forgive me madam Quarmi but when I want the advice from a grey-skinned, honorless assassin then I'll beat it out of you." Orestilla hissed.

Mitzudi drew her falcata as Orestilla stood defensively.

"Mitzudi! Palatine Orestilla!" Syrena yelled. Both women froze in place as more guards rushed in. "Palatine Orestilla, you are lucky that Mitzudi is loyal to our queendom or I'm not sure you'd be able to walk at all." Syrena sat down on her throne. "I'll give you a reprieve for one year on taxes owed to me and Caleope. Other than that, I can do nothing else for you apart from what I already said I would do with the war spoils. Furthermore, I will not approve a tax increase on your lands."

"Very well. Thank you, my lady." Palatine Orestilla bowed and saluted before walking off. Several landgraves from her domain followed behind her.

Syrena sighed. "This is not a good sign."

Syrena heard a few more cases, none as troublesome as what Palatine Orestilla brought to her before the day finished.

"It's a simple matter. Take the spoils owed to your realm through the service of your people. Simple." Syrena commented while stoking the fireplace in her bed chamber.

"It's a political move. Palatine Orestilla was part of the cavalry. She is still part of the cavalry, if you ask her." Mitzudi commented. "The cavalry never thought too highly of the Legion and vice versa."

"Not all of the Legion think like that." Syrena corrected, giving Mitzudi a gaze through the side of her eye.

"The cavalry are all born nobles. Few nobles enter the legion by choice. Only because the cavalry ranks are full." Mitzudi replied. "It's a natural rivalry that has grown out of the years."

Mitzudi was simply recounting the natural order of the military. To be in the cavalry, one must own a horse or two, own arms and armor, and be from the ranking nobles. The legion accepted anyone and everyone that had gone through the Herd. The legion even provided their soldiers with armor and weapons.

"Orestilla will have to be content with what she is given for now. I won't raise the taxes so quickly after a war." Syrena replied, bringing the topic back to the original conversation.

"Perhaps she will be." Mitzudi replied, skeptically.

Night fell before the court finished its daily business and near the outer gate the guards stopped a hooded figure on her horse.

"Halt!" The first guard shouted. "You are entering the town of Caleope! State your business."

"Of course." The hooded woman replied from atop her horse. "I'm Magister Mestra. I'm here to see Viscountess Syrena." She finished, removing her hood to show her diadem of a magister. She also handed the guard a letter bearing the queen's mark.

The two guards saluted. "Forgive us, ma'am. We have to stop everyone after nightfall."

"I understand." Mestra smiled.

The second guard walked up. "Madam Magister, I had the honor of graduating the Herd with your sister Morea." The woman bowed.

"The honor is Morea's, I'm sure." Mestra smiled.

The second guard bowed. "Please make your way to the keep. I'll send a runner to announce you, my lady." The guard smiled.

Mestra returned the smile and rode her horse through the bailey gate and past the town at the base of the motte. It wasn't big, not as big as the town that Mestra was from, but it was active. She smelled the ale from the tavern and the last remnants of dinner being served. Mestra's stomach growled from the aroma.

"Syrena damn well better feed me." She said to herself with a laugh. She saw the rider rushing off before her to let the keep know that there was someone of importance approaching. This guaranteed that there would be food waiting.

Nearly fifteen minutes after arriving at the outer gate, Mestra dismounted her horse, handing the stallion to a stable boy. She looked up at the keep and grinned.

"Mestra!" A voice called. Familiar and caring to the woman's ears.

Mestra glanced over and saw Syrena standing at the doorway of the keep, her arms held out wide.

"Your highness." Mestra replied with a salute, dropping to one knee.

Syrena looked at her friend, disappointed. "Dammit! Not you too."

Mestra stood up and laughed. "I have to." She walked up and the two friends embraced in a hug. "It's good to see you, Syrena."

"And you!" Syrena replied. "Come in and get some food. We have ostrea stew and roasted rabbit."

Mestra hummed. "I'll take one of each" She said with a laugh.

Syrena laughed in reply. "Fetch us some rabbit and stew." She said to a nearby attendant.

Mestra looked to the attendants, smiling. "And several flagons of ale."

The two sat at a table in the great hall and enjoyed a meal fit for a queen. They laughed and drank as much as they could handle. Eventually, the topic of the recent war came up.

"I've heard that Orestilla isn't happy with you right now." Mestra said, pouring another cup of ale, spilling a little on her hand.

"When is she ever?" Syrena slurred. "She's just mad that a legionnaire was named viscountess."

"She knows you're the princess, right?" Mestra asked. Still shaking the ale off her hand.

"That's the other thing, first royal to lead the legion in nearly a century." Syrena laughed. The two women toasted the legion before downing another flagon.

Syrena narrowed her eyes towards her friend. "Why are you here?"

Mestra choked on her ale and coughed. "Do I need a reason to see my best friend?" She asked.

Syrena just starred at the woman.

"Fine." Mestra said, and she put her cup down. "Your mother came to visit me recently, more than once actually. She's worried about a dream she's having. It comes a little too often for her comfort."

"You interpret dreams now?" Syrena interrupted.

"If the queen asks me to interpret something then I interpret whatever she asks." Mestra continued rolling her eyes. "I'm not a dream walker or flayer, but I know a few things about the symbolism. Most dreams are just subconscious visions that we've seen throughout our lives. Nothing very serious. Nothing to stress over." Mestra sipped her cup before continuing. "But, I can also peer beyond the veil if need be, and that's why I'm here tonight."

Syrena leaned forward. "What did you see?"

Mestra shook her head. "War is coming. Your mother's dreams point to a massive war that will see a lot of death and the destruction of nations. The old gods speak of it in whispers."

"Does any of this have to do with what you learned on your trip to Kalisadad?"

"I'm not sure. Honestly, I'm still not sure what I saw then, but this feels different. Your mother's dreams are much more palpable than the nearsightedness of the old gods and their machinations." Mestra took a gulp of ale. "I also think you need to visit Gabriel."

"What, why?" Syrena asked and scoffed.

Mestra rolled her eyes and pursed her lips. "You haven't thought about him since finding out he is back in Jovag?" Mestra asked.

"No." Syrena said unconvincingly.

Mestra slammed her cup on the table and shot up, knocking her chair over behind her. "For two fucking years in the Herd, all we heard from you was about how handsome Gabriel was, how great a fighter he was, how honorable he was. All I remember from you was how melancholy you were that he was to marry your sister! Then, how happy you were that he was gone to the north to fight the Huns, to protect innocent people, and that your sister would not marry him! Now that he is back, you lie and say that you haven't thought about him at all?" Mestra exclaimed.

"Well..."

"Well, nothing!" Mestra replied. The inflamed mage fixed her chair, sat back down and pulled a note from her cloak. "When I told the queen I was coming here to see you, she asked that I bring you this." She handed the sealed note to Syrena. It bore the seal of Lotcala. "It's from King Liam and addressed to you. Your mother had received it before you arrived in Verna."

"She had this?" Syrena yelled angrily. "Why didn't..."

Mestra held up her hand to calm the princess down. "If she had given it to you then, Cecilia might have fussed about you being the favorite or something stupid." Mestra reasoned.

Syrena tore open the letter and read it in a mumbled voice.

"I'm sorry, you said something?" Mestra said, sarcasm dripping from her voice.

Syrena's eyes widened. "Liam, Prince Liam, is asking in the king's name that I come to present myself as a bride choice for Gabriel." Syrena's grin nor her joy could be contained from reading the letter.

"Well now, that calls for a drink!" Mestra yelled. "Bring out the Treshan rye liquor!"

"Hold on!" Syrena replied looking to Mestra. "I never said I would accept the invitation and travel all the way to Jovag."

Mestra smiled as a servant brought a bottle of a golden brown liquid. "Uh-huh." Mestra hummed, pouring two cups of the potent drink. She handed one to Syrena. "A toast to your upcoming engagement and marriage. Shall I call the Furies to our side for the trip?"

Syrena took the cup. "I never said..."

Mestra waved Syrena off. "Yeah, yeah. You never said you were going. We both know that you will fall asleep thinking of Gabriel and by the sunrise you will have packed. It's a bit colder near the Blue Mountains this time of year, so make sure you pack your boar skin."

"Yes, because nothing says attractive bride to be like a hulking, matted boar hide." Syrena said, rolling her eyes.

"It symbolizes your first great triumph!" Mestra said in reply. "Everyone, even in Jovag, knows that story." Mestra smiled at Syrena. "So, are we going?"

Syrena looked down and then back to Mestra, smiling. "Call up the Furies, old and new, we're going."

The two raised their cups in a toast. "To Jovag and to the Furies!" Mestra said. The pair drank their cups and grimaced from the burning liquid.

Syrena put her cup down and took the bottle to pour another cup worth. "First, I need to travel to back to Verna and speak with my mother."

Mestra nodded. "While you're doing that, I'll round up the Furies and we'll meet you just outside the gates in fifteen days."

The pair drank the rest of the bottle until the night was through and the sun was dawning in the east. Both cursed their timing. A day of hard riding was ahead of them.

Mortal Whims and a Love so True

Another thirteen days of traveling for an exhausted Syrena was not a pleasing thought. She put it off for a week. In Syrena's mind, there was still a great deal of work left to do in Caleope. The princess had only been back from a yearlong war for two days when it was decided she would leave again. This time for no less than four, possibly six months.

The morning she was to ride out, her guards presented her with a message just as she had mounted her stallion. Syrena crumpled the parchment and tossed it to the ground.

"Bitch!" Syrena snarled. Kora looked towards the angry viscountess. Syrena returned her gaze. "Orestilla has made an official complaint against me to the queen. Now the queen is requesting us both to convene in Verna to settle the matter."

Kora scoffed. "At least we are heading that way."

Syrena huffed. "This might change my plans. Fetch a levy!" She called out. "Leave a contingent of the levy to guard the town until the bulk of your force can return, Kora."

The older soldier nodded and went about following the orders before joining the princess and her ride south.

The princess was still fuming as she turned her horse towards the road and away from her keep. Thirteen days to stew over a petty lord's insult. This wasn't what she had in mind for the journey. Nor was it how she wanted to approach her mother about a delicate matter. Queen Saria had already rejected one idea of a marriage alliance between the two nations, citing that there was no need, and Syrena wasn't sure how she was to react to this latest request. Now, with Orestilla's complaint, a serious matter, there was even more doubt cast on the marriage request.

Thirteen long days of riding felt like months when Syrena approached the doors to the Queen's Hall. She could not recall much of it, pictures coming to her as a blur when all that was on her mind was dealing with Orestilla. She stabled her horse and left her warriors in the barracks for rest. The road had been long, and the warriors sacrificed sleep for more hours riding.

She lowered her head and sighed before pushing the large oak door open. Several attendants. Dressed in fine linen chitons and laurels approached her. Syrena removed her helm and walked to her mother's throne room. A large warrior stood at the entrance. She struck her right fist to her chest and lowered her head.

"Welcome, princess. I'll introduce you." The warrior said before turning and entering the hall. She slammed the iron buttcap of her spear on the limestone floor. "Princess Syrena, Viscountess of Caleope has arrived my queen." The warrior kneeled in salute.

"Arise Sebula and escort my daughter forward. Orestilla, step forward as well. We might as well dispense with this." Saria said as she sat upon her throne, advisors and court officers stood around the large room. Crown Princess Cecilia, dressed in her golden muscle cuirass, like her sister, stood to the right of the queen.

The large room, painted with mosaics of legends and battles from ages prior, had massive pillars on each side. Aromas of jasmine and sage hung in the air. The queen's throne was almost as intimidating to the queen. Atop marble and gold dais was the imposing Throne of

Mara, a throne carved from ivory and silver. Legends said that the first queen, Mara, had carved it from the horn of a dragon she had slayed during the Age of Cold Sun.

Orestilla walked up and stood in front of Queen Saria. Syrena joined her, the heavy boar skin wrapped around her shoulders and wearing her golden muscle cuirass. A stark contrast to Orestilla's ankle length red peplos, the typical Amazonian tunic, and cloak thrown over her shoulder. Both women kneeled and saluted the queen.

"Rise." Saria waved her hand. "Orestilla state your grievance."

As the women rose, both craning their necks to look up to the queen, Orestilla spoke. Her tone suffered from an air of arrogance, even to the queen. "Your majesty, the people of Anglona suffer under weak leadership. Land owners see crops wither and die while their tenants march in the legion, drink in taverns and fornicate endlessly without paying rents. Landgraves suffocate from the stress of the recent war, praise the queen's victory."

"Praise the goddess." Queen Saria interrupted.

"Of course, your majesty." Orestilla smiled. "I only ask that Syrena allow us to pursue the rights owed to us as nobles." Orestilla turned to Syrena. "It is our rights to raise the rents on the lands we own to feed the families on it!" The older palatine finished with a fist raised in the air. Many from the surrounding crowd cheered.

Saria nodded. The queen was thinking similarly. She looked to Syrena. "What say you, Viscountess Syrena?"

"I say it is her right as it is the right of all landowners, but it shouldn't be done on a whim. Especially not when your liege has offered you her own share of the war spoils." Syrena replied, shrugging her shoulders.

"A viscountess share of spoils?" Cecilia asked, surprised.

"Indeed." Syrena answered.

Queen Saria's eyes widened. "That would feed a county for a year or more." She looked to Orestilla. "Was such an offer made?"

"An insult to my rights!" Orestilla replied. "I did not earn such spoils."

"Woman! Damn your pride!" Saria scolded. "Take the spoils and feed your people." The queen looked to Syrena again. "When can you give Palatine Orestilla such tribute?"

Syrena smiled and turned. She clapped her hands twice. In an instant, four levies carried in two large chests and placed them on the floor. Syrena shooed the levies out of court and then opened the first chest. Gold and silver coins gleamed back at Orestilla. The older woman sneered.

"Shall I open the second chest for you, Lady Orestilla?"

Orestilla put her foot on top of it just as Syrena went to the lock. Syrena stood and smiled back at the angry woman.

"How much is there?" Queen Saria asked.

"Three hundred gold falcons and five hundred silver ravens. Three hundred and thirty pounds of gold and silver." Syrena replied, looking to the queen.

"I trust this settles the complaint?" Queen Saria replied.

Orestilla nodded solemnly. She had won nothing like she had hoped. For her, it was a matter of honor and seeking a personal victory over Syrena. However, the princess had come prepared. Orestilla kneeled and saluted before ordering her attendants to retrieve the chests and walking out of the court.

"That's settled. Moving on then." Saria said while motioning Syrena to move to the side. The princess kneeled, saluted, and did as ordered.

As she stood to the side, Syrena slipped behind the crowd and pulled Kora close.

"Take the guard back to Caleope and shore the defensives around the town, the farmlands and outlying villages especially." Syrena ordered.

"What about you, my lady?" Kora asked.

"I'll be fine here. I'll send word of my destination after this, but I need to make sure that Caleope is safe." Syrena replied.

Kora smiled and nodded. "My lady, I will protect Caleope with my life."

Syrena grasped Kora's shoulder. "Let's hope it doesn't come to that."

The older warrior nodded and then silently exited the court.

Across the court, Cecilia watched the scene. She had to peer and tilt her head slightly, but she could witness much of her sister's movements. She looked suspicious, but Cecilia knew Syrena wasn't one to scheme and plot. At least she couldn't imagine her sister plotting anything.

Saria adjourned the court and waked to her garden, a favorite spot of hers. She liked to walk among the flowers, the statues and the fountains. She would stop and bird feeders and pour seed around. Saria loved to be in the peaceful garden. It was a place few people could go. Syrena was one of the lucky few. Saria granted her family such privilege, but few others. It was her own secret.

That privilege was why Saria was not surprised to see Syrena walking towards her that sunny afternoon. Syrena stopped and kneeled before her queen, saluting.

Saria sighed. "I've taught you and your sister too well. Do you think I saluted my mother every time I saw her?"

"I do, my queen."

"I'm also your mother, now get up!" Saria demanded.

Syrena smiled. "You are my queen first and mother second." Syrena said. "That's what you taught us during those years, standing beside your throne at court. You are our mother and the mother of the queendom all at once and therefore we should act as all our brothers and sisters do."

Saria lowered her head and shook it from the memory. "Maybe I was too strict, like my mother. She was a beast of a woman." Saria laughed, followed by Syrena. "An excellent queen, a damn good mage, but a horror to be around. I don't know how my father did it. Did you know she never called me daughter once?" Saria chuckled. "Cecilia reminds me of her." Saria smiled. "Good women, but to be near them is like being near a demon."

"Mother?" Syrena began. "I'm sure you know why I've come?"

"I figured that letter was one of two things." Saria sighed again. She thought to herself that she had been sighing a lot more lately. "A trade request or a bride request." Saria sat down on a nearby bench. She adjusted her chiton around the stone. She patted the bench next to her, asking Syrena to sit with her. The princess did as asked.

Saria smiled at her daughter. "The craftsmen of old made these benches from stones given to us from the siege of Jovag during Charles I's reign. Six hundred years ago. A war between the Knights of the Silver Seal and Lotcala. We sent aid and the crown princess, Ophelia, asked for two things. These stones and to marry Jakob Gowan. He was the king's best friend and his Lord Marshal. A good pairing, except many here in the Queendom thought him less than worthy. Hard to argue when you think that he was a son of a blacksmith, but Jakob had distinguished himself in battle. He was such an accomplished warrior that he was knighted and given a small parcel of land. Jakob had even fought alongside Ophelia in Orleuns, and she was smitten. Not a simple task."

"Forgive me, but I know the story mother." Syrena said, holding her mother's hand.

"I know. Queen Ophelia and Sir Jakob is a tale that is repeated through the ages, but my point is this; a queen must always know when to polish a rock to make it shine but also when to throw it away." Saria stood up. "You have loved Gabriel for so long now, and no amount of years nor thousands of miles can erase that love. If you wish to travel to Jovag, then I give you my blessing. Just know that not all queens are like Ophelia. They don't know how to polish rocks into gems." Saria turned to a statue of Ophelia. "The future may be darker than any of us can imagine and soon hard choices will need to be made."

"Does this have to do with you visiting with Mestra?" Syrena asked, standing up.

Saria turned back to her daughter, smiling, she clasped her daughter's cheek lightly. "Don't worry about that just yet. Go to Jovag and find happiness in this life."

That was all the encouragement Syrena needed. The queen wrote a letter of introduction and gave a bill of passage between the two kingdoms. Once the other Furies arrived a day later, they made plans to begin the expedition north.

In the first days after graduating from the Herd, there were only five Furies: Syrena, Ino, Melantho, Mestra and Althea. Althea would soon fall in combat against the Demon Boar. However, as time went by, more worthy warriors joined the ranks of the Furies. These were the best of the legionnaires. Any of the original four could offer a spot to their fellow legionnaires and now there were twenty seven Furies.

All, including Ino and Melantho, were waiting outside the queen's hall for Syrena and Mestra to finishing gather their things for the long journey.

"You have to take a gift." Mestra said as she and Syrena packed their gear for the trip within the quest chambers of the Queen's Keep. Syrena looked to her friend. Mestra rolled her eyes. "Same old Syrena." She walked to the princess and clasped her by the shoulders. "You intend to make yourself known as a potential bride and therefore you need an introductory gift."

Syrena shook her head. "Damn these Lotcalans." Syrena grinned. "Alright, what would I take?" She wondered aloud.

"Something meaningful and worthy of a princess' station." Mestra replied. "Horses always worked in the past." She shrugged.

"They have excellent horses in Lotcala, many sired by an Amazonian ancestor." Syrena shook her head.

"What about a spice? I hear that saffron is rare in the brother kingdom. Maybe cinnamon or anise even." A voice spoke up. The two women turned to see Cecilia in the doorway.

Syrena and Mestra both bowed to the crown princess. Cecilia motioned for them to rise.

"I won't say I approve of this journey, but I will say that as a princess, saffron, cinnamon or even anise would be an appropriate gift. All three would mark you as the wealthiest contender, I'm sure." Cecilia looked to Syrena. "I'll also add that I think you're a fool for leaving Caleope. Orestilla will not let this go. She hates you."

Syrena nodded. "Yes, she does, and I'd wager that she isn't alone, but those chests will hold my other detractors over for a while."

"It helped that the queen supported your ploy, but what is the end game with Orestilla?" Cecilia asked.

"I hope that she sees reason before long." Syrena replied. "Why did you come to see me?"

"Are our visits so antisocial that they must have a motive to them?" Cecilia asked. "You're right, though. I came for a reason. Mestra, leave us please."

The mage bowed and then exited the room to join the others.

"You are taking two prefects with you. How you got mother to approve that I'll never know." Cecilia remarked.

"They will return. All who wish to return will, even me." Syrena responded.

Cecilia sat on the bed next to Syrena's pack. "You were three when I threw you off this bed and broke your arm. You remember that?" Cecilia looked up to her younger sister, who nodded. "Mother was angry, but father said that your bones would strengthen. If you had gone to father about this first, he would have told you that a broken heart will heal stronger." Cecilia said.

Syrena smiled. "Perhaps, but it was not his place to approve."

"Of course not, but I would not discount his advice." Cecilia answered back.

"I never do." Syrena narrowed her eyes at her sister. "There's something else."

Cecilia smirked. "Orestilla is going to be a problem for you. I control the cavalry and since Orestilla used to be an officer in that very same cavalry, I asked around and some of her agents are within my numbers now. I won't pretend to love you as a Herd sister, but you are my blood sister and I will be damned if I let my ranks betray my blood family."

"Thank you Cecilia."

"Don't thank me. However, I'd expect the same from you." Cecilia replied.

Syrena thought about it and she had never taken the time to investigate the legion's feelings for her sister. She nodded to Cecilia, who continued her thought.

"With you gone for a few months to Lotcala, I think it prudent that someone speaks with the palatine before she plots further." Cecilia finished.

"I think that wise. Would you have someone in mind?" Syrena asked.

"I do as a matter of fact. Me."

The prospect shocked Syrena. "You? You would go against the cavalry?"

"The cavalry isn't plotting against you. Just a pissed off, retired officer that couldn't finish her career on the field. If so, that is conspiracy to commit treason and I can deal with it before it becomes actual treason." Cecilia responded.

"How?"

Cecilia smiled. It wasn't a pleasant smile, but it wasn't exactly a wicked one either. "I'll simply speak with her. My agents have informed me that she has left the queendom to see family, but they know not where. She'll return and I'll speak with her then." Cecilia shrugged.

Syrena wasn't sure, but she had to trust her sister. One day Cecilia would be her queen and that meant putting her faith into her older sister.

Syrena nodded. "Okay, thank you."

"So, now that is settled. If you go to Aquinas' Apothecary, there you can load up with a crate of any herb or spice you like. Aquinas, the shop owner, had the three I mentioned just this morning." Cecilia made her way out of the room.

"Already needing to stock up on supplies?" Syrena chuckled.

"I needed some silphium." Cecilia grinned, turning back to her sister.

Syrena looked confused. "Silphium? That's a contraceptive?" She smiled. "Have you also found love recently?"

Cecilia turned her head and walked out the door. "No, but you're not the only one that brought home spoils of war." The crown princess said as she walked out of the room.

Syrena stood alone, surprised by the admission. Slaves from war were outlawed, and Cecilia would have known that. Syrena shook her head. It would do no good to protest it and Cecilia was already willing to help her with Orestilla. The princess felt it better to finish packing and join the other Furies. First, however, she would need to stop at the apothecary to purchase the proper amount of spices.

The twenty seven warriors all laughed and joked as they loaded two crates each of cinnamon and anise and one large barrel of saffron into a wagon. Another three wagons, full of supplies, trailed behind the women.

"This should mark you as the most likely contender, commander!" One of the Furies said with a smile.

"So I've been told, but I'm hoping I don't need to buy my way back into his heart." Syrena replied.

Ino, standing alongside Syrena and Melantho, smiled as the Furies finished loading the spices into the wagons. "This will be a fun journey. I'm looking forward to meeting the man that captivated your heart."

Syrena grinned. "Perhaps our last chance."

"Well, if nothing else, we'll smell good. Cinnamon is also a good fragrance for me." Melantho laughed.

One Fury, Polydeuces, looked to the Legion Prefect. "You wear cinnamon, ma'am?"

"Not too often but my husband likes the scent, so I purchased a perfume from an apothecary once." Melantho smiled. "I know, back before my posting, I would never have thought of using something worth so much gold as a perfume.

"Nobles and their fineries." Ino chuckled.

Melantho laughed along with Ino. "If it wasn't for this post I'd never wear the stuff."

Syrena looked to her friends. "I bet you wouldn't." Bringing a hearty laughter to their group. "Come, we have to be on the road before long!"

The princess rode her horse out of the gates of the city, followed by her band, and along the road leading north to Jovag. A few weeks on the road was not something that most weary warriors wanted after a yearlong war, but all their spirits were high leaving Verna. Several of the warriors sung songs of triumph and glories from days past, while others would converse about the latest happenings in their lives. Though they were Furies and sisters, many were not together daily. A trip like this gave them a chance to catch up. The nightly camps were the best place for such joys.

For an Amazon, camp life was part of their culture. This was where bonds were forged and strengthened. Camps provided a place to rest and shelter from the elements, a place to eat and celebrate. It was a common feature of all camps to be filled with the smells of roasting meat and the sounds harmonious singing. Camps also provided a place to mourn and recover. Camps were a second home, to some the only home, for Amazonian warriors. It wasn't uncommon that legionnaires birthed many children in the legion or cavalry camps throughout the years.

For the Furies, this was no different. Each night the warriors would set up their camp, cook fine meals of rabbit meat or guinea fowl, and regal each other with stories or legends. Most of the tales were of Amazonian legends and some of Lotcalan history. Syrena and Mestra could fill in the younger warriors on that immense subject. Each having spent time in the kingdom. Eventually one night, as was expected, the topic shifted to Syrena and Gabriel's past.

Sitting at a campfire one night just north of the border with Lotcala, a young Fury named Leontia asked her commander of her past.

"Your highness, what happened between you and Prince Gabriel?" Leontia asked, bringing the other conversations to a halt.

Syrena looked across the campfire at the young legionnaire, her face framed by the light of the flame. She was a newer member of the Furies, having joined the year before. Leontia, however, was a five-year veteran in the Legion and had proven herself in the war against Tresha. She, along with two other legionnaires from her cohort, had held off an attack from over one hundred Treshans. The princess smiled to her younger compatriot.

"That's a long tale, Leonita." Syrena replied.

Another legionnaire, Esther, spoke up. "It is a long night, your highness."

Syrena looked to the other woman and grinned. "It is indeed. Nights are getting longer and soon the solstice will be upon us." She sighed. "Alright, but I'm afraid it isn't the most exciting tale you'll hear in the camps." Syrena leaned forward to put another log on the fire.

The princess leaned back and sighed, breathing in the smell of charred wood as it crackled from the embers. "Ten years ago, Cecilia and I went to Jovag with an entourage of diplomats. Cecilia was to meet with Gabriel and work out the terms of their betrothal with his father and our mother's representative. It was when the queen was with child, the pregnancy was difficult and if she had traveled, she was certain to lose the child. In the end, as most of you all know, it didn't matter." Syrena sniffed. That memory still pained her and her family. She continued on. "My role was to train with the Crown Prince, Liam. Diplomacy, basically. He is famous for his orator skills and acumen in running a kingdom under his father. Our group met with the royal family and worked our way into their society."

Syrena laughed. "Cecilia hated it, Jovag, like the rest of Lotcala, is ruled by men unlike any place in Amazon. They allow for baronesses to rule the land in place of male heirs who are not of age but more often than not, it is the man that rules. Their inheritance line favors the first-born males. Cecilia wasn't comfortable there, and she wasn't too thrilled with Gabriel. For the first two weeks, I hadn't even seen him since our meeting on the first day, but Cecilia would tell me about their time. She found him boring. She said he would talk about the north and his uncle's adventures. Gabriel had yet to have many of his own except for some mountain patrols. He asked about our queendom, but despite his best efforts to engage her in enlightened conversation, Cecilia was indifferent towards him."

Syrena smiled again. "She dragged me along one day while the two walked around the city. It was a tour for us to see the market and other points of interest. I remember nothing from that walk except for Gabriel."

The other women around the fire laughed and whistled.

"Love at first sight?" Leonita asked. "Didn't think that even existed."

Syrena's smile faded. "I used to think I was unlucky in that area. I always knew that Gabriel and I were meant to be, but my mother and King Liam betrothed him to my sister. How could it ever happen?"

"So what did happen?" Haritha, asked.

"Cecilia was happy to have me distract Gabriel while she kept to the libraries or apothecary shops. Cecilia wasn't interested in marrying Gabriel and maybe I'm being selfish, but Gabriel didn't want to marry her either. Besides, I was happy to listen to his tales of the north and his dreams of adventure. We both had dreams of the future and he would listen to mine just as I did his."

"The heart wants what the heart wants." Leonita replied.

"True enough, but my heart was aching for him with each day knowing that he was to marry my sister." Syrena sighed, and then she smiled. "I remember the night before we were to return to Verna, Gabriel gave me my first kiss. Pleasant and sweet. He was just as nervous as I was. I could face the Herd, but in front of him, I was a ball of stress. I wasn't sure how Cecilia would respond if she had ever found out, besides this was the man I had fallen in love with. Of course I was nervous. Only one other knew of our love. Gabriel's brother, Liam. Apart from all that, I felt so different around Gabriel. I felt like I could be calm and let my guard down." The princess looked to the others, engrossed in her tale, and her smile faded. "We left Jovag the next day. I've never been back, and Cecilia resigned herself to the marriage. Famously, it didn't happen, and that's the end of that." Syrena stood up. "Rest up, we leave at dawn." She said before walking to her tent.

Esther looked to the others. "Well, that took a turn."

Mestra smirked as she played with the fire. Magic wafted through her fingers, making the flames dance and spark up in a mesmerizing display. "You only know one side of your commander. She's a tough woman and will stand against Wohd, Malum or any being from beyond the Thin Place. That much everyone knows and has seen, but once she talks about Gabriel, she becomes a waif of a girl." Mestra shook her head. "She doesn't like that. It's like it's a weakness and she hates weakness."

"A true warrior." Leonita said.

"No, she is a queen that will never wear a crown." Haritha countered. Others around the fire cheered at the admiration and the tribute to their commander.

Mestra stood and looked to Syrena's tent. "Never say never." She whispered.

The others behind Mestra and at the second campfire sang songs they had learned during their times in the Herd. Shanties of glory, love and lust. Many passed around skins of wine while others wrote letters home or sonnets to loved ones.

Leonita, playing a seven string lyre, led her sisters in a tender song about finding true love.

"Minerva gave me a rose, a dear gift from her heart. I promised that no war could keep us a part.

A sea I'll sail for a love so true.

Waiting day and night for my safe return. Her love, the underworld, never felt as high a flame burn.

A sea I'll sail for a love so true.

Ladies so fair could never make me stray. I will return to her before my dying day.

A sea I'll sail for a love so true."

Syrena sat in the tent and listened to the words. She removed an old book from her pack and opened to a dried rose, stuck between the pages.

"A sea I'll sail for a love so true." Syrena said to herself.

The Lost Prince

Gabriel's return was not as joyous as he might have hoped. He rode into Jovag with a Hun woman on one side and a half elf woman on the other. The half elf was easier to explain. She was his protégé, Marluna, from the Rangers. A gifted archer and mage, the masters assigned her to Gabriel as a protégé and during their training, Arana, the Hun woman joined up.

Gabriel wasn't sure about the custom, but somehow she owed him a life debt. He could not remember how, but that did not matter because there she was with him and she had made it clear that she was not leaving his side.

Eight years prior to Gabriel's uneventful, yet fateful return, the young prince took off during the night. Only a handful knew of his journey. His uncle Ragnall, and his two best friends; Miralda Holt and Argyle Elbe. Once he had set out, he ventured north through Panyakuta, Coronado and into the Sile Empire before he found the forests of the Northern Continent. His uncle had warned him the difficulties that he would face in reaching the forests, but it was his training under Kagesuke, the Grey Warrior, which was the real test.

Kagesuke was an older Quarmi warrior, advanced in years to the age of nine hundred and twenty-three years old. Legends told of his great battle against Godfrey the Conqueror, a past King of Tresha and Gotistan. Gabriel and the other rangers put little stock in the old tales, as did Kagesuke, but what they knew was his skill. Even in his advanced age, Kagesuke was a feared leader, having been the second leader of the Rangers after had Aklima passed on from the mortal world.

Gabriel honed the skills he had learned at the War Academy in Sirie, a young town named for the queen from seven hundred years prior. In the Rangers, however, Gabriel excelled in these skills. His archery improved, as did his hunting and scouting. Gabriel improved his swordsmanship with the help of Kagesuke and other rangers. His time was well spent, protecting the villagers from Hun raids and Sile incursions.

Gabriel's status and legend grew in the small towns and villages around the southern coasts and even into the mountains of the continent. As his skills grew, the masters gave him many more responsibilities. They even gave him the rank of master ranger and the new Ranger captain assigned a young Marluna as his pupil.

Not all of his experiences had been good ones, though. Gabriel had seen his share of mistakes and battles. He had led men and women, but first he had to be led. For a prince that had excelled in the world, the Rangers offered a chance at humility and for Gabriel it came at a high price. Kagesuke counseled his young protégé, telling him of honorable defeat, a defeat he knew himself. The wise Quarmi preached caution and humility while focusing on self-improvement to ensure success not only on the battlefield but also in life. Gabriel listened to his teacher and focused his attention to training, a goal that would allow him to strengthen his body and his mind, while also refining his skills.

Eventually though, his past caught up to him and he was called home by his uncle. Many had thought the prince had shirked his responsibilities and many of the barons were upset over the king's refusal to divide Gabriel's lands. Lands that were part of his birthright. It was his obligation to venture back south and protect his lands and his family's honor, an honor that he couldn't help but feel that he had besmirched enough.

Taking their leave from the Rangers, Gabriel and Marluna, followed by Arana, arrived in Jovag amid arguments. The lords from Ter Nog and Canton were pushing King Liam to have Gabriel relinquish his lands in absentia. Liam, a righteous king though strict, refused, which was pushing his barons towards rebellion.

Nearly a thousand years had passed since the formation of Lotcala, but the Gota blood still ran through many of the people's veins. However, once Gabriel arrived, though the chamberlain questioned him at the door, the argument was a moot point. Gabriel, the Baron of Antei, a town long since passed its prime, was home.

Fateful Decisions

The Queen's Court did not go well for Orestilla, and nearly two months later the scorned woman arrived at Gib, the capital of Elysia. Orestilla was seeking an audience with the king. Ahab III was not a kind man, but he was a man of tradition. Orestilla was an Amazonian noble woman with noble Elysian blood from a grandfather. She was welcomed, though it was a cooler welcome than what she believed was appropriate.

Within the great hall of Gib, a dark room with just a few windows, sitting high and providing little light, the king sat on a wooden throne. Candles flickered, and the air was as icy as the welcome had been. At least there would be food. Servers and attendants laid out plates of roasted duck and pork.

The king eyed the woman as the courtiers introduced her. Ahab and his advisors probably thought that she wanted to gloat, and they were not entirely wrong.

"Your majesty, enemies could see such a loss as a weakness. Perhaps they might feel like they can prey on you now." The Amazon palatine said. She donned a silken tunic, dyed blue and trimmed in gold, and the laurels of her position as palatine.

"Madam, do you really think it wise to come in here and criticize my handling of the recent war?" Ahab replied with a sneer.

Orestilla grinned at the king's question. "I think it wise, your majesty. However, I also know that you might feel that defeat's keen sting. Allow me to suggest an alternative course of action. I pride myself on my skills in the botanical craft. Like in raising plants from seeds, we often have to trim away the worthless parts of the plant. This allows for more growth. Such pruning might be in order so you and I can grow to reach our heights of power and success. Perhaps an alliance to help foster this growth?"

Ahab leaned forward menacingly. A scar down his right eye and across his lips, parting his beard, made the Amazon woman shiver.

"Do you think I haven't looked to allies?" The king exclaimed, pounding his fist on the arm of his throne.

"Your majesty, I only meant that I could help in your search." Orestilla tried to point out.

Ahab leaned back in the throne. "How?" He narrowed his eyes.

Orestilla smiled. "I am already one of the wealthiest women in the Queendom, and I just came into another sizeable sum of money. I could finance mercenaries from Gota and even work wonders with Emperor Hel. He is a distant relative of mine."

Ahab stroked his grey beard. Fire burned in his green eyes, but he showed restraint. "Gota warriors, like the Lotcalans themselves?"

"Those days are long gone, your majesty. The Lotcalans are little like the Gota now." Orestilla replied.

"Perhaps, but Hel? You think you, an Amazonian palatine, can sway him?" Ahab smirked, bringing a laugh to members of the court.

Orestilla smiled to the king and his court. "Why do you think he sought such a quick resolution? These seeds, planted so long ago now only need cultivation."

"Let's hope. For your sake." Ahab stood. "Speak with your relative, Hel, and if he will treat with me, then

I'll be happy to use his horsemen to conquer those Lotcalan bastards!"

Orestilla grinned an even bigger grin than before. "Of course, your majesty."

* * * *

It took Syrena and the other Furies twenty-two days to reach the outskirts of Jovag. From the plains just south of the city they could see the tall keep and the outlying towns. Farmland stretched to the horizon. It was still morning, and the sun was not yet at its zenith, but the warm light was already comforting.

"This is like Verna." Leonita said in awe. "Such vast fields!"

"These fields feed the people of the city only. Just like in the queendom, the lords feed their people. Fields like this exist all over the kingdom." Syrena replied. "However, that's part of their tension within the kingdom. The barons can rule their own lands without a lot of oversight by the king. So long as they pay their taxes."

"How many times have you come here?" Esther asked.

"Just once." Syrena replied with a smile. "But it is a place you'll never forget."

"Especially not with your experiences." Mestra joked. "For me, I've been here three times. All to visit the mage guild." She scoffed and shook her head. "At least that's what they call it. It's not a proper guild." She finished, looking to Cassia and Riva. They were the only other mages in the Furies, each woman was a protégé of Mestra's.

As the band of women trotted along the road, they passed traders, laborers and many others going about their day. On any other day, twenty-seven Amazons would be a sight to see, but on this day, the princess' standard was waving in the air as the riders rode by. This brought many more eyes to the women. Many workers in the fields close by turned to the riders with a friendly wave or smile. Children ran up to the woman, bringing flowers to the princess and her companions.

"I heard tales yet I never realized it would be like this. They truly love us." A Fury named Callisto remarked, taking a lily from a girl.

"We are their sisters and they are our brothers. Not just in arms but in life." Melantho responded with a smile. She waved to the people she passed.

"We should have worn our armor." Ino said to Syrena.

It might have made a much more spectacular procession. However, even in the white or beige linen chitons and red chlamys, an Amazonian cloak, and their sandals, the women looked magnificent!

"We are not here as a military envoy." Syrena answered.

Ino looked at her commander. "Yet we brought our armor."

"It is better to have it and not need it than to need it and not have it." Syrena smiled.

"Damn, you sound like your mother." Ino laughed. The surrounding riders joined in the joke.

Mestra rode up to Syrena. "Princess, we're nearing the southern gate. Allow me to present you to the guards."

Syrena raised an eyebrow. "Mestra, I can speak for myself."

"We are here as an official bridal presentation. You should not. It would not be proper etiquette for a princess." Mestra replied before speeding her horse up to ride up to the guard house.

Syrena shrugged.

"She's been here more than us, your highness." Melantho said, riding up to the princess. "She has an idea to their ways."

"Of course, but..." Syrena paused. "It's fine."

"Except that it's not." Ino said, picking up on Syrena's tone.

"I wanted very little pomp to this visit." Syrena said.

"Kind of hard when you're coming to include yourself in the prince's love life." Melantho replied.

Syrena glared at her friend. "Mel, have I told you how happy that you could come."

"Happy to help, your highness." Melantho smiled before riding to catch up with Mestra.

Ino scoffed. "Damn nobles." Syrena turned to the woman. "Well, it's true!" Ino said in response to Syrena's gaze.

The rest of the band of warriors rode up and caught up to the two women.

"We are here to present Princess Syrena to King Liam as a candidate for marriage for Prince Gabriel." Mestra said. "Why is that hard to comprehend?"

"What's going on?" Syrena asked.

Melantho looked at the princess. "These guards are sending a rider to the palace. It seems that our visit isn't at the best time."

"This is becoming a bit of a habit." Syrena murmured.

"Do you need proof?" Ino yelled out to the guard. "We have the letter from the crown prince and a letter of presentation from Queen Saria."

The guard looked to Ino and bowed. "No, ma'am. We recognize the coat of arms and we gladly welcome you all. We received word of Princess Syrena's arrival, but they instructed us to expect a small delegation. Not..." The guard counted.

"There are twenty-seven of us, sir." Ino finished.

"Yes, twenty-seven. We want to make sure..." Another guard rushing from the city interrupted the first guard. The two conversed in whispers. "Yes, of course."

"Please come in and allow Sigur and I to escort you to the palace." The guard bowed, clicked his heels and spun around. He turned back and bowed again. "Forgive me and the delay. I am Sergeant Peter Shortmane." He turned back again and walked to the Amazons through the town and towards the palace.

The women followed the guards as they made their way through the busy streets of the town. The city was vibrant with a diversity not seen in most cities, except for the port city of Ter Nog. However, Jovag was a massive city of stone and brick buildings dating back centuries. The walls of the city predated the Gota invasion and even predated the Yendis. This was a city with bustling shops, schools, hospitals and plenty of guardhouses. As the capital of a great kingdom, Jovag was home to large markets and trading post. This meant that Jovag had to supply protection for the local trade routes.

The Furies with their escorts took in the sights of the large city, passing small shops, baking bread and others putting meat in the windows. Near one shop two men were pulling an enormous pig off a metal rack that was sitting over burning logs.

"Look! They had a whole pig cooked on that rack!" Callisto exclaimed, watching the men lay the pig on a table in front of the butcher. She pulled her horse over to the shop, watching the butcher chop the meat with a cleaver and then spread a red liquid over the chopped meat. The butcher looked over to Callisto and scooped a small piece of the meat into a spoon.

"Tell me what you think." The butcher said, walking to the Callisto.

Callisto took the piece and sniffed it before biting it. She grinned and finished the piece. "Amazing! So tangy, with a hint of spice." She said.

"Give me a moment and I'll give you a pot full. My gift." The butcher smiled before walking into his shop.

In a flash he was back with a small terracotta pot full of meat. "Boucan is my specialty. Whole pig cooked over wood overnight, chopped up and covered with a red vinegar sauce."

Callisto thanked the man and accepted the pot with a smile, taking a sniff of the smoky and tangy meat. She held the warm pot gingerly as she rode to catch up to her companions.

"What's that?" Riva asked when Callisto reached the group.

"Something called boucan. It's pig, and it's delicious!" Callisto replied, offering some to her friend.

Riva reached over and took a pinch of the succulent meat. She bit into the juicy piece and smiled.

"Wow! That is delicious!" Riva said. "We must go back to that shop."

Callisto smiled and nodded as she munched on more of the meat.

The rest of the easy paced ride through the city saw more people coming out to admire the procession, a few brought more gifts of flowers or bread loafs.

"The people are so generous." Esther said after taking a loaf of pumpernickel bread from a Lotcalan woman.

"There is a decent chance that many of them are distant cousins." Melantho replied. "I know I have Lotcalan blood from my grandfather."

"Interesting." Esther replied. "I hadn't thought of our people being so closely related."

"That's right. Your family was from Kesh originally." Melantho remarked.

"Still allies though, ma'am." Esther said, her rich Kesh accent shining through her words, marking her heritage of the southern regions of the continent.

"True enough." Melantho smiled to ease her fellow warrior. "I meant no disrespect."

One hundred years prior, the tensions between Lotcala and the Kingdom of Nashoba reached a climax and a thirty year war between the two nations broke out. Nashoba was an old kingdom on the southern end of the central continent founded by the illegitimate daughter of Charles I of Lotcala, Rowena Enano, during the second century of the Carolyngian Age. Few knew the exact cause of the war, other than the claim that Rowena's descendants pushed for the throne of Lotcala. The Empire of Kesh, neighbor of Nashoba, stepped in as allies to Lotcala so they could claim more lands from their southern neighbors. A costly mistake.

Even with the combined forces of Lotcala, Panyakuta, Amazon, Kesh and Gota mercenaries; Nashoba was too strong. The King of Nashoba had united with the forces of the kingdoms of Biset and Quis against Lotcala. What many expected to be a brief war turned into a thirty year war of attrition that ended with Kesh in ruins and a princess of Lotcala betrothed to a prince of Nashoba. Some years later, the princess died mysteriously.

As for those from Kesh, in return for their help, Lotcala and Amazon offered a refuge. Many took their allies up on the kind offer to find a new home in the north. Others, determined to rebuild their former empire, stayed behind. Esther's family was part of the former group. Her grandfather and grandmother settled in Amazon after the war and prospered in the spice trade.

The band of twenty-seven warriors and the two guards zig zagged through the city, passing many more shops, houses, the mage guild and the Temple of Scholars, one of the many schools within the city. Soon the Furies were at the palace walls, eight yards thick with a massive portcullis to guard the entrance. Syrena dismounted, as did her companions.

"Your highness, our stable hands will see to your mounts. If you and your sisters follow me, I'll lead you into the palace and the chamberlain." Sergeant Peter said with a bow. "The king's throne room is deeper within the palace and no longer in the great hall, your highness."

"Times change." Syrena smiled.

"Yes, they do, your highness. King Liam felt prudent to have a small room for his court." Peter replied, before turning and leading the women inside.

The Furies followed the man inside and marveled at the frescos that lined the walls. Brilliantly painted images that featured royal figures, battles, and other historic occasions. Sunlight filtered in through the large windows along the walls, showing the bright hues in the murals.

"These murals are impressive." Leonita said, walking along the corridors with her sisters. Many Amazons found art to be well worth the skill, marveling at the intricate detailing. During their time in the Herd, academics and art were also taught alongside war. Many famous artists, sculptors and singers came out of the queendom. There, artists, like warriors, sought perfection in their daily crafts.

"That's why this part of the palace is called the Halls of Frescos. Each painting details a great deed or event." Syrena explained. "I would come her and stare at the paintings for hours each day when I was here ten years ago. It's the kingdom's history. Good and bad."

The group turned down a hall and a few of the frescos changed in atmosphere. Now the images seemed to show more recent defeats.

"You are right, your highness." Sigur remarked. "Some more recent additions are of our defeat in the Southern War with Nashoba." He motioned to a painting on his left.

Brightly painted frescos showed the fleet sailing to the south with great enthusiasm. However, the images that followed showed a bleaker outcome. War and death on battlefields. Several feet of the plaster wall were filled with red rivers, fallen warriors, and clashing armies. A wedding was the final image. The princess that was used as a pawn for peace.

"That's tragic." Esther said, stopping to view the frescos. "I never knew the price of my life with you sisters." She said, tenderly touching a painted Amazonian warrior.

"Our people, like the Lotcalans, were bonded in war. Bonds forged in battle can never be broken." Mestra replied from behind, clasping Esther's shoulder. "Come, the king awaits."

At the end of the hall, a tall Lotcalan noble stood at the door with a serious look on his face.

The group approached him and he bowed to Syrena.

"Princess, welcome." The man said, lifting from his bow. His blonde hair flew in front of his eyes, but he was quick to move the strains out of his face.

Peter stepped up. "Chamberlain Cullenhun, I present Princess Syrena of the Queendom of Amazon and her sisters, the Furies."

"Yes, sergeant. I'm aware of who they are." Cullenhun replied. The chamberlain sighed.

"Sir Chamberlain, may I ask your full name?" Syrena said.

"Of course. I am Alaric Cullenhun. Son of Manor Lord Euric Cullenhun." The man replied with a feigned smile and a quick bow. "I am the king's chamberlain."

"I see. You're a new face from my last visit." Syrena reached in her satchel. "Please accept this invite from Crown Prince Liam."

Alaric accepted the letter and read it. He nodded and handed it back to Syrena. "Forgive me, but no one gave us notice of your arrival until just yesterday. However, an entourage of twenty seven is unexpected. Rest assured, we are not completely unprepared."

"We sent a rider." Ino replied.

"Yes, but as chamberlain, I'm not the first to receive the most up-to-date news. Not unless I seek it out. The Lord Steward would have been the keeper of that knowledge." Alaric called over three attendants. "Please allow me to escort you to your chambers for your stay. The king has given me instructions to have you join him for a feast in the great hall tonight. I'm sure, given the reason for your visit, that this will be more than a simple welcoming meal."

Alaric walked the Amazons through more halls, painted with more frescos and portraits. The natural light coming in from the wide windows helped to illuminate the corridor.

"So many tall windows." Riva remarked.

"Terrible for defense." Cassia said, a few Furies nodded in agreement.

"We allow our walls to defend us. That and the keeps around the perimeter of the city." Alaric answered.

"Maybe an army won't breech the walls and maybe they will." Cassia shot back.

"Hasn't happened yet, not for lack of trying." Alaric replied. He stopped and turned towards the women. "These are your chambers. The entire wing is yours for the duration." He walked off but stopped short. "Someone will call upon you when the feast begins and the attendants will be along with your belongings." He started walking off again but stopped yet again. This time next to Callisto. Looking at the young Fury, he noticed her pot. "Boucan?"

Callisto smiled and nodded. She opened the pot and offered Alaric a taste. He took a pinch of the meat and gave her a smile and through a mouth full of meat he thanked her.

"What a nice man." Callisto said. Others rolled their eyes.

"You think everyone is nice. He was a jerk." Cassie put in.

"He's a manor lord's second or third born son." Syrena said. "Chamberlains are never first borns. He won't inherit and he feels that this is beneath his station."

Ino shrugged. "Can't blame anyone for wanting more out of life." The others nodded.

"Well, let's rest until the feast." Syrena said, pushing a door to her right open. "Ino, Mel and Mestra are with me. The rest of you divide out as you wish. Remember to behave yourselves." Syrena warned with a glare. "Show the decorum of Amazons."

As the hours passed, the women rested and acclimated themselves to the palace. Some walked around, finding the gardens or marveling at the art along the walls. Others found the barracks and compared notes with the King's Guards. Callisto and Riva walked through the town, searching the markets for more food to try. Before returning to the palace the two had several crates of pastries, meats, breads and of course, a few more pots of boucan.

"What is this savory meat?" Ino exclaimed. "I can't stop eating it!"

Syrena smirked as she took a handful. "Boucan. A specialty here in Lotcala. I've tried to make it back home, but I just can't get it right." She ate what she had in her hand, reached for more. "It's an old recipe. The cook smokes the whole pig over wood, usually over a pit or in the ground, and they leave it for hours. Overnight, even. Once done, they chop it up and mix it with a type of vinegar and red pepper sauce. They grow the peppers near the coast and in Lostwood. Some of the best soil comes from those regions." Syrena ate more of the decadent meat. "It's from the old way of smoking meat that the Gota used when they used to raid lands around the world. They had to preserve the meat, and smoking was one way. It doesn't last as long as salt curing, like we do, but it's still delicious."

Alaric smiled. "It's the best here in Jovag, but Ter Nog has a variation of the recipe that is close but not as good. Less vinegar and they use the juice from tomatoes. Don't get me started on how they do it in Hardstone." Alaric said, shaking his head at the doorway of Syrena's chambers. "If you are all ready, we can walk to the great hall now." He said before walking out into the hallway. "If you like boucan, then you'll love the compliments to the meat being served tonight."

"We'll be ready shortly." Syrena smiled.

A few moments later Syrena and her fellow sisters walked down the corridor towards the great hall.

Before entering, the Chamberlain stopped them. "Please wait to be announced." Alaric walked in and called attention to the hall by ringing a metal bell near the entrance. "I present Princess Syrena of Amazon." The princess walked into the hall and was escorted to the head table by an attendant. Syrena noticed that the Lord Steward, Sir Edward Alban, was also at the head table. He offered her a smile as she arrived.

Syrena dressed in a white peplos, trimmed in a red and gold band, and clasped with golden pins. This particular peplos, like those of her sisters, was ankle length, as opposed to the knee length of their everyday chitons. Syrena's brown hair was curled and pinned high with thin strains on each side of her face. She wore her silver laurel crown atop her head, showing her position as princess. Like her sisters, she wore a himation, an Amazonian cloak, over her left shoulder and tied near her waist. The only difference in hers and her sisters' was the purple color of Syrena's himation.

Once Syrena was standing at her seat, Alaric called upon the next highest officials of the Amazonian delegation. "Presenting Prefects Ino Selinofoto and Melantho Laskaris. Presenting Magister Mestra Pappas."

The three woman, wearing blue himations over their beige peplos, went to the table to the right of the head table. It took a few more minutes, but finally all the Furies were announced and given seats based on their position. A few of the younger women were seated on the further end of the hall, but they were not lacking for company as several minor Lotcalan lords were seated nearby.

Alaric rang the bell once more. "May I present his majesty, King Liam, her grace Queen Clotide and their royal highnesses, Crown Prince Liam and Lady Theodora."

The Lotcalan royals entered the hall and walked to the head table where Syrena was standing. She noted their dress, different from the style of the Amazons. Each member wore cotton tunics or dresses, with silk robes over them. The king and queen each wore their crowns. The crowd wore similar fashions, though none had as fine of designs on their fabrics as the king. King Liam had golden stags embroidered into his robes.

Queen Clotide had golden ravens in hers. Each an indication of their respective houses.

The king and prince, along with a few other members of the court, also wore livery collars, showing their titles. This was not a simple dinner by any means. This was a royal festival meant to bring out as many nobles as possible. Many manor lords were present and four barons as well. Prince Gabriel, however, was not in attendance.

As the guest of honor, Syrena was seated to the king's left, while the queen was on his right. The Lord Steward was at the far end on the right while the crown prince and his wife were on Syrena's left. The Lord Marshal, Lord Chancellor and Lord Treasurer were away from the capital and wouldn't be back for some time.

Servers brought out large trays and plates of food. Instantly, the hall smelled of mouthwatering meat from roasting fires. Roasted quail and goose, brazed lambs and finally boucan. Along with the meats, the servers brought out trays of cheeses and breads were placed on the tables. Syrena also saw wooden bowls of vegetables being served at the tables. She smiled.

"Vinegar chopped cabbage! I've missed it." Syrena remarked.

King Liam smiled. "Then, please allow me to serve you a healthy portion." He took a spoon and scooped up a mound of the cabbage, carrot and vinegar dish for the Amazonian princess' plate.

Syrena grinned, looking at the green and red cabbage, mixed with the carrots and seasoned the salt and black pepper, stewing in vinegar. She smelled the tart aroma of the vegetables and ate each of the dishes in front of her. Syrena looked around the hall and saw others enjoying the meal. Her sisters were devouring plates of boucan, quail and the chopped cabbage. Syrena smiled.

"For all except Mestra, this is their first time in Lotcala." Syrena said to those at her table.

"Well then, I hope they enjoy their time here in our kingdom." Liam smiled.

"The wonderful food overwhelms them." Syrena chuckled.

"If I remember correctly, Amazons are quite the connoisseurs of meats." Queen Clotide remarked.

"We are, and Prefect Ino is one of the foremost critics on meat." Syrena said, pointing to her friend.

Ino was grabbing a rib of lamb in her right hand and a goose leg in her other hand, laughing and carrying on with her tablemates. Syrena raised an eyebrow. "She's usually much more voracious around meat than this." The princess said, bringing a laugh from the table.

Ino looked up to Syrena and toasted her friend with the goose leg. Syrena took her goblet of wine and returned the toast to the smiling Ino.

The prince turned to Syrena. "I should mention it before it becomes too late in the evening, but unfortunately Gabriel isn't here."

Syrena made a half smile and sipped her wine. It was a red wine, semi-sweet. She put her cup down. "I half expected him to leave before I arrived. Should I be insulted?"

"I understand your feelings, but he did not go far, nor out of any spite. Duty called. He was given and accepted the title of Baron of Antei, his birthright." The prince answered. "You remember how to get to Antei, I assume?"

Syrena smiled. "I do, my lord. A long but friendly road." Syrena's smile faded. "I remember the town not being too full of life, however."

"That has been the case for years. I hope that Gabriel can change Antei's fortune." Prince Liam said. "It is all of our hopes."

Syrena smiled. "He is a bit more resourceful than my sister gave him credit for. He always found ways to get things when needed. I look forward to seeing him soon."

The prince smiled. "Then tonight we'll enjoy the festivities and tomorrow you and your sisters can journey to meet with Gabriel. However, should you decide to stay a few days, you'll be welcomed here in the palace as well."

"Thank you, my lord." Syrena replied. She looked out again as she ate, seeing her companions enjoying their meals and conversations.

"You should know that Gabriel did not return alone." The prince said before sipping his wine. "Two women, a half-elf and a Hun, returned with him. One is his ward or protégé in the Rangers. The other, a bodyguard, I understood it."

"Should I be concerned?" Syrena asked, looking to the prince.

"Only if you seek to threaten him." The prince smiled. "From what Gabriel told me, she is fulfilling a debt to him for saving her life. Nothing more. She's strong and a skilled fighter."

"Good to know. Thank you, my lord." Syrena replied. She then tapped her pewter goblet with her fork. She nodded to Polydeuces, Ester and Cassia, then the three left the hall.

Syrena stood, her goblet held in a toast. "Your majesties, I've come as you know to offer my hand to Prince Gabriel in marriage. Though it is tradition here in Lotcala for the man to ask for the hand, in the Queendom, women take more action in such matters."

King Liam smiled. "I had heard such joyous news. Unfortunately, Gabriel left for the barony, but I'm sure he would be just as delighted as we are. You have my blessing."

Syrena smiled. "Thank you, your majesty and as a proper thank you and groom price I offer you these gifts of cinnamon, saffron and anise." The three warriors brought in the crates and barrel, enjoying the 'oohs' and 'ahhs' from the gathered crowd. "Luxury ingredients from exotic lands."

King Liam stood and walked to the crates and barrel, taking a long whiff. The Queen and the prince joined him. "This is magnificent! Sure to keep our chef busy with exquisite meals." King Liam exclaimed. The crowd clapped at the sight.

Attendants took the spices away and the king and his family rejoined Syrena at the head table. The three warriors went back to their seats, and the party wore on. Within the hour, the Amazons had shed their cloaks and wore only their chitons as they drank as much as they could handle, trying to out drink the Lotcalans. Most did just that.

At the further end of the hall from the head table, Syrena saw that Esther and Riva had already tried to best each other in arm wrestling, including some Lotcalans in their fun.

"Oh, how I've missed this." King Liam remarked, smiling.

"Your majesty?" Syrena asked, turning her head to the king.

"The fun of a feast. We haven't had many in the last eight years." He replied, looking at Syrena. "This is what a party should be about, fun!" King Liam motioned for an attendant. "Bring out the entertainers. We have a fire breather! Bring him out!" The king laughed as others showed off their strength or tell jokes at their tables. A chorus of laughter and cheer echoed around the hall. King Liam cheered on a few of the lords arm wrestling the Furies.

After most had finished eating, the attendance within the hall began to further mix with one another as people rose from their seats to visit with old and new friends. King Liam walked over to the center of the hall and stood next to Ino, watching an arm wrestling match between Callisto and the son of Manor-lord Hubert Blacktower's son, Robert.

"Ten gold falcons on the Fury!" Ino yelled.

"I'll take that bet!" King Liam laughed.

The two shook hands and handed their gold to Alaric. The Chamberlain stood, stoned face, as everyone broke out in merriment.

The hall was lively throughout the night. Court entertainers regaled the crowd while the fire breather was running out of fuel. Celebrations had been rare in the kingdom, so this had been the perfect chance for everyone to rejoice again. A good night for all!

The rising sun was filtering through the narrow windows of the great hall. The large room was a mess with leftover food, spilled wine, mead and ale. Among the mess were several Furies, passed out and hung over.

Syrena, Ino, Melantho and Mestra walked into the hall alongside the smiling king. There they saw the leftovers of their band of sisters. Most still passed out from the alcohol or just waking up from a drunken slumber.

"Figured as much. Poor things can't hold their own yet." Ino said, seeing the warriors sprawled out on the floor or on tables.

King Liam laughed at the scene, his hands tucked into his sleeves. "It's good to have some fun again." He smiled at the scene before him. "We need more feasts like last night. It might bring back the happiness to the palace."

Ino, Melantho and Mestra went to work waking their sisters up. Kicking their sandals or splashing water over the women.

Mestra pulled Callisto up, the younger warrior still wobbly from her hangover.

"How the hell are you looking so fresh and wide awake, ma'am?" Callisto asked, looking at Mestra.

Mestra smiled. "Pappas women know how to hold their liquor." She laughed. "You should see my sister."

"I have." Callisto replied. Her voice raspy from all the wine and mead the night before.

Syrena smiled at the king. "Your majesty…"

The king smiled. "Journey well and tell my son not to be a stranger. He has a home here too. I want him to know that all is forgiven."

Syrena nodded. "I will but you'll forgive me if I give him a good knock on the head before I completely forgive him." She smiled.

"I wouldn't expect anything less from Saria's daughter!" Liam laughed. The two embraced in a hug. "Farewell. Next time we meet I should hope to call you daughter." Liam gave her a smile as they broke their hug. "I better fetch attendants to clean the hall." The king said. "Their probably just as hung over!" The Furies heard the king laugh from down the hall.

A Second Chance

"We have plenty of gold and silver to make the deal. Three thousand Gota mercenaries." Orestilla said to her ward. The two women stood on the docks of Gib.

"My lady, what of the retainers from Nashoba?" The ward replied.

Orestilla squinted, looking to the rising sun. She shook her head. "The treaty doesn't allow for Nashoba retainers. They won't work for me, anyway." She turned to her ward, anger flashed in her eyes. "You should remember that my grandmother was a hero during that war. She rode down many of the Nashobans."

The ward nodded and slunk behind Orestilla as the noble woman walked back to the city. The way the ward heard it through court gossip, Orestilla's grandmother actually rode down innocent villagers, mostly women and children. That is partly why she was stripped of her rank. Her death in battle soon after kept the demotion quiet.

"These mercs will be enough to tip the scales in our favor. Now we just need Hel to come through and this plan will be in place." Orestilla remarked. "Once the contact arrives, be sure to stamp the contract with my seal. I need to visit another contact of mine."

The ward watched as her master disappeared into the town. She waited for a few moments and then whistled a tune. After she stopped, she took a small piece of parchment and scribbled a quick note with a piece of charcoal.

A falcon appeared and perched on a nearby post. The ward walked to the falcon and rolled up the parchment. She tied it to the bird's leg. The ward whistled a different tune, and the falcon lifted off the post and flew away to the southwest.

A short time later, Orestilla reappeared behind her ward.

"Did the mercenaries arrive yet?" The Amazon noble asked.

"No, my lady." The ward replied.

"Fine. I'm going to get some wine. Continue waiting here." Orestilla said dismissively to her ward as she left the docks.

"Of course, my lady." The ward said. She turned towards the horizon. She pulled her black cloak over her head. On her hand was a small tattoo, a blackbird. She stood and waited.

* * * *

Syrena, Melantho and Leonita went out to gather supplies for the road to Antei. It was not an ideal trip; leaving so soon after arriving in Jovag, but it was necessary. The Furies had a limited amount of time in Lotcala and many miles to ride.

"We have plenty of water and ale in the skins." Melantho said. "Leonita went off to purchase cloth and healing herbs." She looked to Syrena.

Syrena was eyeing a healthy portion of beef ribs on a hanging rack just outside a butcher shop.

"Add a couple crates of dried meat." Syrena added.

"Salted pork?" Melantho asked.

"Can we get any beef?" Syrena asked.

"It won't last as long, but yes we can pick some up for the trip." Melantho said with a half-smile. "We'll load up what we can and meet the others by the southern gate."

The Furies had to ride nearly three hundred miles to Antei, the former home of the Goldwater family. The story of their fall was tragic, indeed. Hugo Goldwater was once the patriarch of the powerful family. The betrayal of his eldest and only surviving heir broke the king's most loyal subject. He renounced his position as the Lord Steward and made himself a recluse. He was still loyal to the kingdom, but no longer wishing to be a part of the administration. His nephews, however, had different ideas.

If only one thing can be remembered of the reign of Charles I, was that he was a king during the kingdom's most rebellious time. Hugo's family and new heirs, still reeling from the patriarch's losses, aligned themselves with Elysia and stood against Charles. War broke out.

Charles, older than he had been in previous wars, relied heavily on his son, Alfred, and daughter, Rowena, to lead his army. Both successfully and decisively defeated the Elysian and Goldwater alliance, putting the Goldwater family to the sword. Ending the long line of the previous Barons of Goldwater.

The true war began once Charles' children returned. Rowena, as the oldest and by far the true leader of the army, asked for Antei as her share of the spoils. Charles, however, rebuffed her because of illegitimacy. The court knew Queen Sirie influenced the injustice. Her reputation already tarnished from rumors of fratricide, she harbored an open and growing dislike for her stepdaughter. Sirie's influence over Charles was too great, however, and they scorned Rowena. King Charles awarded Antei to Crown Prince Alfred. In one last insult, the prince's coat of arms changed to a golden stag head, like Canton's, atop the golden fish and blue shield of the Goldwater family.

Though Rowena asked for Antei, she was given a gentry title within the barony instead. A disgrace given her stature as the king's eldest child. A lowely title under a manor lord, not even under the baron himself.

Rowena cursed her family and refused to swear loyalty to the crown prince as the new baron in response. Subsequently, she was banished as a traitor. Already a successful mercenary captain prior to the war with Elysia, Rowena left Lotcala with all those still loyal to her and journeyed south. Eventually founding the Kingdom of Nashoba. Many people think of Lotcala's tensions with Elysia as being their most hated rivalry, but in actuality it was with the southern Kingdom of Nashoba.

The rivalry between the two monarchies ate away at Charles. His only daughter, a girl he loved and cherished, had left because he could not shut out his queen's influence. Rowena became a ghost, floating within his every thought. Finally, after years of torment, Charles succumbed to his guilt.

The turbulent history of Antei was famous and even the Amazons knew of the town's tragic past. A past that was saddled on to every prince or baron, a burden of a title. Once a title for a town and barony that was on the cusp of greatness, only to fall to whims of angry men.

Three hundred miles was a long ride, not as long as their ride to Jovag, but still long enough to take a week. Their pace was slower than their ride to Jovag, but it was just as scenic. Farmlands and rolling fields as far as the eye could see stretched before the Amazon warriors. The area looked little different from their own homeland.

Tiny villages around the roadside offered a chance to let the horses rest, to converse with locals or to have a snack. While Amazons preferred camps, Syrena housed her band in the roadside inns and taverns between Jovag and Antei.

"I want to meet with the people. If Gabriel accepts me, I want to the people to know me." Syrena said to Mestra as the two enjoyed a cup of wine by a roaring hearth on the third night of the journey.

"I can certainly understand that." Mestra replied. "The others seem to like the soft beds."

"Maybe it is better for their backs." Syrena said, smiling.

Mestra sneered at the thought. "But the ground teaches us more than soft beds."

"Just because you prefer to sleep on the floor of your room doesn't mean the rest of us do!" Syrena laughed.

"And yet I can feel when someone comes to call on me." Mestra sipped her wine. "No one gets the jump on me."

Around them, the Furies enjoyed their night, the food and the ale. In the morning they would ride out. Still more miles south, but the air was changing and fields of wheat gave a pleasant smell for all travelers.

Hillsides lay ahead of the riders, but nothing too mountainous. Rolling hills were the typical landscape of Lotcala's southern reaches and part of their defense against Elysia. The hills slowed the war machines that could siege a town or city. The hills also help divert water to the more fertile regions, a boon to the farms in the Antei and Greenfield baronies.

Three more days of riding gave Syrena and the Furies a chance to mingle with the local populace. Like in many other areas, the popularity of the Amazons was clear. Their coming preceded them as well. Many locals were along the roads awaiting the procession. So many people came out to view the Furies that they decided to wear their famous muscle cuirass armor. Syrena donned her famous boar cloak, a story even the Lotcalans knew. Ino, Mestra and Melantho all took prizes from the same boar and they wore them around their bodies as jewelry pieces.

Finally, the Furies came over a rolling hillside and faced a walled town. The wall was not as high as the walls of Jovag, but they looked just as old. Damage from siege engines was visible and plaster was flaking off the wall. The main gate was open and a lone guard sat out front. Travelers, though only a handful, and farmers walked in and out, but it was quiet. The sun was setting, but work was still in full swing.

Syrena led her band of Furies closer and there they saw the lone guard sitting on a stone bench, his back leaned against the war. They could see from his features as they approached that the guard was a Quarmi. Not unusual in Lotcala, given the close friendship between Orleuns and the kingdom. Even closer than just allies, with the Ironhand family marrying into the Mori Daimyo five hundred years prior.

The Amazonian princess rode towards the Quarmi, she could tell instantly by his posture that it was her old friend Minimoto.

Closer to the gate, Syrena and the others could hear his song and the melodic playing of his gottan, a wooden three string instrument with a long neck and plucked with a tortoise shell.

Cheerful wintertime

A beautiful snow dances

because of the fox

Syrena pulled on her horse's reins, stopping the majestic stallion. She leaned in to listen to another verse.

Darkening fountain

A beautiful rain dances

enjoying the fox

Syrena took note of his clothes. A silk robe over his silk shirt, called a jinbaori, embroidered with crescent moons and the traditional hakama style pants of the Quarmi. He was dressed as a warlord's son.

Minimoto looked up from under his jingasa. "Good evening, princess. I see you are doing well and well accompanied." He looked around the princess to her fellow warriors. "The lord said you would not come. He hoped you would, but he doubted. As true as the sun's rise each day and setting each night. That is what I told him about the great Princess Syrena." The Quarmi added.

"You seem to be more faithful to my love for Gabriel than Gabriel is, Minimoto." Syrena replied. "Your playing has improved."

"Practice." Minimoto replied.

"Are you on guard duty?" Syrena asked. "The son of the Usagi Daimyo?"

Minimoto smiled, if one could tell from behind his face wrap, tightly wound around his mouth. "No task is beneath a warrior if done in service of his lord."

"Quarmi wisdom and honor." Ino said. "Such a commendable outlook." She smiled.

Minimoto nodded. "Alas, I'm not on duty, however. Prince Gabriel has removed the guards to the southern front. He doesn't trust the northern Elysian lords. I trust fate, and fate is cruel to those that try to circumvent her way." Minimoto said. He stood and slung his gottan behind him. "Allow me to take you to the lord's manor."

"Manor?" Melantho asked. "Isn't Gabriel a prince and the ruling baron? Wouldn't that mean a keep?"

Minimoto lowered his head. "The years have not been kind to Antei. The lord has done what he can to rebuild. For now a manor, the old manor from years gone by, is what remains of the lord's residence. My lord has gone to great lengths to make it livable. That is why we were not in Jovag for your arrival."

"Duty calls." Syrena said, and Minimoto nodded.

Minimoto walked to his horse, tied up just behind the wall, and he led the Amazons through the town.

"This town must have been beautiful in its heyday." Leonita said.

From the front of the group, Syrena nodded. "It was. I came here a couple times, Gabriel was the baron then too, but he didn't administer to the town at the time. That was left to Daimyo Usagi Katsuichi, Minimoto's father."

"The great warlord Usagi Katsuichi?!" Callisto asked in amazement.

"He prefers just Katsuichi." Minimoto said with a smile. "But yes, that would be him."

The town was lively, given its tragic history. Trade was happening, and many crops were being hauled along the roads in wagons. Life had slowly returned to Antei. The town looked better than the rumors had said.

The market was in the center of town, surrounded by the shops and craft workers that occupied the town. Near the main road, Syrena and the other Furies could hear the sound of metal workers hammer molten steel from their forges. Vendors calling out for their wares.

"Minimoto, how many people live in Antei now?" Melantho asked, looking around and seeing more life than see had expected to see.

The Quarmi looked around. "I'd say roughly five thousand and growing by the week." Minimoto stopped his horse and turned to the Furies. "When my father administered the town, it was surviving and growing, a little. However, in recent years and more so over the few months that Gabriel has been here to run the day-to-day activities, the town has felt more alive." He turned his horse and walked towards the motte where the manor sat atop.

"Why have people begun to come here again?" Ino asked.

Minimoto shrugged. "I guess they think that with the prince they might have a better chance at a good life. These fields are fertile once again, the river is still full of fish and ready for commerce. Really, the only problem was in the old days people didn't want to be associated with traitors, and more recently the people didn't know if it was worth the risk. The fields weren't always so fertile and the region was hurting. The earth healed with fewer people around over the centuries and the lands returned to their former glory."

"Don't the people rotate the fields?" Esther asked.

Minimoto turned his head and from his peripheral vision he saw the Amazon asking the question. "Of course, but those were hard centuries after a devastating battle. Antei was destroyed in spirit and almost completely by Prince Alfred and his sister, Rowena. Leaving the region as a shell of its Goldwater glory. They salted the entire area in almost every sense of the word."

"Rowena." Esther said and she spit to the ground. "She would do that."

Minimoto pulled on his horse's reins, stopping the mount, and turned to Esther. His look had changed from jovial to serious in a split second. "Rowena did not do it." He said, looking to the woman. "Alfred did, and he did it after they won the war. That's why Rowena pleaded to be its baroness. Those of us with longer memories remember the kind hearted Charles and the daughter that resembled his heart. Alfred was too much like his mother. Alfred destroyed this land and he and his mother vilified Rowena."

"Forgive me good Quarmi, but Rowena was a monster." Esther said in reply. "She killed…"

"Anyone who went to attack her or her family, including my uncle." Minimoto interrupted. "Sirie sent him on orders to assassinate Rowena and her newborn child. Rowena sent my uncle's head and the heads of the other assassins back on a boat. Rowena left the kingdom and started over. She lost everything here and instead she wanted build something away from Sirie." Minimoto said. "The kings that came after Charles could not allow her to build anything substantial and that's why she was seen as a threat. Her line still has a claim, though weaker after all these years. Did you know that she had a gorgon fighting by her side? A most interesting woman Rowena was."

"So who really started the war one hundred years ago?" Ino asked.

Minimoto shrugged. "That is a mystery, but it's safe to say that it won't be the only war we will fight against them." He turned his horse and rode again.

"You'll fight in a war, knowing that Lotcala might have started the entire thing?" Melantho asked.

"If it comes to it." Minimoto shrugged again, without turning around. "I'm loyal without question to King Liam and the throne of Lotcala. Like my uncle, if I'm told to go, then I will."

"Unquestioning loyalty. That's what you'd expect from a Quarmi warrior." Leonita said with a smile.

Syrena nodded, but she wasn't thrilled at the thought. She knew that wars often had very convoluted causes, and no one was sure who had really been wronged in the last war between Lotcala and Nashoba. Still, this was a thought that unnerved her. Sirie Bow-Breaker had been a heroine even to those in Amazon, where they had erected statues in her honor, but her honor was now in question.

"It's hard to fathom how a queen could justify sending assassins to kill a royal family and newborn." Syrena said.

"Dear princess, it is a dark matter but one that unless we face the consequences of the action or inaction, that we may never understand." Minimoto said. "If my uncle had succeeded, then the war one hundred years ago would not have happened and your friend would probably not be here. On the other side of that, perhaps the retaliation of such an act would have come back to destroy Lotcala. Only the Creator knows."

During the conversation, the group rode through the entire town and up the motte to the gate of the manor house.

"Here we are, princess." Minimoto said, dismounting.

Syrena and the Furies did the same. Walking into the courtyard, the Amazonian princess took an assessment of the surroundings.

"Start setting up tents along the north wall there." Syrena pointed. "Polydeuces, please unpack my horse. Ino, Mestra and Melantho, come with me."

"Allow me to introduce you properly, princess." Minimoto said.

"Of course." Syrena smiled.

The group entered the two story manor house and walked into the main hall. It wasn't a large hall, no bigger than thirty by fifty foot with a kitchen off to the side. The upstairs was a bedroom for the lord. However, it was the main hall that was the occupied living space.

Four tables spread out in front of Syrena, two women playing chess with stone pieces at one end. They looked up to her and her band. Both stood looked to the Amazons, a half elf no taller than five feet and a towering Hun woman at least six inches taller than Syrena. Sitting on a chair and smoking a long, wooden pipe in front of a burning hearth on the far end of the hall was Gabriel.

"My lord. The princess has arrived." Minimoto said, bowing as Gabriel shot up from his chair.

"Syrena!" The prince said. He dropped his cup and his pipe fell out of his mouth as he rushed over to her.

Syrena jumped towards him but just as the two met to embrace they stopped and stiffened.

"My lord, Prince Gabriel." Syrena said with a bow.

Gabriel bowed in returned. "Princess Syrena, welcome."

The three Furies, along with Minimoto, stood confused.

"What the hell was that?" Ino asked.

Syrena turned, shooting a glare and a sneer at her friend.

"It's polite." Mestra said, understanding Syrena's glare.

Syrena turned back to Gabriel, blushing. "It is good to see you. I hope we are not imposing."

Gabriel smiled. "No, of course not. The cooks were just making dinner. You are all welcome to join us."

Minimoto cleared his throat. "What about the other twenty some of them?" He said pointing over his shoulder towards the door.

"Twenty some?" Gabriel said while Syrena and the other Furies smiled.

"Introductions might be in order." Melantho said, bowing.

"Yes." Gabriel said. "You brought a delegation?" He asked looking to Syrena.

"My sisters." Syrena replied.

"Cecilia is here?" Gabriel asked with a tone of concern.

The Furies standing behind Syrena chuckled.

"No." Syrena smiled. "These are three of the Furies. Melantho, Ino and Mestra. My sisters." The three women bowed. "The other twenty-three Furies are outside setting up our camp."

"There are twenty-seven Amazon warriors here?" Marluna asked from behind Gabriel. He amazement was unmistakable.

"Yes... I'm sorry but I'm at a bit of a disadvantage lady elf." Syrena replied, coolly.

Gabriel took the cue. "Forgive me. This is Marluna, Ranger protégé on her way to third class." The blue-haired Marluna bowed at the introduction, her green cloak flowing low towards the floor. "And this is Arana." Gabriel said, turning towards the tall blonde woman next to him. The leather clad woman stepped up, standing above everyone in the room.

"The Hun woman I've heard so much about." Syrena said.

Arana smiled and extended a hand to Syrena from around Gabriel's left side. Syrena looked at the woman for a second before clasping her hand. The grip from Syrena was tight but Arana did not show any discomfort, Syrena could feel the Hun's strength in return. After they broke their clasp, Arana stepped back behind Gabriel.

For a moment there was an awkward silence.

"Should we meet with the rest of the Furies?" Mestra asked, breaking the silence.

Gabriel smiled. "Yes, let me just inform the staff that we will have more guests for a while." He walked into the kitchen. A moment later there was a clash of iron pots as Gabriel rushed out of the kitchen with the sound of the cooks cursing and yelling.

"They're happy to add a few extra plates." Gabriel said sheepishly. "Shall we?" He said, motioning towards the door.

The people left the manor and stepped out into the courtyard. There they saw several large tents. A few campfires had been or were being lit while in another part of the yard, four of the Furies had practiced wrestling with one another.

Callisto was the first to see the princess and the prince. "My lady princess!" She exclaimed, dropping to one knee and saluting. The other Furies followed suit, dropping to one knee in salute.

"Wow." Marluna replied. "They're so in sync." She said, amazed.

Syrena and her closest friends smiled. "Yes, they are." Syrena whispered.

The sun was setting as Gabriel was introduced to the group, and the food was served around the campfires. The cooks and attendants brought out guinea fowl stew with carrots and potatoes. They stretched the ingredients as far as they could, considering the new and unexpected arrivals. Many of the Furies produced their own treats to hold them over before getting a share of the stew. They also passed around bread loaves, mead and wine.

"The mead here is delicious." Gabriel said, pouring some for Syrena, Ino and Mestra. "They mix in blueberries from the banks of the river into the barrels."

Everyone sat around a campfire and ate the stew while talking about the past ten years.

"Northern Rangers? So, is that were this scruffy beard came from?" Syrena said, smiling to Gabriel and playfully pulling his beard. "You always talked about your uncle Ragnall and wanting to join. Still, I was surprised when you did."

Ino, Mestra and Melantho laughed to themselves.

"What?" Syrena said, glaring to her friends.

Ino, her mouth full of bread, was the first to speak up. "You drank yourself silly in celebration when you found out!" The others burst out laughing at the memory.

Syrena's face turned beet red. "I did not!" She shot up, standing over her friends. "That was in celebration of killing the Demon Boar!"

"Sure it was!" Mestra laughed. "Your face when Cecilia told you he had disappeared to the north was all smiles that day. I thought she was going to slap you for being so happy about it."

"Although killing that boar was fun." Melantho said, trying to hold in her laughter.

Syrena narrowed her eyes and sat back down on her chair.

Gabriel looked over and lightly tugged at her fur cloak. "This boar?" He asked.

Syrena nodded.

"It's a big hide. Must have been a formidable beast." Gabriel said, trying to calm Syrena's embarrassment.

The courtyard grew silent, and the laughter softened.

"It was a splendid victory." Syrena said. "But a costly one. We lost our sister, Althea, fighting that beast. She sits in glory, awaiting us on the Blessed Isles."

"I'm sorry to hear that." Marluna said.

Ino spoke up. "Don't be. We should all be so fortunate to have such a destiny."

"Ino was Althea's sword sister." Mestra said. "She feels the pride more than any of us. The loss too."

"I see. Then let us drink to her glory." Gabriel said, raising his cup followed by all those in the courtyard.

After drinking Minimoto, sitting along the manor wall close by, interjected a thought. "A culture surrounded by warriors and a warrior's mythology. Sound familiar, Arana?"

"Yes, that reminds me." Syrena said, wiping her mouth from the mead and looking to Arana. "I'd love to hear about you, the Huns, and how you came to know Prince Gabriel."

Again all other conversations ceased and a few of the Furies from other areas walked over for a better seat to hear the story.

Arana scoffed. "The Huns are dying, wasting away in the north. There is nothing much to tell about them anymore."

"Surely, there is a story of glory that you know. How is it you are here in this great kingdom?" Melantho asked.

Arana sighed. "Fine." She said. Her tone gave away her annoyance, but she continued, anyway. "I was from the Grey Bear Tribe, but we were weakened from years of warfare. The Blood Wolves hunted us. They hunted everybody. We wanted to live in peace as did some of other tribes, but Ruga was an honorless warlord. He sought to unite the tribes, and he killed those who did not fall in line."

"Ruga was the Blood Wolves chieftain?" Mestra asked.

"Aye, he was, and he was a murderer that only wanted to bring destruction to the Hun people." Arana answered.

"You keep saying he was this or that. He failed to unite the tribes?" A Fury named Eurydice asked.

"Aye. He gathered many warriors around him, but the Rangers laid a trap for him. They killed his army, but I'm the one that cut his throat out. He was lost in all the confusion, a worthless leader." Arana replied. "His brother, Temu, caught me right after and tried to rape me. He almost did, but Gabriel killed him before he had the chance. I still took a prize from Temu's corpse so he isn't whole in the afterlife."

The Furies around the fire grinned and a few openly shared their approval.

"I've followed Gabriel ever since." Arana finished.

"What about your tribe?" Mestra asked.

Arana looked to Mestra. "They are dead. My father refused to join the Blood Wolves. I had gone to take vengeance for my tribe when I found the battle. I have nowhere to call home."

"Of course, I welcome here you. Besides, Creator knows I need the help." Gabriel smiled, clasping Arana on the shoulder.

"Help? It seems like the town is doing well." Syrena said, furrowing her brow.

Minimoto laughed. "The town is doing well even with Gabriel in charge."

Gabriel chuckled, nodding his head along with the jest. "Yes, the town is fine. It's the other title I have now." Gabriel sighed, coming out of his amusement. "I am now the commander of the Thousand Man Battalion."

The comment confused many of the Furies, while Syrena looked down and shook her head.

"For the life of me, why do they keep such a force?" The Amazonian princess asked.

"It's a tradition and could be an excellent group of warriors. The problem is that most of the men and women in the battalion are not as one. Most of them are cast offs the barons didn't want or criminals." Gabriel replied.

"We'll train them, my lord. Have no worries to that." Marluna said, trying to bring encouragement to the conversation.

Arana stood up, as did Marluna. "It is late." The Hun woman said. "I plan on getting the battalion ready in the morning for training. We will see you at dawn."

"Good night." Marluna bowed, though Arana simply walked off.

When the two had mounted their horses and rode off, Syrena looked to her fellow Furies, some feeling insulted at the Hun's lack of manners in front of nobles.

Syrena looked to Gabriel. "I take it the Huns don't bow to their superiors, or is there a lack of manners on the Northern Continent?"

"She will learn southern ways." Melantho remarked, wishing to diffuse her commander's anger.

"Doubt it." Gabriel replied. Minimoto laughed. "I was happy to leave Jovag a few weeks back. She pissed off a few of the lords there and throughout since our return. She's a formidable fighter and she'll get the battalion trained eventually, but she won't bow. It's not her way. It's not the way of the Huns."

Minimoto sat down where Arana once sat. "Nor are we asking her to change. To temper her might not be like tempering a blade. Tempering a Hun warrior could cause her to lose her strength. Huns fight with rage, unseen by most every other culture." Many of the Furies nodded at the reasoning.

"My lord Gabriel, I was hoping you could tell us more about the rangers." Mestra asked. "I had heard tales that a siren had started the order."

Several of the other Furies nearby came around. Ravi scoffed when she heard about the siren. "A siren? That's just a legend."

Gabriel chuckled. "Many think that, and some used to think it." He leaned over to move the logs on the campfire with a nearby poker. "Oh, yes, she is real. Was real? I don't think anyone knows if she is alive anymore, to be honest. Aklima was a siren from the Middle Sea, sent by Wohd to kill Oleg, Theodorif and Theodorif's mother, Carolyngia. Oleg found her and took pity on her for being cast out of the sea and sent on a mission that would lead to her death."

"She was a child of an old god?" A Fury asked.

"All sirens are children of Wohd, or so the old stories say." Mestra answered.

Gabriel nodded. "It was Oleg's kindness that made Aklima see that Wohd was evil. She never converted to the Creator, but her knowledge of the truths of the world won many followers. She saw a need to defend the world from the damage that the old gods could do if they felt that mortal kind deserved their wrath."

Riva shook her head lightly. "But the old gods protect us."

"Some might." Gabriel conceded. "And I pray that is true, but some have shown themselves to be enemies of mortal kind. Because of that, Aklima started the rangers to help those that cannot defend themselves and to teach newer generations."

"What happened to her?" Riva asked.

"She left one day. A couple centuries ago she walked away from the rangers and left them to another, Lord Kagesuke." Gabriel sighed. "No one has seen her in this area since the reign of Charles I, in the second century of the kingdom. It was probably a hundred years later that she left the rangers."

"She can't still be alive all these years." Ravi remarked.

"A child of an old god can be immortal or as close to it as any being can become." Mestra answered her sister. "Thank you, my lord, for the story." She finished turning back to Gabriel.

A Fury approached and knelt in salute to Syrena.

"My princess, we are wondering if you have news with regard to the reason of our visit." The Fury, Nyx, asked.

Syrena's eyes widened. "Nyx, I have yet to speak on that subject with the prince. Perhaps in the morning. For now, enjoy your slumber. Tomorrow I want to see the Furies training and preforming drills." Syrena rose and all the Furies knelt and saluted her. "My lord, I trust you have made the master chambers ready for my visit."

Gabriel stood. "Yes, you may use my chambers. Of course." He stammered.

Syrena nodded. "I expect and thank you for your hospitality." Syrena looked to her friends. "Ino, Melantho and Mestra shall we retire for the evening?" The three women stood up and walked towards the manor. "Nyx, you and Callisto shall take first watch tonight." She said before walking inside the manor.

The Furies grumbled as they put their fires out and retired to their tents. Callisto sneered at Nyx, tossing her mead cup to the woman, hitting her in the shoulder.

"Thanks, Nyx." Callisto huffed.

"I just wanted to know." Nyx said, following her sister.

Gabriel and Minimoto looked at each other.

Minimoto shrugged his shoulders. "I can only imagine my lord, but I take it you will join me in the great hall tonight?"

Gabriel nodded.

"Fair warning, I talk in my sleep." Minimoto said before drinking some mead.

"Yeah, I know." Gabriel sighed.

Tries Nychtes Prin

"He composes poems as he goes to sleep." Gabriel said as he and Syrena walked through the town the following morning.

"Minimoto always had a charm to his thoughts and actions." Syrena smiled.

"That is true." Gabriel replied. "Part of being a Quarmi warrior. Poets all."

Syrena smiled to Gabriel. "I know that more than one of my sisters are a bit smitten with him. Amazonian men, for all their honor and passion, are not so poetic." She giggled. "It must be something here in Lotcala."

"He composes poems in his sleep too." Gabriel continued. "As he drifts off and throughout the night while sleeping."

Syrena laughed. She enjoyed the peaceful walk through the town and seeing all the people out during their daily routines. A pleasant change from the rigors of Amazonian life. While she loved Amazon, the way of life was war, work and toil above all else. Yes, they would enjoy celebrations, festivals and other events meant for fun, but life in Lotcala seemed much calmer. Syrena felt more at ease in Lotcala.

The pair passed by stalls of vendors and the many artisans that had flocked to the growing town. The sight of many of the Furies drew attention. Most of the Amazons wore their full armor comprising muscle cuirass over a leather war skirt, iron greaves and forearm guards. They strapped their shields and corinth helms around their shoulders. An impressive sight, to say the least.

However, Syrena and her closest friends, Ino, Melantho and Mestra, choose to wear less warlike outfits. Instead, they decided on wearing white linen chitons, trimmed in red or gold for Syrena, and their himation cloaks. Purple cloak for Syrena and red for the other three ladies. All the Furies wore their falcata swords on their left sides. That was part of their right being within the warrior class of Amazons. No Amazon warrior would ever be without the falcata.

Gabriel, on the other hand, wore his usual blue tunic and leather breeches under a green, black trimmed cloak. He displayed his livery collar around his neck and shoulders.

The two were enjoying a walk when something off to the right caught the princess' eye. Syrena stopped by a jewelry vendor, noticing a golden pin with an engraved image of what appeared to be a divine figure. Someone or something with wings wrapped around the figure.

"Whose image is this on the pin?" She asked the stall vendor.

The elderly lady squinted and then smiled. "That is an image of Blessed Mother Hagar, Blessed Oleg's sister."

"Oleg, the man that converted the Gota from the old gods?" Syrena asked.

"Yes, your highness." The vendor answered with a smile and a heavy accent from one of the eastern kingdoms.

"How much is it?" Syrena asked, picking it up and admiring the craftsmanship. "I like it, though I'm ignorant to her importance."

"She is a great woman to us from the eastern lands. Please accept it as a gift, your highness." The vendor said. "We are grateful for your visit."

Syrena stiffened a bit at the offer. "Such craftsmanship should not be parted with without proper compensation." She said. "Please allow me to pay a few gold pieces at least."

"Thank you but you chose this pin of her image and I think it was meant for you." The vendor said. "Hager was a leader among Gota women and she was the one, with her son, who led many of the southern Gota people to prosperity in unknown lands."

Gabriel looked over to Syrena. "She is an important figure to many of the eastern peoples. Those past Zaragoza and Telaram revere her as their mother."

"Yes, she is our mother." The vendor smiled.

Syrena returned the smile and noted the woman's features. Darker hair and eyes, naturally tanned skin and fading red ink lines on her hands and wrists from a recent ceremony or festival related to her home culture.

"This is from your homeland?" Syrena asked, lifting the pin up.

The vendor nodded. "Yes, it is from Farush, in the Burning Sands. Though, I consider Antei my home now. Many of my people do."

"Then I'll accept this gift. For blessings upon what I hope to be my new home as well." Syrena smiled and walked away, fastening the pin to her himation.

Gabriel stood for a second before catching up to Syrena.

"Your new home?" He asked.

"Your brother, Liam, didn't tell you the reason of my visit?" Syrena said. She stopped and turned to Gabriel. "Your father and brother think it is past time for you to marry. I agreed, you're not getting any younger, you know." Syrena flashed a grin. "They've asked me if I wanted to come and present my case."

Syrena stepped in front of Gabriel and extend her arms out, as if showing herself to him. "Here I am, Gabriel. I am the second born daughter of the Queen of Amazon, the Viscountess of Caleope and Commander of the Amazonian Legion. I have won nineteen battles and collected no less than thirty thousand pounds of war spoils from those battles. I already presented a crate each of cinnamon and anise and one barrel of saffron to the king. I don't think you will find a better bride that can offer more in material fineries. I also think that I can provide you with strong daughters." Syrena put a finger up. "Children." Aligning to the Lotcala thinking of progeny.

"I agree. There is no one else I could have ever wanted to marry, but you said ten years ago that you couldn't marry me." Gabriel replied. He looked down, pain and remorse etched on his face.

Syrena tenderly touched Gabriel's chin and lifted his face up. She looked into his eyes, an inch lower than hers. "You were betrothed to my sister. We kissed, a kiss I remember each day that I awake alone in my keep or in a camp, but it was a kiss that should not have happened. It was a dangerous moment that almost destroyed an alliance. You were meant for Cecilia."

"And so now?" Gabriel asked.

Syrena dropped her hand and started walking again, with Gabriel following along. "Now, Cecilia has said you are not worthy of her, or me, though I disagree. She still thinks you are a coward for running off to the north, yet I see honor in your journey. Whatever her feelings, she has decided on finding an Amazonian noble to provide her with heirs, however, she will not stop us from marrying. We have her word on that."

"So, we are free to marry?" Gabriel grinned. "Why didn't you tell me last night?" He asked, gently touching Syrena's arm causing her to stop walking.

Syrena smiled. "I wanted to see who your two companions were first, and then it didn't feel like the right time to speak of it. We were both drinking a lot and maybe it wouldn't feel true. Here we are sober and talking honestly."

"I see." Gabriel pulled Syrena into his arms for a deep embrace. She returned the hug. Both pulled back slightly before joining for a long kiss. Once they broke, they both smiled at one another.

Syrena looked at Gabriel. "I've waited ten years for that kiss again. Just as sweet as I remembered. It felt like you enjoyed it too." She said with a wink before walking off again. Gabriel blushed and strolled alongside Syrena. She wrapped her left arm into his right as they walked, enjoying the beginning of their new life together.

The Furies enjoyed their celebrity status among the people of Antei as the days passed into two weeks.

Many brought gifts of food, wine or mead and even some jewelry. More than one adventurous man even proposed marriage, taken by the Amazonian beauties. While most were just smitten young men with little experience in the real world, one was a landowning farmer. Nyx, the Fury that caught his eye, took the proposal a bit more serious.

"He can provide better than some men in the queendom." She said to Ino as the two walked around the town. "You're my aunt, the family matriarch, what would you do?"

"He isn't really my skin of wine, as you know, but if you want to have daughters, I suppose a few nights wouldn't hurt. Besides, it's good to know that the father is of healthy roots." Ino replied to her niece.

"That's my quandary. We've spoken these last few days, and he is a Sir under Prince Gabriel and one of the manor lords. I forget which one." Nyx said, waving her hand dismissively. "I know what our family had to go through. What you and my other aunts and father had to go through. I want better for us too."

Nyx's father, Datis, was the youngest of Ino's siblings and just an infant when their mother left for the last time. Their father died not long after, and Ino and the next oldest sister, Artemisia, were left to raise the younger children. This bonded the siblings more than most Amazon siblings. Ino took care of and tutored Nyx when Datis found success as a goldsmith in the queendom and traveled around selling his wares until the queen granted him the right to own a permanent shop.

"You needn't worry about that. Between your father, Artemisia, Gorga and I, our family is secure." Ino reassured her niece." Ino clasped Nyx's shoulders. "Marry for love, not position. My youngest sister Amytis married for position. A Treshan lord, but she died heartbroken. Love, even if it is only for a short time, a fleeting romance, is the joy that you will remember on your deathbed." Ino replied, holding back her memories and a few tears. She let go of her niece's shoulder and smiled at young warrior.

"Thank you, aunt. I would have to finish my time in the legion, anyway. If he will wait, then maybe he would be worthy of me." Nyx replied with a smile.

Ino returned the smile. She eyed her niece. "You look like your grandmother did when your father was a babe. Full of life, black hair, dark eyes and pale skin." She gave a playful smack to Nyx's shoulder that made the younger woman stumble. "But you're as light as a feather, just like your dad." Ino laughed, followed by Nyx.

By midday, the two had finished their walk and met back up with some of the other Furies in the courtyard. They split up with Nyx joining Cassia and Riva practicing their spells under Mestra's watchful guidance. Mestra was a strict teacher, and this was no exception.

"Moving pebbles is nothing! I want whirlwinds of boulders flying around!" Mestra yelled to her students as the dirt flew around her.

Ino found Melantho and Syrena enjoying a bowl of soup.

Ino sat down on a chair and grabbed a bowl, spooning some soup for herself. "So are we going to talk about that Arana woman?" She said, sitting next to Syrena. "Have you seen a woman as tall as her?" Ino exclaimed.

"There is a legionnaire, Sebula, that is taller than me, but I don't remember her being a foot taller.

Arana has to be nearly seven foot." Syrena replied. "I spoke to Gabriel, and she is not a threat to me."

"You believe that?" Melantho asked.

Syrena shrugged. "I have to. If I'm to marry him, then we need to build marriage on trust. Besides, she doesn't sleep in the manor. I asked around and she and Marluna stay in the battalion camp just outside of town." Syrena took a spoonful of soap and sipped it. "Speaking of which, you two and Mestra will need to sleep out in the camp in another night or two." She said.

"And tonight?" Melantho asked.

Ino raised an eyebrow. "Gabriel returns tonight."

"He and Minimoto should return, yes. With a royal entourage and a priest for the ceremony. Mestra will give us the Blessing of the Goddesses afterward." Syrena answered.

"You're not marrying him tonight." Ino said in return.

"No, another week at least, but it's our custom of Tries Nychtes Prin. Those nights are my right between my future husband and I." Syrena responded.

"I never knew you to be one for tradition." Melantho smiled. "I only spent one night with Solis before we wed." She said of her own husband.

"Why do we even have such a tradition?" Ino asked. "It's hardly mentioned anymore, I don't even think I know the true origin of it."

"Nobles." A voice said from behind Ino. The voice soon revealed herself to be Mestra taking a seat next to her Fury sister. "It's archaic from the nobility when the women would fight for the men of excellent stock. Once the man was wed, another woman couldn't take him unless offered. You had a limited window of time, but you could legally steal a man away before the marriage."

Ino rolled her eyes. "Let me guess, three days?"

Mestra nodded. "Women in the old days would take the men they wished to marry and confine them to the bedrooms and try to get pregnant. That way if the man was taken by another before the marriage, at least a child would still be born. Preferably a daughter. The nobles rarely lost men because they had the gold to pay for more guards than the poorer classes."

"That is some of the most ridiculous crap I've ever heard." Ino smiled. "I don't think I'll ever get used to you nobles."

The friends all laughed and joked for a while longer. Syrena put her bowl down. "I'm serious though." She said, changing her tone. "I've waited ten years for this and I want it to be just as I had always imagined it."

"Fair enough." Melantho replied. Turning around, she saw two Furies doing nothing important. "Haritha! Leonita! Come over here!" She ordered. The two Furies walked over, knelt and saluted their leaders. "Make up a tent for Ino, Mestra and I. We will be in the courtyard for a few nights."

The two stood and grinned, understanding the meaning, before rushing off to unpack the prefect's tent.

"What of the Lotcalan traditions? What if he does not wish to share his bed with you until you and he are married? You might be the first he has shared a bed with." Mestra asked.

"If you believe that, then I'm not sure you'll do well as the Magister." Syrena laughed. "We've all heard the tales of the towns of the Northern Continent and their many lust-houses." She picked up her bowl and spooned in more soup. "He is no more a stranger to the female form than I am to a man's. Still, should he wish to wait for marriage, Tries Nychtes Prin doesn't have to be about getting pregnant. It is also a time for getting to know one another's thoughts and habits. There will be plenty to do without sex, just not as fun."

"Very true." Mestra replied with a grin.

Far-off movement had distracted Melantho. In the lower bailey, the Thousand Man Battalion was running drills. Melantho stood and walked over to the lower wall and climbed the ladder to the wall's walkway. The others followed her, wondering what she was looking at.

"They could be formidable again with proper training." Melantho said. "That Hun might be a decent fighter, but she can't train one thousand soldiers. The ranger either. Not alone at least."

"Then let's offer some help." Syrena replied, turning back to the ladder. Ino and Melantho joining behind. Once on the ground, Syrena looked back and saw Mestra still on the wall. "Are you coming?"

"What and miss this view? No, thank you. Besides, phalanxes were never my forte." The mage replied with a sheepish grin.

Pawns and Kings

Dawn came and went, but for Orestilla nothing mattered. Her work was going well with no hitches, but something nagged in her mind.

"Persephone!" Orestilla called out. "Where the hell is she?"

Suddenly her ward, Persephone appeared from around the corner of Orestilla's keep.

"My lady?" The younger ward said with a smile.

"Where the hell have you been?" Orestilla yelled.

"I was tending your roses, my lady." Persephone bowed. "Is there an urgent matter that requires my assistance?"

Orestilla sneered. "My niece told me that Crown Princess Cecilia has been asking about our trip to Gib. I want you to send a letter to the princesses to meet with me." Orestilla waved her hand in the air dismissively. "Say for some sort of goodwill banquet."

"I will my lady, but I believe only Cecilia will come."

"Why do you say that?" Orestilla frowned.

"The servants have been talking about it since our return but it would seem that Syrena has traveled to Jovag to seek a marriage with Prince Gabriel." Persephone replied.

"What?" Orestilla screamed. She grabbed a nearby vase and was about to throw it across the room when Persephone stopped her.

"My lady! That is your mother's vase!"

"And?!"

Persephone bowed. "Perhaps this is a chance to take advantage of Princess Syrena's absence." Persephone gently removed the vase from Orestilla's aging grip and placed it back on its marble pedestal. "Let the crown princess come and see how well you administer to the lands and sow the seeds of Syrena's mishandling."

Orestilla glared at her ward. "I've tried that."

"But this will be a firsthand look. We can also foster discord among the people to turn on her and Honora. That way when the time comes for war, you can take Caleope for yourself." Persephone smiled.

Orestilla grinned wickedly in return and nodded. "Yes. Send the letter to Cecilia and let her come. Once here, we will win her to our cause."

The satisfied palatine walked off, leaving Persephone behind to ponder her next steps. She watched as Orestilla turned the corner and then she went back out into the garden.

Persephone took a rose and cut the bloom from the stem. "My lady will see that her whims are meaningless to the world's true rulers."

* * * *

Syrena walked down to the training field below the motte of Antei. Leaving the lower bailey, the princess, along with Ino and Melantho, passed by the ruined keep that had once been the Goldwater seat of power.

"Why build a keep on the lower level." Ino asked.

Syrena looked to the crumbling structure and shook her head. "The Goldwater family built it nearly a thousand years ago and Rowena the Dwarf knocked it down during Charles I's reign." Syrena stopped and pointed. "I remember Lord Katsuichi telling us when we were young that they built it there to show they weren't scared of an attack from Eylsia. It is still in a defensible position when facing a southern march. However, Rowena came from Jovag in the north. Lord Katsuichi said that the manor house, used by the lords since, stands as a humble reminder of where you come from and where you can go. That's why the manor house is still in use and why the ruins were left to crumble."

The women continued on to the training rounds where they approached Arana and Marluna, trying to teach spear attacks. Marluna saw the Amazons first.

"Your highness!" She called out and then dropped to a knee in salute.

"Thank you, young Ranger, but a simple bow is all that is needed. You aren't one of my subjects." Syrena smiled.

"Not yet, your highness." Marluna replied, grinning.

Syrena nodded. She looked to the soldiers, and they all bowed to her. All but Arana.

"My good Hun, won't you bow to the princess? She is to be your overlord soon." Melantho said.

"I bow to no one in this land, princess." Arana answered in as much courtesy as the tough woman could muster.

"Arana, this is an Amazonian princess and Gabriel's future wife. Maybe it would be okay to bow to her if no one else. Plus she's a famous warrior. You can respect that." Marluna said, trying to reason with her friend.

"Famous? I hadn't heard of her." Arana smiled. A gasp went out from the soldiers behind her, and the looks on the faces of the Amazons gave away their thoughts.

"Have you killed a dragon? A Kraken? Maybe manticores? No?" Arana said, shaking her head. "Those are the deeds of famous warriors in the north. My father killed ten manticores before he died. My grandfather slayed a water dragon. Them I would bow to, but they didn't have to ask it of me. You killed a boar, a big boar. I've done that plenty of times." She finished.

Some soldiers behind her snickered.

"Not just a big boar. A big fucking boar." Syrena replied with a smirk. "A few armies and plenty of Hun cast off bandits running with their tales between their legs from Fesian riders." Syrena unfastened her himation, leaving only her chiton on. "How about a show of strength? You and I."

"I have nothing to prove, besides I would get executed when I kill you." Arana replied.

"No, no." Syrena said, holding her hand up to calm the woman. "We grapple. Wrestle. No weapons, and not to the death. Just until one of us proves who is better." Syrena clarified.

"And what's the point?"

Syrena smirked. "If I win, you have to bow to me as is proper. If you win, I won't ever ask you to bow again."

"Fine." Arana accepted, dropping her spear and unbuckling her armor.

"You highness?" Melantho said, but Syrena just put her hand up to silence her. "Fine." Melantho said, returning to Ino's side.

Syrena looked at the towering Hun and squared up against her. Arana cracked her knuckles. She wore only her loose fitting leather breeches and a cotton tunic. Arana cracked her neck and lowered her body.

Both women rushed into each other and grabbed at whatever they could. Each taking a fistful of cloth, trying to buckle the other woman down to the ground. The crowd around them cheered while Marluna and the Amazons tried to keep the people back to give the fighters room. Both women buckled and pushed each other, trying to gain ground. Syrena was trying to slip her right foot behind Arana's left foot to trip the larger woman to the ground.

Arana was more muscular and taller, but Syrena was a skilled fighter and trained to defeat opponents of all sizes. Syrena locked her left foot in place and twisted her hips into Arana's waist, using that leverage to flip the Hun woman to the ground. Syrena landed on top of her as her sisters cheered her on.

Arana landed with a cloud of dust and Syrena was on top, straddling her. The Amazon was throwing punches, landed them with precision across the face of Arana. The Hun's nose erupted with blood, but she was still in the fight. Arana reached up and violently pulled Syrena's hair, dragging the princess down to the ground, allowing Arana to reverse the position.

"That's why the grandmothers used to shave their heads before battle." Ino remarked, and Melantho nodded. Others joined them on the field.

Arana pummeled Syrena with vicious fists, but the Legion had trained Syrena to defend herself. She kept her forearms up, blocking the punishing blow from Arana. Once Syrena figured she had an opening, she wrapped her arms around Arana's neck and pulled her down into a reverse headlock. Syrena tightened her grip on Arana's neck, but she could feel the Hun's strength. Arana put her feet and hands under her and she pushed herself off the ground.

Syrena felt the movement as she was slowing being lifted up and she tightened her grip around Arana's neck and Syrena wrapped her legs around the larger woman's waist. Suddenly, Arana dropped to the ground, slamming Syrena onto her back. Syrena, however, did not break the hold. Arana lifted herself up again as Syrena remained firm in her grip.

Atop the motte at the manor house, Prince Gabriel and his family, plus their entourage, entered the courtyard.

"Where is everyone?" Gabriel said, dismounting from his horse. His father, mother and brother were walking up behind him. He looked around and saw Mestra and several of his guards along to motte walls.

Walking over, he called out to them to see what they were looking at. "Lady Mestra? What's going on?"

Mestra turned, along with the guards, and bowed. "Your highness, Princess Syrena has gone to the training guards to provide a lesson in Amazonian martial arts." Mestra smiled. "The other Furies joined her. I chose to stay here with the best vantage point."

Gabriel joined her on the wall and looked over, down to the field. There he saw Syrena and Arana trading blows back and forth. As the king and rest of the royal family came up to the wall, Gabriel called out to the two women, but neither heard him. "They're killing each other down there."

Mestra shook her head. "This is more of a comparison of techniques, your highness."

"We have to get down there!" Gabriel said, shocked.

"Your highness, I assure you that they need this so they can air out their grievances." Mestra smiled. However, the prince was heading away to the field and not listening to her. "Fine." Mestra looked to the guards. "Save my spot and remember I have ten gold pieces on the princess." She said, smiling to her new friends.

Mestra rode down to the training fields with the princes. Liam accompanied his younger brother while the king and queen waited at the manor house. There they found a large crowd of soldiers around the two women. The Furies were keeping the rest of the crowd back.

Gabriel was leading the way into the crowd, moving people aside and shouting orders. Once he reached the front of the crowd, he saw the fight first hand.

Both combatants were bloody and bruised. Syrena was on top of Arana's back and had her wrapped up in a choke hold.

Gabriel tried to rush in, but Polydeuces and Esther stopped him.

"It is a challenge that has to be finished." Esther replied.

"I will not have my bride fighting my lieutenant!" Gabriel roared.

Syrena looked up to Gabriel. "Don't worry, I'm almost finished."

Arana tried to lift herself off the ground. Syrena sent a knee into the woman's side. The impact slowed Arana, but she continued to stand up. Syrena kneed her again.

"Give up!" Syrena yelled!

"Never!" Arana gasped.

Syrena tightened her grip around the Hun woman's large neck. Arana pushed with all of her might and flipped herself onto her back, landing on the ground with a colossal force. Syrena broke her hold. Both women laid on the ground exhausted.

The crowd was quiet as the Furies went to their princess and lifted her up. Several of the Lotcalan soldiers did the same for Arana. Both women were spent and barely able to keep their eyes open.

"You're a damned beast from Hell." Syrena gasped. "I've fought no one stronger."

Arana nodded. "Nor I, your highness." Arana nodded to Syrena. Arana clutched her wounded side and licked the blood running down from her nose.

"Then that's it." Gabriel said definitively. "It's done and when you're both rested, you can explain what the hell all of this was about." The prince said before returning to his horse with his brother.

Ino, Mestra and Melantho stood by their princess. "He's going to have to get used to living with an Amazon." Ino quipped.

"It'll be fun breaking him in." Syrena grinned through her bloodied mouth.

Hours later, a bruised but smiling Syrena and Arana joined the royal family in the manor house's main hall. The hearth's fire was roaring along with many candles. The sun had long ago set, but the atmosphere was light and joyous.

King Liam was laughing along with his wife. "That's what we need, a grand tournament and melee! Just like the old days!" He took a bite of the chicken leg in his hand. "A grand melee, feats of strength and ale all around. Food too! Can't forget about the meats." He finished.

"Of course, dear." Clotide smiled. "Maybe it's time for us to retire for the night."

The king furrowed his brow. "What?! I'm just starting to plan this tournament."

Clotide laid a hand lovingly on her husband. "Let the young ones have this night."

"I'm young yet!" The king protested, but he pouted and then rose from his seat. The others rose and bowed, but King Liam waved them down. "Enjoy your night and tomorrow we'll finish the tournament plans. We have very little time." He said before walking up the steps to the bedchamber.

Prince Liam smiled, and he looked to his younger brother Gabriel. "I guess I'll be here with you and Minimoto." He said knocking on the bench seat. "How do you sleep on these benches?" He laughed.

Gabriel smiled. "We get so drunk that it doesn't matter what it feels like." He laughed.

"Here, here!" Ino slurred.

Melantho looked to Syrena and whispered. "So much for Tries Nychtes Prin."

"It's fine." Syrena replied, coolly. "At least I've made a new ally today." She replied.

"What's Tries Nychtes Prin?" Marluna asked from the table next to Syrena's.

Syrena and Melantho turned to the elf, shocked at the question. The others in the hall stopped and looked on.

"What do you mean? What're you talking about?" Syrena said, trying to pretend ignorance.

"Melantho said 'so much for Tries Nychtes Prin' and I just wanted to know what that was." Marluna clarified.

"It's nothing. An old saying from Amazon." Syrena said, her face letting the young elf know that the topic was not for discussion.

Marluna knowingly nodded. "Sorry I bothered you, your highness." She turned around back to her table with a few of the other Furies.

Later on, as Marluna and Arana were heading out to go back to their camp, Mestra met up with them.

"The princess is a bit stressed. Things back home were uneasy when she left, and coming here has her a bit anxious. Take no offense in her words tonight." The Amazonian mage offered a smile to the pair.

Marluna smiled in return. "It was just a moment of curiosity."

"Questions are how we learn. She's not used to this concept. Many Amazon nobles aren't used to having to answer questions." Mestra explained the ritual to the women as they walked.

When she was done Arana paused, looking confused.

"They don't love each other first?" Arana asked.

"For nobles, rarely. It can develop, like for my parents, and the Tries Nychtes Prin tradition helps with that. However, without such a tradition the couple will be complete strangers when they meet to wed." Mestra explained.

"Meet to wed?" Marluna asked.

Mestra nodded. "Some couples don't have the time for Tries Nychtes Prin, and they meet on their wedding day. Lower classes, in the cases of weddings, have more luxury that the nobles aren't afforded." Mestra smiled. "Now you know and you can be discrete I'm sure." Mestra saw the two women nod. "Good. Have a restful night." She finished before walking to her tent.

In the manor house Prince Liam and Minimoto were already asleep and snoring on the benches. Now and then Minimoto would blurt out a line or two of a poem. However, given the amount he drank, Gabriel was sure that his Quarmi friend would not recite too many lines.

The Furies that had joined them in the main hall were mostly passed out from the five barrels of wine that had been tapped. Syrena pushed herself up from her seat and Gabriel helped her up.

"You've drunk a healthy amount tonight." Gabriel laughed, feeling the effects of the wine himself.

"I have a reputation to uphold." Syrena replied. "Mestra's sister is supposedly trying to challenge me, and I can't have that." She laughed.

Gabriel helped Syrena walk out into the cool night air. "Where is your tent?"

Syrena pointed to the tent where they could see Ino's feet sticking out of the entry flaps. "That's the one." Syrena slurred.

They walked over and he led her in, guiding her to the open cot that was probably Ino's.

"We can still have Dyo Nychtes Prin tomorrow night." Gabriel said.

Syrena looked at him, confused. "You heard all that?"

Gabriel shrugged. "I remember a little old Amazonian." He said with a smile. "Sleep well. We have a lot to do the next couple of days. Just try not to challenge anymore of my vassals." Gabriel laughed, but Syrena was already asleep. Gabriel left the tent and said his good nights to the other Furies that were still awake.

* * * *

"An invitation?" Cecilia remarked, reading the letter from Orestilla. The corridor she had met her mother in was dimly lit from just four candles, and night had long fallen over the keep.

"A ploy." Saria replied. "Trying to incur your favor over your sister."

"Of course." Cecilia whispered. "There is more."

"More?" Saria asked and narrowed her eyes to her daughter.

Cecilia handed her mother the letter she received from a falcon recently. Saria read it and crumbled it in her hand. Her face betrayed her calm exterior.

"Treason!" Saria yelled finally.

"It would seem." Cecilia replied.

"I'll burn her keep to the ground!"

Cecilia put a hand on her mother's shoulders. "Mother, if I may. Doing so might invoke her allies in Elysia. Fe is still our allies and we cannot think they are turning on us for her whims, even if they have some distant relation."

"I will not let her go, unpunished." Saria resolved firmly.

"Allow me to accept her invitation. I'll give her the option of standing trial or the honorable path."

"This isn't enough to bring her back for a trial." Saria said.

Cecilia nodded. "Then I'm sure when confronted she will take the honorable path out of this. Then her work will crumble."

Saria nodded. "Go to Anglona and present what we have. Do not return with her left there unpunished." Saria said before walking off down the corridor.

The hall grew dimmer and a soft hiss was heard as an unknown shadow extinguished all but one candle in the dim corridor. Cecilia's father Agis came from another hallway from behind his daughter.

"You understand what you need to do?" Agis whispered.

"I do, father." Cecilia answered.

"The vial is in your chambers and marked. One drop is enough." Agis said. "The wind blows in the west during the summer storms."

"The wind blows in the west during the summer storms." Cecilia said.

"Again." Agis said.

"The wind blows in the west during the summer storms."

Agis smiled. "Good. Chaos is our religion, and the old gods grant us blessings for our work. Orestilla threatens not only your family, but she treats with traitors to the old gods. You know what we must do."

Cecilia grinned wickedly. "I do, father."

For the Good of the Queendom

Cecilia made the long trip from Esto to Orestilla's keep in the town of Anglona. Not far off from Caleope but still ways enough away for the traitor's safety. Cecilia dismounted from her horse and walked up the stone steps to the large wooden doors, marking the entrance. A skilled craftsman had carved the large oak doors with scenes of mythical beasts and religious imagery.

"A bit too opulent for my tastes." Cecilia remarked, walking into the highly decorated halls of the keep.

Along the plastered walls were detailed reliefs of Amazon cavalry glory. Cecilia was not opposed to seeing the cavalry glory throughout the years. However, the common thread with these reliefs were that most were images of Orestilla and her family members.

An attendant came from around the corner to greet the princess.

"My lady, Princess Cecilia." The attendant saluted and bowed. "My mistress has been expecting you."

"You may rise." Cecilia said without a smile. "Thank your lady for the invite, but there are other matters than a banquet for me to contend with. Since my sister is away, I am to administer to her lands." Cecilia eyed the woman. "That is an interesting mark on your hand." She said, looking at the small tattoo of a bird in black ink.

"Yes, my lady, it is." The woman replied.

Cecilia looked the woman in the eyes. "The wind blows in the west during the summer storms."

The attendant bowed. "Fear not, for the storms will fade before the first harvest."

Cecilia nodded, pulling the sleeve of her tunic up to her elbow, exposing her own blackbird mark. "Then you are the one that called to me."

"For the good of the queendom, your highness." The attendant, Persephone, replied.

Cecilia smiled. "Of course. For the good of the queendom."

Orestilla came around the corner and greeted the princess warmly.

"Princess Cecilia, welcome to Anglona!" Orestilla said with an elegant bow, her hand tight against her cane. "I hope the journey was not too rough for you."

Cecilia smiled. She couldn't tell if Orestilla was being sincere. To be honest, many people never knew if the woman was being sincere.

"The road was pleasant and your domain is just as beautiful as I remembered it from my previous visit." Cecilia lied. She couldn't remember the last time she stepped foot in Anglona and she really didn't care if she ever did again.

Orestilla bowed her head. "I'm happy to hear that, my princess." She lifted her head and smiled. "If you'll join me in the main hall, the other guests have already arrived."

Cecilia lifted her chin slightly and her tone changed. "Am I to understand that I am running late?" She asked, annoyed.

Orestilla stammered but remained as calm as possible. "No, your highness. Of course not. Everyone simply wanted to be here when you arrived."

Cecilia smirked. "Then, let's not keep them waiting."

Orestilla and her ward bowed to the princess as she walked past them towards the main hall.

Once she entered the hall, a magnificent room with more of Orestilla's family history adorning the walls, the other guests all stood and bowed. Cecilia smiled and nodded, allowing everyone to return to their seats. Orestilla trailed in behind Cecilia and guided the princess to the seat at the head table.

"Thank you, your highness for joining us." Orestilla smiled as she took her own seat next to the princess.

Cecilia smiled. "Of course."

Servers went around to each table, bringing food and wine to all the guests. It was a lavish meal, goose and white-tail deer. Cecilia enjoyed the tastes, but she was careful. Her father had taught her well enough to detect most poisons by the look of a piece of food or in a cup. Agis had also trained his daughter to improve her olfactory sense, and she could smell many poisons. The plate in front of her looked harmless, it was indeed.

The other guests all enjoyed the meal and the two leaders heard laughter throughout the hall. Orestilla was pleased, and she felt confident that she would have allies in the coming months. She wasn't sure what the goal after the war would be, but Orestilla knew that the victors would hail her as a hero in the queendom or in Elysia, if not both.

"Lady Orestilla?" Cecilia asked, breaking Orestilla from her daydream. "This is a superb feast. I see that you have served the finest meats, an abundance of sweet pastries and now the minstrels have come out to entertain us."

"We have silk dancing maidens from Biset, as well." Orestilla bragged.

"The ones that dance seductively like the waves on the ocean?" Cecilia asked, raising her eyebrows with interest.

"The same. They weave coins into their fabric so that the trinkets jingle as they move." Orestilla smiled.

Cecilia smiled and looked to the minstrels. She turned back to Orestilla. "Tell me, how are you able to afford all of this?" Cecilia asked, trying to lay a trap for the elder noble.

"Your sister helped me in that regard." Orestilla said bluntly, before sipping her wine. She looked to Cecilia and noted her expression. "My dear princess, those spoils are here for the people. We bought our grain, and we used some left for this party for the gentry of our region."

"I see." Cecilia said before raising her cup to Orestilla. Both smiled and let the party carry on.

An hour later, as the festivities carried on, Cecilia looked around but couldn't find Orestilla within the hall. Excusing herself from the conversation she was in, Cecilia picked up a cup and filled it with fresh wine. She removed a small vile and emptied it into the cup.

Cecilia ducked out through a side door and heard the raised voice of Orestilla. Cecilia crept close to the door. Orestilla was trying to force herself on a dancer, who repeatedly refused her advances. Cecilia sneered. She couldn't stand a person in authority pushing herself onto a servant or entertainer. Still, her goal was unchanged, so she made herself known.

Clearing her through. "Ahem, Lady Orestilla?"

Orestilla turned, surprised. "My princess!" The dancer rushed off as Cecilia's presence distracted Orestilla.

"I hope I'm not interrupting anything."

Orestilla frowned. "A pay dispute. Nothing more."

Cecilia smiled. "Figured as much. Here, I brought you a cup of wine."

Orestilla thanked the princess and accepted the cup, swallowing the wine quickly. "Thank you, this hot air from the kitchens have parched me." The two walked out of the hallway towards the main hall. "I should get ba..." Orestilla stopped and bent over, clutching her cane tightly for support.

"This wine is a particular vintage. One I'm sure you're unfamiliar with." Cecilia said as Orestilla coughed and gasped. "Víaios Ypnos." She smiled.

Orestilla looked up to the princess, recognizing the name of the poison.

"Plot against my family and you plot against me. Plot against me and I'll kill you before you even finish your sentence." Cecilia smirked and kicked Orestilla's cane from under her, causing the woman to fall onto the stone floor. Cecilia looked down at Orestilla. "You were a worthless captain and an even more worthless person, but in your death we will find a resolution."

"Fe is coming..." Orestilla tried to gasp. "They will be here in less than a fortnight." The dying woman gurgled through bile and blood. She laid her head down and her breathing slowed to a snail's pace.

As Orestilla breathed her last breath Cecilia turned and saw Persephone.

"Who are you to me?" Cecilia said to the Blackbird agent she had met earlier.

"Cloaked in shrouds I am a servant of Chaos and none other." Persephone said, bowing.

Cecilia nodded. She understood the meaning and welcomed her new ally. "I need a message delivered to the queen." Cecilia remarked. "Fe is coming to attack."

"Consider it delivered." Persephone bowed to Cecelia.

Cecilia and Persephone walked out of the hallway and outside to the stables.

"It's funny that I never met you. Have you been in the area long?" Cecilia remarked as they mounted their horses.

"Yes, your highness. I have served your father faithfully for years." Persephone caught on to Cecilia's meaning. "Fear not, your highness. I will not betray you. I am loyal to your family as were my parents and their parents before them." Persephone replied. "What of Princess Syrena? Should she be made aware?" She asked changing the topic.

"I will send her a message on the matter. She should be a married woman by now. Let's give her a few days of bliss before a new war erupts."

"My princess, war is here. Orestilla lied with her dying breath. Fe has already crossed the border and is camped only a few miles north. Orestilla was to lead them to Verna."

Cecilia grinned. "The lady cannot fulfill that task. I'll inform the queen of this development and ride out with the cavalry at once." Cecilia nodded to the woman before the two rode out of the town and in opposite directions into the dark night.

The New Life Begins

It was two days before Gabriel and Syrena's wedding, and the Furies were making sure that the two would have two days and nights to get reacquainted. It was not like in the older days of the queendom, but within a private tent Syrena and Gabriel talked with each other, shared wine, a few tears and enjoyed some time away from the town's life. Given the other occupied tents in the courtyard, the couple did not have the same amount of privacy that Syrena's mother had.

This didn't deter the couple, however. Within the tent, in an atmosphere of love and familiarity, Syrena and Gabriel talked of their coming life together. Sitting upon silk pillows brought in from the queendom, Syrena thought to her future with her soon to be groom.

"Children? How many do you think?" Syrena asked Gabriel with a smile.

"As many as fate destines us to have." He replied with his own smile. "I think the fun is in the trying." Gabriel winked.

Syrena laughed and leaned in and kissed Gabriel. "Then I suspect many children." She whispered. "This beard will take some getting used to. It tickles a bit." Syrena gently stroked Gabriel's beard before giving him a playful tug on it and a second kiss. "But I like it."

They shared a few more kisses. The mood was romantic and one that the couple savored for the moment. Many duties awaited them in the coming days and then in a month's time, they would have to travel to Caleope to resume lordship. That is where some anxiety for Gabriel had sprung from.

"What of me in Amazon? What of this town while I'm away?" He asked.

Syrena leaned back and took her cup. Filling it with more wine, she smiled to her soon to be husband.

"Don't fret. In the queendom the queen will give you a comfortable position. You have a mind for logistics and diplomacy, so I'm certain you'd find a place within the region easily." Syrena replied. "I'm certain that with your past in the north that my sisters in Caleope will welcome you as a brother."

Gabriel smiled. "I'm happy to hear that. It's encouraging, but that doesn't answer the question of my duties here? I can't just run off again. Even if it is with you. I'm needed to remain here."

Syrena put her cup down and stood up. Her chiton was wrinkled and unbuckled, exposing her left breast as she rose, but Gabriel tried not to notice. Syrena realized it and reattached the buckle.

Syrena scoffed. "Even with me?" She said. "I've been through hell for this love that I've had in my heart. Torment most foul, yet you find it so hard to leave for just two seasons a year. Could it be that your subjects might understand, rejoice even, that their lord has found love?"

Gabriel stood up and embraced Syrena from behind her. "I never meant to say I didn't want to leave with you. People felt threatened with my return and this land, though poorer than most others, is highly contested over. This is still the most valuable target for the Elysians."

"You think I don't understand that?" Syrena shot back, shrugging Gabriel off her as she turned around. "I've seen the reports of those seeking to usurp your place. I defended you to those in the queendom that doubted you!" Syrena yelled, almost in tears. "I ask nothing of you than to be close to me during our years together here in this world." Syrena looked Gabriel in the eyes. Her face softened and her anger mellowed. "I only asked that you stand by me as I've always stood by you. I know you didn't see it, but I never left your side and I never stopped loving you."

Gabriel clasped her hands and brought them up to his lips, giving them a gentle kiss. "I'll spend the rest of my life by your side, no matter where we are." He said before the two fell into an embrace.

They had time to think of all that and a lifetime to figure it out. The next couple of days were all that mattered. Spending as much time together before they were married to reconnect from a long absence.

That time was welcome because two days later, the couple stood in the church within the town of Antei. While the royal family wore their normal attire for formal affairs, linen tunics and dresses with fur trims, Gabriel opted for the Amazon style himation over his royal tunic and linen trousers. Syrena, as was fashionable for brides in the Central Continent, wearing her blue peplos and white himation. The Furies dressed in their finest armors and himations for the occasion.

"I never figured I'd step into a Creator temple." Esther whispered to Nyx a few rows back from the altar.

"They call them churches." Nyx corrected.

"Think we'll build one in Amazon?" Callisto asked.

Nyx shook her head. "The queen is staunch in her faith to the old gods. Cecilia, more so. We might have a missionary every few years but never a permanent church."

The ceremony was brief, as were most under the Creator's church, but the reception lasted all night and into the following day. The entire town closed up their shops and stalls, going into the main square for a parade, and feasts were held throughout Antei. Gabriel and Syrena did their best to visit each of the feasts, but they too wanted to attend their own private feast.

King Liam and Queen Clotide adjourned from the manor house and took residence in the town's largest inn, an inn that saw more festivities than any other in the celebration. This gave Gabriel and Syrena the manor house to themselves and allowed the newly married couple a chance to consummate their marriage. However, that was only after Mestra said the Amazonian blessings over the marriage bed.

While Gabriel and Syrena laid naked in their bed, Mestra prayed over the couple, burning incense while anointing the pair in oils and oak ash. The oils, heavily fragrant, represented the seal of the marriage pact while the ash from oak trees symbolized the beginning and end of all living things. Once she finished the rites, Mestra bestowed a simple blessing for fertility by having each eat a pomegranate seed before leaving to give the couple the rest of the night to themselves.

Syrena giggled. "Now that we smell of oak and perfume, I guess we should make use of this bed."

Gabriel grinned and wrapped his arms around his wife, enjoying the night as the two made love into the wee hours of the morning. All around them, throughout Antei, celebrations were heard, but for them the only thing that mattered was their expression of true love.

* * * *

Three more days passed before the parties wound down. Training slowly resumed in the courtyard and below the motte, as life returned to normal. Though many, Minimoto and some Furies in particular, still showed signs of their hangovers. However, much was to be done and there wasn't any time for being sick.

The Furies took to their training, Syrena leading the drills, and several of the Furies helped the Thousand Man Battalion in their own formations and training. They gave assistance right after Syrena and Arana's duel, but took some time off during the wedding and celebrations. The king watched the drills from atop the manor house alongside his sons, enjoying the view of the expansive fields when a cloud of dust came into view.

"What is that over there? Are there soldiers training?" King Liam asked.

Gabriel put his hand up to shield his eyes from the sunlight and looked across the open plain that stretched along the Moonstone River. "No. All of the battalion is just beneath us. Is your cavalry riding Liam?" Gabriel asked.

Prince Liam looked around, rushing to the northern side of the wall and saw his horsemen, two hundred strong, still camped. "No!" He shouted as he rushed back.

In a split second a horn sounded from the southern outpost that blew for a tone but went silent abruptly.

"Elysia." King Liam snarled. "Form the defenses!" He shouted. His sons went to work, Prince Liam to his camp and the king to the manor house. He found the queen quickly. "Stay in here with the attendants!" The king shouted. He looked to his steward. "My armor and sword, now!"

The king rushed out with his steward moments behind him. He stopped and the steward helped him slip on his chain mail shirt. Fastening his greaves and gauntlets, the king then attached his sword before putting on his nasal helm. Mounting his horse, Gabriel walked up to him.

"What do we have for soldiers?" King Liam asked of his son.

Gabriel was sliding on his chainmail with the help of Syrena, already in her armor from training.

"With the Thousand Man, the Quarmi battalion, Liam's horses and your twenty king's guards, we're sitting at two thousand regular soldiers and three thousand town militia and levies. Antei supplies five hundred of its levy as horsemen." Gabriel answered.

"Twenty seven Furies, the best the Amazonian Queendom has to offer at your command, my lord." Syrena said to the king.

"Thank you. We'll show them the might of our mighty alliance!" King Liam replied with a smile.

Gabriel was not so sure. "Father, this manor has stood on this motte for centuries. Even Rowena couldn't take the manor house. We can defend from here."

"This is just another Elysian skirmish. Get used to them because they come like the tides." Liam answered before unsheathing his sword. "King's Guard, on me!" He shouted, riding out of the courtyard to the field below.

"We should defend from here." Gabriel remarked, watching his father rush out with a handful of other riders.

"Maybe he is right, and it's just a skirmish. I'll take the infantry down." Syrena replied. She kissed

Gabriel and parted as the two went in separate directions.

Gabriel rushed on his horse to the area where the town militia was gathering. "Riders, come with me! All those on foot, you'll be with Captain Minimoto!" The group broke off as every able bodied man rushed to the field south of the motte and rendezvoused with the Thousand Man Battalion and the Furies.

Syrena, on her horse and shouting orders, saw Gabriel riding up with his riders. "Your father and brother already rode out to meet the Elysians!"

Gabriel cursed their want for such haste. "Damn it! Fine, let's ride!" The horsemen from Antei rode with quickness as the infantry units rushed at a double time march. Minimoto left some militia and Quarmi behind to guard the town, but he joined in the march south.

On his horse, Minimoto stuck an impressive figure in his tatami chest armor and greaves over a silken robe. His robe bore his family's crescent moon crest while his helmet had deer antlers attached. He rode up to Syrena.

"This will be a day with much death." Minimoto mourned.

"I though the Quarmi wanted to die in battle."

Minimoto looked to Syrena. "Not me. I prefer to die old and drunk by a warm fire, writing a poem. Your husband was right. We should have defended from the motte."

"Where is the honor in that?" Ino asked from behind him.

Minimoto shook his head. "Many fathers will not return home today."

"Are you a seer, Minimoto?" Syrena asked.

"No. Just in tuned to the world around us." The Quarmi answered.

Mestra looked on to the field before them. "He's right." Everyone looked at her. "The dust cloud is too big for a skirmish. This is a battle with a full fighting force. We need to hurry."

Sensing the same danger that Mestra could feel, everyone rushed on, spurring their soldiers into a run. All to reach a battlefield already bloody from horse and human death!

"Form a phalanx! Furies dismount!" Syrena ordered before sliding her corinth helm on, followed by a disciplined but slow line forming up around her.

Minimoto rounded up his soldiers similarly. "Militia, get behind the Quarmi line. Quarmi battalion, shield wall!"

The two forces formed and stood in defense as an Elysian infantry charge bared down on them quickly. The Quarmi took the brunt of the charge, but the Furies shouted taunts and hurled insults at the Elysians to bring them their way.

Syrena stood in the phalanx's front next to Mesta and Ino. "Did either of you see Gabriel?" She asked before the second charge came. Neither could answer yes.

"Damn." Syrena cursed before the next charge hit them. Again their shields stood strong.

Little to nothing would break a phalanx supported by Amazons, no matter how few there stood. For the Amazons, the phalanx and the entire battle was a part of life itself. Their armor, bronze, iron or steel, was as much a part of their bodies as their skin.

Horsemen rode in front of the combined lines, but it was hard to make out who was riding the beasts. Most of the Lotcalans had on blue or green surcoats or tunics over their mail or gambesons. The Elysians wore red over mail. Still, with the amount of blood, the blue and green had turned to a darker hue, making the patterns hard to see and the colors even harder to distinguish.

Gabriel rode by the Amazons, but he couldn't afford to be distracted by his wife or his other soldiers. Now was the task of beating back the surprise attack by an age-old enemy. Gabriel led his horsemen into an advance cavalry charge, meeting the opposing forces head on. This was not a simple task and Gabriel tried to meet up with his brother's cavalry, a force made up from members of the Lotcalan heavy horse. Nobles able to afford the heavier steel and mail for both themselves and their mounts. With the more armored cavalry, Gabriel and his lighter horsemen would fare better, but as it was, Elysia was gaining the upper hand.

Elysian heavy mounts, like their riders, were always armored, usually iron lamellar armor made to look like feathers. The horses were typically large drought horses or coursers, known for their strength. Gabriel's horse, and many of the Lotcalan riders, were destriers, faster yet smaller horses built for quicker attacks.

The fight amongst the cavalry was harder than Gabriel had expected and he still couldn't find his father, his brother or their men anywhere. Riding and thrusting his spear into a nearby warrior, Gabriel unsheathed his sword, calling for his men to advance alongside him. Gabriel was determined to drive the Elysians back to the south and past the Southern Hills.

"Charge!" Gabriel ordered, spurring his own horse faster, his sword in right hand, and his round shield in his left.

The Lotcalan cavalry collided with the Elysians, the Lotcalans took most of the force but they stayed on their horses. The swifter Lotcalan mounts dodged the lumbering Elysians once they passed the first line, and shields blocked spears and lances while swords swung with abandon. Gabriel reached the other end of the Elysians and saw his brother's and father's men fighting with more of the Elysian cavalry.

Gabriel risked a glance around. "No archers They meant this to be a quick strike." He said to himself before turning back into the battle.

Nearby, Syrena looked out over the field. "Advance!" She called and in a slightly disjointed movement the Furies and the Thousand Man Battalion ran into the battle, breaking the phalanx they had set up. However, with the Furies at the front, the provided effect of the shock was working. Elysian soldiers saw the rushing horde and braced for the impact. There was little they could do to shield themselves from such a deadly force, however, and the Furies, backed by the Lotcalan soldiers, slammed into the Elysians, mowing them down with ease.

Most of the Elysians had seen the ferocity of the Amazons in the recent war, and few wanted a repeat experience. However, this was a smaller number of Amazons and the Elysian confidence was high. Minimoto arrived with the other Quarmi and town militia to provide a hand to the Lotcalans. A new phalanx formed, wrapping around the Elysian foot soldiers. Chaos erupted from the entrapped soldiers. The Elysians outnumbered the Lotcalan and Amazon warriors, but the advantage was to the phalanx.

"Mestra!" Syrena called out. "It's a matter of time until this dissolves. Anything you can do to put the fear of the goddesses into them?"

Mestra nodded. Looking up into the sky, the Amazonian mage, a high ranking magister, called out in an ancient tongue and slammed her spear into the ground. A blue light sprang from the ground where her spear pierced, sending lightening into the Elysian mass and killing many of the soldiers in front of Mestra's spear.

"That should do it." Mestra said with a smirk under her helm.

The Furies took advantage of the scared Elysians and rushed into the mass of soldiers, running over those already dead and stabbing at any that stood in front of them. The Quarmi and Lotcalans joined in the mayhem, but the Furies reigned supreme in this sort of warfare.

Melees like this were part of daily life within the Herd. While the many warriors that came from the queendom were skilled in phalanxes because of their extensive training, the muck and bloodied mud of battle was when their warrior mentality and ferocity would take over. A bloodlust, engrained in the fearsome women from an early age, blinded them. Expert precision based on instincts pushed the Amazons forward, thrusting spears into the less armored Elysians. Syrena bashed her shield into any coming foe, sending them hurtling to the ground. A last stab of her spear to the man's neck finished the job.

The other Furies were following suit, and soon the Elysians were running from the approaching Amazons and their allies. The fight continued, with Quarmi and Lotcalans joining the fray. Several of the Furies were wounded and two were laying on the ground. Many Lotcalans and Quarmi were also wounded or dead. However, many more Elysians lay on the ground dead or dying.

The battle was raging on when a horn sounded and the Elysians retreated. For good measure, Syrena leveled her spear and hurled it into the back of a running Elysian.

Syrena looked around and called out to her sisters. "For the goddess!" She roared, followed by a loud 'Alala!' from her sisters.

Syrena looked across the field and saw the dirt settling as a coming rainstorm brought a down pour. There she saw a soaked and broken ground around a mass of bodies. Syrena rushed over and saw what was left of the twenty king's guard standing over the king.

Just then a man in heavy chain armor came up to Syrena. "My lady!" He said, bringing her attention to him. "The prince is there with his brother. You should go to him, he mourns."

Syrena rushed the fifty yards to find her husband sitting next to the body of his older brother.

"They said he fell in the second charge." Gabriel said, wiping tears, leaving mud and blood smeared on his face. "I tried to reach them in time, but they caught me between their heavy horses and retreating foot soldiers."

"Gabriel..." Syrena began. "You need to know something." Syrena knelt down beside her husband and held him. "Before I tell you, know that what happens today, from this moment on, will define you more than anything else in your life. Stand up, look your country in the eye with bravery because today everything has changed."

As news of the crown prince's death spread, Syrena knelt with her husband a few minutes more before she guided Gabriel up. The prince did what he could to stand. Exhaustion and grief weighed him down more than he had ever felt before. He clutched a spear that he had found nearby and used it to steady himself. His legs were weak from the hard riding on the muddy ground, but he stood as proud as he could with his wife's loving and steady hand. Still, he wasn't prepared for what came next.

A crowd gathered around Gabriel as he stood, looking over the battlefield. His childhood friend, Minimoto, walked up to him and presented him with the king's crown.

"My lord." Minimoto said, lowering his head. "The king fell in the battle."

Gabriel dropped to his knees and lowered his head. Minimoto placed the crown, a golden band with five raised points, on Gabriel's head. "May you honor your people as your father did, and his father before him back until the days of Theodorif. Long live the king."

Whether Gabriel knelt for that or because of the weight of what was happening isn't known, and there he was on his knees. Gabriel was the new king.

The crowd echoed Minimoto's final proclamation. "Long live the king!"

War

The Lotcalans sent out scouts to the south to find the reach of the Elysian army just as soon as the battle was over. They found that the Elysians had retreated further back to their outposts and border forts nearly three days' ride. The scouts also came across valuable information in the form of a wounded rider left behind. By the time the scouts returned, the world was a different place.

After the battle, Gabriel and the Furies carried the bodies of the fallen king and crown prince back to the manor house while the soldiers buried the other fallen in the ground where they fell. One Fury, Livia, fell honorably during the battle. Nyx and Polydeuces carried her back to the camp.

"I'll give her the rites. We have to set up a pyre for her." Mestra said in a somber tone once Livia's body reached the courtyard of the manor house. "To the ashes of our ancestors will we all return." This wasn't common for Amazons, most practices preferred burial in the battlefield. However, for the Furies, cremation was the quickest way to meet the ancestors and the old gods.

The Furies that stood within earshot instinctively replied to Mestra's words. "As was with our grandmothers."

Ino looked on. "We will miss her. Her bow was nearly the best I've ever seen."

Melantho nodded. "I must send a letter to the archer prefect." Melantho sighed. "Artemisia will be angry for her loss."

"Then let me." Ino responded. "I'm her older sister, she'll accept it from me."

"I'll inform Prefect Artemisia. Lavia was ultimately my responsibility." Syrena said walking up to the Furies. "However, right now we have other matters to deal with." She looked to the manor house. "I must see to Gabriel." She said, walking away from her sisters.

Ino looked to Mestra and Melantho. "What do you think she'll do now?"

Mestra shook her head. "It pales compared to what the Lotcalans have lost, but I believe that we've lost our commander."

Melantho stood next to her sisters. "Let's tend to the wounded and to Livia's pyre. Gabriel is giving us the courtyard for the ritual. It was a blessing enough that Syrena didn't have to ask, let's not dwell on the task any further." The other two Furies agreed and went to work for their fallen sister.

Syrena waked up to the manor house, pushing the door open she could hear the wailing cries of Clotide. She walked to her husband and sat on the bench next to him, remaining as stoic as possible. Gabriel looked to her and clasped her hand.

"We have to act." Gabriel whispered.

"My love, maybe…"

"We must mount an attack of our own. The barons will expect us to fight." He continued.

"Do you really think now…" Syrena began, but stopped. "Gabriel, think of the people here. The numbers of dead and wounded are coming in and they keep growing."

"We weren't prepared." Gabriel stood, releasing Syrena's hand. "That won't happen again. We barely won this battle, but the war is beginning anew and I won't rest until the Elysians feel my pain."

Syrena stood, but before she could walk to her husband, two Quarmi riders burst into the manor. The scouts that rushed after the retreating army had returned. These particular Quarmi scouts hauled in a wounded rider and tossed him on the wooden floor. The hurt man landed with a painful thud.

"What the hell is this?" Gabriel exclaimed. "You bring this filth into my presence!" He unsheathed his sword, but one of the Quarmi called out.

"My lord, wait!" The Quarmi quickly bowed to Gabriel's anger. "Before you execute him, he could have information." The Quarmi went over to the man and removed his helm. "He is Fesian!"

Gabriel sneered at the man on the ground.

Syrena went over to him. "What say you then, rider?"

The man was defiant and silent. Syrena saw his wounded side just below his ribs and stepped on it.

"Anything you wish to tell us?" Syrena asked.

The man groaned in agony, but he remained defiant.

"Take him to the headsman. If he won't talk, then he'll die." Gabriel ordered.

The Quarmi lifted the man up, but Syrena stopped them. "My lord, allow one of the Furies to pry the information out of him."

Gabriel fumed, but he nodded an acceptance of her idea.

Syrena looked to the Quarmi men holding the wounded rider. "Take him outside and find Riva."

The Quarmi looked to Gabriel and with his nod they followed the order. Outside of the manor house, they asked around and finally found the mage that Syrena had directed them to. Mestra walked up to the Quarmi just as Syrena and Gabriel joined them.

"What's going on, Syrena?" Mestra asked. "Why are you taking him to Riva?"

Syrena looked to her oldest friend. "Forgive me, Mestra, but you once told me that Riva could enter people's minds. We need that here."

Mestra frowned. "That is dangerous, not only for him but her as well." She looked to Riva. "Do you think you are ready for this?"

Riva was silent for a moment. She rubbed her hands, still bloody from the battle. Then she nodded. "Set him down. What do you want to know?" She asked, looking to Gabriel.

"He is Fesian, so why is he wearing Elysian armor and colors? What is the plan? He is a rider and one with many scars, he isn't a commoner." Gabriel answered.

"Yes, my lord." Riva replied. "Please know, that I'm not used to mind flaying and it could do damage."

"I don't care." Gabriel replied.

Riva looked to Syrena and Mestra, noting the look of shock on their faces from his coldhearted reply.

Riva turned back to Gabriel. "It could also damage me, my lord."

Gabriel looked at the Fury and softened his stance. "Then stop if that happens, be careful. The information he isn't telling us might be more valuable than his life but do not hurt yourself."

"Yes, my lord." Riva replied. "I'll try."

Riva knelt down beside the man and grasped his face with both hands and stared into his eyes. Suddenly, he was gasping for air as she entered his consciousness and probed within the man's mind. She was as still as a statue, locking her eyes in place, unblinking and focused on his eyes.

Within the man's mind, Riva fell into what felt like an abyss. She centered herself and her feelings, stopping the free fall, and from there she saw images. The battle, riding a horse on the open desert and camping under the stars. She walked through his memories. Everything was so fluid. She reached out and touched a tree, feeling it dissipate from her fingertips.

"Shit!" Riva said, her voice echoing. "Touch nothing." She said to herself.

Walking further through memories of the battle, an enemy camp, and a long journey from Fe. Finally, she found the one she had been looking for. Fesian riders putting on Elysian gear and speaking in their local dialect. Riva knew enough Fesian to understand some of what they were saying. She grasped enough before the man fought back. A natural reaction of anyone under a flay spell.

Riva turned and rushed from the memory, back to her starting point. She jumped back into the abyss and let go.

Coming back to reality, Riva let go of the man's head and they both fell back on the ground. She rolled backwards and landed on her feet, crouching, as her battle instincts took over.

She looked around, collecting herself and stood. "He's part of an expeditionary force. Testing your strength. They were led by Elysian knights, but Fesian riders made up the bulk of his compatriots. He and his fellow riders are from the Helot Tribe." Riva said, standing up.

"Mercenaries?" Syrena asked.

Riva shook her head. "No, my lady. He is a vassal of Warchief Gelimer, nephew to Emperor Hel."

Gabriel turned to his guards. "Send word to Jovag and all the holds! Elysia and Fe have declared war."

"There is more." Riva said. "They aren't the only ones."

"I have to send word to the queendom!" Syrena said as she hurried into her tent. "My mother needs to be warned!" Inside, she retrieved a roll of parchment and a quill and sat on the ground to write a hasty note.

"What should we do?" Ino asked her commander.

"We'll return with the Furies and storm Orestilla's keep." Syrena replied, never looking up from her parchment.

"We should go to the queen first." Mestra said, walking into the tent. "Even with this, it's just hearsay. The queen will need proof of Orestilla's treachery and she will need more provocation to invade Fe."

Syrena stopped writing. "Damn." She stood up. "Then we ride for Verna and mobilize the queen's forces into action. We'll bring the prisoner."

"There is more." Mestra said. "You're married to a king now. What of that?"

Syrena thought for a moment. "I'll speak to him before we ride out. In the meantime, prepare the Furies." Syrena exited the tent, followed by her sisters.

The Amazonian princess walked up to the manor and entered. She could still hear the queen wailing over the loss of her son and husband. She mourned for her, but her stoic exterior wouldn't allow her to show any cracks. None of the Furies could. Any emotions that followed tragic loss were snuffed out of the Amazons during their training in the Herd. This gave Amazons their infamous tough exteriors, but on the inside they still felt the sting.

Syrena walked up to her husband, who was sitting by the hearth, his head hung low and the king's crown in his hands.

"Gabriel?" She said, as softly as she could.

"You're leaving?" Gabriel asked, keeping his head low. His hair was still matted with blood, mud and dried sweat. "I can understand why. We need to prepare."

"No. I'm staying by your side." Syrena said, betraying her reason for coming into the house. Her sisters looked at her in surprise. "You need me here." She said, surprised in her own voice uttering the words.

Gabriel stood up and looked to his wife. He gave a slight smile, but his pain was still too great. "You're needed in the queendom. It's fine. When all this is over, I know you'll return and then we can figure out how this marriage will work. This wasn't at all what I had expected to be for our lives. I never wanted a crown or be called a king."

Syrena embraced him. "Those that seek a crown rarely deserve one and those that deserve a crown rarely seek one."

"Syrena..." Gabriel begun, but a voice from behind cut him off.

"The king will need a queen beside him."

Everyone turned to regard Queen Clotide, descending the stone stairs.

"I can no longer fill such a role. My husband is dead. My king is dead." Clotide sighed. She slipped the crown from her head and walked over to Syrena. The Amazonian princess stood nearly a foot taller than the Lotcalan queen. "You must take my place as queen." She said reaching up to place the crown on Syrena's head. "I'll remain with your father and brother, but I don't have the strength for another war." She said, looking to her son.

Syrena leaned down and accepted the crown upon her head. "My lady..." Syrena began.

"Just promise me you'll guard the kingdom with your life. The kingdom does not rest with the king alone, nor with the queen. This kingdom is its people. They are strong and they will follow you into hell if they know you'll give your last breath for them." Clotide said sorrowfully. "Liam knew that. The great kings of the past knew it, and the great queens knew it and guided their husbands with a firm hand. You are the right hand of the king now. It's up to you to decide if you will be the nurturing hand or an iron fist of a tyrant. Neither is right nor wrong and both are right and wrong." Clotide turned and walked back up the stairs. "Rule well, King Gabriel and Queen Syrena." She said before disappearing.

Minimoto stepped up to the group from behind Gabriel. "My lord, there is a rider from Amazon. She arrived just a short while ago."

Everyone left the manor house and walked over to the area where an exhausted rider sat drinking water from a ladle and bucket. The woman stood up and saluted Gabriel and then dropped to one knee when Syrena appeared.

"My princess!" The messenger said.

"Queen now." Melantho spoke up. "Queen Syrena of Lotcala."

The woman looked up. "Forgive me." She replied, standing up. She looked to Gabriel, now wearing the king's crown. "My condolences, my lord Gabriel." She said, looking around, she saw the wounded and the battle beaten warriors. "This may not come as a surprise, my lady Syrena, but I come on orders from your sister." The messenger took a breath. "Orestilla has betrayed the queendom, and Fe is en route to attack both the Queendom and Lotcala. Orestilla also treated with Elysia and Gota mercenaries."

"Elysia has already attacked with Fesian riders." Syrena replied, already knowing of Orestilla's treachery through Riva's magic. "What of Orestilla? Has she slithered behind her walls or will we meet her on the field?"

"Orestilla has died." The Messenger replied. "She was hosting a banquet when she died. The healer couldn't say how. Your sister was there, but she left by the time they found Orestilla."

Syrena nodded. "Thank you." She turned and walked to her tent, leaving the messenger with Ino to settle in for the night.

Mestra caught up to Syrena. "You're thinking it was Cecilia." Mestra said bluntly.

"She was going to help with Orestilla, that's what she said. This isn't helping." Syrena said, packing her bedding into a cloth pack. "She killed her."

"In Cecilia's defense, Orestilla was a traitor. Practically plotted against you before your own eyes." Mestra replied. "This is a favor."

Syrena turned and regarded her friend with pain in her eyes. "How can you say that? I never wanted her dead!"

"I know that, but what if she forced your sister's hand?" Mestra reasoned. "We both know that Cecilia isn't a murderer. She'll kill on the battlefield with reckless abandon, but she will not kill anyone in cold blood. It's possible that she discovered the true plot or perhaps Orestilla attacked her."

Syrena ceded the point. "I need to return to Verna. I still command the legion. No matter what happened, war is coming."

Mestra nodded. "Then we'll ride out tonight."

"First, I must speak with my husband." Syrena said, looking to the manor house. "I need him to know."

Syrena walked into the manor house as a priest and Minimoto were arguing. Gabriel was nowhere in sight. The argument sounded heated, but once the priest saw Syrena walk in, he stiffened.

"What's the matter?" Syrena asked.

Minimoto scoffed. "Our dear priest is refusing your coronation blessing." Minimoto walked to the nearby table and poured a cup of wine. "Say's he won't perform it until you convert. I told him that this wasn't the time to discuss it and that you had the queen mother's blessing and of course Gabriel's." Minimoto shook his head. "King Gabriel's. That'll take some getting used to." He finished before gulping his wine.

"So what of my beliefs?" Syrena asked to the priest.

"Our throne is a throne that follows the Creator." The man said. "Since the earliest days."

"And Theodorif?" Syrena countered.

"The Blessed Olaf converted him." The priest grinned, raising his hands up. "We can look into your conversion...

"Shit, I do not have time for this." Syrena interrupted. "Minimoto, where is my husband, the *king*?" She emphasized the word king for the priest.

Minimoto was still drinking his wine. "My dear *QUEEN*." He said, gasping from the wine and, putting emphasis on the word queen for the priest to hear. "He is in the town preparing for a journey to Jovag, so he can begin mobilizing the barons against Elysia."

"Dammit!" Syrena cursed. "Fe is in an alliance with Elysia and are marching on the queendom."

"That could be a problem." Minimoto said, putting his cup down. "I'll fetch the king." The Quarmi warrior rushed out of the manor house, leaving Syrena and the priest alone.

The priest smiled to Syrena. "Shall we discuss your conversion to the faith of the Creator?"

Syrena scoffed before turning toward the door. "No, we shall not." She said before walking out of the manor.

An hour later, King Gabriel and Minimoto arrived back at the manor.

"Where is that damn priest?!" Gabriel shouted as he dismounted from his horse. Everyone in the courtyard looked to the king, many stood and saluted with a bow. "Is he still here? I need a word with him."

"He's gone to the battlefield, praying over the dead, my lord." Melantho replied.

"Fine, I have another here anyway. She's a little less steadfast." Gabriel replied, bringing a priestess to the group.

"It's not that big of a deal, Gabriel." Syrena said. "My king." She corrected. "That will take getting used to." She said with a look to Minimoto, who nodded.

"No, it needs to be done. Here and now. This way you can lead in my name should I..." Gabriel stopped. "Should I be unable to fight?" He finished.

Syrena leaned into her husband with a hug. "Gabriel, we won't let that happen." She said, but the look on Gabriel's face told her that his mind was made up.

"If it's that important, then I will." Syrena looked to the priestess. "Shall we?"

The priestess bowed. "Y... yes." She stammered. "May I have the crown?"

Syrena handed the priestess her crown as Lotcalans and Furies crowded the royal entourage. It was a heavy ring of gold, molded with four points rising from the band.

"Please kneel." The priestess said. She then took out a vial of water and poured it over the crown.

Looking at Syrena, she began the coronation. "Syrena of Amazon, daughter of Saria of the line of Mara, I stand to give this crown, and you as the bearer of the crown, the blessing that Oleg gave to Theodorif, the first king of Lotcala." The priestess cleared her throat and raised the crown above Syrena's head. "Our ancestors named this land for the old goddess of the hearth. Our home, our sanctuary, is yours to safe guard as ruler. Yours is the rule of law, of protection and of the people. As we trust in you, so to do we ask you to trust in us. With this crown, do you swear to honor Lotcala as you would a brother or sister, your own child?"

"I do." Syrena answered.

"Do you swear to defend the kingdom and its people against all foes, physical and divine?"

"I do." Syrena answered.

The priestess placed the crown on Syrena's head. "Then rise my queen. Rise and be known as Syrena I of Lotcala." The priestess smiled. "Long live the queen!" She said aloud.

The surrounding crowd repeated the proclamation. "Long live the queen!"

Syrena rose and everyone in the courtyard bowed or dropped to a knee in salute. Syrena lowered her head.

"Thank you everyone, but get up. This is going to be hell and we have little time to waste." She said.

As everyone rose, Syrena took Gabriel aside. "I have to return to Verna. Fe is mobilizing against the queendom and for now I'm still the Legion commander. I'll meet with you here as soon as I can."

"I have a plan for that." Gabriel grinned. "Come inside the manor house."

The royal couple, along with Minimoto, Mestra, Ino and Melantho all went into the manor house. Gabriel laid a map out on the table, throwing cups and plates on the floor.

"We have forces close to here in Greenfield, just south of Estan." Gabriel began. "General Miralda's Southern Division is there, stationed as border patrols. They and the force from Ter Nog, under Commander Bulwyf, can lead a strike into Elysia's northeast region. If the queendom can spare the warriors and mount a strike near Varus-dun, then we can hold them back until we finish with Fe."

"You want to go into Fe first?" Minimoto asked.

"It's the largest of the targets and the one with the biggest army. We hit them hard and fast while holding Elysia off in the south, then we could fight this war on two fronts. They have crossed into Amazon already, and while they're fighting in the south, we'll take the battle to them in the north." Gabriel answered. "I'll spearhead our move into the desert and Minimoto you can take command of the forces from here, keeping the border fortified."

"My lord, your grace." Minimoto stuttered. "I'm a Quarmi, I can lead a battalion but the entire border forces? Few would follow me."

"Miralda would, as would Bulwyf. Both trained with you and know your worth as a military leader. They are also friends from the academy. Besides, you can remind Bulwyf that as my cousin he is required to do as I say." Gabriel said with a smile, but Minimoto wasn't so easily won over. Gabriel clasped his friend's shoulder. "You're the eldest son of the great warlord Katsuichi, you are born to lead the forces. You know firsthand the might that we are dealing with. Bulwyf has been in Ter Nog, and Miralda hasn't been on the border as long as us. You have been with me every step since my return. I need you to be my eyes, ears and mouth here now."

Minimoto nodded. "Then I am your man, your grace." He said with a bow.

"Good. Trust this manor and the people of Antei. It has repelled many invasions." Gabriel said. Letting out a sigh, he looked to the Amazons. "What do you think, Syrena? Will Amazon be able to help us defend against Elysia?" Gabriel asked.

"If the queen can spare it, then we will push in at Varus-dun." Syrena answered.

"Good. We don't have time for second guessing, so trust your instincts from here on out." Gabriel rolled up the map. "I've sent out riders to gather the barons in Jovag. I need to leave today for that meeting, but I would like some time with my wife before I go." The others bowed and left the manor, and Gabriel pulled Syrena into an embrace.

"I look forward to the day we will see each other again." Gabriel breathed.

"Come back to me, my love." Syrena answered before joining her husband in a kiss.

A Foreign Queen

Two and a half weeks later an exhausted Syrena and the rest of the Furies arrived in Verna. The city was bustling with war preparations and excitement. News had reached the capital of Fe's advance within the queendom, though turned back by the northern border forces. However, in the capital, not a moment was wasted in gearing up a sizable defense and counterattack.

Syrena sent the Furies to their normal posts while she went straight to the queen. The Queen's Keep was a hotbed of anticipation over many of the soldiers marching off to war. Syrena overheard many of the conversations, and the topics mainly revolved around venturing into the desert. A few didn't even notice the princess as she walked through the halls. Those that did notice Syrena also noticed a queen's crown atop her head.

Sebula, guarding the door to the throne room, stopped Syrena as she approached and then knelt in salute.

"The queen is in council with her advisors. I must announce you, my princess." Sebula said in a booming voice as she stood up.

"Please make haste." Syrena replied. She wrung her hands. A nervous energy, uncommon for the normally stoic Amazon.

Entering the throne room this time was different for Syrena. She entered as an equal of sorts with her mother, but she was still the queen's youngest daughter.

Queen Saria listened to reports from the prefects that had stayed in Verna when she noticed Syrena walk through the door. Sebula knelt and announced the princess, but Queen Saria cut her off.

"That won't be necessary, Sebula. As you were." Queen Saria waved Sebula back and motioned for the prefects to step aside. "Who is this now that comes to treat with me? My princess? No, a queen I see." Saria gave a half smile. "To what do I owe the honor of being visited by the Queen of Lotcala?"

Syrena knelt and saluted. "I come as the Legion Commander."

"Then rise and tell me why you come with a crown upon your head." Saria said.

Syrena rose and looked around the court. Many familiar faces looked to her and sought guidance. She saw her other three prefects, Artemisia, Leda and Philyre, each looking at her and waiting for her next words.

"My queen, I come because my queendom needs me more than my husband does. Fe is advancing as we speak." Syrena replied.

"Aye, they are. We've had fighting at our borders, but we've pushed back and they've retreated. Our scouts say that this retreat is just a ploy, therefore we'll push further." Saria paused. "Tell me though, what of Gabriel? King, now I understand. He doesn't wish for his wife at his side during this time?" Saria asked.

"We mourned for the former king and prince, and we will mourn yet again when we defeat our enemies. For now, King Gabriel is mounting his own invasion into Fe. He doesn't have time to cry." Syrena said, lowering her head. "Mother." She said. "My husband needs me, but I am a loyal daughter of Mara. Where else but here can I go?"

Saria nodded. "We will honor King Liam and his fallen son with prayers that King Gabriel is every bit the man his father was." Saria stood from her throne, her silk himation fell to her ankles. "The battle, was it fierce?"

Syrena nodded. "Yes, my queen."

"Did they fall with honor?"

"They did." Syrena replied.

Saria nodded. "There is little more we could ever ask for in life." She walked down to her daughter. The two women stood eye to eye. Saria embraced Syrena in a hug. "Welcome home, your grace." Saria smiled. "Now, we have a plan in place. Where are Ino and Melantho?"

"They are mobilizing the artillery and infantry cohorts." Syrena answered.

"Fine. Then mobilize your forces and march out before first light tomorrow. We cannot waste a moment. I've sent your sister to bolster the border forces in the north. They will probably need to resupply." Saria looked to Leda. "Prefect Leda, you will take your cohort of pikes out first and assist with the cavalry. Once we reach Caleope, then Syrena, you will form up the legion as a full force and march on Karum."

"Karum? Shouldn't we stick to the mountains?" Syrena asked.

Saria shook her head. "Karum was the staging point for the southern invasion force. We defeat their forces at Karum and we cripple their southern advance. Now everyone begin your preparations. Be warned that should any of you ever leave this world and journeying to Tartarus to spend your eternity, just know it will look like the deserts of Fe." The queen spoke grimly before waving everyone out.

Everyone saluted before leaving.

"Syrena, a word?" Saria said, stopping Syrena from leaving.

"Your coronation? Was it blessed or did my new son-in-law simply drop the metal band on your head?" Saria chuckled.

Syrena smiled. "No, there was a Creator priestess willing to offer me the blessing."

"A battlefield blessing, that's a true Amazonian blessing." Saria smiled. "What of the wedding night? Did Mestra give the rites?"

"She did, mother."

Saria grinned even wider. "Then will I see some grandchildren soon?"

Syrena gave a laugh. "Time will tell."

"Let's hope they're born in battle. Good omen for a child born in the heat of a battle." Saria said before turning around, back to the throne. She stopped and faced Syrena again. "That crown looks good on you, like the goddesses meant it for you."

* * * *

Gabriel spurred his horse onward as fast as the steed would run, reaching Jovag in five days. He had little time to spar, but he reached the capital city while the barons were arriving. The atmosphere of the city was full of anxiety but also ready for a renewed war. The rumors had spread that the Elysians, age-old enemies of the Lotcalans, were behind the war.

Additional information was trickling in, but all of it was hard to verify.

Gabriel rode through the city, many of the citizens looking to him with curiosity. So recently returned to the kingdom and now a king. He was not alone, the King's Guard rode into the city with him and other soldiers.

Baron Roland Ironhand, from the Barony of Pern, was walking out of Grimwolf Castle when he spotted Gabriel riding up.

"Gabriel!" Roland yelled out. He saw Gabriel dismount and saw the crown. "Forgive me, my grace." Roland said before bowing.

"Stand straight." Gabriel grinned. The two men clasped hands and gave each other a hug. "Blessed it be to the Creator, it's good to see you, Roland." Gabriel said when the two separated. "It's been too long."

"Yes, sire it has. Congratulations on your wedding, but also you have my condolences for your father and brother." Roland lowered his head for a second. "We will miss them."

"Thank you." Gabriel said. "When did you arrive?" The two men walked toward the palace, passing stately homes of nobles and a temple dedicated to the Creator.

"Just this morning. I've set up my men in Grimwolf and was about to head over to the palace to meet with the other barons. Barons Harbor and Coldwood have yet to arrive."

"We will need Harbor to buy in on the plan to commit Ter Nog's forces, yet he might be the hardest to convince." Gabriel said.

Roland stopped walking and grabbed at the king's arm to hold him.

"Did I read your notice correctly saying that Minimoto is in command of the border forces?" Roland asked in a hushed voice, letting go of the king's arm.

Gabriel nodded. "That is correct. Is that a problem?"

Roland smiled. "My lands incorporate the former Mori Daimyo's domain, Minimoto's mother's family. You know that I have no qualms with his people, but I can't speak for the other barons. I know Captain Minimoto well and I consider him to be a friend. I also know that he has the skill to command such a large force, if the eastern and southern divisions will follow him is another story. Harbor will not."

"Bulwyf commands one of the infantry battalions in the eastern division. I plan on sending him to Miralda's division. Doing so eliminates Harbor's opinion. As long as he defends his portion of the border, then we'll be fine." Gabriel replied.

Roland looked at his friend. His brown eyes pierced through his long hair. He rubbed his brown beard before speaking up. "Is this a ploy to bring more of the military under the throne's control?"

"Not really a ploy. More of a necessity. I need to know that things are going along with my plan. If not, then we might lose our throne." Gabriel answered. "I'll need your support."

"And my army." Roland smirked.

Baron Ironhand wasn't wrong. The Barony of Pern had nearly five thousand men at arms when all the banners were counted. Ter Nog had almost eight thousand on their own. These were the two largest of the baronial armies. The king had twenty-five thousand men at arms and knights at his call, apart from the baronial armies sworn to the barons but also to honor the king's orders. However, the feudal and centralized workings of the military were often at odds with one another.

The two went inside the palace, followed by several guards. They passed the same halls that the Furies walked just weeks earlier. The throne room was down a long hall, but the walk seemed short given the lively action throughout the palace.

Upon entering, Gabriel was bombarded with questions and comments. Some well-wishers and others arguing for their rights. Gabriel passed by all and gave curt smiles until he reached the throne.

"Your grace." Chamberlain Cullenhun bowed. "The throne is yours."

Gabriel walked up to the throne and saw the surrounding crowd. To the left of the throne was Sir Edward Alban, the Lord Steward and Manor Lord Charles Laoch, the Lord Marshal. To the right of the throne was the Lord Treasurer, Sir Julian Navegar and the Lord Chancellor Baron Jacob Canton. Each man wearing their livery collar and grim looks on their faces. Gabriel saw the older men, the same men who had been placed in their offices when his father became king. A stark contrast to the young king.

The Lord Steward approached as Gabriel sat on the throne. "My lord." The steward began. "You've given us news most dire and we are making arraignments for the king's and former crown prince's bodies as we speak. Yet the news of a renewed war distresses us."

"Distressed? How are you distressed?" Gabriel asked. His eyes left little wonder to his thoughts on any distress towards war.

"Why attack Fe?" Sir Alban asked. "They've been a steadfast ally for some time and we've received no declaration of war."

The crowd grumbled. The Empire of Fe had been firm allies to Lotcala, Amazon and Panyakuta, but now that seemed to be different.

"We can't just invade Fe without more cause than this, your grace." Baron Paul Walafrid of Greenfield said aloud. "My lands border Elysia and if we are in danger, I need to be prepared."

"The border forces are in place, my lord." Gabriel responded.

"Under whose command?" Walafrid asked.

Gabriel hesitated for a second. "Under the command of a trusted leader."

"In the command of a Quarmi, you mean." A voice from the far end of the hall shouted. Everyone turned to see Barons Harbor and Coldwood enter. "That's the truth, isn't it your grace? Minimoto, fine captain to be sure and of excellent lineage, is leading the entire border forces, including the entire Southern Division." Harbor continued.

The arguing lords in the crowd were of a mixed bag. Many disapproved of Quarmi commanders in the military, while some were more welcoming. Gabriel sat on the throne and watched the crowd, eyeing them carefully. These were Lotcalans through and through, but the Gota blood and pride ran through their veins. That meant that there was a streak of independence and a feeling that a new monarch had to earn their loyalty.

Baron Ironhand moved around the crowd and up to the throne. He nodded to Gabriel.

"My lords!" Baron Ironhand called out. "My lords, you are in the king's hall and you will show him the same respect that we all expect in our own halls!" The baron waited for the arguing to die down. "I will proudly vouch for Minimoto. Baron Harbor is correct that Minimoto is from fine lineage and is an excellent military leader. I know Minimoto well, and I trust his skill to guard our borders. I also trust our king to guide us into Fe."

"On what grounds?" Baron Oric Coldwood asked to Baron Ironhand. A few other lords agreed to the question. "We've followed the throne for centuries, but most kings had a familiarity with Lotcalan workings. Our current king spent his youth adventuring in the north and without training in Lotcalan politics." Others nodded and agreed.

King Gabriel stood up from his throne. "Many of you know of my recent marriage to Princess Syrena of Amazon..."

"Ah yes, the foreign queen. Are Lotcalan women not good enough for the well-traveled man anymore?" Baron Harbor interrupted.

The Lord Steward, a man known for his short temper and fierce loyalty, Sir Edward Alban walked up to the crowd. "The king was addressing you, my lord, stay your tongues or lose them!" He looked to the king and nodded.

Gabriel smiled faintly and continued. "I trust it won't come to that, but as I was saying, The Furies accompanied my wife here and with their help we were able to defend Antei. These are the best of the best Amazonian warriors and within their ranks is a mage with flayer abilities. She could enter the mind of one captive, a Fesian rider."

The revelation of a Fesian rider made the lords pause.

Harbor looked at his fellow nobles. "And this flayer saw the truth of the attack? Fe is truly allied with Elysia?" The Baron of Ter Nog asked.

"Aye, it is true." Gabriel answered. The crowd murmured. "We have to march on Fe first. They have the largest army and they are threatening our dearest ally as we speak. Minimoto and the border forces can hold off the Elysians at the border for now."

"How so?" Harbor asked skeptically.

"I'm asking that Hardstone, Greenfield and Ter Nog move their forces along with the Southern Division. Ironhand will join me in the invasion of Fe with Coldwood, Canton and Lostwood." Gabriel replied.

"And what of the king's personal army? This central army that we have sent men to for centuries?" Harbor asked.

Manor Lord Charles Laoch, the Lord Marshal spoke up for that answer. "I, under the guidance of the king, will lead that force and we shall ride alongside our king, into the afterlife if we must."

The crowd talked over one another, shouting their thoughts on the matter with few adding anything of importance. That is, until Baron Ironhand shouted louder than any of the other lords.

"You have my men, your grace!" Ironhand replied with cheers from others around him.

Baron Sigmund Hardstone stepped up. He towered over the other lords at nearly seven feet. The Hardstone family were imposing and gruff but they were the throne's closest allies, a loyalty that stretched back to Theodorif. "Ye have me men as well! I'll lead them to the south and protect yer borders, milords!" Sigmund Roared.

"That's fine for you, your grace, but you're expecting my forces to be led by a Quarmi?" Baron Harbor spoke up. "Ter Nog has a long history of fending for ourselves, and I'll be damned if I take orders from a Quarmi now!" A few other lords echoed agreements. "Those blue and grey skinned bastards and rot in the pits of the underworld for all I care."

"You'll disobey your king's command?" Gabriel asked.

Harbor paused. "Your grace, I was merely pointing out Ter Nog's long history of strength." He replied, backing down from his previous comments.

"My lord Harbor, good man and true you are, but let's think first that you would not sit upon your baronial throne had it not been for the king's ancestor." Baron Paul Walafrid of Greenfield said. "My house might be young yet, but I remember where my gratitude for my station lies even if it was my grandfather that earned it." He turned to the king. "My grace, if you trust in Minimoto's abilities, then so do I. You have my men."

The hall erupted in cheers as more nobles pledged men to the king's plan. Eventually, so too did Baron Harbor. Though, he was begrudged to do so.

"We have all the supplies needed and are ready to march north at your command, your highness. Er... your grace?" Prefect Philyre said.

"Your highness or commander is fine, prefect." Syrena answered.

"We are stretched thin with funds, however. The tithe from the fiefs was not large given the recent war with Elysia and to think of the march into their kingdom again…" Philyre paused and shook her head. "It will be hard to pay for supplies and soldiers if we are to march from Fe to Elysia; even with war spoils."

"How bad is it?" Syrena asked.

Philyre noted her commander's concern, and she tried to smile to reassure Syrena, but Philyre couldn't hide her own trepidation. "We would have to borrow from a foreign bank."

"Then let's look at cutting costs until we can figure out what to do to bring in more gold." Syrena replied.

Philyre bowed and left the room. Syrena was glad for the veteran's presence at such a time when experience might be a winning factor. Philyre, a veteran legionnaire, was an expert in logistics and had seen service in many battles, with the scars to prove it. However, wars had taken their toll and Philyre requested the supply prefect post once available. A chance to rest her bones before retirement.

Syrena poured over notes and movements, unsure where to turn next. Her mother had already taken the Queen's Legion north and Syrena would leave in the morning, but the something in the moonlit night left the warrior pondering. She knew the costs of going into the desert of Fe. An unforgiven place in the best of times and a hellish nightmare in the worst of times. Philyre's expertise would probably be Syrena's most valuable weapon, but this was something that even the veteran of the legion going on thirty-eight years might have trouble with.

Syrena rolled up her maps and gathered her papers, stuffing them in a leather satchel. She breathed a sigh and whispered a prayer to the old goddess of wisdom, Ema. She often prayed to Guerra, but rarely Ema. Most mages sought Ema or one of the other goddesses, but within the Legion, Guerra was their guiding mother.

Walking down the stairs to the courtyard she caught scents of the breads and salted pork the cooks were preparing for the journey north. At the courtyard Syrena found Artemisia in her armor and looking at a scroll.

"Trouble, prefect?" Syrena said coming up to the woman. She was Ino's younger sister, one of the best archers in the legion, and she was the youngest prefect in the queendom's history. Also one of the strictest.

"My budget report." Artemisia said, looking at Syrena. "Your highness, how am I to provide arrows for my bows if the fletchers are short changing us?"

"You think I have miscalculated my budgeting and discretions, prefect?" Syrena said with a scowl.

Artemisia wasn't one to be intimidated, especially by a superior, but she also knew that this was not through Syrena's budgeting.

"No, Commander, however, the fletchers are over charging for normal goods. Talking about demand increasing during war time. This is inappropriate and Philyre isn't budging on increasing my funding." Artemisia replied.

"I'm sorry that the gold isn't coming in as we would normally expect. However, I agree with the fletchers having more demand, they aren't wrong. Why were these supplies not requisitioned prior to the outbreak of the war?" Syrena asked in return.

"Was it too much to think we could have peace in our lands?"

Syrena eyed her prefect for a second. "No, it's never too much to ask for such a lofty goal, but we are a society built upon war."

"And I have just enough arrows for every member of Fe's army." Artemisia said.

"Then?"

"Some of our legionnaires miss."

Syrena grinned. "I see. Then purchase what you need and give me the notes of transaction. I'll reimburse you from my spoils."

Artemisia shook her head. "Commander, that's not…"

Syrena clasped Artemisia's shoulder. "Consider it an order." She smiled as Artemisia bowed.

The two women walked out of the courtyard and to their waiting horses. It was the eve before riding out to war, but they were calm. Most would not feel so relaxed, but this was the life that Amazons led. War was their culture.

Syrena was still not happy, however, by the revelation of a lack of funds for one of her prefects. This would not do, but Syrena was sure she had a workable solution, Domino Eolas.

Once the two leaders parted ways, Syrena rode her stallion over to the dungeons under the Queen's Keep. She found the halls damp and desolate. A cold, stone hallway, lit by only a few oil lamps. It wasn't a place that she liked to visit, and thankfully it wasn't a place that she needed to visit often. However, this was a dire need.

There weren't many sounds coming from deep with the stone halls and though she wore sandals, Syrena's footsteps echoed off the stone walls. Walls that were built during Queen Euryale's reign to house rivals and Quarmi enemies. These days just a few people were housed within the cells. A few humans and a harpy. Syrena could hear the faint scratching of talons on the walls, telling her that the beast was still trapped within the prison. She hated the dungeons, but Syrena conceded their purpose and now she needed one of its occupants.

Syrena quickly found herself standing in front of an oak door with a short but stout guard on duty.

"You're the jailor, Megara?" Syrena asked.

The guard snapped to attention. "Aye, your highness!"

"I need to speak to the prisoner."

The guard stiffened under her helm, the slits for her eyes caught the light and Syrena saw the confusion. "Ma'am, the queen gave orders that he is to be left alone."

"I understand, but know that war has been declared against Fe and the queen and crown princess have both left to the front." Syrena said calmly. "I leave in the morning, but until then I need him."

Megara nodded and produced a key from her belt loop and unlocked the door.

"Careful, his charm is his weapon, your highness." Megara warned as Syrena walked into the cell. Megara followed with a torch from the hallway.

"Domino Eolas." Syrena said to the silhouette that stood in the dark cell, moonlight streaming through the bars on the small window high on the far wall. "I need to know where you left your gold."

The imprisoned man stepped forward, his ankles shackled to the wall behind him.

"My, you are blunt, your highness." Domino replied. He smiled, the torch light glistening on his sweaty face. His hair was matted and dirty from his time without a bath. Dirt and grim caked his face.

"I don't have time to beat around the bush." Syrena said. "I need your gold."

Domino smirked. "I'm sure you do. I've been able to overhear the whispers. War has come. Well, that's too bad because I don't have my gold on me." He shrugged.

"I'm sure. I could have Megara entice its location out of you." Syrena grinned. She looked to the shorter Amazon.

"I'd be happy to knock him about for a minute or ten." Megara responded.

"And here I thought you and I had something special, Megara." Domino jested and chuckled, but the joke fell on deaf ears. "Well, let me say that my gold isn't here, as in here in the queendom."

"Okay, then where is it?" Syrena asked, folding her arms.

"Safe."

"You really have nothing to gain in staying quiet." Megara said.

"And I have nothing to gain, yet, with telling you the truth." Domino replied.

Syrena nodded. "What do you want? Freedom, I'm sure."

"Yes, that is number one. Safe passage out of the queendom and a pardon."

Syrena eyed the man. "How much gold are we talking about?"

Domino sighed. "One thousand pounds of gold, silver and copper. Enough to start a new kingdom."

"I'll accept seven hundred pounds." Syrena said.

"Four hundred." Domino balked.

Syrena held firm. "Seven hundred."

Domino relented. "Five hundred and fifty pounds."

"Seven hundred pounds gets you a pardon, freedom and safe passage through Amazon and Lotcala." Syrena replied.

"Lotcala? You can do that?" Domino scoffed.

"Yes, I'm the new Queen of Lotcala. That's why there is a war, Fe and Elysia attacked and King Liam is dead. Gabriel is now the king and I'm his wife."

"Well then, okay, deal." Domino said, sticking out his hand for a confirming handshake.

Syrena ignored him and looked around. "Bring some guards and unlock him. He'll take you to the gold." Megara nodded before she passed the torch to Syrena and left the cell.

"This is going to be interesting." Domino said, backing away from the woman.

"Why?" Syrena asked, raising an eyebrow.

"The gold is not in the queendom."

"So you said already."

"Yes, but the gold is actually in Lotcala. In my uncle's bank." Domino grinned slyly.

Syrena grimaced at the revelation. "I figured it wouldn't be easy." Four guards arrived with Megara behind Syrena. "I also wasn't planning on going with you, they are." Syrena turned. "The Queen's Legion are the toughest warriors in the queendom and they are brutes, for lack of a better word. They are larger than you and much stronger than you. I'd liken them to orcish in size. Megara here, though short in stature, is stronger than most people I've ever met. The other four I'd count in that same list. They will escort you to your uncle's bank and you will bring the gold to me. I will be in Fe, but your escorts know how to find me."

"Yes, if there is one thing you Amazons do better than anything else, its coordinate a war." Domino joked.

Syrena smirked and looked at the man with piercing eyes. "I'd go easy with the jokes, Domino. These ladies are not known for their sense of humor. Enjoy your journey." Syrena turned to walk out of the cell but stopped short, turning her head to address Domino. "If you don't arrive with the gold, I will hunt you down with the might of both nations and then I'll take what's owed from your uncle and your family in the Sile Empire while you watch your family become nothing. Then I'll finish collecting what's owed by ripping it from your skin. Do we understand each other?"

Domino nodded shakenly. "Perfectly, your grace."

"And give him a bath. He stinks." Syrena said before walking out of the cell.

The jailors looked at each other after that last order.

Domino grinned to the women. "Who'll be doing the honors?"

Hell is for Heroes

Legends and glories had driven the tales of the heroes from both Lotcala and Amazon for centuries. Famous names like Sirie the Bowbreaker, Ophelia Brightblade, Sir Rickard the Knight of the Waters and many more dotted the literary landscape of the two nations. Still, war was hell and few knew that better than King Gabriel.

The royal traditions raised Gabriel to lead, but he deplored fighting. He hated violence, but he lived and ruled in a violent world. It was his nature to protect and unfortunately that meant to kill to keep others alive. That is the grim truth that he learned from his former teachers; his uncle Ragnall and Master Ranger Kagesuke. The truth of the world was a simple one; mortal life was full of pain. Still, some fought to ease the suffering.

The king rode his horse west towards the Sunset Mountains. The ridge nestled on the border of Lotcala and Fe, a former home to thousands of nests of wyverns, but in recent centuries their numbers had dwindled. Rarely did the reclusive beasts leave the safety of their mountainous home. This did not make the roads any less dangerous. Bandits and brigands walked the paths, searching for easy targets. Luckily for the bandits, they were smart enough to know that a King's Army was not an easy target.

Gabriel sent scouts ahead, and a handful came back with reports of sizeable forces amassed at the southern Fe border. However, there was something different in the east.

"The Fesians are being harassed by Cavall tribesmen." One scout reported.

"Cavall? Chief Wenceslaus Braga's tribe?" Gabriel asked.

The scout nodded.

"The enemy of my enemy..." Gabriel mused.

"Maybe, maybe not." A large man from behind Gabriel said.

Gabriel turned and saw a familiar face walking up to his command tent. "Argyle! Glad you could finally make it." Gabriel said in a joyous tone, extending his hand out to his friend.

Argyle smiled and accepted the handshake. "It's been a long time." Widely known for his size and intimidation throughout the kingdom. The kingdom also knew Argyle as a kind man with a bright smile and cheerful disposition.

Rumor had it that one of Argyle's ancestors was a giant. While that was the case for some folks, with Argyle he wasn't sure. However, it was suspected considering the famed military officer, who stood well over seven feet tall and was as wide as two average men, was from the mythical bloodline.

"You're thinking of treating with the Cavall tribe? They've raided our merchant caravans just as much as the Fe caravans." Argyle pointed out.

"True, but if they are fighting the Fesians, then we can try to employ them along with us." Gabriel reasoned.

Argyle nodded, accepting his king's decision.

Gabriel clasped Argyle's arm. "How was it leaving Ter Nog?"

Argyle sighed. "Difficult. I'm happy to be here alongside you again. Fighting beside you was always a good time, but Miralda isn't too thrilled about joining the border forces."

"Don't tell me she isn't happy about answering to Minimoto." Gabriel said.

"That's not it so much. She's a soldier to the end. You tell her where to go and who to answer to and she'll do it. She'll follow him well enough, but she would rather be here with you on the front." Argyle answered. "She sent a battalion of horse archers. She felt they would have more use in the steppes and desert out this way than on the border." He chuckled. "As long as they didn't stay in Ter Nog. She doesn't trust Baron Harbor with them."

Gabriel folded his arms. "Anything I should know?"

Argyle shook his head. "Nothing much, really. When I left, Harbor was yelling about sending battalions away. Sounds like he wanted to fortify Ter Nog instead of sending troops to the border."

"I see. Well, I knew he would be the hard sale." Gabriel replied.

The two walked into his command tent and joined other commanders. Argyle was the son of a gentry-knight in Lostwood, the Elbe family, a noble and old family loyal to the Baron of Lostwood. He was one of Gabriel's most trusted friends from their time at the War Academy in Sirie. Argyle's wife, General Miralda, was the daughter of Sir Victor Holt, a gentry-knight for Baron Ironhand in Pern. The pair were a match made in heaven. Argyle was calm and happy-go-lucky while Miralda was fierce, aggressive and zealous.

Coming up behind Argyle was a horse archer. She wore leather armor over her tunic and leather trousers. Her bow and quiver were slung on her back and she tied her dark hair up high on the back of her head.

The guards stopped her as she approached the command tent. Argyle caught sight of her and waved her through.

"Your grace, this is Carladias. Miralda gave her command of the horse archers." The large man said as the woman approached.

Carladias bowed. "Your grace. I look forward to fighting at your side."

Gabriel smiled. "Welcome." He turned and led everyone back into the tent where he could council on his plan.

"We are going to make our push into Fe through the steppe. We'll send diplomats to speak with Chief Wenceslaus Braga of the Cavall tribe." The king and his commanders looked over a map. "This is the quickest way into the desert and we can follow this river."

"They will probably fight us along the river." Baron Oric Coldwood, said. "That's what I'd do."

"I would too, that's why we're going to push them there."

"Your grace? I'm not sure I see the reasoning." A confused Baron Harold Lostwood responded.

"The Amazons are pushing north, so if we hold their attention in the east, Fe will have to fight a war on two fronts." Gabriel answered.

Roland Ironhand spoke up. "So how will we take the upper hand if we fight them to stalemates?"

"Lord Marshal Laoch and I will lead half our force to Cavall lands and treat with them. Ironhand, you'll lead the rest of the force along the river. Once we finish setting up our alliance with the Cavall, we will march to the river and flank the Fesian forces." Gabriel planned. "Our scouts have said that there are two larger forces and a few others scattered around. The desert can't support larger scale troops, so they have to cluster near water sources, but so do we. The larger of the two main forces is in the south near Karum. That's the one that the Amazons will contend with. That leaves the capital for us."

"This force along the river, they're the emperor's own guards?" Argyle asked.

Lord Marshal Charles Laoch answered that question with a grim tone. "They are, and they are the best riders in the desert. Several thousand along riders with thousands more infantry. We might have the numbers, but this is their home and their preferred style of fighting."

"We need to appeal to the lost tribes." Carladias spoke up.

Everyone turned to regard her. A junior officer, a woman even, wasn't often active in strategy meetings. The kingdom accepted women into the military society of Lotcala. Queen Sirie helped with that centuries before, but they were still vastly outnumbered in the camps.

Carladias wasn't deterred. "The Fesians are practically born on horses, the lost tribes are too. There isn't much love between the two groups."

"How do you know so much of this region's people?" Baron Jacob Canton asked, raising an eyebrow.

"This is where I'm from. My father found me as an infant in the caravan that had been attacked. My birth family dead, all the other merchants were too, and

I was all that was left. He raised me as a merchant and for my first ten years I rode in a trade caravan between Fe, Amazon, Elysia and Lotcala. We finally settled in Lotcala." Carladias grinned. "The Fesians ride light and fast, like the wind over the sands. However, their infantry is lightly armed as well. The Bohiems to the north of the river ride just as fast, but they arm their riders and infantry. It might be hot on the sands, but the Bohiems wear chainmail like we do. If we ally with them, then we can match the Fesian skill."

Everyone looked to her, most skeptically.

"She's Lady Miralda's most trusted sergeant. If she says it, then I'll believe it." Argyle put in.

"We have little choice but to think of alternative plans." Baron Ironhand agreed. "This must be why Miralda sent her to us, plus to keep her away from Ter Nog." He finished with a wide smile, looking to Gabriel.

Baron Canton looked to Carladias. "Can you get us in so we can speak with the chieftain?"

Carladias nodded. "I can, my lord."

"Maybe the best course would be for the sergeant here to be our way into the heart of the lost tribes. We'll meet with them north of the river and then cut south." Canton said. He was a distant cousin to the king and a brilliant strategist. Canton was also one baron wanting to strip Gabriel of Antei.

Gabriel was unsure. It was a minor change to his plan, but still a change. The crowd around the table seemed to be amicable to the idea, however. As the gathered leaders agreed on how to proceed, Gabriel pulled Argyle back.

"Is it wise to trust Carladias?" Gabriel asked his longtime friend.

"If Miralda sent her, then I'd say wholeheartedly, yes." Argyle replied. "Miralda and I have always been at your side since the day we met, and that doesn't happen lightly for Miralda. If she vouches for this sergeant, then I know we can trust her." The large man sighed. "Canton, however, that's another story I think."

Syrena marched her legion north, passed her own lands. She did, however, make a quick stop at a small villa set within the rolling hillside east of her own keep. Honora lived there peacefully and content to send her levy and conscripts with her liege. But Syrena had one other request.

"I can't trust anyone else with this matter. He has to make it to the bank and then to me on the field as soon as humanly possible." Syrena implored to her trusted advisor.

"I will not let you down, my lady." Honora smiled.

Syrena bowed to her friend. "Thank you. I've mentioned to Megara and the jailors that you would meet them on the road. This Eolas man is crafty and charming. The jailors don't see many men and you know how things can happen."

Honor chuckled. "I haven't met a man that can charm me out of my robe. Not yet at least." She grinned. "I'll make sure they are all behaved."

"I don't mind a bit of relaxation on Megara and the others' parts, but the priority is retrieving the gold that we're owed." Syrena clarified.

"Understood, my lady." Honora smiled.

Syrena left the villa and rode back to her legion. Honora made haste in packing for her trip. The older Amazon guessed that she could make it to the main trade road leading to Jovag in a week. There was a roadside tavern and inn, frequented by many of the merchants, and that was where she was to meet with the jailors and Eolas.

That was what was intriguing her. Honora had served for years alongside many in the legion and she led many missions, but this was a first. Transporting a prisoner to a bank on the orders of a queen.

Honora was welcomed since Syrena was needed elsewhere. She knew that as the commander, she needed to be at her best. Syrena rode quickly to catch back up to the front of her column. Thousands of warrior women marching in full iron and steel armor was a sight to behold. Even the levies that marched alongside in bronze or iron, for those lucky enough to purchase it, was impressive.

Anyone familiar with the geographic border of the two nations could tell that the Legion was crossing into the steppe region of southern Fe. This set well with Syrena, knowing her legion was making excellent time.

That was of little comfort for many, however. Marching to war was usually a time of excitement and energy, but this wasn't like most marches. This time the legion was marching off towards a desert that was infamous for its inhospitable climate. Many people had ventured into the desert in the past, not completely unsafe along the trade routes. Though only three major trade routes existed, and these were often filled with bandits. Some intrepid adventurers tried to strike out on their own, off the trade routes, and that's where their troubles really began. Most disappeared, and those that didn't come out of the desert scorched from the sun and near death, few lived more than a few days afterward.

Karum was on the southern end of the desert, mostly a Saxe trade hub, but it was important to the Fesian Empire because of its location. The largest populated area and close to Amazon, Karum housed the bulk of the southern army. Much of that army comprised Saxe tribesmen, their allegiance to Fe was strenuous. This could play into the Amazon's favor.

Having a large force of skilled warriors coming at you for the crimes of your overlord might put things in perspective. And that perspective might be not dying for another man's sins.

The prefects met in Syrena's command tent two miles south of Karum. Queen Saria joined them. She had been waiting for the legion to arrive, but that was standard practice The legion marched slower than any other Amazonian group, and this meant that the battle plans had to revolve around their time. Such battle plans did not sit well with the cavalry, but that did not matter as the queen was not willing to battle without her strongest and largest force behind her.

"That's the plan, plain and simple." Syrena said, peering over a large map of the region, rolled out on a table. Dim candle light was all she had to use on a moonless night. "We attack the city head on and siege it. It won't last an extended siege."

Ino bit her lip. In her mind, she wondered if she would last an extended siege herself.

Others nodded. Philyre rubbed her chin. "Can we be sure to resupply that far into the desert?"

"Between what we've brought along with us, collected along the way and what we plan to pillage; it must be enough." Syrena answered. She pointed to a spot on the map north of Karum. "There is an oasis in this area. We can resupply our water reserves and hopefully some game. Along the small rivers and the steppe borders are farms. We can scrounge from them as a last resort."

"What's the purpose here?" Queen Saria asked, standing up from her chair, behind the prefects. She was letting them have their time to strategize. "Are we to seek plunder and leave a growing list of enemies behind in our wake, or are we here to conquer?"

Syrena looked to her mother. The question had never occurred to her. For Syrena, this war was about stopping the invasion. Yet the question now loomed; what would they do after the war was won? If they won it.

"Leave that for Lotcala to answer." Syrena replied. "I want no part of this desert."

Her commanders looked shocked. Land spoils going to another nation wasn't common or welcomed, but their discipline was too engrained to speak up. The queen, however, had another thought.

"The desert is a parched landscape that holds little value except as a buffer between other, not so friendly, nations. However, I wouldn't be so quick to refuse gained land." Queen Saria looked over the map. She pointed to an area of steppe land just south of the desert but north of the queendom. "This land here."

"That is where we are now, my queen." Syrena replied.

"Yes, and this will be land hard won. We must hold on to it once claimed. Furthermore, I don't think we should so easily leave it." Queen Saria answered.

Just then, Cecilia entered the tent. "Karum's main force just retreated within the walls of the city!" She threw her helm to a nearby attendant and grabbed a goblet of wine. Swallowing the liquid and tossing the cup to another attendant, she continued. "We need to unload the artillery and hammer the hell out of those walls. Sandstone won't pose too much trouble, even for you Ino." Cecilia quipped.

Ino sneered but wisely let the insult go. Syrena was not so forgiving. "We'll unpack the siege equipment once and only after I've accessed if that is the best course of action."

Cecilia grinned. "Fine. Then how do you plan to defeat the city?"

Saria spoke up before Syrena could surrender the point to Cecilia. "Karum is not your decision, Cecilia. The legion will handle this city." Saria walked around the table to her eldest daughter. "I want the cavalry to ride north east. Link up with the Lotcalans and storm the eastern territories."

"Why would we split our force? Karum is the price!" Cecilia protested.

"A price that the legion can claim without your help." Saria said in an optimistic tone.

"This battle, here, is ours. Let the Lotcalans have the lands in the north, but I will be here taking control of this city!" Cecilia protested further. "You cannot deny me this!"

"You have your orders or do you wish to disobey your queen?" Saria answered in a stern voice. "Perhaps you think my time has come, and you are queen now. A better one than I even."

Cecilia knelt and saluted. "No, my queen. I'll led the cavalry north and rendezvous with the Lotcalans." She stood up, her head lowered.

"Rest your horses and sisters tonight. Leave prior to dawn to give you better cover." Saria said, placing a motherly hand on Cecilia's shoulder. Her daughter nodded before exiting the tent. Saria pursed her lips. "She's angry. She'll use that, if not in this war then some day in the future we'll feel her anger."

"Everyone leave." Syrena ordered. "Ino, begin thinking about a siege." She ordered before she was alone with her mother.

Saria sat down on her chair and smiled to her younger daughter. "You think I was wrong to embarrass her?"

"Why did you?" Syrena asked, sitting next to her mother.

Saria sighed heavily. "One day she will be queen and she must understand that there is not one path in life."

"I think she sees that already, mother." Syrena tried to reason.

"She doesn't. She sees that an Amazon fights and to wage war. If she isn't fighting, then she isn't happy. That is not our way, however."

"The goddesses breed us for war." Syrena replied.

Saria smiled. "They breed us for greatness and that comes in many forms. Is the sculptor that carves the human form any less valuable than the warrior who stands as the model? What of the builders that erected the Queen's Keep? Without that keep, without our barracks, would our warriors be as strong as they are? What of the farmer, the bakers, apothecaries or herdsmen? In all these things we are stronger because of our greatness in the mundane. Without them our queendom fails, yet she sees only war. Your father's family was the same, and I fear she took too much after him. They never understood that to be human meant to be fierce and vulnerable all at once."

"What of me? I am now to be a queen of another great people, yet today I'm to conquer this city."

Saria pat her daughter's knee. "We can be fearsome and yet vulnerable at the same time. Let Karum see that in our conquest." Saria stood and walked out of the tent, leaving Syrena to ponder the lesson.

Outside the tent, campfires were lit, and many warriors were cooking their evening meals. Hares, quails or squirrels roasting over open flames brought memories to Saria of years past during her days as a soldier. The time would soon come for her to bring back all of her experience.

Carladias led her battalion, along with Baron Canton's force, north of the river. The terrain was becoming more sandy and full of grit as they rode further away from the river. Still, the young sergeant pressed on into a land she was becoming reacquainted with. Carladias felt little worry among her fellow archers, but with Canton's troops and the baron himself, she was feeling like an outsider. She had been in Lotcala for more than a decade and she gave her adulthood to the King's Army. Carladias still needed to prove herself to the barons.

That was it. Carladias thought, in a nutshell.

The King's Army was still gaining acceptance when the barons had their own forces. Strategically it made sense, but infighting caused more than a few to skirmish against each other. This drew the king in so he had to take matters in hand, putting a stop to the fighting.

Alongside the baron, Carladias knew to watch her back. Even though a central army, the King's Army, had a history stretching back six hundred years or more, the division was palpable. The young sergeant was warned before leaving Ter Nog that the barons of Canton and Ter Nog would not be so easy to trust any of the soldiers from the King's Army. Except when the barons feel they need them.

Baron Jacob Canton wasn't too sure if he was willing to die by the king's side just yet. They were cousins, but Antei was becoming a source for trade and Gabriel held on to that land. Canton saw two options; help the king win the war and petition that Antei be absorbed into his barony or betray the king, risking riot and life. Winning the war was preferable to the traitors' wall. Still, following the advice and the lead of a Fesian born soldier in the King's Army was a difficult task for the proud baron, but one he was willing to do. Of course, that was in the hopes of securing the lands of Antei through favorable actions.

Three days from breaking with the king, Carladias and her party found themselves on the southern age of Bohiem land. She stopped the advance of the horsemen, pulling the reins of her horse and putting a hand up.

"We're here." Carladias said, putting her hands up.

"How do you know?" Baron Canton asked, looking at Carladias.

Just then an arrow whistled through the air and landed in the sand, directly in front of the baron.

"Just a hunch." Carladias replied, her hands still in the air. "You might want to raise your hands, my lord."

Baron Canton sneered but did as suggested. A moment later riders appeared over a hill and stopped in front of the two leaders.

"Who are you?" A rider demanded, his bow leveled at the Lotcalans.

"Allow me, my lord." Carladias said. She kicked her horse gently and walked him a few steps. "My name is Carladias, I'm a sergeant in the King of Lotcala's army. This is Baron Jacob Canton, and we are here to speak with your chief about an alliance."

"The Chief would welcome you himself, except that you are allied with the Fesian dogs. You look like them. A Fesian dog." The rider chided.

"We are at war with Fe." Carladias clarified. "They've attacked us and killed the king's father and brother. Gabriel is now the king."

The rider looked to his companions, and they all nodded. "King Liam was a good and fair man. He held our respect. You kingdom has our sorrow in his death." The rider responded. "If your words are true, then we welcome you and the baron to treat with our chief, Aron. Let him be the judge."

Carladias nodded and waked her horse, with Canton, towards the riders. She turned to her men before ascending the hill. "Set up camp and rest here. We'll send word soon." She turned back toward the hill and went with Canton to the Bohiem village.

The village was kept well and lively as family units exited their houses, hoping to see the Lotcalans. Curiosity filled their minds as the visitors waked through towards the chief's sandstone house. Several village guards and riders joined them, but neither Lotcalan felt like they were in any danger. The mood was more inquisitive than threatening.

The pair sat on cushions and rugs, their chainmail and leather bulking up around their midsections.

"You may take off your armor. I'll protect you in my village." Aron, the chief said. This was a relief to Canton and Carladias, as they did as suggested before sitting back down. "Comfortable?" The chief asked.

He was a burly man with a grey, bushy beard, but he had a welcoming and warm smile.

"Thank you for the audience, you grace." Canton said.

The chief held up his hand. "First we eat, then we talk." He clapped his hands and servants began walking in with platters of food and pitchers of wine.

Canton raised an eyebrow at the morsels laid out in front of him. Carladias leaned over to him.

"That's okra. It's a hardy vegetable from this area, and that's squash. They season both with peppers and other spices." She said, picking up a piece of bread and smearing some vegetables onto the bread. "Take the barley bread and just spread the okra or squash on it." She bit into the bread and a rush of flavors from her youth returned to her, producing a satisfying smile. Canton followed suit, and though it was not what he was used to, he enjoyed the meal.

The chief grinned. "I'm glad you like it." He said. "Now the main dish."

Servants returned with a large platter with slices of whitish meat.

"That's snake meat." Carladias whispered to Canton. "A delicacy here in the desert." She took a slice with her fingers and ate the juicy meat. Again, Canton did as she did, though he was not as pleased with this as he was with the vegetables.

"Enjoy, my friends, and tonight we talk about Fe." The chief said, ripping a piece of the snake meat from the platter and munching on it happily.

Dancers came into the tent and moved rhythmically with drum beats and songs being played on woodwind instruments of musicians. Canton enjoyed the show, being swayed in the intoxicating rhythm of the dancers' hips, while Carladias took pleasure in more of the food from her youth. Once the sun had set, the chief put his goblet down and shooed away the dancers and servants.

"Let us discuss what it is you have come to ask me." The robust and bearded man said once the three were alone.

Canton nodded before beginning. "Sir, we seek an alliance against Fe."

"Lotcala and Fe are brothers in arms. Centuries now. Why fight and why should we care?" The chief asked in reply.

"King Liam was murdered by their betrayal and we need help fighting on the sands." Canton answered.

"Your riders are lighter and far more skilled in desert fighting."

"You're flattering for a baron. I met your grandfather once, and he was far less cordial. That was in our rebellion against the oppression of Fe. King Liam, a prince then, stepped in before your grandfather took my head. I was but a youth of fourteen years and Liam not much older. I owe my life to him." Chief Aron rose from his cushion. "I believe in your intentions. I'm proud to say that I owe a debt to Liam. If Fe's treachery indeed took his life, then I must answer in kind." The chief called to his men, waiting outside. "Send off the riders and call the warriors to prepare. We will march alongside the Lotcalans." Chief Aron turned back to Canton and Carladias. "Know this, if you are lying and try to betray me, I'll take your heads first before I let any of my village suffer."

Canton stood and extended his hand to the chief. "Understood."

The battle to the south of the river had raged for the past two days. A large contingent of Fesian soldiers coming from the western capital had stopped King Gabriel's army. The citadel in Fe sent out many of the famed infantry units, marching with pikes and javelins. The Lotcalans were dug in at the high dunes of the eastern region of the desert, but supplies were running short. The Fesians cut the river off from the Lotcalan advance and this meant that replenishing stockpiles would be difficult, if not impossible.

King Gabriel rode his horse along the battle lines, caring little for the arrows and javelins that whizzed past his head. All that mattered was defeating the defending army and moving on to the capital. He was certain that his wife would be there, sieging the fortified city.

Baron Roland Ironhand rode at the head of a heavy cavalry brigade. His armor covered in dust and grit from the arid atmosphere. His helm had splashes of blood and his nose was broken from a blow he took to the face. Though this caused him discomfort and pain when breathing the scorching air, he ignored it to continue the fight. As desperate as the battle was, the desperation drove the men to fight on.

"Sire, we're being pushed further away from the river. Without the river we will perish." Argyle said, walking up to the king.

"We have to hold. Baron Canton will meet us here and we can regroup then." Gabriel said. He took off his helm and saw the grim expressions of Baron Coldwood and Argyle. The stress, pain and heat were cracking his tough façade. He threw his helm to the ground and yelled out. "What the hell do you expect me to do?! We stay and fight and die or we run and leave the Amazons to fight the empire alone!"

Oric Coldwood was not overly emotional, nor was he a man of many words, yet he was spurned to speak at the moment.

"Surely your time in the north taught you something of battles." Coldwood chided. "What is happening here is a setback, but we can't rely on Canton returning before they force us to surrender."

"We can't surrender." Gabriel replied.

"Then what is your plan?" Argyle asked. He looked to his friend and saw the pain and fear.

"I don't know. All I know is we have to hold and push back." Gabriel said.

"Then push back." Coldwood responded. "Let your men see you ride in front of them. Let them follow a man that is afraid but has summoned enough courage to face the odds."

Gabriel nodded and stormed out of the tent. Argyle leaned over and scooped up the king's helm. "Did you think that would work?"

"Basically the same thing his grandfather told his father one day before a battle. Not having any fear isn't the challenge. Fear is a part of life. The challenge is using that fear doing the impossible." Coldwood replied, walking out of the tent with Argyle.

Argyle tossed the helm to Gabriel just after the king mounted his horse.

"Call for all riders and infantry. Behind me for the charge!" Gabriel called out. He rode through the camp, gathering his soldiers and officers.

Lord Marshal Laoch followed behind with Coldwood and Argyle. Soon, thousands of Lotcalan soldiers stood with their king, amassed opposite the Fesian line.

"Use the terrain. Lancers, ride their infantry down! Archers unleash hell on their flanks!" King Gabriel ordered. "Spearmen, give them all kinds of hell! Today we break their line and march to the capital or we die in the sands. Either way, this will be a day of glory!"

Cheers echoed from the Lotcalan warriors as the riders galloped toward the enemy. Archers let loose barrages of arrows to the flanks as the king ordered, and soon the Fesians were in a desperate hurry to mount a defense. The desert terrain was marked with soft, rolling hills that did not slow the riders up, but it provided cover. As the riders made their way closer, the lead horsemen would maneuver around the hills, creating an unpredictable pattern to their path. The Fesian archers could not pinpoint where to aim. Firing arrows helplessly was not the best idea, but given the tactics of the Lotcalan riders, it was the only one that the Fesian archers had.

Gabriel led his men through the field and he felt the arrows fly by him. In the corner of his eye and within earshot, he could tell that some of his compatriots were being taken down, but he knew that others, many others, still rode alongside him.

The Fesians positioned barrels and wagons as a makeshift fortification, but once the Lotcalans reached it, they shattered the defensive structure. Gabriel's horse hurled over a wagon and he thrust his spear into a nearby Fesian. The point entering the chest through the heavy cloth. Other riders followed over the barrels and wagons, sending men running away from the heavy beasts and their deadly riders. Broken spears were traded for swords, some curved and others double edged, but all deadlier than the long spears or lances.

Argyle and the infantry spearmen appeared at the broken wooden wall and entered the fight with a ferocity that was unmatched by the defenders. Blood coated the sand and the first wave of the attack had been a success, but Gabriel knew that the Fesians still outnumbered them.

"Rider to the flanks!" Gabriel ordered the lancers and other horsemen. "Defend the infantry!"

Laoch called for the riders to follow him as he rode to the left flank, ready to meet the Fesian cavalry, arguably the world's best, head on.

It was a fatal encounter, but one that was necessary. The Fesian riders, skilled horsemen that rode through enemies with deadly sabers, had to be stopped. This meant that the heavy horsemen from Lotcala, lancers with heavy chainmail and leather or iron plate riding on armored steeds, had to withstand the best in the world. It could have been a one sided fight, but the Lotcalans were desperate, hungry and ready to die for their king, the man that was in the middle of the battle.

For many of the Fesian riders, the emperor was a man that they would never see in person. He was just a myth of a man that may or may not care of the outcome of a battle. These men, therefore, were not as desperate as the Lotcalans, men fighting for someone that for all they knew would be dead on the same battlefield as them in a few moments.

He hasn't, not yet at least.

"Oric, Roland!" Gabriel called out. "Protect the right!"

Ironhand and Coldwood both lead their men in the ordered position, clashing with more Fesians that were coming in to help in the battle. Spear against spear and sword clanging on sword. The sand provided little traction for the fighters. The sand ground kicked up into the air, choking many of the fighters. The lack of visibility from the dusty air turned the fight into a disorganized melee. A bloody brawl.

Gabriel rode through the camp with his men, cutting down any Fesians that appeared, but with every Fesian killed, two more appeared. Soon, Gabriel was cut off from his main army and the Fesian riders split his force in three.

"Damn, what have I done?" He breathed, realizing his mistake. "Form up and make our way to the left!" He ordered. A line of spearmen gathered and pushed against coming Fesians.

Just then, a multitude of horns sounded from the north and a rumbling sound grew. The horns increased and Gabriel could hear war cries coming. With a crash that echoed around the desert, Bohiem riders and Lotcalan horse archers stormed into the Fesian camp from the north, sending the battle into a feverish and bloody spectacle.

Canton led the force as the riders bored a hole deep into the Fesian defense, sending bodies to the ground and trampling anything in their path. The tents and the encampment burst into flames, Fesian scrambled to react but the surprise of the Bohiem force was too much to overcome and the new wave of riders forced the Fesians to organize a hasty retreat. The hatred was deep, however, and the Bohiems rode down many running away or fired arrows into those fleeing. Without order, Gabriel knew that the battle would turn into a slaughter, but he also did not want those fleeing to become added resistance at the capital. He allowed the Bohiems a few more minutes before rushing to stop the massacre.

Once the battle was ended, the fires were dying down, and the Lotcalans rounded the prisoners up, Gabriel walked through the camp and took stock. Barons, Canton, Coldwood and Ironhand walked with him, along with Argyle. It was a moment of peace as he surveyed the damage.

"Laoch fell in the fight with the Fesian riders. The lancers were all but slaughtered." Gabriel remarked.

Argyle nodded. "But they held." He said.

"They held." Gabriel replied, looking to his friend. "They held like heroes of old."

The men watched as caches of supplies were being rounded up and carted to the Lotcalan camp. The Bohiem chief approached Gabriel with Carladias at his side.

"You are now king?" Chief Aron asked.

Carladias bowed.

"I am." Gabriel answered. "You are Chief Aron?"

"I am." The chief said. "Your father would have been proud, I'm sure. He was a good man and I hope you are as well."

"Creator willing I am." Gabriel smiled. "Thank you for agreeing to fight alongside us."

"The enemy of my enemy can be my friend." Aron said in return.

"Then let's figure out how we will attack the capital." Gabriel responded. The two men walked off, leaving the barons, Carladias and Argyle alone.

Before long, it was only Argyle and Carladias.

"You did well. Miralda was smart to send you." Argyle remarked. "Of course, she is the smartest woman I know. The scariest too."

"Forgive me, my lord, but it amazes me that the largest man I ever met is the nicest and he is married to the fiercest woman I ever met." Carladias laughed.

Argyle laughed along with her. "You should have met her mother." He laughed. The laughter died down and the world got quiet. "Was this your first major battle?"

"Yes, my lord." Carladias said. "I've always heard it was like hell. The old warriors talk about what you see and smell. I've been in a few skirmishes but never anything with this many dead."

"Tresha was like this. The king and I couldn't stop throwing up after the first day we entered the city. The rotten flesh eaten by gangrene, the smell of shit and bile after we won the siege. That's a smell you never forget. Battlefields, those are something else entirely." Argyle lowered his head at the memory. "Fields like these, never seem to heal."

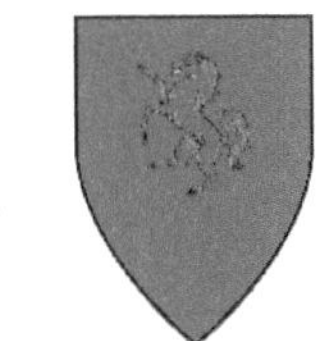

Boulders flew in the sky, and arrows soared to the city walls of Karum. The negotiations had failed, and that left the Amazons with little option but to advance with a full scale siege. This meant that the walls were going to have to fall. Syrena tried to negotiate peace but time was not on anyone's side and after several failed attempts, Syrena ordered Ino to unleash the might of the siege engines.

Saria looked on as her daughter walked back into the camp. "They will buckle."

Syrena gave her mother a grim look. "Maybe."

"They will. Eventually we all have to break." Saria replied.

"These are Saxe and they are much tougher than most Fesians."

Saria nodded. "I don't doubt their will. I do, however, doubt their supplies. We can wait longer than they can. Cecilia captured the oasis."

Syrena turned back towards the city. "We can storm it. Finish it quickly."

"True." Saria answered. "Storm it and capture the city in one night but lose a third or more of the Legion."

"We have to at the capital with Cecilia and Gabriel. They do not have the force to take it alone." Syrena responded, looking back to her mother.

"No, they don't but a boulder is always overcome by the stream." Saria answered.

Syrena shook her head at her mother's wisdom.

Just then Mestra approached Syrena. "We found a small opening on the eastern rampart, commander."

Syrena and the Legion wasted no time in shifting focus to that opening. In less than two hours, the infantry had massed near that area while Ino kept the barrage of boulders and stones flying toward the main gate. Artemisia ordered her archers to line up and provide cover for the soon to be advancing infantry. This would have to be a shift move and one that would need to employ the Legion's best tactic; shock.

"Give cover for the sappers and make that opening bigger." Syrena ordered.

Several sappers from Ino's cohort ran out, under a hail of arrows, to set barrels of black powder smothered in pitch. Two sappers fell to the enemy arrows, a terrible volley that darkened the sky around them. Syrena counted them lucky that more hadn't fell to the defense.

Once the sappers returned Syrena gave the final order.

"Light it and blow that wall to hell." Syrena yelled.

A sapper threw a torch on a crate of black powder that was near several other crates and connected by blankets smothered in flammable tar. That set off the chain reaction that was needed to ignite each crate and eventually the wall. The fire burned hot, and each crate exploded until it reach the wall and the mass of barrels and crates covered in the opening.

From a safe distance Syrena and the Legion watched as the wall burst in a scene of mud bricks, bodies and blood. Black smoke rose in plums, but the Legion remained poised.

"Attack!" Syrena yelled after a few moments, watching the smoldering mud-bricks cave away, giving more space for the attacks to rush into the city.

The opening had increased in size from just six or seven feet to nearly sixty feet wide, allowing room for multiple legionnaires to rush in at once. Shouts and war cries rose from within the city, but Syrena knew that Melantho could maintain the fight while Ino continued to press the siege from the main gate.

Within the city, Melantho was coordinating the attack and pushing her sisters onward. She had been the first through the opening and met with the toughest resistance, but she wasn't a prefect for nothing. Melantho was by far one of the best warriors in the queendom, and she was showing her skills to any brave Fesian soul that stepped up against her. The phalanx had yet to form, but that was of little consequence when matched with skilled warriors. Melantho and her sisters battled with their spears, thrusting into any enemy that stood against them, bashing shields into coming bodies and causing general mayhem as more legionnaires stormed through the gaping wall.

The defensive forces turned into rag dolls against the shock filled might of the Legion. A usual tactic, but one that was as reliable as the phalanx. Screaming and hollering Amazons with blood rage filling the city gave many of the defenders pause before counterattacking.

Loud horns blew in every direction and the combined with the noise from the Amazon war cries and siege bombardment, the battle had taken a devastating turn for the Fesians. Time would soon tell how much they could take in the losing affair. The Saxe that occupied the town were Fesian in location only, and many held little regard for the Fesian overlords, just another rival tribe than the emperor. This was their land, however, and that meant they had to defend it. Never had they had to defend it against such hostile forces.

Syrena watched from outside the wall, Mestra walked up behind her.

"My healers will be busy. Shall we look to the townsfolk as well?" Mestra asked.

Syrena never looked to her friend. "I gave them a chance to surrender."

"You did, but that doesn't answer my question."

"Doesn't it?" Syrena replied to Mestra.

Mestra lowered her head. "I suppose." She paused. "You don't have to be your sister."

Syrena shot her friend, an old and trusted friend, an angry glare.

"I mean to say that we don't have to be enemies of everyone on the continent." Mestra continued.

Syrena nodded. "This has to be done. The Saxe tribe invaded our lands."

"They did, you're right, but does that fact negate our humanity?" Mestra asked.

"The queen ordered we make an example." Syrena said, solemnly.

Mestra lowered her head again. "That way other tribes move out of our way as we move north. Speed us up."

"We'll take no prisoners."

Mestra sighed. "And what of this land once we finish the conquest? Won't they be rebellious?"

"The queen has agreed to give this land over to Lotcala in exchange for lands further east near the steppe." Syrena answered.

"Convenient."

"You object?" Syrena asked.

Mestra crossed her arms and leaned back on her back foot. She smirked. "There is a library here in Karum. I would like that it not be torched if possible. It might prove valuable in the future."

"Then I'll send the word." Syrena called another officer over and gave her the order to spare any library. The officer ran off to spread the order at once.

"Thank you."

"Something I should know about?" Syrena asked.

Mestra shook her head. "Nothing yet, but if that changes, I'll make sure to make you aware." Mestra then walked off back to her fellow mages and healers.

The Last Dragon

Karum was the jewel of southern Fe and a beacon of hope for travelers of the expansive desert. A glistening city full of exotic wares and tales from centuries past, of magic wafting in the streets. Ancient buildings decorated with beautifully colorful motifs and banners strung in between the houses. Karum was a wondrous sight to behold in the middle of a virtual wasteland of sand and scrub bushes. On this day, however, Karum burned!

It had been every intention of Syrena's to leave the city as beautiful as she had found it, but time had forced her hand. Messengers sent word of the cavalry's battles further north and some reports came in of her husband's fight. She had to hurry. Syrena's goal now was to march her Legion north towards her sister's army and then meet her husband, King Gabriel, in Fe. This idea solely depended on Cecilia's battered and bruised cavalry holding out until the Legion arrived.

Cecilia was far less concerned with the fate of a city as she was with the fate of her life and that of her sisters. The cavalry took heavy and key losses. She was bruised herself, having been unhorsed just a day prior and still feeling the pain. Agis gave her something for the pain from his medicinal stores, but her pride hurt her most. Of course, that was what she loved about her father. Agis was there for his daughters, mostly Cecilia, for advice, remedies and a shoulder to cry on. He accepted their ways and was more than happy to walk into battle alongside them.

Agis commanded a unit of horsemen that comprised Amazon noble men. These were sons and husbands of the main cavalry units, and they were quite effective. Still, they were not the primary unit and though noble; they were thought of little better than levies.

Agis walked into his daughter's tent and looked at her sitting on a chair, bottle in hand.

"The future queen drowning her sorrows in wine." He smirked. "Appropriate."

Cecilia smiled. "I'd say so." She stood and tossed the bottle to her father, watching as he took a swig of the potent liquid. "It's from the queen's stores."

Agis let out a content sigh. "I thought it tasted familiar." He handed her the bottle. "And your outlook for the coming battle?"

"The Fesians will charge again. It's their way." Cecilia answered.

Agis grinned and nodded. "Horsemen through and through."

Cecilia spit on the ground. She walked to a basin with water and pulled a dagger and rubbed a soft cream on her head. She then pulled the edge of the blade over her head to shave off the short hairs that had been growing.

"Those horsemen are more trouble than I originally gave them credit for." Cecilia said, looking into a small mirror. "Those bastards are quick and nimble on these sands. We're too heavy."

"Yet if we ride with no armor, then we are vulnerable to their arrows and sabers. Thankfully our armor is far superior to theirs." Agis replied, sitting on the chair.

"That's what I thought about our cavalry too." Cecilia pulled the blade smoothly across her head from the front to back. "At this rate my baby sister, the

Queen of Lotcala, will have to come and save me. I feel like such an insignificant ant."

Agis chuckled.

Cecilia spun around and eyed her father. "What?"

"No one, not even the ant, is insignificant, Cecilia. You're far too concerned with the musings of a love struck newlywed." Agis told her.

"This is serious. How can I claim to be queen when I can't even lead my cavalry to victory?"

Agis walked over to his daughter and wrapped her in a hug. "You will be an excellent queen, but you need to get out of your own head. You are a resourceful and cunning woman. Few could ever hope to stand in your way. Orestilla already found that out and with my training, you have excelled in ways your sister could never imagine. Our family seal is the dragon, not for its strength but for its intellect and cunning. Remember that. You are a daughter of the dragon, and the only daughter of the dragon."

"The only daughter?"

"You sister, my youngest daughter, is a wonderful daughter that I love, but she and I are not the same. You are the heir to my mind and spirit." Agis answered.

Cecilia smiled at his words. Comforting of a loving father, but there was another meaning behind it.

Agis' family, Corvino, were elder nobles from the earliest days of the queendom. The Corvino family were followers of Viri Al Sim, a god from the south and a patron of dark arts. Agis was the last member of the line, an ancient one that sought power through marriages and often ill-advised ones involving family.

Agis was different however, his grandmother and mother would raise him different and away from the failed political tactics of the formally powerful family. Instead, he shunned the family and married the crown princess. All a ruse since he never turned on his family and instead embraced their strongest ideals; duplicity and chaos. Cecilia carried on that legacy for Agis and the dragon mantel was her's to carry on.

"I have trained you as my successor because you have the aptitude that your sister lacks. Make no mistake. Syrena will be a good queen, but you shall be a great one!" Agis said to reassure his daughter. The pair hugged, but in an instant they cut it short by the sound of a horn blowing from outside.

"An attack!" Cecilia shouted. She rushed outside, followed by her father, finding a scene of chaos surrounding the camp.

Cecilia rushed to her horse and mounted the steed. She grabbed her helm from an attendant's hand and rode to the front, shouting orders and calling for riders. Agis watched as she disappeared into the fray. His next reaction was pivotal. He rushed to his fellow noblemen and rallied them to an attack of their own. It was desperate and uncoordinated but brutal.

Agis, followed by no less than fifty fellow nobles, rode his horse into the heart of an oncoming Fesian charge. Heavy oak lances, tipped with steel points, pierced the light cloth and thin armor of the Fesians. Many fell just from the weight of the impact, leaving gaping holes from the spear points as added damage. However, the lances would break, leaving the stronger, heavier and slower Amazon men at a disadvantage to the swifter Fesians. What was left was a simple arrow barrage that sent over half of Agis' force to the burning sands?

"Ride to their center!" Agis called out.

The men rode into the center as their commander called. A feverish charge that sent them deeper than Agis expected. A simple diversion by the Fesians to surround the Amazonian riders and cut them down. Agis saw the ploy, but he was too late.

Across the field Cecilia was leading her riders with heroic bravery that would be spoken about for years to come. Bleeding and without a shield or lance, Cecilia pushed further into the Fesian, slashing her sword with precision across any warrior that faced her. It was a sight for the bards to sing about. Cecilia's eyes stung from her blood as well as her foes covering her face. She ignored the pain and loss of vision as she fought on. Even after her horse was killed from under her, she stood and pulled a Fesian off his horse, mounting his steed and continuing the fight.

Cecilia held little remorse for those that fell to her blade, nor to her sisters'. She was not merciful, even to those that begged with final breaths. Cecilia was concerned only with victory and claiming glories untold. Another horse killed under her did little to slow her. She looked around the field and saw other Amazons fighting on foot, their steeds also killed.

Cecilia rushed into Fesian infantry and hacked one's arm off at the elbow with her deadly falcata. She slammed her shoulder, guarded with a plate of steel, into another Fesian and sliced at his throat. The head rolled onto the ground. Cecilia did not even flinch or let him roll too far before she moved on to her next foe. Her sword sisters came in and provided support for her. It was a glorious battle, and one that left a smile of Cecilia's face.

Death would not take the crown princess this day. This was a day for her to send many to the god or goddess of their choice. She didn't care, if they opposed her they would die.

Fesians riding against Cecilia and her equally fearsome sisters lost a taste for the battle, seeing so many of their own fallen on the field. Red sand, mixed with the entrails and limbs of loved ones and comrades, wore on the Fesian men. Wonders if the Amazons even saw the battle-field like that. Perhaps this was what they ignored to fight on, or maybe such sights meant that they had fought well and earned a place in the afterlife. Whatever the case, even the cold hearted and cruel Cecilia couldn't hide her emotions from the sight that awaited her.

"Princess!" A voice called to Cecilia as she watched the remnants of the Fesians ride away.

Cecilia turned on her heels and rushed to the voice. She saw her father's banner, tilted where it had been in stuck into the dirt and she felt a pit in the bottom of her stomach. Her legs were heavy, and she felt like her pace was slower than she knew she could run. Each footfall sunk into the wet ground and became a tough task to make it to her father's side. Cecilia made it to the crowd and everyone parted as the crown princess collapsed beside her father's body.

Cecilia's second in command, Ria, called orders to clear the area and set up for a possible renewed charge. She looked down to Cecilia, tears streaming down the face of each of the women around the scene. Slowly, everyone dispersed to follow the orders, leaving Cecilia alone, kneeling as the wind kicked up dust and sand all around her.

Cecilia didn't notice the glow of the desert moon as night fell around her. Within her tent, attendants worked at helping her remove her armor. She received more hits and bruises than she originally thought. The shock of her father's death faded, though slowly, and soon the realization of injuries overcame Cecilia and her body.

The princess winced as an attendant removed her cuirass. Cecilia's lips curled in an angry snarl, but she remained silent. Another attendant walked to her with bandages and clean water.

"Wine." Cecilia rasped. "Now, levy." She stared at the woman, a lower classed member of the society. Cecilia's gaze left nothing to the imagination of what would happen if she had to wait too long. The woman rose and bowed before rushing out the tent to bring several bottles of wine and a goblet.

Cecilia downed the poured wine and took another goblet before standing up and staggering towards the tent flap.

"Your highness? You mustn't…" An attendant began to protest, but Cecilia's glare stopped her short and the woman bowed low.

Cecilia snarled to the attendant, then turned away. "I'll return soon. Make yourself scarce before I come back." Cecilia exited the tent and walked over to her father's tent. She pushed the flap aside and limped to his cot and sat down.

"The gods are crying tears of daggers." Cecilia said to herself before finishing her wine. Tears streamed down her cheeks. Her skin itched from the liquid rolling over her dry skin. The dirt on her face cracked from the wet trails of tears. She sniffed and looked across the tent and saw her father's lockbox.

Sitting her empty goblet down, Cecilia moved to the metal box and took it from the table. She recognized the seal on the top. It was the dragon insignia from her father's family. Cecilia even incorporated it into her own sigil. The lock on the box was intricate, a combination design. The symbols carved into the four moveable, interlocking discs weren't from the common tongue but were instead of an ancient Amazonian alphabet. She could feel the movement and could hear the clicking of the internal gears as she rotated each disk. Cecilia recognized it as one similar to one that her father built for the queen's vault. This was an important box to have such a lock.

Turning the discs along the dial, Cecilia felt her instincts guide her with each click until she knew the point to stop. Four times she trusted an inner voice to the right combination and then after the final click, the latch opened and the box was free for her to explore.

Cecilia pulled out old pieces of parchment and a couple of phials of liquids. Each labled in ancient Amazonian.

"Elixir of death." Cecilia read. "That's simple enough to know what this does." She took out a few more and read similar titles. After a few moments rummaging through the box, she found a small scroll and broke the wax seal. Cecilia's eyes widen upon reading the words.

"This is from Nicodemus Corvino's private collection!" She gasped. Cecilia read the rest of the scroll. "The first Blackbirds were Corvinos members, and this is the sacred writ of their founding of the order." Cecilia groaned as she stood up, still reading the scroll. "In the absence of peace the righteous find solace in chaos." She read. Cecilia lowered the scroll and thought back to something her father said often. "Chaos is our religion." She said of the memory.

Cecilia gathered the materials from the box and locked it back up. She took the lockbox back to her tent. A moment later, her second in command joined her.

"My princess, the scouts have come in reporting that the Legion is a day out. We still are preparing the body of your father for cremation."

"No." Cecilia said. "He and his men deserve to be buried in the field were they fell. They've earned that rite."

The officer looked confused. "My princess, our tradition dictates that men are cremated. Only women are to be buried upon the fields."

Cecilia turned to her officer and gave her a grim look. "My father and his men rode with us and bled with us. Their sacrifice is the best any of us can hope for. If any of our sisters protest then tell them to come to me, but I expect my order to be followed." Cecilia turned away from the woman, but turned back, grabbing the officer's attention. "Also make sure that our soldiers scour the outlying areas for aloe vera and arnica. We need to make sure we have enough to help stave off infections." The officer bowed and left the tent.

The crown princess might have felt a depressing pit within her stomach over the loss of her father, but she wasn't about to see more death under her command. Not from infections, at least, and not when she could help guide the healers to ointments and salves to comfort those in pain. The desert was teeming with life for those that knew where to look and what to look for. This was a chance for Cecilia's other skills to play a role in the coming victory.

Cecilia went to the box again and opened it. "This recipe looks promising. Dragon's tongue. Dwarf laurel, bitter Denos almond and rotten elder tree leaves mixed with port wine." Cecilia paused for a second before continuing. "Seems easy enough. Causes the blood vessels to burst under the skin." Cecilia grinned. "The origin of the name, I suppose. This will come in handy later, I'm sure."

Cecelia poured another cup of wine and smiled. "Don't worry, father, the legacy of the dragon, our legacy, is assured." She grinned and sipped her wine.

The Second Wave

"Captain Constantine, move those palisade stakes to the southern front." General Miralda ordered one of her captains, as she rode along the main entrenchment of her army. "The king is expecting the bulk of the kingdom to still be here when he returns." She finished before riding back to the manor house on top the motte in Antei.

Miralda dismounted once in the courtyard and walked into the manor house. There she saw Minimoto looking over maps and missives from other leaders. Entering the manor, she removed her helm. Her bronze tinted skin blended in the dimming light of the fireplace. For ease when wearing the helm, Miralda kept her hair, naturally curly with small curls, braided tight against her scalp.

Miralda poured a goblet of wine and sat on the bench in front of the Quarmi's table. "You look like a cartographer that noticed a mistake in a trade route on his best map." She smiled before sipping the wine.

"That's what's bothering me. I think I missed something and someone slipped through," Minimoto took a scroll and passed it to the general. "The scouts reported troop movements."

Miralda read the scroll. "This is saying Ter Nog troops are riding this way. Bulwyf wouldn't have moved an inch without Gabriel's word. Not counting you, me and my husband, you'd find no one more loyal to Gabriel than Bulwyf."

"That's my concern." Minimoto sat across from Miralda. "I think it's Harbor."

"Why move from a secured position?" Miralda wondered aloud.

"He is no fan of Gabriel's and certainly not of me and this post. I'm worried." Minimoto replied.

"He is a baron of this kingdom. If he dares to incite a rebellion, then he will be executed as a traitor." Miralda responded with a grim look on her face. "Ironic if that is the case, given that the Harbor family only came to prominence once Seabane was executed for treason against Charles I."

"The entire Seabane family were cousins to the Coldwood Family. That is the origin of Harbor's family." Minimoto added. The two leaders looked at one another, knowing the implications.

"I'll rally the division. Will you be able to manage here without me?" Miralda said, standing up.

"Leave me some engineers and we'll be fine. The fighting is sparse now."

Miralda nodded to Minimoto before walking out of the manor house.

"If Harbor is plotting a rebellion, then I'd hate to be him when Miralda finds him." Minimoto smirked before returning to his maps.

Miralda gathered her officers and went over the new orders. "We march to this route." Passing around the scroll, each saw the location of the Harbor army. "This has to be done quickly. Elysia has already tested the king's strength, and they are likely to begin another attack anytime now. We'll march back to the east and intercept this army and we have to do it before Elysia returns."

"Ma'am, is this the Ter Nog force?" One officer, an older veteran of the border wars with Balenor, asked.

"I don't know, but let's hope not." Miralda answered. She turned and walked to her mount.

"Perhaps it is Ter Nog offering assistance." The man persisted.

"The king ordered Baron Harbor to maintain the position at the port. If he has left that post, then that's disobeying the direct order. He is also not marching here. He is heading to Lostwood. That's your hometown, isn't it captain?"

The veteran nodded.

Miralda gave a slight smile. "Then let's ride and find out what the baron is up to."

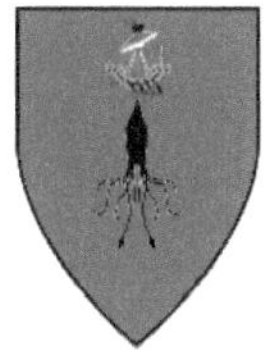

The fighting on the southern border was mostly minor skirmishes and a few supply raids. Nothing like what had been expected. Boredom in the camp had been the worst of it, but that didn't leave anyone feeling any better. At some point, the bulk of the Elysian army had to march north.

In Elysia's capital of Gib, King Ahab III cursed his luck at the renewed war.

"Damn! I trusted that woman and she disappears with no mercenaries!" The Elysian king fumed. "Where are those Gota warriors she promised?" His anger boiled over and he threw plates and goblets across his hall. His attendants and advisors watched the now common scene unfold.

"Your grace, the ship is en route. Until they arrive, we can hold the Lotcalans with strikes on Antei and Ter Nog." One advisor said, trying to placate the angry king.

Ahab turned and glared at the young man. He seized him by the throat and pulled him close. Ahab's hot and foul breath engulfed the man.

"You dare think I hadn't thought that?" He said through gritted teeth. Ahab tossed the man to the ground. "Orestilla lied to me, and now I have to fight a war with Lotcala and Amazon again. As long as Varus-dun holds and we pressure the northern border, we can prolong their suffering. At least until those damn outcasts arrive."

"Your grace, what of Fe?" Another advisor asked.

Ahab grunted and waved his hand dismissively at the question.

"Hel is a coward and all know it. He'll send his army out and they'll be slaughtered in the desert." Ahab sat on his throne and gripped the arms of the stone chair. "No, here is where the war will end. I will end it by ending Lotcala and Amazon in one fell swoop." Ahab clenched his right fist, tight enough that his knuckles whitened. "Now the question is to funds. Where is that Eolas boy?"

That was the question; where was Eolas? At that moment Domino Eolas, second son and least favorite of Constantino Eolas, was riding north from Verna to Jovag with an escort of Amazonian jailors and one crippled yet dangerous Amazonian veteran.

The group camped along the roadside and were enjoying a warm meal by the fire, sitting on down logs and relaxing after a long ride.

"So, Megara, have you found the right man to settle down with yet?" Domino asked. It should be noted that the imprisoned man, hands still shackled, had not stopped talking since leaving Verna. The only exceptions were when he slept and eat.

Megara glanced to the talkative man and spat at his feet.

"That's a no then?" Domino smiled.

"What's it to you anyway?" Megara growled.

"I figured we've been spending so much quality time together and that my father would be more than pleased to have an Amazon warrior for a daughter-in-law. Do you have any gold? You know for a dowry?"

Megara sneered and gripped her spear, but Honora calmed her.

"Men like him make life fun and interesting. Not much for settling down, but they keep you on your toes." The older woman said as she sat next to Megara. "I had my share during my days in the Legion."

"So you were a legionnaire too?" Domino said.

Honora smiled. "Aye, I was. The Commander, actually." She replied, but without vanity. Her time as the Legion Commander was one that many remembered well and with honor but not one that Honora, herself, gloated over. "That was many seasons ago, and it was fairly uneventful."

"Uneventful, not counting the war with Tresha and River Port." One of the other jailors, a woman named Celaeno said.

"Well, there was that one war. Oh, and the few with Nara and Tresha again." Honora laughed. She looked to Domino. "Now, this one here." She said pointing with a pewter, two-pronged fork. "This one is a bit of a talker."

"His charm is part of his weapons. That and his gold." Megara put in.

"Gold that I do not have on me at the moment." Domino added.

"No matter. He could be of use later on, so make sure to not damage him too much." Honora smirked.

The jailors all grinned to one another at the implications. Domino raised an eyebrow, inquisitive to the new tone of the camp.

After three days of riding along the southern border of Lotcala, Miralda and her soldiers found signs of another army. This army, however, was marching east to west.

"What in the Creator's name is Harbor doing?" Miralda said.

She knew the baron to be ambitious and more assertive than others, but this time he was out of line. The king's commands were law, and now that seemed to be exactly what Harbor was breaking.

Miralda pulled on her horse's reins, seeing the dust of an approaching army. She turned to one of her captains. "Wait her and set up a defense." Miralda snapped the reins of the horse and trotted the steed closer, followed by her house guards, brave warriors from the village that Miralda's father ruled over. These would be fearless men and women that would fight to the end beside their liege.

After a while a silhouette of an army gave way to figures walking towards the steady general. At the front, Miralda could see a large man riding a large draught horse.

"That's Harbor." She said calmly to her guards. "Be ready."

Within thirty minutes the baron reached Miralda. "My lady general, to what do I owe this surprise?" Baron Harbor asked smugly.

"Somehow I think we both know the reason you're marching west along this road." Miralda replied.

"You have me at a disadvantage then. I'm simply protecting the border."

Miralda lowered her head and chuckled. "It's never wise to think me a fool, baron. The border is that way." She pointed to the south. "This is the road to Antei."

"Then it should be well guarded just the same." Harbor remarked.

"It is." Miralda grinned. "King Gabriel has given lord Minimoto command of the southern border forces."

Harbor scoffed.

"You doubt your king's decision?" Miralda asked.

"You put gold and silver on a Quarmi and you may get a pretty Quarmi but it's still a Quarmi." Harbor spat on the ground. "You think that the people, the humans, of Lotcala wish to follow a Quarmi?"

"They will follow whoever the king commands them to follow, as will I." The general replied.

"That's the problem, then. Even an entire division being led by a woman. Too much consorting with the Amazons for true Lotcalans like those in Ter Nog and Coldwood. Those in Jovag and the western part of the kingdom have gone soft. Allowing women and Quarmi to command would never happen in Ter Nog."

Miralda sniffed and tightened her grip on the horse's reins. "This road is being guarded by the Southern Division. I must ask that you return to Ter Nog, my lord, or I'll be forced to escort you back in shackles."

Harbor sneered. "Do you realize that you're threatening a baron of the kingdom? You, a daughter of some lowly gentry-lord."

General Miralda remained defiant. "My lord, I respect your title, but the king saw fit to leave me in the post that our current king's father saw fit to place me in. I am the General of the Southern Division and I am the authority on this road during wartime." Miralda raised her hand and her guards all pointed their spears to the baron.

"You dare?!" Harbor snarled. "You speak to a baron in such a tone?"

"I am a general in the King's army. I have such authority in times of war as written in the charter that founded my position centuries ago by King Charles I."

Harbor grunted. "Perhaps, but those with me are part of the baronial army of Ter Nog. They only follow my orders."

"That is why my commander Bulwyf is not with you, is it not?" Miralda asked. "Do you agree to return to Ter Nog or do you wish to continue with this folly?" The general finished.

"I will not be pushed around by some woman!"

Miralda nodded. "Then I shall have to place you under arrest and hold you until the king can pass judgement."

"What?" Harbor scoffed. "Where is the honor afforded to a man of my position?"

Miralda nodded slightly, but in a flash drew her sword. She held it to Harbor's neck. "Dual in an hour. We'll let the Creator determine our fates."

"Agreed." Harbor responded, backing his horse away slowly.

Harbor turned his horse and rode back, leaving Miralda with her guards.

"Was that wise my lady?" One guard asked. "He is a skilled duelist."

Another guard spoke up gruffly. "As is our lady."

Miralda nodded to her guards and smiled. "He is skilled and he will be a challenge." She paused and took a deep breath. "Send word to Minimoto that we will need to be prepared, just in case. If I fall, give them hell and make sure the baron dies." Her guards nodded at her order.

The hour passed quickly and the two leaders met back in the spot of their earlier confrontation. Each left their armies a few yards behind them, watching and waiting for the outcome.

"You're brave to come yourself. I thought for sure one of your champions would do the honors." Harbor taunted.

"This is my duel. Besides, none of my champions have bested me yet." Miralda smirked.

Miralda adjusted the pauldrons on her shoulders and the bracers on her arms. Each were made of steel plates, interlocked and covered with cloth. On her chest was her black brigandine. Interlocked steel plates riveted together and covered in cloth. Underneath she wore an arming doublet with chain mail sleeves and a chainmail skirt. Miralda bent down and tightened her metal greaves.

"Strong words." Harbor said commending her.

Miralda looked to the older baron. He looked burdened with a chainmail hauberk and plated metal greaves. Harbor also armed his arms in plate metal. Miralda took stock of him as he put on his helm. It wasn't a small helm, but a great helm with a closed face. It would give him blind spots, unlike Miralda's nasal helm.

The general put her helm on and walked to the baron. "Your army, should I win, will lie down their arms?"

"Aye, and yours the same, I'm guessing?" Harbor asked.

Miralda nodded.

Harbor smiled. "Good." He said removing his arming sword from its sheath and taking up his shield. He moved closer to Miralda.

The general pulled her longsword and gripped it with both hands, raising it above her head. The baron was surprisingly quick in heavier armor and tried to slash at Miralda's center, but the general was quicker to defend. She brought her sword down swiftly, blocking his strike and then followed through, pushing his sword low towards the ground. Miralda kicked the baron back and swung her sword up, but the baron brought his shield up in time to block.

Harbor stepped back. Miralda allowed him a moment before she sent an attack of her own. The general slash downward, but Harbor caught it with his shield. He pushed against her and knocked her back a few steps before slashing at her with his sword. Miralda dodged the attack and retaliated with a sword slash that glanced off of Harbor's chainmail.

The two regained their balance after the last attempt.

Harbor grinned. "Chainmail is still good for something. Swords can't beat it." He chided Miralda.

"Let's test that!" She roared before striking again.

This time Harbor deflected the hit off his shield and he leveled a strike on her. His strike also glanced off, only tearing the cloth but leaving the gleaming metal underneath unharmed.

Miralda wasted little time in going after the baron again and throwing her shoulder into him. The baron staggered back but remained on his feet. Miralda went for another charge, but Harbor stepped away, allowing Miralda to stumble onto the ground.

Harbor stood over the downed general. He smirked as he pointed his sword to the woman.

"Anything to say now?" He asked snuggly.

Miralda kicked out her right leg and smashed it into Harbor's left leg at his knee. The baron buckled and lowered his body to a knee on the ground. Miralda lifted herself on to her knees and grabbed Harbor's shoulders. She pushed the man down and Harbor fell onto his back, dropping his sword. Miralda crawled onto him and put her knee on Harbor's chest.

The general pulled a thin dagger from her belt and put it to the baron's neck and pushed it in until it stopped on the Harbor's spine. She watched blood flow from the wound and from under the helm. Miralda stood up.

"That's why you don't gloat." She said before picking up her sword and removing her dagger from Harbor's neck.

Miralda looked to Harbor's army, standing across the field and watching. She raised her sword high and then quickly lowered it, giving her army the signal. Her captains let out war cries and a volley of arrows flew from her army out towards the Ter Nog soldiers. The confusion sent the men scrambling with little defense. This allowed Miralda's horsemen to ride down from the hills and send the Ter Nog soldiers running back to their camp.

One of Miralda's house guards rushed to her side. Miralda removed her helm.

"Gather those that surrender and chain them up for the king's judgement. For those that won't surrender show no mercy and set an example." Miralda turned to walk back to the camp but stopped short. "Also, send word to Minimoto that I handled the threat."

Miralda's order was followed, but she had little knowledge of the threat that was coming to Ter Nog and what Harbor had failed to prevent. Just then a distant horn blew from the south.

Commander Bulwyf rushed to the outer wall of Ter Nog. His plan had been to reinforce the southern border, but his scouts reported a mass of soldiers marching north. Baron Harbor's force had marched further west and Bulwyf knew that Harbor wouldn't be able to intercept the coming Elysians. Not that Harbor wanted to intercept any of the Elysian force. His goal was to outmaneuver the southern border forces commanded by Minimoto. Harbor failed at that task, but Bulwyf had yet to be made aware of the fact. What Bulwyf did know was that a force of ten thousand Elysians was marching to Ter Nog!

Bulwyf surveyed the area along the southwestern gate.

"Dig those trenches deep and dig the timbers in! I want to see points at the ends of those timbers. Cover them with salt and shit when you have them carved." Bulwyf ordered. He turned to one of his captains. "We have two days at the best case."

"Aye, sir." The captain replied. "The town's militia is asking about Harbor."

Bulwyf clenched his fists in frustration. The young man was hot tempered and as fiery as his red hair. "Tell them he went to bolster the border forces.

Remind them that the king has ordered that I am in charge of the defense of this town."

"Sir, people are talking of rioting against our army. Against the king." The captain said.

"Then round them up and let them decorate our new defensive trenches and fields with their treasonous bodies. Their children too." Bulwyf said without a smile. He was grim in his tone. The guard looked worried. "I will not try to defeat an enemy double our size. I will, however, attempt to defeat their will to fight us."

The captain saluted before rushing down from the wall's walkway and to the town center. Bulwyf watched him before turning back to field.

"This field needs to be a place that inspires fear in those bastards' souls. A killing field." Bulwyf remarked to himself. "Break their spirits and their army will break before the battle begins."

Fe

The southern approach was hostile to any infantry, it did not matter that the Amazonian Legion was well trained or well supplied. The desert of Fe was a treacherous place for anyone not moving at a gallop, and this left little option for the Legion. However, nothing was impossible for the noble and determined Amazonians. Syrena marched her soldiers on, deeper into the scorching sands and dust of the Fesian desert. She knew the stakes, and she knew the plan. March until the rendezvous with Cecilia and then onward to the capital. There her husband, King Gabriel, would join the Amazons in the final conquest. It was a battle long time in the making given the turbulent history of the area.

The nations fought wars in the past, all leading to treaties and alliances. The Fesians were fickle with long-term alliances. Though the empire had a central government, the local chieftains ruled under the elected emperor, who was a chief from the local tribes. These chiefs were the true seats of power for their people, and it directly tied their influence to who the emperor might end up being. This also meant that the next emperor could break an alliance with one nation. One could think such a complex government of as a weakness, especially when the elected emperor might not have been the best option.

Amazon chose not to exploit this weakness like Lotcala did in recruiting the Bohiem tribe into their alliance. This was a masterful tactic, but one that Syrena was not willing to do.

"We will march through to the capital and leave the people out of the war. Fe's problems are their own."

Syrena remarked to her prefects. "Our goal is the capital and nothing else."

The camp was full of life as Cecilia's cavalry joined the Legion. Mourning for their father had to wait, though Cecilia looked more somber. Syrena pulled her sister aside after the prefects and captains had left.

"Mother mourns alone tonight." Syrena said to her sister.

Cecilia looked up from her seat and gave a slight nod. "As do we." She sighed. "Father would not want us to cry over his bones."

"No, but it is hard not to cry." Syrena sat next to her sister. "I think it was right to bury him in the field."

Cecilia nodded. "Others do not."

"You're the crown princess and you decide. Mother agreed with it."

Cecilia smiled to Syrena. "Thank you." Cecilia stood up. "Tomorrow we reach the capital and Gabriel. It will be tough to break the walls of Fe."

"I was thinking we'd have more resistance than what we've seen." Syrena commented. "A few towns and little defense from the locals."

"Fesians are not as united as we are. Elysia is the one we will have trouble with, I think."

Syrena nodded at Cecilia's assessment.

Cecilia continued. "This war is something that they tricked us into. Honestly, I'm not sure it was worth us getting involved in once Orestilla was dead, but here we are anyway."

Syrena stood up and approached her sister at the center table and poured two goblets of wine.

"Lotcala and Elysia have had bad blood for centuries. This was the breaking point."

Cecilia accepted an offered goblet. "And yet if you hadn't married Gabriel, it wouldn't have been our war."

"No, perhaps not, but we haven't fought in Elysia." Syrena countered.

"And I plan to keep it that way." Cecilia sipped her wine. "You are the Queen of Lotcala and I can respect that, but keep your kingdom's politics out of Amazon." Cecilia put her goblet down. "Mother will expect you to remove yourself as commander once this war with Fe is over."

Syrena hid the hurt and the anger within her. She knew that Cecilia was right, but Syrena also knew that much of her sister's reasoning was out of spite.

"I will do what mother asks when she asks." Syrena answered, putting her goblet down as well.

Cecilia and Syrena locked eyes for a moment before Cecilia smirked and walked out of the tent. Syrena stood there and shook her head at her sister's words. The tension between the two was still very strong and would likely not fade soon. Syrena only hoped that leaving to start a life in Lotcala might calm the relationship.

Syrena had little time to think of it, however, for now she was off to see her mother, alone in her tent and mourning the loss of her husband.

The camp looked and acted as if all was normal, and for most people it was. Agis' death and the deaths of those he led were accepted as part of the war. This happens in battle; you fight with a fifty percent chance of a premature death. Syrena knew it, and Cecilia did too, as did others in the camp. Still, this death hit the royal family much harder than others.

Queen Saria's tent was near the center of the camp, not far from Syrena's. The princess walked in and saw her mother sitting by her cot with a cup of tea in her hand. Her head was to the floor and her eyes were closed.

"Mother?" Syrena said, quietly. "Is it alright to join you?"

Saria looked up and sniffed back a few tears. "Of course." She replied in a raspy voice, fighting back tears.

"I wanted to check on you."

Saria smiled and motioned to a chair. "Sit. Would you like some tea? It's from your father's stocks."

"Are you sure it's tea." Syrena smiled and pouring a cup for herself.

Saria chuckled. "I might not approve of his craft but he taught me enough to know the difference between tea and poison." The queen sipped the hot green-yellow liquid. Saria sobbed. Syrena went over and embraced her mother.

"I'm sorry, mother." Syrena said through her own tears. "I never thought of a day like this coming."

"No one does. He was still so full of life that we could have ruled seven kingdoms." Saria boasted. "Why did he have to be so brave?" The queen mused.

"He was brave." Syrena smiled as she wiped away her tears. "Anyone would have to be to marry the Queen of the Amazons." The mother and daughter laughed and hugged again.

They broke the hug and Saria wiped her eyes. "He was the finest man I ever knew." She cleared her throat and wiped her eyes before standing up. "We arrive at the capital tomorrow. I should walk around and encourage the warriors. They don't need me in the tent sobbing like a toddler."

"No one blames you for staying in here right now." Syrena said in a supportive tone.

"No, as queen I must be with my sisters and ready to die if it's my time." Saria stopped. "I didn't put enough stock into Mestra's warnings. She told me my dreams foreshadowed a great grief. A fallen dragon."

"You mean father?"

Saria nodded. "I believe so. There was more, but I didn't head it and now I can't remember. Did I will this?"

Syrena shook her head. "Did you will father's death? No. This is fate." Syrena walked up to comfort her mother. "Orestilla did this."

Saria looked down for a moment before turning back to her daughter. "Fate has a way of making what it wants to come to fruition, happen."

"Death is something we can't control."

Saria smiled to Syrena. "Then speak with Mestra and be ready for whatever fate may bring us."

Syrena walked out of the tent and towards her friend's tent. Mestra had been keeping to herself since returning to the queendom, and Syrena wanted to know why. Syrena found the mage sitting on her cot and reading a tome.

"The camp is prepping for a major battle and you're reading. Just like our days in the Herd." Syrena remarked as she walked into the tent.

"Just like in those days, my skills are less useful than yours and our sisters." Mestra replied, never taking her eyes off her book.

"That isn't true."

Mestra looked up and raised an eyebrow. "Isn't it?"

"Is that a book from the Karum library?" Syrena asked, trying to avoid the topic. Mestra's role as a mage relegated her to a healer, though she was a skilled warrior and powerful with attack spells. Still, in the queendom the sore point for mages was that their skills in battle often went unused. Some saw it more honorable to fight with a weapon as opposed to magic.

Mestra nodded. "It is, I saved several ancient tomes before the building caught fire."

"I am sorry about that. We tried to prevent it."

Mestra looked to her friend and sighed. "Not all causalities in war are people's lives. So much history can be lost by invading armies."

"That's true." Syrena wrung her hands. "I want to talk about my mother's dreams and what they mean for us here in Fe."

Mestra closed her book and sat it next to her on the bed before standing and walking to a nearby table. "This pendant," she said, picking up a rather large jewel on a silver chain, "is apatite. It allows me to read what isn't seen. This has allowed me to see beyond our mortal realm, just as it did for my mother and her mother before her, all the way back to the first Pappas woman. Carved from a stone washed upon the shore by her husband and offered as a gift on their wedding night." Mestra put the pendant on. "Your mother asked that I use its power to read her dreams and see the truth in them."

"I knew she wanted you to interpret the dreams, but that's just speculation, right?" Syrena asked.

"No, with this I can see them as she saw them, and then with training I can see more. I told her the warnings the dreams gave."

Syrena looked at Mestra. "You told her my father would die? Gabriel's father and brother?"

Mestra nodded. "In a way. They were only symbols. It could also mean the kingdoms, bloodlines or armies."

Syrena gasped and clenched her fists in anger, but she calmed herself. "Why didn't you share this with me sooner? You're my friend, my best friend, and you kept all of this from me?"

Mestra sniffed as a tear ran down her cheek. "This lets me see some things, but not everything. I saw their deaths and the end, but not the beginning. Had I known that it began with Orestilla's betrayal, I would have stopped you from leaving when you did. However, nothing is ever set in stone. Fate is but our journeys to fulfill a destiny that is ever changing."

"Do we win this war?"

Mestra shook her head. "So much has changed now, I don't know. Some things are not as I saw them."

"Such as?"

"Your sister is alive. The dragon was dead."

"She's the last dragon now." Syrena reasoned. "She was always father's favorite and I never had the same desire to learn his craft." Syrena sighed at the memories wafting in her head. "Anything else?"

"Elysia is silent. The griffin fell first."

"Could things happen out of order?"

Mestra shook her head again. "Our dreams are a reflection of our lives and everything we see within them are things we've seen in life. It might be a symbol for something real but it is something real. Most things like this are more straight forward than people realize. If you see a dragon, then look within your life for a dragon. Only con artists make vague statements because they are protecting their lies with confusing readings that could be interpreted as true to the desperate."

Syrena nodded and sat down on a chair near the table. She felt confused at all that was happening. Was it fate or was her destiny changing? She looked to her friend, still standing nearby.

"How has the healing been going?" Syrena asked with a smile, changing the subject.

Mestra sat down across from her friend. "Better than we expected. The goddesses have blessed us with few casualties."

"Then let's be grateful to the goddesses for that." Syrena smiled. "The coming battle will not be easy."

"We're ready, my queen." Mestra said with a grin.

"I'm not your queen. I'm queen of Lotcala."

Mestra chuckled. "I know." She said, standing to fetch a bottle of port wine and two pewter cups. She sat the cups down and poured the wine for Syrena and herself. "I plan to journey with you back to Lotcala. I'm a magister no matter what guild I am a member of, and I believe I could do well in helping Lotcala rebuild theirs to incorporate more mages."

Syrena took the cup and sipped the wine. "You'd be a welcomed addition to the kingdom." She said with a wink.

* * * *

The levity of that night soon gave way to a scene of another siege. This time it was the capital of Fe burning. Gabriel and his gigantic war machines entrenched themselves deep within the dunes just below the ridge that the city sat upon.

Cecilia's cavalry rode ahead of the Legion. The horsewomen finished setting up the camp near Lotcala's camp when Syrena's Legion arrived.

Syrena went to work ordering her soldiers to their duties. She surveyed the scene, knowing from day one that challenge would be in besieging the capital.

Syrena looked to Ino on her left. "That ridge will be a problem." She said to her friend.

"Maybe King Gabriel has an idea?" Ino replied. "If not I might have a suggestion."

Syrena looked to the tall and steep rock wall. The famous Fesian Ridgeline was a granite that rose three hundred feet in the air.

Syrena turned and looked around at the camp forming. "This was something I did not consider in depth."

Ino looked to her friend. "We discussed this ridge."

"Yes, but we never said how we would conquer this obstacle." Syrena remarked. She turned her horse and rode towards the camp.

Ino stayed behind, looking at the ridge. "I'll break us in." She said to herself.

The camps were separated, but many walked through each of the two camps, talking and enjoying the break from the marches. Stories of the recent battles were exchanged and different souvenirs were passed around and traded as signs of friendships forged. Some Amazons and the Lotcalans took the time to become acquainted with one another, enjoying a much needed respite within the bounds of passion.

This was a time of relaxation as the Lotcalan trebuchets launched boulders into the air, trying to reach the fortifications atop the ridge. The effort was fruitless, given the height of the ridge and the range of the trebuchets.

"We'll never reach the wall this way." Baron Ironhand said as he and King Gabriel conversed in the king's tent. Several of the other barons were present, as well. "We can do some damage to the granite below, but that's minimal and would take us years to make it matter." Ironhand was leading the artillery for the Lotcalans, and he wasn't a stranger to granite.

The Barony of Pern, Ironhand's home, was built of cut granite. This, however, was a monstrous wall that had never been taken. The logistics and the stakes couldn't be any more different. In Pern, the miners had years to quarry the stone that was needed and they would work at the leisure of the deadlines, often a reasonable time. Here, however, was a solid stone ridge that might as well have been a mountain that they had just a month to break open.

The barons and the king continued their strategy when Syrena walked in, followed by her prefects, Cecilia and Queen Saria. Everyone in the tent bowed and greeted the Queen Saria and her daughters.

Gabriel bowed and extended his hand to his wife, Syrena. "Welcome, my queen." He said, kissing her right hand. Gabriel then looked up to Queen Saria. "Your grace, Queen Saria, welcome and please accept my deepest sorrow for your husband."

"Well met, your grace, King Gabriel, and thank you for your words. I will miss him more than the moon misses the earth with each dawn." Saria replied with a warm smile. "I should say, before we become mired in the war and our own grief, congratulations on your nuptials. Welcome to our family." Saria smiled. "It has been many years since our nations have shared a camp." She finished.

The rest of the occupants of the tent grinned at the words. Cecilia feigned a smile. In the weeks preceding this meeting, her smile faded. The war had taken a heavy and personal toll on the crown princess and she was not at all herself, but she rode on as a loyal princess and soldier would.

Gabriel smiled to her. "Princess Cecilia, it is good to see you here alongside us." He remarked. "You have my condolences on the loss of your father. He was a man that I wish I had known more, but I could tell he was an admirable man."

Cecilia gave another fake half grin and a slight bow to her new brother-in-law. "Thank you, your grace." She lifted herself up. "May I offer mine to you as well?"

"Yes, yes, we all got dead people, your grace. Might we continue with the task at hand before we bog ourselves down in condolences?" Lord Marshal Laoch said. "We have a mountain to climb, you know."

The Amazons looked to the man. Queen Saria grimaced at the man. "You must be a Hardstone."

"My grandmother was actually a Hardstone daughter. She married into the Laoch family." Laoch replied.

"This is Lord Marshal Charles Laoch." Gabriel said. "As good a man that I've known, but he is rather blunt like his forefathers. Also, he is rather frustrated about this ridge."

Saria nodded but eyed the rude Lord Marshal before turning to Gabriel. "Does anyone have an idea or two?"

Ino, from behind Saria, stepped up and spoke to the group. "I think I might." Saria walked to the table with a makeshift model of the fortress and the ridge. "Looking from this southwestern ridge we have the height to contend with, but from the west and northwest we have a gorge. To cross the gorge, we'd have to storm the bridge. We would be bottlenecked of course, but that would be the perfect battle for the Legion."

"You're saying that we should storm the bridge?" Syrena asked. "It's been awhile since I've been on that bridge, but it's maybe twenty soldiers wide."

"Yes, but that's not the actual attack." Ino continued. She pointed back to the ridge. "Here is the attack. Prefect Leda if you take your cohort of pikes and Artemisia's archers, you can distract them on the bridge and Prefect Melantho your force can swing around to the northern approach to cut off any reinforcements from the river tribes I think we can sneak in."

"This is the part that I've been waiting for in all of your rambling." Laoch remarked.

"Then listen up Lord Marshal." Ino grinned. "We'll attack the ridge here from the northeast." She pointed to a part of the ridge that was just around two hundred and seventy feet high. "That's where we send in the best of our army to secure the wall and drop rope ladders down for others to climb and join in the surprise attack."

The rest of the tent looked grim and doubted the plan, but Ino smiled as wide as a child getting a new toy.

"I have the perfect group in mind for this and if you have any climbers, they're welcome to join us. All I need is your artillery to continue bombarding the area they're hitting now. I'll get mine set up and join in. We have to pull them off that side." Ino finished.

Gabriel held his hand to his chin and thought. Others from Lotcala were looking to him for his response. Syrena looked to her husband and then back to her friend.

Syrena touched Gabriel's arm. "Ino is–"

"Out of her mind!" Cecilia interrupted. "That ridge is too tall and it is suicide mission."

"No, I was going to say she was trying to think of something new." Syrena answered.

"She is thinking like a lunatic! She'll get whoever is foolish enough to climb that ridge killed." Cecilia shook her head before looking to Ino. "If you can't keep up with the prefects then you shouldn't be one." The princess paused for a moment and put her fists on the table in front of her. "This whole war was a farce for us. We did our job and snuffed out the traitor and even pushed through the desert gaining lands. Yet now when our task is done we are still here trying to breach an impregnable fortress based on an idea from a six year?" Cecilia turned to Syrena. "She's only here because of your nepotism."

Ino turned to Cecilia. She would not stand to be insulted by such a disgraceful term as six year. A name meant to shame those that leave the legion after the minimum commitment, like Ino's mother did.

"You might be the crown princess but just five minutes is all I'd need to teach you some respect just like back in the Herd." Ino replied angrily.

"Respect? You want to talk about respect? Let's go then *six year*!" Cecilia shouted angrily. "Teach me some respect!"

Cecilia and Ino began pushing into each other's bodies and faces. The Amazonian entourage was trying to hold the warriors back while Saria went and sat down on a chair. The Lotcalans stepped back, except for Gabriel, who inched closer to help.

Saria sighed. She looked on for a moment before deciding the time was right to speak up.

"That's enough, dammit!"

The group of Amazons stopped and regarded their queen.

"These Lotcalans know us to be hotheaded and that's fine." Saria said, motioning to the others in the tent. "Gabriel, you need to watch yourself with this one. She has a temper too." She said pointing to Syrena. "Now if we can get back to this plan. Ino, why don't you finish. I'm sure you had something to add about who you want to send."

Ino straightened up and adjusted her armor. "Yes, my queen." She said with a salute. "Forgive my anger."

"Nothing to forgive, you and your family have more than made up for your mother's legacy and cemented your own. As for Cecilia, my eldest is a bitch on the best of days but it would be best to make a good name for yourself in this battle just in case."

Ino nodded. "I would lead the climb. A climb like this is nothing with the right tools. Artemisia will come with me." She said looking to her sister.

"With the commander's blessing." Prefect Artemisia remarked.

"Can you make this climb?" Gabriel asked.

"We used to climb heights like this as children in Verna. The towers of the mage sector are around the same height, and we'd climb them for fun." Artemisia replied.

"That was you?" Mestra yelled from behind, shocked. "We used to throw rocks up at you!"

"We know!" The two sisters replied, simultaneously looking at the mage.

Ino turned back to the Lotcalans and Amazons. "This is dangerous, I know, and it is a long shot, but we do not have the time for a long drawn out siege. I know how Cecilia feels about me and I know she isn't alone. I'm not a great Artillery Prefect, but I can fight and I'd say I'm one of the best fighters in the Legion. I also know that I can break into that fortress."

"How many men do you need?" Argyle asked from the Lotcalan crowd.

Ino stared at the model on the table. "Fifteen would be fine. Just to get in, clear the area, and then lower some more rope ladders."

"That's still a hell of a climb." Artemisia said. "Whoever goes needs to be the best we have."

"I'll go." Mestra said.

"Fine." Ino said. "That's three."

"I'll go as well. Been a while, but I can still climb a mountain." Gabriel smirked.

"Your grace." Ino began to protest, but Gabriel stopped her.

"I'm going."

"And if I say no to that?" Syrena spoke up.

Everyone turned to regard her, but Gabriel smiled and clasped her wrists. "I'll be fine. Ino will protect me." He said.

"Then take Carladias." Argyle said. "Miralda sent her to protect you after all."

Carladias stood next to the large man. She bowed and then stepped forward.

"At your side, sire." Carladias said.

"Good. Now just gather a few more of your best warriors and climbers. We leave just after nightfall tomorrow to give us as much cover as possible. It's going to be a new moon so that'll give us much more darkness." Ino replied. "Until then, I'll set up the artillery I led here, and then we can meet with the climbers to go over more details tonight." Everyone in the tent exchanged their goodbyes and went to work recruiting. Everyone except for Syrena, Gabriel and Saria.

Gabriel looked to his wife. "That's a few hours away yet." He said holding her hand. "These couple months have been long without you near me."

Saria rolled her eyes. "I'll leave you two to your young love. I must speak to Ino, anyway."

Syrena stepped back from Gabriel and towards her mother. "Go easy on her, please. Cecilia has liked no one from the labor class."

"I know." Saria said with a reassuring smile. "However, if this plan fails, I'll have a tough time protecting her from Cecilia's wrath. I can't protect her I after I'm no longer queen. She must think of that."

Syrena nodded and Saria left the tent. She turned back to husband. "I suppose we are alone for a while." She said with a grin.

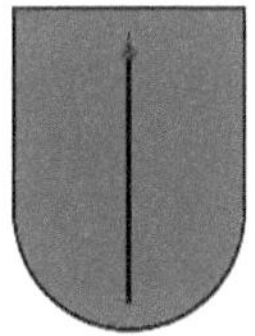

The Climb

The moonless night fell upon the camp. It was a dangerous time to climb a small hill in a hostile land, but a two hundred and seventy foot tall rock wall; it was near impossible. Especially with archers atop the wall and a forty-pound pack on your back. Still, it was the best plan that Ino had. During the day, the archers and the pikes maneuvered to the bridge. Though they hadn't reached the bridge and set up just yet, Ino could not wait. The moonless nights would not last, and they had to begin the climb.

It was never a good idea to climb in the dark, and this was as foolhardy a plan as anyone could ever think of. It was, however, the only plan that took them into the fortress within a day or two. That was time they would desperately need. The only light the group would have was from atop the ridge and coming from the flaming projectiles hurled by the siege engines, several hundred yards to the south.

Ino stepped up to the ridge. She pulled her pack tight and gripped the rope on her back. "This will keep us together and should help us if anyone slips. If too many people slip, then it won't matter." She said.

Everyone that joined her was ready. Nervous, but ready. They wore cloth or lightweight leather. Everyone had picks and thinner blades or daggers. Anything to keep the weight down. Only Carladias and Artemisia carried their bows with a handful of arrows strapped to their sides.

"Let's go." Ino said. She stepped up and gripped a piece of rock, pulling herself up with ease.

Artemisia followed on her left, doing the same. The two women, filled with experience from a youth of daredevil antics, made it look easy, even when they used the pickaxes. Two more climbers, Carladias and Gabriel, followed next. After them, two more. Baron Ironhand was one. Laoch was also in the group, leaving the siege to Baron Canton.

The climbers pulled themselves up the steep rock facing and struggled at areas with little to no outcroppings for gripping. Weariness took over from the hands, forearms and into the shoulders. Soon the pain and fatigue would reach their backs. Even Ino and Artemisia were feeling the effects. Still, they soldiered on. At the tail end of the group, anchoring the climbers, were Nyx and Riva. They were two experienced climbers and strong enough to support any weight that might fall their way. They could also provide excellent offense if needed once over the ridge.

Ino's knowledge of the task placed the two in the rear. It was also her idea to tie everyone in each group together, and it was a blessing that she did. Halfway up the ridge, a slow climb to maintain as much silence as possible, and Laoch lost the grip from his handhold. The man tried to hold on to his pickaxe, but his hand slipped from the sweat and he fell. Ino gripped the rock tightly as she felt the tug on her rope. His weight was heavy, but she could hold with the help of Gabriel and Ironhand below her. His freefall stopped near another Amazon warrior, Helen.

"My lord, grab my hand!" Helen called out to Laoch. She strained to catch the dangling man, finally gripping his hand on the third swing close to her. She pulled him in. "There, my lord, grip the rocks there." She said. Helen handed him a second pick, and they climbed back up again.

"Thank you." Laoch breathed to the woman.

As they returned to the climb, Ino slowed her pace, assuming that someone near the top had heard Laoch's scream. She tried to flatten out as much as possible to limit anyone catching sight of her. Artemisia had the same idea and was doing the same. Ino could almost see the top of the ridge, and just beyond was the fortress of Fe. Another hundred feet and they would crest over the ridge and climb up the fortress wall itself.

That was another task that Ino left off of her original plan. A sandstone fort was easy to climb, but doing it quickly and quietly might be another thing all together. However, the wall itself was only forty feet high and there was a narrow ledge that they could stand on. That meant a small amount of rest for the group.

Artemisia was the first to reach that ledge. She pulled herself over and shimmied to the side. She held herself, distributing her weight to allow for more support for the next climber who made it up with ease. Ino followed several feet away. Soon everyone had made it to the ledge. Each climber staked in the rope ladders and then lowed the long ladders down the ridge towards the ground. This would allow others an easier climb to the top.

"What now?" Gabriel asked Ino after the ladders were in place.

"We finish the climb." She replied looking up. She turned to the wall and drove her pick into the sandstone. Again and again until she was near the top, the others did the same thing until they too had reached the top.

Ino gripped her picks and hoisted herself to the top ledge. She could hear men talking close by. She peaked over the edge and saw two men about ten feet away. The light from a nearby torch was too dim to show details in their features, but she could see their silhouettes. She knew that if she was quick, they wouldn't see she was there until she struck them. Ino lowered her head and looked to the others. She mouthed for them to be quiet before she turned back, picked herself up and shimmied over the ledge.

Ino was quiet on her feet for a woman that was heavier than average. Her muscled frame was perfect for the heavier weights of armor and weapons, yet, she was nimble and quick. Ino was quiet and stealthy as well. A useful trait when she was inches behind one man, a dagger in each hand. It was over in an instant, a flash from the torch that glinted off the blade. Neither man knew it, not even when one's throat was slit horizontally, while the other received a dagger tip into his throat.

Ino waved to the others to come up. Before he started the last climb up, Gabriel looked down and saw that other warriors had started their climb. He lifted over the final ledge and joined the rest of the advance force.

"We have to hold this area and begin clearing nearby areas so we can have a foothold for the final attack." Ino said.

Laoch looked around. "What about patrols?"

Gabriel saw Nyx and another Amazon moving the two bodies to the side, far off from their group and dropping them over the wall and out of sight.

"We'll keep Nyx, Riva and Helen here to guard the ladders." Ino said. "We have to place the last ladders on this wall before anyone comes up." She finished.

"I'll go with Ironhand, Laoch and Carladias down this way to clear the path." Gabriel said pointing toward the northern walkway. "A few other warriors might be helpful."

"Alright. Artemisia and I will take the others down through the alleys, heading to the city center. We should avoid the bombardment area." Ino replied.

"Why are they not around here more in force?" Carladias wondered aloud.

"More than likely they've put more men to help rebuild areas damaged by the siege. Other reasons might be that Leda must have reached the western bridge, or at least been seen. Perhaps Melantho was spotted from the northern ramparts." Artemisia answered. "Either way, they have moved their men away from here thinking that this ridge made it secure for them."

"That's their fatal mistake." Laoch replied.

"Right, so let's make sure our force isn't in danger when they reach the top. Quiet and deadly." Gabriel said. "We can't cause any alarm."

The two groups broke off, leaving the three Amazons to guard the ropes.

Gabriel and his warriors reached an intersection in the walkway and looked around for anyone coming. They could hear voices, but no one was patrolling the area. The dialect was different, but Carladias knew enough to translate. Artemisia was correct in the assumption that Leda's force had been spotted. The bulk of the Fesians had moved to the western gate. Carladias whispered a quick translation and then they moved off.

The city was further in, but along the walls they had expected to encounter soldiers guarding. However, with the diversion, it was possible that the surprise attack could maneuver under more stealth than they had expected. A pleasant revelation.

A lone guard wondered close by and Laoch wasted no time in dispatching the man as he appeared around a corner. Further away, a few more were walking on patrol. Carladias removed three arrows from her quiver and clutched two while nocking one. She drew the bow string and let an arrow fly. With incredible speed she fired off two more arrows, each finding their marks. Blink and her companions would have missed her skill and speed. The three Fesians did not, but they were no longer alive to tell anyone about it.

"We have to guard this area." Gabriel whispered. He looked to two other warriors that joined him. A young Amazon and a Lotcalan. "Go back to the last intersection and wait there. Guide others that come up but hold that area." The two nodded before rushing off.

Ino and her band had similar success, but they had more fighting coming their way than Gabriel's, at first. A group of seven Fesian warriors walked by while Ino and her group hid in the shadows, waiting for them to pass. Once the Fesians were in front of the Amazons, Ino and the other sprung out from the darkness and dispatched the Fesians with swift and precise attacks. The stealthy Amazons used their short blades and even hand to hand attacks. Ino was more than happy to snap an opponent's neck if given the opportunity.

While Ino and her sisters were handling anyone unfortunate enough to get too close, Gabriel and the Lotcalans found their own challenge. When few patrols walked by, Gabriel and his fellow warriors made quick and silent work of any Fesians that wondered their way. Daggers were the most efficient, and a slice across the throat was the quickest method.

This tactic provided them with a way to remain hidden. However, that wasn't to last.

Suddenly, a woman shrieked and screamed in a Fesian dialect, pointing to the area where Gabriel and his warriors were. The screaming woman blew their cover. Carladias nocked and arrow and let it loose towards the woman, striking her in the heart and dropping her. It was too late, her screams alerted nearby patrols.

"Get back to the intersection!" Gabriel ordered. "We can hold them there and provide a cover for those still coming up the ridge!"

The Second Invasion

Ter Nog was the jewel of the Falcon Coast. The city was home to traders and merchants from around the globe. This helped it become the epicenter for commerce for the Kingdom of Lotcala. Many commoners sought their fortunes among the busy markets and new the hub of trading that could be found throughout the city and along the docks.

A massive wall surrounded Ter Nog, protecting the city from inland invasions, a long ago threat from days when the land was fractured. Most scholars thought the wall to be close to a thousand years old, yet still standing as if it was no younger than a decade. That wall had repelled invasion and was as strong as the people that grew up in the city. A people that held to their proud roots of a Yendis and Gota mix. These were a people that had never been conquered in the traditional sense. They were too stubborn to surrender and too strong to conquer outright. This was a matter of pride for the people of the city.

For many in Ter Nog, they may have been citizens and subjects of the King of Lotcala, but they were as free as anyone could be without a king. If one wanted to take the city, they would have to find another way other than war to do so.

During the War of Conquest that saw the Gota take control of the land, Jarl Uffe negotiated a peaceful surrender, which was really more of a cohabitation. That deal only came after days of fierce fighting along the docks. The citizens of the city had pushed the Gota back, yet the city leader saw the need to negotiate for the future. A wise choice but one that came at a heavy loss to the Gota invaders.

Two centuries later, King Charles fought a rebellious Baron Seabane, sparing the city, after sieging the city and bursting through a small section of wall. Infamously Charles decree saw the city population subjugated after executing the Seabane family. He then gave the city and the barony to the youngest son of Baron Coldwood, who took the name of Harbor.

Yes, the people of Ter Nog had a long and brutal history of standing up against the king or anyone foolish enough to attempt an invasion. This time, however, was different. Baron Harbor stoked the flames of resentment that had burned for centuries for the royal family and their attempts to centralize the monarchy. The torch was lit for a rebellion. Not only that, but Elysia crossed the border and were marching with thousands of men north to Ter Nog. Should they take the city, they would have Lotcala in a chokehold.

Commander Bulwyf, the king's cousin from the Hardstone family, was not about to let either happen. Bulwyf was every bit as hard and cold as his family name suggested, perhaps more so than any other since the founder Maeve. History knew the legendary woman that had fought alongside King Theodorif I for her ruthlessness and staunch loyalty to the king. Not much had changed in the last seven centuries.

Bulwyf first dealt with the rebellious citizens. He knew that the king had many loyalists within the city, but he had to quell the dissention so he could focus on the coming Elysians.

His captain rushed up the wall where Bulwyf perched himself for the past two days. "My lord, we have placed the prisoners on the field." The man said with a grim tone.

Bulwyf looked to the man, he was younger but the captain had seen plenty of skirmishes in recent years. The young captain looked paler than usual.

"Are you alright, Finn?" Bulwyf asked.

Captain Finn, turned and vomited over the wall's edge. "My lord, it's not right. What we did… those people were–"

"Were spreading sedition during a time of war." Bulwyf interrupted. "I could not abide that, nor should you." The scowl on his face told Finn that it would not be a good idea to press the issue.

The two men turned to face the southern field. The once pristine landscape was now scarred with trenches, pits of flaming tar and pitch, and large spikes. Upon those spikes were the bodies of the rebels that were captured the previous day and tried in a mock show trial. Along with the rebels were their families; husband, wives, parents and children. Many were still moving, left alive to suffer and to set the example for the Elysians.

Bulwyf stared, unblinking. "Finn, I will be damned for this without question. The old gods do not take these matters lightly, and your Creator will not accept my pleas for mercy. No, I will burn for this act but I will not loss this city and this will ensure our victory." He finished motioning to the field.

"My lord, how?" Finn asked in utter shock at his commander's unnerving demeanor.

Bulwyf pushed himself away from the wall and walked toward Finn, stopping just a few inches away. "I will break their will to fight. I will defeat the spirit before we fire an arrow. Without the will to fight, the Elysians will find it impossible to mount an offense."

"That field?"

"That field is there to show them the lengths I will go to achieve victory, and I will do worse if I must." Bulwyf finished before walking down to the lower ramparts.

He was certain that after the war was over and if Lotcala was victorious, that he would find himself on the headsman's block. King's cousin or not, one of the finest military minds or not, this was an unnatural act that would be hard to justify. Until then, however, Bulwyf would fight for the kingdom.

"Victory at all costs." Bulwyf remarked.

Miralda had barely sent a message to Minimoto in Antei before the bulk of Elysia's force crested the southern hills. Normally, these green and soft sloping hills were a beautiful sight to see, but for Miralda they held no beauty, only war and coming death. Miralda mobilized her force and gave a quick ultimatum to the Harbor troops that had been in chains. *Fight now with Lotcala or die before the battle begins.'* A tempting and what many would assume was a painfully obvious choice.

Many took the former option and fought side by side with their countrymen but others, just a handful, chose death. Miralda was glad to oblige, and she did so in full view of the Elysians.

"Let them see what we do to those that stand against us!" Miralda yelled out. "No quarter and no surrender!" She shouted before beheading one prisoner kneeling in front of her.

The Elysian army stood atop the hills and watched as the Lotcalan army put several hundred prisoners to death in front of them. If it intimidated them, they did not show it. Horns and drums continued to play on throughout the mass of soldiers. Familiar songs of war and war cries meant to rattle the nerves of their opponents.

When the prisoners were dispatched, Miralda and the others that completed the gruesome task walked back to their line to be ready for the coming charge. There had to be a charge, they had to run down the hill and attack. What else could they plan?

Miralda lifted her sword and waved it high above her. "Shieldwall!" She ordered before joining the warriors along the front line. "This is an expeditionary force." Miralda said to her captains, standing close by. "They wouldn't try to push the main force with siege equipment so far north along this road." It hit her like a stone on her forehead. "They sent that force to Ter Nog or Antei!" She reasoned aloud.

The horns from Elysia blew out in unison, a call to arms for those that knew the sounds, and the warriors cried out in a bloodlust that echoed around the shallow valley.

"Here they come!" Miralda shouted to her warriors as the Elysian force rushed down the slope and toward her force.

Miralda was a strict and disciplined leader. She was bred to fight by her father and her grandfather. She graduated second in her class at the War Academy, only behind Gabriel. Miralda knew that the shieldwall was simple, yet effective. It was her preferred tactic when she was lacking in a suitable cavalry, and during this battle she did not have a suitable cavalry. Miralda did, however, have a large force and one that could match the Elysians in a pitched battle. On the field, few armies were better than the Lotcalan and repeatedly they had proven that attacking head on was not always worth the risk.

It was a gamble that the Elysian commander was willing to take, however. That thought alone played into Miralda's strategy. She had to expect that her opponent would sacrifice men to gain a victory. For those unwilling to sacrifice, victory would not and could not be achieved. Perhaps Miralda admired something in that thought. If her opponent was willing to sacrifice so much, then perhaps he was capable of victory and that was something she wanted to find out.

The march was a thunderous stampede of warriors, screaming like devils, coming down the southern hills. The defiant cries from Miralda's brethren on the Lotcala side deafen the ears of the members of the shield wall. Somewhere behind the Lotcalan line, a commander gave the order to fire off a volley of arrows. It did little good. Miralda saw the arrows bounce off the heavier armed Elysians.

"They're wearing steel plate!" She shouted. "Brace yourselves!"

A few seconds later, the Elysian army crashed into the shieldwall in a violent impact that set the wall back a few steps. Miralda urged her warriors to hold the line, but the force behind the Elysians was too strong. She knew her wall was doomed.

Miralda pushed with all of her might, but she was pushing against a larger and stronger force. Even with the force from Ter Nog, she couldn't hold much longer. Her ploy to execute the prisoners was not enough to deter the attackers. She yelled in frustration and thrusted her sword out into the neck of an attacker directly in front of her. He fell back, and it gave Miralda time to break away and access her situation. She looked out over her moving line and saw it breaking. She looked back to the hills and saw the banners of the force that descended on her own soldiers.

"Gota?" Miralda exclaimed. "How?"

Around her the carnage was causing her wall to break and some stragglers on the line were running. Miralda knew that her time was limited, and she had to make a fateful choice.

"Retreat!" Miralda yelled out. "Vanguard with me everyone else, full retreat to Antei."

Her loyal soldiers fell in around her to form the vanguard while others broke off and ran back to the northwest. Miralda would hold out as long as she could, give the others time to reach Antei, but it was a desperate decision.

"We give our lives so they can prepare the defense!" Miralda yelled, her soldiers around her gave a battle cry, raising their swords, in unison at her command. "Let this be a stand worthy of history!"

War cries from the Lotcalan vanguard rose out above the valley, signaling that they would fight to their last breath as they charged to meet their enemies head on.

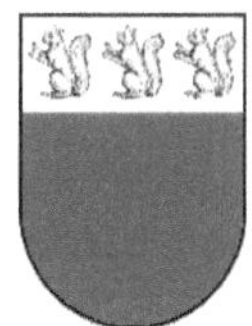

Elysia's commander riding north to Ter Nog was the famous general and King Ahab's nephew, Isidore. Never had there been a better general to carry the banner for the Elysian Kingdom. Though many, including his own uncle, felt he was far too merciful. King Ahab had sent away him in the years prior to Gotistan as an envoy. Had he been on the Falcon Coast during the previous war, many in Elysia felt he would have led the kingdom to victory. The respect that he carried, even in Lotcala, was on par with the kings and leaders from the ancient legends.

This is why Bulwyf was concerned as reports came to him of the advancing Elysians. However, Bulwyf's plan was already in place and Isidore would be the first to see it in action.

The brilliant general rode his steed ahead of his army. He was a thin man with a lightly sunken face, very much the opposite of his uncle, the king. Isidore's red hair, with a touch of grey, waved in the wind, but that wind brought a putrid stench to his nostrils.

The general rode closer to the city, exiting a thicket of trees he then saw the horror in the midday sky. Isidore's face paled at the sight of hundreds of helpless people, some still suffering the slow and agonizing death, that Bulwyf sent them to. His officers, coming from behind him, stopped and stared at the horrific scene.

"My lord?" One began. "What is this?"

Isidore shook his head. "Hell." He breathed.

Other Elysians emerged all around, and they too saw the horror of what the Lotcalans had prepared for them. They didn't just see it, they could smell it, and they could almost taste the burning flesh in the air. Last, the Elysians could hear it. They heard the voices, weak and dying, of the people Impaled on spikes, hanging by their arms, slowly bleeding to death.

"What monster could do this?" Isidore asked, just as the main gate opened and a lone rider with a white flag approached.

Bulwyf was brave, cruel and uncaring. He rode alone to the Elysians, stopping one hundred yards away. Isidore rode to Bulwyf.

"What the hell is this?!" Isidore demanded.

Bulwyf sat upon his horse, stone-faced. "This is the lengths I will go to protect this kingdom. These were rebels that were loyal to Baron Harbor and his insurrection against King Gabriel."

"Gabriel is king now?" Isidore asked. "A weak little boy wants to play war, and he sends his best butcher. Bulwyf, the illegitimate son of a Hardstone sodomite. Your father was a failed commander too, resulting to murdering prisoners to win battles." Isidore looked around. "The children?" He sneered.

"Examples." Bulwyf replied. "For you and your men."

"Examples?" Isidore scoffed. "You've murdered people to show off to me?"

Bulwyf caught the tone of the man's voice. His pitch had raised a bit. Not much, but enough that Bulwyf could tell his ploy was working.

"I killed these people as criminals would be in any kingdom that cared about its safety. Perhaps your king would rather let rebels run wild. We do not, however." Bulwyf smirked.

"No, you impale women and children!" Isidore shouted back. "King Ahab would never do such an unspeakable thing!"

"Then he is weak and doesn't need to sit upon that throne."

Isidore's nose and upper lip quivered. "Such barbarism. It's a wonder that your people ever developed from the primitive tribes of Gotistan."

Bulwyf grinned. "This is just a taste of my barbarism."

"What does this prove?"

Bulwyf turned his horse to return. "Victory at all costs." He remarked before returning to the city. He half expected a spear to pierce his back, but his gamble was correct. Isidore was an honorable man and so as Bulwyf returned to the city he knew his plan was in place. Make the battle as honorless as possible and Isidore would only know defeat.

Bulwyf gave the signal and a dozen archers let loose flaming arrows to the ground below the wall, igniting the pitch. The fire spread quickly around the bodies and the prisoners that were still alive, sending cries and screams of agony into the air, echoing off the city's stone walls.

Isidore watched as the blinding flames engulfed the field. His repulsion and anger only matched his feelings of horror over the scene. It was too much, and he had to hunch over and vomit on the spot. His men not only saw the flaming corpses but their famed leader, unable to control himself. No matter the cost, Bulwyf was happy to know that his diabolical plan was successfully in motion.

Along the battlements, Bulwyf's men wondered what the next life would have in store for them as they committed such acts during this life.

Isidore composed himself and returned to his men. He saw their stares and wondered the same thing as they did. Was he able to lead under such conditions?

He turned to his second in command. "This Bulwyf plays with emotions, but we can't break our resolve." Isidore began, knowing that he had already cracked. "We will storm the gates tonight! We can't wait!"

"Sir?" His second started, but Isidore hushed him.

"Now is not the time for any restraint. He tortured these people and now we have to liberate them from this horde of demons!" Isidore yelled. He stormed off within the camp, leaving his young second in command to issue out the orders.

Within the city, Bulwyf took a gulp of water. He looked to his own officers and nodded. "He is taking the bait. They will rush an attack and we'll beat them in their disorganized state."

Two days after the battle in the valley, Minimoto was adjusting to the large influx of warriors returning. Battered and beaten, they were dehydrated and hurting. He ordered his soldiers to do what they could to heal their coming comrades and provide rites to those that wouldn't heal.

The sun was setting as Minimoto walked up the stone steps to the top of the manor house. He could see beyond the ruined keep and the open field. His mind went back to the previous battle that saw his friend become king, only after the deaths of the former king and crown prince. A terrible price to pay, but one that was paid and no amount of wishing could change it. However, the Quarmi warrior spied something in the distance.

A small group of riders rode fast from the south. He squinted to see, and he barely made out the banner of General Miralda.

"To the southern gate! General Miralda approaches." Minimoto yelled down to the guards.

An hour later, the general and her vanguard joined Minimoto in the courtyard of the manor house. Miralda was covered in blood, a fresh scar across the left side of her face oozed blood and pus. Her hair was knotted and matted, caked with blood and sweat. She accepted a water skin and gulped it down before sitting on a stool near a healer. The young woman cleric was shaking as she neared the general, but she did her best to attend to the famed warrior.

"It was a surprise attack from the south." Miralda gasped. "Thousands of Gota!"

Minimoto couldn't hide his shock. "Gota?! Here?"

Miralda nodded. "These are all that got away. We took some Harbor prisoners and conscripted them into the army. I won't worry about loyalties now. They proved themselves, but we were beaten before the battle even began." Miralda stood up, leaving the cleric undone. Miralda looked to the woman. "Don't worry, scars are signs of honor and aren't something to hide." She turned back to Minimoto. "Creator damn us, those Gota were fierce and in steel plate. These weren't simple mercs."

"That Amazon woman said that the traitor Amazonian had treated with Gota mercenaries." Minimoto said, but Miralda shook her head. "Then the Gota have turned on their cousins?"

"These were regulars. Too many with the same uniform." Miralda replied. "I can't say if they've turned on us, but these were harden warriors. We were lucky to get away."

"How did you?" Minimoto asked. "Hearing the stories, I feared the worst."

Miralda sighed. "They're Gota. I had one trick I could pull on them."

"What?"

Miralda smirked. "Gota respect the old magic, Sven over there can cast plenty of damn powerful spells." She said pointing to one of her housecarls. "We couldn't risk the attack with so many of our men there, though. I won't be a cause of that much collateral damage. My housecarls know the cost of riding with me but the others don't so I called for a retreat and then Sven blasted half their army off the field with a scorching fire spell."

"Impressive, the ancestors would be proud I'm sure." Minimoto smiled.

"True, but I can see in your eyes you're not relieved with the time I've bought us."

Minimoto motioned for her to join him in the manor house. The grey skinned warrior placed a token near Ter Nog. Miralda was right, his black eyes gave away his true feelings.

Minimoto sighed, lifting his hand off the token. "Baron Harbor taking his army out of Ter Nog left a void that Bulwyf is filling. Prince Isidore is sieging the city."

"That wall will stand until the king returns and the people of the city will hold out."

"Maybe, and it isn't Isidore I'm afraid of. It's Bulwyf."

Miralda furrowed her brow. "Why? The king trusts him as true as any other, you and I included."

"The scouts that reported the siege reported the scene outside the city walls." Minimoto handed the missive documents to Miralda. He noted her eyes as she read the damning document.

"He…" She breathed. "He wouldn't do that."

"He did."

Miralda was shaking from anger. In her eyes Minimoto say the fires of the underworld burning and her anger seethed like molten steel in a forge. "I'll ride there with the army and lift the siege at once. Then I'll arrest Bulwyf."

She dropped the missive and turned out, but Minimoto ordered her to stop.

"We have an army ready for retribution coming this way. General, you and the king's army are needed here unless we give Antei to Elysia."

"I will not let history repeat itself. This kingdom's peace and stability is always hanging by a thread with the barons. Once this gets out, more barons will revolt unless Bulwyf is put down by a king's man." Miralda reminded Minimoto. "Every king has to deal with some barons and lords over reaching and I will be damned if I let that happen to Gabriel!"

Minimoto lifted his hands to calm Miralda down. "I understand and I agree. We have to do something in the king's absence, but we have a war on two fronts and both armies are dug in behind walls."

Miralda kicked a chair from the table in frustration. "Dammit!" She yelled out. "Those damn Hardstones always have to be so wretched!"

"Bulwyf is a son of Carolyngia too." Minimoto pointed out regarding Bulwyf's ancestry and the relationship to the king's family line.

"He is too much like Maeve. This is her trick to deal with rebels. King Haakon I used her to deal with the rebels during the Barons' War." Miralda replied, sitting down at the table.

Miralda reached for a goblet and a wineskin to pour herself something to drink. "Haakon was a bitch of a king, would rather fight his own people than anyone else, and he broke the alliance with Elysia, so here we are with that. But his worst moment was when he kidnapped a gentry-lord's daughter, fathered a child with her, and then turned them away. That was the final straw for the nobles. Heavily taxed, a lack of true leadership, and now an insult such as that. The barons rose up, all but Hardstone, Maeve was the baroness, sort of. Her husband was the baron, but he was dead by then and her son had yet to assume the baronial throne, because of Maeve."

Miralda sipped her wine. "Haakon couldn't fight for shit, Theodorif I wasn't exactly the best teacher or father, so he left his son to his own devices. That left Haakon fighting with a small force against almost his entire kingdom. Ter Nog, Baron Seabane's hold, stayed out of the fight, yet stayed loyal, but they were too far away when the war turned. That's why Haakon rushed to hide under Maeve's cloak. Hardstones are nothing if not loyal to the crown, blind loyalty. Maeve beat it into them, I guess. Whatever the case, he was safe in the Hardstone Barony. The other barons and lords sent a force in to find him and bring him out to face a tribunal. The first-born son of Baron Ironhand led seven thousand men into Hardstone, and they never stood a chance. Maeve slaughtered them. She then called for the barons to meet with her and the king. She wanted to talk of peace." Miralda scoffed.

"That bitch wouldn't know peace if it took her by the hand and led her off of a cliff." She continued. "The lords arrived with their men to the field, the battlefield littered with thousands of their kin. Ironhand's son was on a pike, impaled. Maeve treated other nobles the same. No ransom or mercy for birth. Heads piled up in mountains and bodies laid out for the vultures to feast upon. The woman, evil as ever, wore the fallen warrior's fingers and tongues around her neck and even wore the ring of Ironhand's son on her finger. The lords didn't have it in them to fight anymore after that. Maeve just laughed at the lords' pain and disgust as she gave them her terms. *End the war with the king or she would ride out and bring fire to each of their holds.* She'd barely lost a man, but she had defeated an army of thousands. They all knew her skill. What else could the lords do but accept after seeing the aftermath?" Miralda shook her head. "Their own grief beat them."

"Within a year, Haakon was dead. The sick, lecherous king had it coming, but it was the flea plague that took him. His son, Kjetill Stonebreaker, was a better king, called for Maeve to be executed, but she died before they got the chance. Lucky bitch." Miralda finished. "Her son offered his apologies, which the king forced the barons to accept. He was a much better and stronger king, so few protested. Still, those Hardstones got off easy."

"Ironhands don't like the Hardstones?" Minimoto asked.

"We came over here with them, following the three kings, as brothers and sisters. They were friends, family even, and she killed them without remorse. It's a pain that isn't easy to forgive." Miralda answered. "I'll stand with them for the king's sake, and Bulwyf has been nothing but a brother to me, but I will not risk another war with the barons. Gabriel has a chance to be our best king and this could ruin that."

"You're right, this could damage his standing, but Gabriel will not let this slide. Bulwyf knows that." Minimoto took a goblet of his own and poured wine for himself. "We have to prepare for the Elysians to come soon."

Miralda nodded and stood up to gather her forces to begin defense preparations.

To Kill an Emperor

The fortress that housed the Emperor of Fe was nothing if not massive, leaving Gabriel and his warriors little time to waste before being out of time within their surprise. Already threatened, their ambush was being alerted to guards. That could not deter the King of Lotcala. He had to press on and reach the Fesian Emperor, or the entire battle was lost.

Gabriel led his warriors back to the previous gathering point and waited. More Lotcalans and Amazonian warriors crested the battlements and joined the assault. Soon there were one hundred armed and ready warriors along the outer wall of the fortress, and more were still scaling the wall.

"We need to attack now." Laoch said. "Prefect Ino and her band must have already breached the city."

"We haven't heard an alarm, though." Carladias said.

An Amazonian joined the strategy. "If Ino was leading it, then the attack was silent. She'd be able to get in and out without a guard being alerted."

Gabriel and the others were just about to begin their push when horns blared as loud as the trumpeting of the heavens.

"Shit!" Gabriel exclaimed. "They've been alerted."

"Seems so." Laoch rolled his eyes. "We need to push now!"

Gabriel agreed. The King led his war party in between barracks and buildings, killing any Fesian that they came across. Many were rushing to the city center, but a few turned to stand face to face with oncoming warriors from Lotcala and Amazon. Fierce and merciless, the allied soldiers battle-hardened and fearless in their attack. This was a war waged from pure emotion and bent on revenge.

The Lotcalans fought with swords and shields, leaving the Amazons to their spears and shields. The alleys of the city were perfect for phalanxes. Tight and long, the alleys would provide the best choke point for the Amazonian warriors. Their fury rushed through their limbs and reddened their cheeks. Perhaps the Fesians could see it in the dim light of the dawn, but under the corinth helms of the Amazons, probably not. The last thing the Fesians would see would have been the point of a spear thrusting towards them.

Lower on the ground, Syrena watched as more and more warriors climbed the rope ladders. The Fesians hadn't yet caught on to the attack and she kept the trebuchets and mangonels firing, providing a distraction and another form of an attack. Cecilia rode off to the north, keeping the Fesian infantry and cavalry soldiers busy in their defense of the city.

That defense was wearing thin. Gabriel rushed through, but he and his compatriots noticed a lack of spirit from their opposition.

"They've retreated further into the city." Carladias said as she also noticed the lack of defenders.

The city of Fe, a stone complex atop a granite ridge that gave its name to the empire, was big but not as large as Jovag or Verna. There were fewer places for the defenders to hide if that was indeed what they were doing. The city itself was mud-brick and sandstone, apart from the outer wall. It could house thousands, but most were not soldiers, those were out in the deserts, with their tribes. Within the city of Fe the people were conscripts and others pressed into service when needed. Not everyone was a trained soldier, and that was the advantage that Lotcala and Amazon held because what Fe could bring to war, numbers far greater than other kingdoms, was neutralized in a siege.

That was why the assault was so critical. This was a battle that, for both sides, had to be won. What many outside of Fe had little knowledge of was how badly the Fesian populace loathed the imperial structure. While some pockets of resistance held out against the Amazons and the Lotcalans, many settlements stayed out of the fighting and left the centralized tribes to fight alone. Others, like the Bohiems, joined the invaders. The Bohiems rode north to assist with Cecilia's cavalry attack.

Ino and her sister Artemisia, along with their warrior band, stalked the guards and other soldiers running towards the center of the city. They knew that if they followed them, picking off a few at a time, then they would reach the main housing district of the city. It would take some time, but they would eventually reach their prey.

Gabriel was doing the same, searching for the emperor's lodging. The reclusive Hel was not one to venture out with his army, but they feared him anyway, almost with a godlike respect. However, many of his subjects, especially further out in the desert, did not share that view. To them Hel was another despot elected by the leading tribes that would never even step foot into their territory. That was a vulnerability that Gabriel and Syrena would exploit to its breaking point.

Hours after first breaching the wall, hundreds more warriors infiltrated the city with hundreds more coming, but the ruse was wearing thin. The Fesians were putting up more of a resistance, but the damage had been done.

Gabriel inched along a mud-brick wall near the central tower. It was eight stories high and heavily fortified. Across the courtyard, Gabriel saw Ino and her warriors scanning the courtyard. She looked over to him and motioned with her head to the right. He knew she had a way in.

"Watch Ino and move with her." He whispered to Carladias. The young archer nodded and crept out of the dark corner with a handful of archers and snuck over to another dark alley.

Artemisia stepped out from behind her older sister and shot an arrow, with a rope tied to the end, up to the top of the tower. It struck in the mortar between two bricks, the rope trailing behind it. Artemisia tugged at the rope and felt its tautness. Confident in the rope, she nodded to her sister and under the cover of darkness they rushed to the tower. Gabriel waved his warriors to follow as Carladias and her archers silenced the guards in the courtyard.

Gabriel and Laoch went to the main entrance and secured it from several more guards as arrows flew around them. Soon, guards were alerted to the invasion and now Ino and her sister were in danger.

"Carladias, keep the archers off the Amazons!" Gabriel ordered.

The young captain order her soldiers to do as commanded, and they fired volleys into the coming ass of warriors. More Amazons and Lotcalans fired rope tied arrows up to the tower, giving more secured lines to climb up.

Laoch heaved with his large shoulder and burst through the wooden door, right into the guards' quarters. The startled men shot up from their seats and turned to the man that rocked them from their rest.

Laoch drew his sword. "Well, come on them, you bastards!" He shouted before rushing into the group of guards.

Gabriel and four other Lotcalans burst into the room and joined their compatriot in the melee. The fight was intense as the Lotcalan king, his sword already bloody, pulled his ax from his belt and chopped at the Fesians. A sword in his right hand and an ax in his left, the king was a fearsome sight. His fellow warriors fought only with their swords, the area too tight for a shield to be effective. The element of surprise was enough to give them an advantage, however. Soon the fight was winding down as Gabriel pulled his sword from the belly of a Fesian man.

He looked around, seeing one of his men dead but the others okay, panting for air but okay. That is, until he heard a groan to his left. Gabriel turned to see Laoch clutching his side and huddling to the wall. The veteran warrior propped himself up against the wall and threw his sword down.

"Damn!" Laoch said, pulling his helmet off. His cloth coif stilled, tied under his chin. "Shit, they got me with a lucky strike on the side." He said, turning to show the blood to Gabriel. "It's a deep one, sire." Laoch fell to the ground, landing in a sitting position.

"Charles!" Gabriel yelled, rushing over to his friend. "Don't move, we'll get you a healer!"

Laoch coughed and chuckled, blood coming trickling from his mouth. "A healer won't fix this. Damn, shame I had to leave my mail." He said as Mestra rushed into the room.

The Amazonian mage knelt down beside Laoch and unfastened his gambeson. She looked at the wound, putting a hand to the bloodied area and feeling around the puncture, but she shook her head before standing back up. "I'm sorry, your grace but there is little I can do to heal him. The wound is too deep and the amount of blood loss and the other fluids flowing out tell me that they punctured his stomach and kidney. All I can do now is minimize the pain."

Laoch grinned. "I told you, sire. This is a wound you don't come back from Gabriel, my boy." Laoch sighed a labored breath and stood back up. "I hear plenty of fighting out there." He motioned with his head to the courtyard where more Fesians had started putting up a resistance. He looked back to the king. "Up those steps is the emperor, and that's where you need to go. I'll head out there and die like a loyal son of Theodorif!" Another warrior handed him his sword and Laoch staggered back out the door.

Gabriel hung his head, waiting.

"It's a warrior's death from a warrior's wound no matter where he falls." Mestra said from behind Gabriel. "We don't have the numbers to hold out with this plan. He is giving you time, your grace."

Gabriel gave a sign that he understood before running to the steps leading up to the tower. Mestra and Carladias, with ten other warriors, followed close behind.

Near the top of the tower Ino, Artemisia and several other Amazons neutralized the guards along the tower railings and walkways. Coming together, they burst into what they assumed to be the emperor's throne room. A few guards rushed them, but the Amazons struck them down with expert sword strikes and bludgeoning from the blunt handles on their falcatas.

The swift fighting was what the Amazons trained for and for Ino's band it was a deadly and surprise strike that served them best. The guards didn't put up much of a fight, and the Amazons hadn't suffered a loss.

Yet, the emperor was gone.

"They've moved him." An Amazon said within the empty room.

"Was he ever here?" Artemisia said looking around the gilded room decorated with gold leaf and exquisite silks. "This looks like a throne room, but is it?" She kicked down pillows and pulled silken sheets from ornately built divans and daybeds.

"How do you mean?" Ino asked.

"Look around and tell me that this is the throne room of a desert emperor. This looks like a room for concubines."

The others look around and agreed.

"Come out!" Ino shouted.

Nothing happened at first, but then a curtain moved and a group of women slowly walked out into the open. Ino and the other Amazons sheathed their swords. The thirteen Fesian women, one from each of the tribes, huddled together, scared. Each dress in fine fabrics and adorned with jewels. Their faces made up with pastels to give them an unfamiliar face than their natural beauty.

"Spoils?" Ino asked to Artemisia. The younger sister rolled her eyes and shrugged to Ino. "I'll take that as a yes then." Ino grinned.

Gabriel ran up the steps, but he didn't encounter any real resistance. Things were quiet as he and his band passed empty rooms and corridors along the way. As they entered the sixth story, a few more guards appeared and put up a defense along the stairways.

"We're getting close!" Gabriel yelled, cutting down a defender.

The lightly armed Fesians stood little chance against the heavily armed Lotcalans and Amazons. However, the tighter corridors were helping the Fesians level the playing field. Mestra saw a chance to turn the tide back to their favor.

Clutching a stone that hung around her neck, Mestra uttered a spell that darkened the tower and extinguished the flames on the torches. The fight subsided for a moment.

"Your grace, companions, shield your eyes!" Mestra yelled. "*As yparxei fos sto skotadi!*" She chanted in ancient Amazonian, bringing forth a brilliant light that burst throughout the corridor and blinding the Fesians. "Now, attack!" She yelled, stabbing a nearby guard.

Others squinted in the mage light but saw well enough to attack the temporarily disoriented Fesians. Entering the brightly lit hall, the Lotcalans thrusted forward with deadly precision and force, attacking with such violence that the last moments for many of the Fesians were filled with absolute dread.

Soon the torches returned to normal and the mage light flittered away, leaving the attackers standing within a pile of bloodied bodies. Carladias inched to a window and looked down.

"The tide is turning in the courtyard, sire! We have to hurry and end this before we're trapped up here." The young archer said.

Gabriel nodded and readied himself to break down the door leading to the last room. Mestra and Carladias stood to his sides as he burst through. Archers awaited him and his band. Arrows flew in an instant, one directly towards the king. Carladias was as quick as the arrows and knocked Gabriel out of the way, catching an arrow in her right shoulder. Her fellow archers launched a barrage of arrows through the doorway. Gabriel and Carladias, trapped on the other side, slid away. Gabriel flung his ax into a Fesian archer while Carladias used an overturned table to shield the both.

"Mestra!" Gabriel called out. "Burn the room!" He ordered as more arrows flew from both directions.

"My lord, I can't!" Mestra replied from behind the doorway. "I might hit you!"

"Do it!" Gabriel yelled in reply.

Mestra breathed a heavy sigh and steadied herself. She was an expert mage, arguably the best in the Queendom of Amazon, perhaps one of the best in the world, but she was not a battlemage. Her skills weren't as honed as those that trained to fight sorely with magic and magical weapons. She had little choice.

Mestra brought her right hand up and cupped it to her lips, reciting a spell taught to her by a southern mage. She closed her eyes, focusing on the warmth in her hand, and she turned to the doorway, ignoring the soaring arrows whizzing by her head. Instinctively she let go and whipped her hand forward, letting a plume of fire flew into the room, taking the form of an eagle.

"Gabriel, Carladias, come back now!" Mestra cried out to the two behind the table.

They did as she commanded as the room was engulfed in a searing flame. Gabriel dove out after Carladias and ducked behind the wall, along with the others from his band of warriors. They could feel the heat and for a moment they could hear the screams, but those agonizing wails silenced after a moment in the fire. Then it was over.

The heat stayed and a scent, putrid and acid, lifted into the air. It was the scent of flesh, burned and ripping from bone. More than one warrior bent over to vomit, but Gabriel sat and put his head down. Mestra had watched it all. She saw all the violence, the death and the burning. She watched each Fesian warrior turn into a blackened husk of flesh, bone and ash.

"I..." She stammered.

"You saved us." Gabriel finished for her. He stood and clasped her shoulder. "We have to find the emperor."

The warriors walked into the smoldering room and saw the remnants of the throne room, burned and still smoking from the lightly burning flames.

"There isn't another door." Carladias said, chocking from the smoke still lingering. "He must be here."

A Lotcalan that had joined them pointed with his sword to a body in the corner. "There, sire. The Fesian crown."

They all turned and saw in the back corner, crouching low, was the body of a man, burnt beyond recognition but still with the golden crown, though partially melted, upon its head.

"Emperor Hel?" Gabriel asked. No one really could tell, but the crown was unmistakable. "Throw the banner through the window. Let them all see." Gabriel ordered He then walked over to the body and pulled at the crown, removing it and part of the head with it. "This will be proof enough."

Walking out of the throne room, the warriors met up with Ino and the roped concubines. Once the women saw the partial head, and crown of Hel, they wailed and mourned. A few cast fearful eyes to the king as he walked past them. One dropped to the ground, dragging two other tied with her to the stone floor.

"Up!" Ino ordered, but the women were inconsolable.

Gabriel ignored it. He knew war had a price that had to be paid by one or both armies. Hel paid for his empire, and it was time to see if others would join him. There was little time to wonder as he neared the bottom of the tower.

A Lotcalan knight, a gentry-knight, Sir Gowan, joined Gabriel. "Sire, the Fesian have seen our banner and they've retreated to the alleys." The man reported. His armor was bloodied, and he was panting. "The remaining area of resistance is the bridge. The army there is holding strong."

Gabriel looked at the knight and acknowledged his report, but he remained silent. The king walked to the first floor of the tower. He looked at all the bodies, Fesian, Amazonian and Lotcalan. He saw amongst the Fesian bodies, the body of his former Lord Marshal, Charles Laoch. The price had been high on both sides, he thought.

"Find me a horse. We march on the bridge." Gabriel ordered. "We'll show them what is left of their emperor, and then they can gaze on their new king."

Outside, Gabriel saw the courtyard engulfed in flames and his own warriors and their allies running through the city trying to find any more pockets of resistance. Many of the conscripted tribesmen from throughout the empire threw down their weapons, surrendering to the attackers. The king smirked as his soldiers brought him a horse, the emperor's horse, saddled with a purple cloak and bridled silver and golden reins.

Gabriel rode through the town, Emperor Hel's broken head and crown held aloft in his right hand. Amazonian and Lotcalan warriors, atop stolen horses, rode behind him, shouting for all to turn their attention to Gabriel.

He was bruised, bloodied, cover in blood, both his own and from others, and he looked like a warrior as fierce as any from the days of the Gota conquest. He was the true king of the land and as he rode by the Fesians, cowering from the attack, they could see that Gabriel was the man they would now come to fear above all others.

Scorched Fields

Ter Nog was holding out from intense and desperate attacks by Isidore and his army of angry Elysians. The attacks by the Elysians were swift and disorganized, much like Bulwyf had predicted. It was as he planned it, with a perfection that even he was surprised by. Still, with little hope of breaking into the city, the Elysians stormed to the gates, battering ram poised and armed but they could do little within the smoke filled field.

The air was thin and black smoke covered the land that stretch into the Elysian camp. The choking smog even wafted to the Elysian camp, filling their tents and lungs, further demoralizing them with the smell of rotting corpses.

"Push!" Isidore ordered as his men tried for a fourth time to ram the gate down.

It did not help that the main gate of Ter Nog was the thickest in the kingdom, and the wall was the heaviest in terms of fortification. In fact, the baronial families took such care during the previous centuries that few nations could ever hope to bring the gate down.

Isidore ordered siege towers to be wheeled out, but the men always stopped short. Seeing bodies of women and children amongst the dead on the field pulled them out of the warrior mentality and gave them thoughts of home to their families. The towers were then easy prey for the ballasts, firing flaming javelins from atop the wall. Isidore was quickly running out of options and his men were running out of resolve. Bulwyf's plan was working better than anyone could have expected or hoped, and it looked as if he saved the city.

Many miles to the south, General Miralda and Border Force Commander Minimoto were having much more trouble holding back the thousands of Gota mercenaries and the Elysians that had invaded from the south.

Arana and Marluna joined in with the Thousand Man Battalion as a defensive unit, but no matter who would be sent out to fight and hold back the invading force, they'd come back battered and beaten. The good news was that they'd come back.

"We can't go on like this forever. Hardstone has to send his force down." Minimoto said to Miralda.

The two leaders were sitting atop their steeds overlooking the battlefield that lay before them. Bodies strewn across it.

"We need to glean the field." Miralda said, ignoring the comment about Hardstone, a baronial family that she held a great distrust for.

"And what of..." Minimoto began.

"They'll come, I'm sure and Creator help us when they do." Miralda answered, cutting off her friend.

Night would come eventually, but each day that broke was a day for more fighting and more death. Nothing but death. That was all that was known as each rising sun gave way to more sorrow. Miralda woke from her slumber, her tent small and sparsely kept. A warrior's tent. Miralda felt the cool of the air, her small fire pot had gone out and she wrapped her wool blanket around her. She crept out of her tent when a clamoring noise piqued her curiosity enough to make her move more than her need to relieve herself.

Upon leaving her tent she saw a mass of warriors, clad in chain mail hauberks and steel pot helms. Their armor looked like hand-me-downs, and for some they wore incomplete sets. Some didn't even have armor, only cloth and handmade weapons. Others, most in truth, had axes or pickaxes. Men and women, gruff and dirty. She saw the mark of miners, castles, horses and moons upon their shield and banners. These warriors were unmistakable.

"Fucking Hardstones." Miralda mumbled.

The warriors were loud and rowdy, undisciplined and fighting amongst themselves. Still, they had spirit and seemed to be energetic. Something in short supply.

Miralda returned to her tent, thinking little of the recently arrived warriors apart from her disdain for the barony. She finished her morning routine of calisthenics, washing herself, and dressing in her armor. Exiting the tent with her helm under her left arm, Miralda strolled through several groups of warriors standing between her and the manor house. All looked at her with trepidation. Miralda had a reputation for her strictness and temper. Her recent feat against Harbor and the invading army was also becoming well known. Whatever the relationship between her and the Hardstones, it was plain to see that they held a warrior's respect for Miralda.

The general walked into the manor house and stopped just after entering the doorway, spying Baron Hardstone in conversation with Minimoto and the Hardstone manor lords. He and his lords were not the giants that their ancestors used to be, genetics had a way of changing the younger generations. Hardstone still kept the reddish hair of his ancestors but as of late, due to age, his hair was greying more and more.

Miralda rolled her eyes and walked closer, putting her helm on the table. She matched or stood taller than everyman at the table, except for Hardstone himself.

"Baron Hardstone, welcome my lord." Miralda said, feigning a smile. "We were wondering when you and your lords would grace us with your presence."

Minimoto braced himself for the reply, but relaxed when he saw Baron Hardstone grin.

"Tis good to see ye here General." Sigmund Hardstone said. "What of yer baron? Is he still playing at war while we here fight to protect the kingdom?"

Miralda chuckled. "You're correct on the latter. We are here protecting the kingdom, from the south. My lord, Baron Ironhand, also a descendant from the conquest, is fighting to protect our home from the west." Miralda looked to the other lords and sneered before turning to Minimoto. "My lord commander, what is our plan now that Baron Hardstone and his noble lords have arrived?"

Minimoto cleared his throat, though, under his face wrap it might have been difficult to tell.

"We'll march south, meet the invading force head on and dig in. Develop a foot hold about ten miles south of the river." Minimoto answered.

Everyone around the table nodded or made a noise in affirmation of agreement. Baron Hardstone looked to Miralda and motioned with his head for her step to the side and join him in a private conversation.

"They tell me that there are Gota fighting with the Elysians? Bannermen at that. What truth did ye see?" Hardstone asked once the two had stepped away from the table.

Miralda looked around the room and guided Hardstone's gaze to something she pulled from her belt pouch.

"This was being carried but one of the fallen invaders." She said, handing the cloth to Hardstone.

"A black hammer on a green and white field. That's the ancient symbol of Thorifsonn." Hardstone said in a whisper. His accent on the name was strong with a gruff sound on the 'f'.

"I know that name." Miralda replied.

"They're an ancient hold from central Gotistan. They sided against Godfrey's choice of successor and were exiled along with other jarls." Hardstone answered. "That's the story, anyway.

'Could they have joined the Elysians as mercenaries then?"

Hardstone was quiet for a moment, but then looked to the woman. "It is possible, but so many years have passed, I'm surprised those Gota families are still alive."

"We are." Miralda pointed out.

Hardstone nodded. "Aye, yer right about that, lass."

From the table Minimoto called out to the two leaders asking for them to rejoin the strategy, but the plans had been decided and it was merely a formality.

"If we can develop a hold deeper into the southern lands, then we might be able to have a stronger staging point once the king joins us." Minimoto said to Hardstone and Miralda as they walked outside.

"Give me two weeks and I'll get ye yer staging point." Hardstone boasted. He mounted his horse and rallied the troops he had within the courtyard and marched them down to the field below.

Miralda watched, along with Minimoto, as the men and women left, arching to war.

"I know you don't like him much but I prefer him on our side." Minimoto said.

Miralda scoffed before walking to the stables and mounted her own horse. She trotted to where Minimoto stood.

"I'm taking the Thousand Man Battalion with me and my division. In four days' time I plan to have the south secured and ready for your arrival. Travel safe and Creator keep you my lord Minimoto." Miralda said before riding off with her housecarls following behind.

Minimoto watched them ride off, wishing them well and safety in their own travels. He knew that the war was only beginning for them, but he had no idea what of his king in the west.

"Sire, the city is nearly under our control." Sir Gowan reported to King Gabriel and Queen Syrena.

Gabriel's plan of showing the head of the emperor, atop the emperor's horse, worked to force the Fesian to drop their weapons. However, there was much to do before the invasion could be called a success and the war won. Gabriel was sitting on the bench in the tower's courtyard, watching Amazonian and Lotcalan soldiers move prisoners. He had a good vantage point to watch the healers go about their work, a welcomed sight.

The order went out the night before to round up any and all resistance, but to do so without harming the populace needlessly. That was the tricky part, but not unpopular by any means. The desert heat and sands had taken their toll on the two armies. This was a chance to rest, and with a small but important task of making sure the city was safe. King Gabriel wanted as peaceful a transition of power as possible, and judging by the lack of screams throughout the city, he felt confident that peace was maintained. Though, he was uncertain, he couldn't show it as he sat on a bench.

The king regarded the gentry-lord and waved him off, back to clearing the city of any resistance. A difficult enough job on most days, but an even more daunting experience given the nature of the city. Almost a labyrinth, yet organized, ruled by a tyrannical despot that bled his people and openly showed nepotism across the land. Still, the Lotcalans and Amazonians were the invaders and they might not always be greeted as liberators. The labyrinth of a city could prove to be more of a deathtrap if dealt with coarsely. That was why Gabriel had urged for peace in working with the residents of the city.

Syrena walked up to Gabriel and sat next to her husband. Both were dirty and bloody. Syrena, not content with managing the siege camp, had joined the force at the bridge, even after the proclamation of the emperor's death. Some held out and fought on. Syrena was caught within that fighting. Though brief, that final desperate battle was intense. She looked to her husband and then laid her head on his left shoulder.

"We'll leave a cohort here to help maintain the city." Syrena said. "I heard you were going to leave Ironhand and Coldwood here to garrison the lands."

Gabriel nodded. "Aye. I have to march back quickly."

"Yes, we do." Syrena added. She lifted her head up. "Ino and Mestra plan on joining us. I'm taking five thousand legionnaires with us, as well. A loan from the queen to help with the fighting."

Gabriel looked confused. "You're needed in the queendom." He said, looking to his wife.

"I will still be the Palatine of Caleope, and I'll visit as often as duty allows. However, my place is next to you for as long as I might live and your place is next to me. The queen has already given me my leave from the command post. She's ready to return to Verna anyway and rest." Syrena answered. "As for Ino and Mestra, they see things differently. Ino feels that she has worn out her welcome with my sister and Mestra wishes to improve upon Lotcalan mage guilds. They've asked and received their resignations from the queen, and I've given them approval as the Queen of Lotcala." She continued.

Gabriel protested, but Syrena stopped him. She clasped Gabriel's hand. "This is my decision, and the queen supports it. I'm your queen now, and that means that the day that we leave for Lotcala is my last day as the Legion Commander. It will also mean that two capable and confident Amazons will join us. Do not take that lightly. Both are giving up their positions and titles in the queendom, though Ino seems relieved to do so."

Gabriel stood up, still holding Syrena's hand, lifting her up as well. The two hugged, holding for a moment.

"Then we should prepare." Gabriel said, breaking the embrace. "We leave in five days." He finished before deeply kissing his wife.

An hour later Syrena walked to a small tavern where Ino, Mestra, Melantho and a few Furies had set up a makeshift headquarters. The women drank tankards of ale. Syrena sat down and pulled a pitcher of wine close, pouring some into a goblet.

"To our future!" Syrena toasted. The others cheered, raising their goblets in a toast. Syrena drank the cool wine and sighed. "The end of a career."

"You told him?" Ino asked. Syrena nodded, drinking more wine.

"You'll be missed Syrena." Melantho responded. "I'll visit when I can. Maybe I'll buy a plot of land near Jovag and farm."

Ino and Mestra laughed, along with the others in the tavern.

"What the hell do you know of farming?" Ino snorted.

"You put a seed in the ground and add water. What's to know?" Melantho answered with a laugh.

More laughter erupted from the group as a contingent of Queen's Legion burst in through the doors. The Furies shot up and guard themselves until they saw who was entering the building.

"Princess Syrena of Amazon, Queen of Lotcala. Your mother requests your audience." Sebula, the Queen's Legionnaire said.

"She does?" Syrena said.

"Yes, I do." Queen Saria answered from behind the tall legionnaire. Everyone dropped to one knee and saluted their queen. "Stand down, stand down everyone." She said, taking a chair from the next table. "Be a good subject and pour your queen a goblet from that pitcher there will you Melantho." Melantho quickly did as commanded, as the other Furies sat back down.

"Mother, what can we do for you?" Syrena asked, her left eyebrow raised inquisitively.

Saria drank the wine and gave a satisfied smack of her lips when finished. "This Fesian stuff always tasted damn good." She said, putting her cup down and motioning for a refill. "I used to be able to drink cask after cask in my younger days."

"That's impressive." Syrena replied. "Is that why you've come?"

"You think because I'm the queen that I can't drink with my subjects. I heard that King Liam often drank in taverns throughout his kingdom."

"Aye, he did, some." Syrena said.

"Yeah, well. I guess, I know time is short, and I wanted to enjoy a few tankards and pitchers before you and your sisters left." Saria responded, raising a toast to the ladies at the table and around the tavern. "Another thing brought me here." Saria continued before she took a sip of wine. "I know Ino and Mestra plan to leave with you, but I want you to take a few others. Still, Legionnaires mind you but to act as your personal guards."

"The king's guards in Lotcala –" Syrena began.

"They're fine and capable, but I want to send a few Amazons to be watchful as well. Especially during such a time as this war." Saria answered. "You'll take Leontia, Callisto and..." She paused and looked around the room. "Nyx!" She shouted, bringing the surprised Fury to her feet. "Sit down." Queen Saria said, and she waved her hand to the woman. "I heard you met a gentry-lord out in Antei that you've been enamored with. Better to go now than to wait for another few years. Besides, this way you can hold your oath to the legion and still make a way for love. You three will be Syrena's personal guards."

Nyx dropped to a knee and saluted. "Yes, my queen. Thank you."

"You're welcome, dear. Call me sentimental, but we should all be so lucky to find love, right?" Saria said before pouring herself another goblet of wine. "Now, one more before I head back."

"Mother." Syrena said. "Stay as long as you like with us here."

Saria smiled. "Of course." She motioned for her guards to sit and join them. "We should rest easy for a little while."

Entering Jovag during a time of war wasn't easy, even with a queen's letter of passage. Yet, Domino Eolas charmed his way past three city watches, two of the king's own guards and a small contingent of Quarmi watchmen. Honora was impressed, as was Megara and her fellow jailors, at the man's charisma.

"Now we have to get into the bank." The Amazon said to Domino. She stood at Domino's left while Honora followed closely behind. The other jailors stayed in the inn, resting from the long journey.

"That's the easy part." Domino smiled. He greeted the guards at the front entrance, then strolled right in once they moved to allow him and his band to pass.

"That's it?" Megara asked. She stepped closer to Domino and tried to keep up. The taller man hurried through the crowded building but the nimble Amazon was able to keep step with Domino.

"That was it. Now to see my uncle." Domino replied. He stopped and looked around for a moment until spotting a tall, grey-haired man near the back of the building.

Domino walked over to him, with Megara and Honora following behind.

"Uncle Vincenzo!" Domino exclaimed.

Vincenzo Gabon was an unremarkable man from a very remarkable family and in charge of a remarkable bank. He controlled the finances of many of the lower families of Aran and Lotcala. Some Coronado and Panyakutan families even reached out to him for loans.

Vincenzo smiled when he saw his nephew walking up to him. "Domino! Welcome, welcome!" He said, happily. "You've come to see your uncle at a great time. Interest rates are at a high and I can get you a great return on your previous investments." Vincenzo looked at the two women with his nephew, eyeing Megara mainly. "Domino, did you get married?!" He shouted, wrapping the younger man in a hug.

"What?! No, no, these ladies are..." Domino paused. "Uncle, we have to speak, privately."

Short time later, Vincenzo looked to his nephew from across his wooden desk. An iron scale and several sacks of coins rested atop, next to some official-looking documents and scrolls.

"You're not enough like your father." Vincenzo said. "You've been lucky and you're still lucky to have this way out of this mess. Selling arms to both sides during a war is punishable by death!" The older man stood up and looked out the window. "I should send all your gold north, to your father. Gods knows he could use it."

"I'm sure, and I plan to head back as soon as we settle this. Pardon withstanding." Domino said, with a look to Honora and Megara.

Vincenzo sighed. "Seven hundred pounds to the new queen. I've heard of her, but I've yet see her."

"She's an honorable woman, you can be sure." Honora said.

"I don't doubt, but this isn't normal, you understand?" The older man sat back down. "I'll retrieve your funds and we'll have them sent to the queen under your guards here. That I would have little option against, though I will say that I don't oppose it. Money wins wars and if this helps the war end sooner than later, then I agree with your request. However, as your uncle, I will say what will happen with the remaining three hundred pounds. I will send the remainder north to your father and my sister. They'll put it to good use. I'm sure better use than you would."

"Uncle." Domino protested.

Domino's uncle put a hand up to silence his nephew. "No, Domino. This is what I must do. Your father deserves much more. This money could help your family rise in their station. You'll be named as the benefactor. You might even be accepted home again." Vincenzo responded. He looked to his nephew. "Please understand that I do this because it is what's right and I'm doing it for you, Domino. Even if you don't understand now, you will one day."

Domino grimaced but relented. "Very well. Might I have fifty pieces to at least payback Honora for the inn and food along the way?"

Vincenzo nodded. "Of course. We are men that pay what we owe and we remember those that gave to us."

With the business concluded, Domino, Megara and Honora left the bank and returned to the inn. The funds were being assembled and would be ready the next morning. That left an evening to spend waiting.

"It was a good thing to send that gold to your family." Megara said to Domino over a plate of mutton at the inn. She saw his disappointment and though she was still his jailor, she had developed a friendship with the man. She was trying now to help him ease his mind.

Domino tried to smile at the gesture, but his embarrassment was greater than his humility.

"It was ill gotten." Honora reminded him.

"Yeah. That's why I was kicked out of my home in the first place. Selling ill-gotten goods." Domino joked. Half joked, anyway.

"You can't stop getting into trouble, can you?" Honora smirked. "You need a strong woman to set you on the right path and knock some sense into you." She smiled with a wink to Megara.

"No matter. We will deliver the gold to the queen and I'll have my pardon with a few coins to be on my way." Domino said. "Maybe I'll stop back by one day." He finished, looking to Megara.

"Just maybe?" Megara said. "Maybe we won't be there to welcome you." She huffed.

"Of course, I might find some use around here or in the queendom." Domino quickly corrected.

The two woman shot him suspicious glances.

"No, not the queendom." Domino said, catching their meaning. "Let's just get through this delivery and then we'll see what happens next."

"That sounds like the smartest idea you've had yet." Honora smiled.

Miralda and her thousands of warriors joined Hardstone in battle several days after leaving Antei. The fortified town was too small to support such a large force, but was been necessary. Ter Nog was the planned supply route, but with Bulwyf being trapped within the sieged city and Harbor having been killed in battle, there was no one left to provide the needed support. Lose in a battle on the southern front and it would be almost a week to get to the closest fortified position.

That is why Miralda and Hardstone had to win in the south and why they had to create a temporary fort. The fort that the baron and general were going to build would be of earth and wood. These weren't meant to stay forever, but in times of war these sorts of forts were useful in creating a barrier of defense.

Hardstone and his manor lords rode down with over a dozen housecarls each, a common practice in the old Gota traditions. Miralda watched them, flanked by her own housecarls.

"We've a lot of work to do here." She said to those around her. "Bring me Constantine. He'll take the lead in securing this area with a border fort." Miralda finished.

One of her riders accepted the order and rode off to find the engineer. At the same time, Hardstone approached atop a large brown steed.

"General, this place is hardly suitable for the other lords or me-self." The baron complained.

"And yet, it is quite suitable for me." Miralda answered, never giving the baron any eye contact. She looked past him to the rolling hillside. "In the previous battle, we slowed them by using the landscape of these hills. We were lighter then and we are lighter now. This hill is the tallest around and we'll use that to our advantage."

Hardstone bristled at the woman. "We need to meet them on the open field!" He shouted. "That is the warrior's way. Not hiding in a fort!"

Miralda now turned to regard the baron. "The warrior's way is to win the war by whatever methods results in as few people as possible dying. They fight as a shock and impact force. Against an earthen wall they won't have as easy of a time attacking as they do against a shieldwall. We can hold a defensible position like this for weeks on end. We tried an open field battle, and we lost."

"No general, *ye* tried an open field battle and *ye* lost." Hardstone replied.

Miralda ignored the baron's insult. She turned and pulled her horse's reins. "Do whatever the hell you want. You're a lord and I can't command you like I can those from my hold or the King's Army." She stopped and turned to the baron. "Just know, with these lords and warriors as my witness under the eyes of the Creator, I warned you." She finished before riding off to begin preparations for the fort.

Hardstone snorted and turned off, his lords in tow. Soon after, he mobilized his army and with the sun at its zenith, he marched them further south, trying to locate the Elysian army and their Gota outcasts.

Work on the fort began around the same time and continued on throughout the day and night. Miralda hoped for the help of the Hardstones. She wasn't a friend of many of them, but she would never deny their skills. In fact, that was part of her dislike. She had to respect their skills as warriors and as builders. Here, building the fort, that skill would be missed. However, she was consoled by the thought that if Hardstone met with the Elysians that they would buy her and her army some valuable time.

For Baron Hardstone, this was a chance to show his new king, a boy he knew little compared to the former king, Liam, that he could be the savior of the kingdom. Hardstones had been fighting beside the king since the first days of the kingdom, and even before the conquest. He had to continue the tradition of being there for the king, though he had been sent south instead of accompanying the king.

"Move, lads!" Hardstone shouted. "Sing a song for the march and move them legs as fast as they can go. We'll take Gib if we move fast enough, lads!"

His confidence was infectious and his men were in good spirits marching along the ancient trade roads that connected the two kingdoms. In times of peace, the road was well travelled by merchants. However, in recent months the roads were subject to raids on both sides. Baron Hardstone wanted to find some raiding brigands. He wanted a fight.

Soon, he'd have his fight.

The Lotcalan camp was still being set up as the horns from the Gota and Elysians blew in the distance. Terrible sounding omens of war, echoing throughout the hillside, drawing the attention of the Lotcalans. Hardstone mustered his warriors together, forming a shieldwall, facing the direction of the horns. His lords did the same, falling into line their lines.

The banners appeared over the hilltops, first the Thorifsonn banner followed by a few more that Hardstone thought looked familiar. It didn't matter because under the banners appeared the Gota warriors, standing alongside Elysians.

"Traitors!" Baron Hardstone yelled out.

The Gota and Elysians answered with their own yell before running down the hill. Like before, the Gota were armed with steel plate armor and heavy round shields. The Elysians wore their typical chainmail. The thunderous pounding of their run shook the ground. It could even be felt where the Hardstone army stood waiting.

Poised for the impact, Hardstone ordered his men to hold, but less than thirty seconds later the Gota army smashed into the Lotcalan shieldwall and again they knocked the human wall back some steps.

"Hold men!" Hardstone yelled out.

The fighting was already bloody and intense. The Lotcalans relied heavily on the shieldwall tactic, aligning themselves side by side and locking shields. It was often strong and allowed for the spearmen to make aimed strikes at the attacking soldiers.

However, spear points on the steel plate did little, and the Lotcalans were finding themselves on the losing end of the battle quickly. The Lotcalans stood their ground and dug in as deep as they could, but the push from the Gota mercenaries was too strong. Spear point thrusted out and found their targets' vulnerable areas. Blood flooded the ground, trampled men lay flat, while those still fighting ignored their fallen comrades.

The Gota mercenaries, fighting with spears and axes, tore through many of the Hardstone warriors. Superior numbers and weaponry gave these warriors from a far off land the distinct advantage. That did not mean that Baron Hardstone was out of the fight. The crafty Hardstone was a veteran of the wars with Balenor, and he knew about fighting warriors armed with heavy arms and physical strength. This was a moment that he could not afford to slink back. It was then that he did what any commander would tell their subordinates not to do. He broke the shield wall!

"Estan, Strongmotte!" Baron Hardstone called out. "Flank to the east! Curr and Highwind, flank west!" He ordered.

It was desperate, but he had to switch tactics at this point. His men could not hold the line, and he knew that, but he was willing on taking the gamble that they could be quicker than the Gota and Elysians.

"Draw them off the center and pull them to the flanks!" Hardstone ordered.

His manor lords and those that had come from Greenfield did as commanded. Each shifting their attack to the outer flanks of the invading army and exposing their weakness, speed.

"That's it, boyos! Strike fast at their sides and keep moving!" Strongmotte yelled, as his men fought on the left flank and pulling a portion of the Gota warriors with them.

Spear thrusts kept many of the Gota at bay and out of sword reach. Some battled through, finding holes in the Lotcalan ranks, but not all Gota were as lucky. With the Lotcalans spreading out and staying mobile, the Gota and Elysians had a harder time hitting their targets. Some invading warriors, out of frustration, rushed the Lotcalans and tried to fight on equal footing, some finding success. The Lotcalans that could capitalize on the fighting found that the steel plate had some weak points. Spears and swords pierced the sides under the ribs. Excellent swordsmanship could win a duel and with the shieldwall broken down, some Lotcalans cornered their opponents into duels.

The truth was that the Gota and Elysians were still better equipped than the Hardstone army and that would eventually turn the battle back into the invaders' favor.

Hardstone recognized this as well. He knew that for every man he chopped down with his ax, another would be ready. He also saw the distinct answer to their armor problem. The ax.

Baron Hardstone searched out and found his manor lord, Strongmotte.

"My good lord Cullen." The baron said. "Take yer men back and tell the general to prepare for the invasion with axes, polearms and hammers!"

"My lord baron, we can win." Strongmotte said.

"Nay, lad. I'll be staying put, buying ye some time, but ye need to go and tell the general how to beat these bastards." Hardstone said. "I'll be seeing ye one day though." He looked around and spotted his son, Sigurd. "Take Sigurd with ye." Hardstone said. "The barony will need a baron."

Strongmotte nodded. "Aye, my lord." He said, running off to grab Sigurd. The young man protested but saw his father and then gave his affirmation before calling out to the other warriors to retreat north.

"Hardstones!" Baron Hardstone called out. "Time to show these bastards who the true Gota are!" He yelled before leading his army into the main host of invaders.

The remaining warriors gave a hell of a fight, battering the invaders with a ferocious skill and expert fighting prowess. The battle had broken down from a pitched battle into a bloody melee and muddy brawl. Desperate still and not wanting to give the invaders a single second, the Lotcalans hit and slashed at anything that stepped in front of them. Whether it was a helmet or a chest plate. Even strikes on the arms and shoulders if need be. Any location they could find, the Lotcalans would strike and try to cause pain and if possible, death.

Valor, honor and chivalry had left the world during this battle, none wanting to give an inch or show any mercy. Warriors on the ground, bleeding from wounds, knew not to ask for quarter, for none would be shown. A man on the ground was simply a stepping stone to stomp into the muddy ground. If anyone walks again after such a battle would be only by the will of the Creator or the old gods. No mortal could say.

"Mages! Release yer spells while ye still can!" Hardstone ordered.

A few of the mages with strength still left did as ordered. Most of the Hardstone mages dealt solely with earthen spells, and these men and women sent shock-waves through the ground, toppling the warriors that could not move out of the way quickly enough. A few others could control fire and they sent flames through the invaders. A terrible sight, men burning in the steel plate armor, roasting from within and screaming in agony as they caught fire. Another putrid smell to add to the already thick air full of blood, flesh and shit.

The field was looking worse and worse from the splitting and shifting earth to the scorched landscape etching around the battle. The damage done by the magic would be hard to heal, and the damage done by the mortal warriors would leave spiritual scars that would never heal.

Baron Hardstone fought tooth and nail, losing the feeling in his right arm and relying on his shield to bash into his enemies. His helm still on his head, he would head-butt those that stepped close enough, but he was short on time and losing too much blood to continue for much longer.

The job was done, however. The Lotcalans had slowed the Elysians and the Gota enough and dealt more than enough losses. They had to stop and regroup. There would be damage to the countryside from the resupplying, but Hardstone grinned as he took an ax to chest, splitting his gambeson. He spit the blood that he regurgitated at his killer.

"Good one." He mouthed before falling to the ground.

Sigurd Hardstone looked down from a distant hill and saw the battle still raging, but he had to turn back before the temptation to return took him.

A Long March to Destiny

"Sister." A young mage said, walking up to Mestra as the Magister mounted her horse. Alongside Mestra was Ino and Syrena.

The two Furies nodded to the mage and rode off to the main gate of Fe, leaving Mestra with the young mage.

"Morea. You've fared well, I see." Mestra answered to her younger sister.

"I have. I had hoped to see you before now, but…"

"The war." Mestra finished. "The prefect has reassigned you, I heard." Mestra steadied her horse. "The light horse cohort."

"Actually, I refused it. I've joined the supply cohort. Mother won't be happy. Two daughters to shun the cavalry." Morea grinned.

Mestra chuckled. "She still has Meeka. She'll graduate this coming spring and she'll make a fine horsewoman."

"Aye." Morea nodded. "Perhaps we'll see one another again soon. There are things I wish to learn."

"I thought you passed your magister exam. You should have all the knowledge you need."

"It's not that sister. Our curse." Morea answered.

"A blessing if used properly." Mestra corrected.

Morea shook her head. "These things, the darkness connects us and you've ignored my pleas for help." The younger woman felt the weight of emotions stir.

Mestra turned her horse. "I must go with the Queen of Lotcala. She awaits and you know she is not always a patient woman. Is there something you need of me?"

Morea looked to her sister. Tears formed in the corners of her eyes. "I've seen what must happen." She said with a sniff. "I know what others could never imagine."

"I have seen it too."

Morea fought back her tears. "Then what do we do?"

"Nothing." Mestra answered.

"How can you say nothing? These are images that tear at my soul and mind, leaving me in cold sweats during the night! For all of your knowledge, tell me how to stop these images!" Morea pleaded.

Mestra dismounted her horse and wrapped her sister in a hug. "Do nothing." She said into Morea's ear. Mestra pulled back slightly to look into her sister's eyes. "The more you try to stop something, the more inevitable it becomes. Nothing that you've seen is written in stone. That is the best and only lesson I could ever teach you. When you do nothing, then you've done what is meant to be." Mestra said before hugging her sister again. "It is a blessing to know that the world has its own plan and we simply need to do nothing to find happiness. Look beyond what you see and look for what you don't see." She finished before breaking the embrace and mounting her horse.

Morea wiped away a tear and waved to her sister as she rode off to the gates.

Mestra turned around and looked back to her sister. "I'm sorry, I was wrong. There is one other lesson I can teach you." She called out. "Always be loyal to those that are loyal to you, before you're loyal to any crown." Mestra yelled to her sister before turning back toward the gate and speeding off.

Morea watched her ride away and then grabbed her helm and other gear. She walked over to the supply train and found the sergeant the prefect assigned her to.

"Magister Morea Pappas reporting in." She introduced herself.

A young but confident legionnaire turned to Morea. "Well met Magister Pappas. I'm Sergeant Garra Leos. I was just welcoming in our other recruit. This is Sebula Kouris. Welcome to the supply cohort." Garra said with a smile to the two women.

Gabriel and Syrena marched at the head of the host of warriors, numbering close to thirty thousand. While the Saxe and other tribes, originally loyal to Fe, were still being fought in the outskirts of the former empire, the Bohiems sent a contingent of riders along with the king and his army. This would help to offset the men Gabriel had to leave behind to protect and subdue the nearly conquered lands.

Syrena rode at the head of the five thousand legionnaires that Queen Saria sent with her. The other legionnaires were busy in Fe, helping to settle the lands. Three Prefects stayed behind to help control the populace, while the fourth, Melantho, rushed off to Varus-dun. She took half of the infantry cohort and most of the artillery cohort to lay siege on the fort. That fort, if won by the prefect, would be given to the queendom after the war was won. If they won the war. Until the army reached the Sunset Mountains, Melantho would march alongside Gabriel and Syrena.

The land that the fort guarded was long contested between Amazon and Elysia. Each laid an ancient claim over the old fort and the surrounding lands, but neither could secure it for long. This was Amazon's chance to do so.

For Gabriel, the war itself was far from won. While Fe put up much less of a fight than he expected, Elysia was stronger than anyone imagined. His reports were growing more worrying with each day. News reached him of Ter Nog's siege and of Miralda's defeat along the southern border roads. Now he heard that the Hardstone and Greenfield army, minus the absent Baron Walafrid of Greenfield who was ill within his manor, was marching off to fight the supposed Gota army. That was the most troubling development.

Gabriel, and some barons, had heard tales of exiled chieftains that sailed south in the centuries past. These were still Gota, but they were not related, symbolically at least, to the Lotcalans like the jarls of Gotistan were.

Gabriel welcomed all the scouts that came. He needed the news; it broke the silence of his tent. Leaving Argyle in Fe left Gabriel with no one to talk with. Queen Syrena, though she'd visit, was often with the Legion since that was their tradition and there was still work to be done in transitioning the command of the Legion to Melantho. It would still be a couple of days of marching before the army would split and

Melantho would take the lead of the Legion and march her cohorts to the Elysian fort.

Gabriel was sitting, reading a missive that had come to him earlier in the day, when Syrena walked in.

"My king, are you indisposed?" Syrena said, pulling the flap of Gabriel's tent back.

Gabriel looked up and smiled. "For you, never."

Syrena walked in, pulled a stool and sat next to Gabriel. "You have news?"

"Nothing new. Hardstone marched south and split from Miralda's army. He intends to battle the Elysians in Elysia." Gabriel said, handing the missive to Syrena. "My concern is the lack of resistance we found at Fe. Why was so much of their army not their guarding the city?"

Syrena read the note but put it to the side. She looked to her husband and put her hand on his forearm.

"You're tired. Rest." She said to him. "There is still a long road ahead of us."

"I know, but there is much to do." Gabriel replied, smiling. In truth, however, he was exhausted, as was she, but he had to maintain his strength for his kingdom.

"This burden is larger than either of us could have imagined." Syrena began standing up. "Right now we should have been preparing to travel back to Caleope for the winter season. Warm wine and game each night by a roaring fire." She said, unfastening the greaves on her shins.

"What are you doing?" Gabriel asked, looking at his wife undressing.

"I'm getting ready for bed. I know it has been a while since we've shared a bed but you don't sleep in your mail, do you?" Syrena quipped.

Gabriel chuckled softly. "No, I don't." He answered, standing to remove his gear. He looked at Syrena, having trouble with her cuirass' side fasteners. "Let me." He said, reaching over and undoing the buckles.

The metal chest armor fell with a thud to the floor. Gabriel stepped back to remove his tunic and breeches while Syrena finished undressing. Gabriel gently took Syrena by the hand and pulled her close to him, kissing her deeply. They laid down on the cot that was beside them and enjoyed a quiet night together before the weight of the world took over again in the morning.

Megara walked out her room in the tavern, trailed by Domino, joining the other jailors and Honora near the cart of gold.

Honora and the jailors gave her knowing smirks. Megara ignored them at first, but when their smirks turned to laughter as Domino grimaced from a pain in his hip, she shot each a glare.

"It was one time." Megara said, rolling her eyes. She gave a shy grin over to Domino.

"Well, one night. Several times from what we could hear." Honora joked, bringing a laugh out of everyone but Domino. She looked to the man as they mounted their horses. "Relax Domino." The veteran said. "It's an honor to have the love of an Amazon." She smiled. "Alright then, let's head on to Fe and to Princess Syrena." Honora said, snapping the reins of her horse and urging the beast onward.

The group of Amazons and the Sile noble exile left the city, weighed down with seven hundred pounds of gold meant for the new Queen of Lotcala. The ride would take a couple weeks at least and the last reports had Syrena near or at Fe, depending on who you listened to. However, Honora was certain that would change.

"Be on the lookout for trade caravans and official riders. They will give us news on the princess' movements." Honora said, driving the wagon onward.

"This much gold puts a target on our backs." Domino said, sitting next to the veteran Amazon. He looked around, trying to see his surroundings. "Bandits are common along the sunset mountains."

"Aye, that is true. However, most wouldn't be fool enough to attack a group of Amazons." Honora smiled. "Besides, I have a feeling that we won't be going through the mountains."

"Why not?" Domino asked.

Honora smiled to the Sile man. "More traders are travelling the roads than when we road into Lotcala. A few weeks ago the roads were lonelier. Now the roads are coming back to life."

"They've won." Domino reasoned. He was happy at the thought.

Perhaps a victorious queen would be a happy and merciful queen, Domino reasoned, thinking to Saria of Amazon. He wasn't sure just how much authority Syrena really had over his release, and he wondered how loyal Megara would be, even if she professed her love for him. Still, the thought of peace to the land was something that sat well with the man.

"So we should head closer to Amazon or Elysia?" Domino asked.

"I believe so, yes." Honora said. "Watch for riders bringing news, but I think soon we'll be turning south."

Miralda welcomed Sigurd and his warriors into the fort. They were battered and beaten. The young Hardstone, just nineteen years old, was distraught and weary. Miralda saw his demeanor and that of his fellow warriors.

"Damn." She said to herself, watching the men and women trickle into the earthen fort. "They didn't stand a chance." She commented to one of her housecarls.

"They died protecting the kingdom." The guard said.

Miralda nodded. "Yes, but they didn't have to." She replied.

The housecarl looked to his lady. He respected her, but he was more experienced in the ways of war. He'd felt the sting of defeat and he knew what it was to lose so many in one battle.

"My lady, with all due respect, these men and women need a kind and supportive hand right now. You've led us and many others faithfully for years and your ferocity is what we love about you, but the army sometimes needs the hand of a mother." The housecarl said.

Miralda eyed her guard and sighed. "You sound like my father."

"A wise man if there ever was one." The housecarl grinned. Miralda scoffed before walking over to Sigurd.

She grabbed a pitcher of water and handed it to the young man.

"I was about your age when I was handed my first real defeat." She began as Sigurd accepted the offered pitcher. "I was riding west with Baron Ironhand, right into the heart of Balenor, when we were ambushed by an orc legion." She sat next to the young man. "Those bastards were merciless, and we barely made it out of there with our skins."

Sigurd looked to the general. "Did your father die in that battle, my lady?"

She shook her head softly. "No, he didn't."

"I'm sorry, my lady, but I don't think you're the one that can console me right now."

"Perhaps not, but you're not the only that lost a father today. Others have lost that, a son, a mother, a daughter or sister and brother." Miralda said, standing up. She looked down to the young baron. "If what we've heard is correct, then you are now the Baron of Hardstone and it is up to you to now lead those men and women from the barony." She then grabbed Sigurd's gambeson and hauled him up and onto his feet. She pulled him so fast that his surprise was plain on his face and he dropped the pitcher. "Now, stop acting like the world is ending and lead these men and women as your father would want you to." Miralda said, pushing the young man back a step. "Ready your men, my lord, we have a defense to prepare." She said before walking back to her tent.

Sigurd quickly went to work, gathering his men and ordering them to various areas of the ramparts, having them help finish building the fortifications. It was hard work for the weary warriors, just back from a disheartening defeat, but the King's army welcomed and shed tears alongside them as brothers and sisters. They offered hope and consolation in the tragic time, but they also offered a chance for revenge.

"These were Gota plain as day." Sigurd said, as he and Manor Lord Strongmotte joined General Miralda and her officers in her tent. "They were stout as us and their banners all should the markings that our fathers and grandfathers spoke about."

"Exiles?" Miralda asked.

"Aye. The exiled chieftains." Strongmotte answered.

"The king is going to love this." Miralda said. She looked to everyone there. "Form the garrison and be ready when they come. Bulwyf is holding Isidore and he can, but be certain that if he fails or Isidore sees another option that we'd be powerless to stop him." She looked to one of her housecarls. "Send a rider to Minimoto with news. He must get word to the king as fast as he can."

Sigurd looked to the woman and raised an eyebrow. "What do we do if Isidore breaks from the siege and heads to Coldwood or further in?"

"That would be for Minimoto to defend and for any king's soldiers to stop." Miralda answered. She crossed her arms. "Let's hope it doesn't come to that. Most of the king's men are here with me or in Antei."

She looked to the baron and manor lord. "You can bet that the king will call on the lords for more men after this war."

Just then a young woman rushed into the tent. She was only twenty, red headed, short and stocky.

"Forgive me, but I rode as fast as I could from Antei." The young woman said.

"Who the hell are you?" Miralda asked, scowling at the woman.

"Cwenwyth?" Sigurd asked. "Cwenwyth Highwind?"

"Aye, it's me, my lord Sigurd." The woman smiled and curtsied. She looked to Miralda. "Forgive the intrusion, but I received a rider among the others that my father and brother fell in battle." She said, handing the note to Miralda. "I'm the last of the Highwind family and so I'm the new manor lord... umm... lady, I suppose."

"Well met then, Lady Cwenwyth." Miralda said. "Do you have any knowledge of warfare?"

Cwenwyth shook her head. "My brother was the fighter."

Miralda faintly smiled. It was as she had suspected looking at the woman in a fine linen dress. "Then allow us this time to..."

"I can heal, though. I've trained as a mage." Cwenwyth interrupted.

"Then perhaps you'll be of use." Miralda said. "Let's continue on." Miralda looked back to the map. "The king's army will march from the west, most likely along the Amazon road toward Antei. Minimoto must direct him here and as our force here relieves Antei. Once the king arrives, then Minimoto will march with the king and resupply us here. We have to hold out until then."

"Will we stage our forces here for an invasion?" Sigurd asked.

"If the king deems that to be the proper course of action." Miralda answered. "Until that happens, though, we should prepare for an attack."

"An attack?" Cwenwyth inquired.

"Yes, my lady Cwenwyth. I'd advise you to prepare your best potions and spells while we finish this fort. Baron Hardstone, if I might ask you to direct your men that can move well enough to help with the fort's construction."

Sigurd nodded. "I'll direct them right away." He said before exiting the tent with Manor-lord Strongmotte and others from their homeland.

Cwenwyth stayed behind with the general and her guards.

"My lady, is there something else. I believe I gave your orders."

Cwenwyth stiffened. "Forgive me, but I believe that as a manor lady that I outrank the daughter of a gentry-lord."

Miralda smirked at the words. She knew that she'd always have to fight against the hierarchy. In truth, it was a hierarchy she loved and fought to protect.

"Normally, my lady, that is true. However, here in this camp, a camp commanded by a general in the King's Army, appointed by King Liam, Creator keep him, and confirmed by King Gabriel, I outrank everyone."

Cwenwyth smiled curtly, accepting the reasoning but not liking it. "Very well then, general. I just thought maybe you had forgotten your place." She said before turning to leave.

"Good lady Cwenwyth, my place is where the king assigns me. My father taught me that. He also taught me the value of being grateful for what I have and for my birth status because those things are fleeting." Miralda said, walking around the table and looking down on the shorter manor lady. "One more thing, my lady. When Minimoto comes, as the king's appointed commander of the border forces, he will be in charge and he knows his place as well. A Quarmi warrior will outrank you. Does that sit well with your ladyship because if it doesn't then too damn bad." Miralda grinned as Cwenwyth left the tent.

"She controls a large swath of land that supplies many minerals and metals to the kingdom." A housecarl in the tent mentioned.

"Then she really should start acting like a lady now. It seems that she spent too many days away from the courts." Miralda replied.

The general thought to her time as a youth and a teen. Often, Miralda was invited into her father's court to see how he would rule over his small patch of land. Life was different for most gentry-lords when compared to the other noble ranks. While most had land and tenants, few had actual courts like the Holt family did. However, all manor lords had courts and ruled over land. In Miralda's mind, Cwenwyth should have had some practice in courtly life. Even as a lowly gentry-lord's daughter, Miralda had practice and knew her place in the kingdom.

Riders were spreading out throughout the lands. Some rode west from Fe to treat with outreaching tribes or the other kingdoms in the west. Some went north to Coronado, while others rode east and south to the safer lands of home for Lotcala and Amazon. These were the riders heralding the good news of victory. Queen Saria of Amazon had returned home to Verna, Princess Cecilia was to join her shortly, leaving soldiers behind to help bring a peaceful transition.

Honora spotted one Lotcalan light horseman pushing his horse hard along the road between Fe and Antei. She waved the man down and welcomed him to her entourage.

"Good rider, you look famished, as does your steed. Rest a while and eat with us." Honora said with a smile.

"Forgive me, but I'm too busy to stop. I must report the victory in Fe to the baronies." He replied.

"Good news indeed." Honora smiled and smiled to her band. "We're taking this wagon to your new queen." She said, handing the papers with her name and her orders from Syrena to the rider.

"We'll met, my lady." The rider said, bowing his head. "My mother is from Amazon and has told many tales of you, Lady Honora."

Honora blushed. "Those tales were exaggerated, I'm sure. Was she in my Legion?"

The rider shook his head. "A levy."

The jailors gave a knowing look. Levies were rarely welcomed in the ranks of the legionnaires. Honora, however, smiled at the young man.

"Our army would be all the less without the support that the levy gives us. Too bad many from today's generation ignore their contributions." Honora said.

"Thank you, my lady." The rider said. "My mother spoke of your kindness and honor in leadership."

"Please join us for a meal before you continue on. I'd be honored to repay your mother for her support by offering you food and rest." Honora implored.

The man smiled and nodded, dismounting to join the Amazons and Domino.

"Since this is for the queen, might I suggest that you travel to Antei instead?" The man said, taking a seat on the blanket between two of the jailors. "The queen rides with the king for his baronial home."

Honora and Megara smiled at one another. "Thank you, good rider. We'll set out for Antei once our meal is done." The veteran said, gratefully, handing the rider a water skin.

Gabriel and Syrena made excellent time riding to Antei. They were just a day out when word came of Hardstone's loss and Miralda's encampment. The king urged his horse onward, wishing to reach Antei as soon as possible. The situation was dire, even as the king read the report of Gota mercenaries, knowing the old tales, he felt in his heart the reason that Fe had so few soldiers was soon to be revealed.

"The Gota exiles have risen from the south and have stormed our lands!" Gabriel shouted at the camp that night. "Worshippers of gods that twist the minds of men and followers of false prophets!" He continued.

His barons and lords around him all listened to his anger and frustration. Ino and Mestra looked on but felt compelled, as followers of the old gods, to fall back a few steps. Syrena stayed beside her husband, willing to accept any sort of scorn from the surrounding lords. There would be none.

Even in the Kingdom of Lotcala, a home for those that believe in the Creator, shrines and temples to the old gods still existed in many areas of the kingdom. However, a darker tale was often remembered of the Gota exiles. A tale that spoke of their faith in Hul, the Goddess of the Night. It was her priests and priestesses that still practiced human sacrifice, and even tales of feasting upon those sacrificed were told in whispers around the lands. Most traders avoided the lands of the exiled, but few knew where they called home.

Gabriel hunched over his table, maps and reports strewn across. He stayed like that, in silence, with those around him, for several moments.

"Sire, would it be prudent that we let the lords sleep now?" Baron Canton spoke up. "The ride here was long and tomorrow promises to be just as long of a ride."

Gabriel looked up and saw their weary faces. The war was taking its toll, but most of it was from the riding as opposed to the fighting. The king nodded and then waved everyone off. The lords and Amazons bowed before leaving the king and queen alone.

"We'll get there in time." Syrena said to Gabriel. The king simply smiled in reply.

Less than a day's ride away, Minimoto was amongst his army. He'd spent the weeks since the war began preparing the town for another attack, but he was grateful for Miralda's defense to the south. That fort would provide the town with some breathing room, however, it wouldn't hold forever. Especially not with added soldiers from Fe.

Minimoto prayed that the king would arrive soon, knowing that he was not far off, but each moment mattered. His garrison suffered with each passing day, wanting to fight to avenge their fallen friends, brothers and fathers. No matter how wounded, these were soldiers still ready to march and die for their kingdom.

Fighting alongside the king again would be a blessing. The king's own battalion marched with Miralda, but Minimoto was ready to ride to Elysia and to the glory of what the future held. All he could do now was mobilize any fighting men and women that were willing to go into Elysia, not a hard task. However, Minimoto was up against time. He knew that Miralda needed relief and her days would be numbered without reinforcements soon. His duty now was to make sure that the king would have an army ready to march as soon as he arrived.

Winds from the north brought little relief from the smoke of previous battles choking the sky. The air was heavy with the smell of burning flesh and char.

Constantine, a captain within Miralda's army, walked up to the general. "The smell burns my nostrils."

Miralda was sitting on a stump, sharpening her spatha, a long one handed sword with a stout handle and guard. Her other sword, the longsword from her duel with Harbor, sat to her left side. "You'll never get used to it, either." She commented.

"Why do they burn the bodies?" Constantine asked, looking towards the black smoke rising off to the south.

"Old traditions of battlefield tactics." Miralda said dismissively. "Just a way to demoralize us. They act like demons and we run scared."

"Yet, we aren't running." Constantine replied.

Miralda looked up to her captain. "Run where?" She replied stoically.

The blowing of war-horns and Miralda's own scouts gave her fair warnings of the approaching horde, but nothing could prepare her or her army for the totality of what was coming. The King's Army and the baronial armies were outnumbered three to one.

The general stood and looked to the south.

"Ready the defenses." She said to the captain. "We hold here or we die for the kingdom."

The hills around the earthen fort rumbled with life. Deer rushing through the meadows and birds flocks flying away from the torrent of feet running to take their place along the rolling hills. War cries and taunts followed the bloodthirsty warriors down the hills, their banners waving through the air.

This was the stand that General Miralda knew she would have to make, eventually. Maybe something inside of her had hoped that the Elysians would hold further south, but she knew that wouldn't be true. The hardened general stood on the rampart and watched down as the Elysians drew closer.

"Time for something from Bulwyf's book." Miralda said. She raised her sword and then dropped it quickly, shouting her order. "Loose!"

A volley of flaming arrows soared passed her and down onto the pitch soaked grass just passed the fort, igniting the land in a terrible blaze. Luckily, this caught many of the Elysian and Gota warriors in the torrent of fire and flames, burning them in their heavy plate.

Miralda saw the darkening skies and then looked down from the rampart. "This will not last." She said to herself before walking down and back into the fort. "Prepare for rain." The general told one of her captains. "When it comes, so will they." She said before walking back towards the stump she sat on earlier. She picked up her longsword, a true two-handed sword, and buckled it on her waist.

The general was wise enough to understand the changes in the weather and how to plan for the enemy's tactics. As sure as the rains came, so too did the Gota and Elysians!

"To the ramparts!" Miralda ordered. She unsheathed her longsword and stood atop the earthen mound. "Give them hell or die trying!"

A horde of Gota stormed up the muddy hillside where Miralda and her army were waiting for them. The Gota, with their axes, did little to mount an attack up the hillside, but the Lotcalan archers rained down as many deadly volleys as they could. The rains poured down, limiting the archers' visibility and hampering any offense. This was going to be a factor, and Miralda knew it.

The Gota regrouped at the base of the ramparts and let loose their own arrows. Aimed at the fort, the arrows evened the battle for the invaders. While arrows flew on both sides, the Elysians stacked timbers, to give a foothold up the muddy embankment of the fort. Within two hours the Gota and Elysians had a way up the ramparts and into the fort.

"On the ramparts, now!" Miralda ordered, leading her army to the defense.

The fearsome general wasted little time rushing to the top of the fortification and dispatching several incoming Gota warriors. Other Lotcalan warriors followed her lead and joined her in a frantic defense of the fort.

Miralda swung her longsword with all her might. She kicked one warrior in the face as he tried to climb up close to her. Others tried to cut and chop at her feet, but the general was quicker than their attacks. Miralda's housecarls joined in the battle with many other warriors from within the kingdom. This would be the fight to hold back the invading horde. If Miralda and her army failed, then the capital would be left exposed. The King's Army had to hold!

Turning the Tide

Honora, Domino, and their band found the town of Antei ready to ride out. The king and queen having just arrived and ready to move south to relieve the general.

"We must get to Syrena." Honora said as they pulled the wagon into the main gate of the town.

Megara looked around the busy marketplace, seeing so much commotion she reasoned the queen had to be up the motte.

"That is the baron's manor." Domino replied. "If she is anywhere in this town, it would be there." He agreed.

Honora drove the wagon past the lower bailey of that surrounded the motte. Many of the Lotcalan soldiers gave her strange looks, but the Amazons that came with Syrena bowed and saluted. They knew exactly who was driving the wagon.

The wagon stopped at the top of the motte, met by two legionnaires. "My lady Honora, what are you doing driving the wagon while those beneath you sit in the back?"

Honora smiled at the guard. "My dear, there is no greater honor for someone than to do the duties that are needed. Truly, none are beneath me, a broken down old woman with a cane instead of a sword."

The guards smirked. "Only a fool would think you are a broken down, old woman."

"A fool may the world be. Alas, I need the ladies in the back of this wagon and upon their horses to watch the goods we carry. This wagon is for the Queen and King of Lotcala and none other." Honora replied.

The guard nodded and motioned for the wagon to be let through.

In the courtyard they found many lords and officers rushing off to ready their soldiers. In the middle was Queen Syrena, standing with several legionnaires.

"We'll push to the capital while you need to take your warriors east to Ter Nog. The king will spearhead the attack and I'll ring up the rear with the siege equipment." The queen was ordering when Honora approached, Megara and Domino in tow. Queen Syrena looked up to see her former commander. "Lady Honora, you've arrived. I wondered if you would get turned around."

The veteran smiled to Syrena. "A kind rider pointed us in the right direction, and here we are." Honora bowed.

"Well met, Commander Honora." Mestra said, walking up to the group. "I have missed your tales and lessons of yesteryear. All the whimsical advice seems to be in short supply lately."

Honora smiled to the mage. "I have a few more if you're interested."

Syrena turned to regard her friend. "Have some legionnaires unload the cart. That is the army's pay." She smiled.

"The fabled gold from the swindler." Mestra winked to Domino. "Not how I pictured him at all. Much more handsome than you described him, Syrena."

"Careful there, Mestra. Megara has laid her claim to this one." Honora pointed.

That brought a laugh from around the group. All except Domino.

"I believe there is a pardon for me to accept. Safe passage as well." Domino said. He had his arms crossed and ignored the rolling eyes of the Amazons around him.

"There is indeed." A male voice said from behind Domino.

Everyone turned to regard the man. Domino knew the voice from a previous encounter. He lowered his head and turned. His red tunic, embroidered in silken designs, was a stark contrast to the dirty and worn mail and leather armor worn by King Gabriel.

"You are Domino Eolas, correct?" The king said.

Domino bowed. "Yes, your grace."

"We met once, a year or so ago when I first arrived home." Gabriel said, motioning for the man to rise.

Domino nodded slightly. "We did. I sold your garrison here some iron ore for spear points."

Gabriel grinned. "Yes, you did. Fine materials. You have my thanks for that and for dealing fairly with us."

"Oh... of course, your grace." Domino stammered.

Gabriel took the man by the shoulder and walked him away from the Amazons. "Your uncle sent a letter ahead of you and my wife has filled me in. I'll let you have a place here in Lotcala and the past crimes will be forgiven here in the kingdom."

"Thank you, sire..."

"But," Gabriel interrupted Domino, holding his hand up, and he turned to look him in the eyes. "If you do anything to betray us, I will personally execute you." Gabriel looked at the man and motioned for him to return to the Amazons. "We have an accord." Gabriel announced to the group.

Megara walked up to Domino and stood close to the scared man. He did well to steady himself and feign a smile. The others went about unloading the wagon and gathering more materials for the next march.

Gabriel conferred with the other lords and the officers. "We leave before the first light. I want to be there as soon as possible and relieve the fort."

The other lords agreed and went about readying themselves.

Hell hath no fury as an outnumbered army, surrounded and with no hope of survival. That was what the Gota mercenaries found awaiting them as they attempted, repeatedly, to storm the constructed earthworks. This was the battle that none of the invaders expected. Not after the last pitch battles. Here the Gota mercenaries, known worldwide for their battle prowess, learnt the might of their long-lost cousins.

General Miralda, covered in blood and screaming with the wail of a demon, ordered more troops onto the ramparts. They were sorely needed to relieve the tired or wound or replace the dead. However, she found that fewer and fewer could answer her orders. She did not hesitate to jump in, but she was feeling the fatigue herself. Those first hours turned into two days of brutal fighting, and the victor was as far off as when the battle first begun. That, however, was a blessing for Miralda. For every hour they held, the better chances Minimoto and hopefully the king would have in the coming days.

Let no one say that the bravery of either side failed in any respect during that battle. As fierce as the Gota legends spoke of the warriors, the Lotcalans put fear into the hearts of their kin. With so few to stand against them, the Gota thought the battle to be another victory, but Miralda showed the true grit, killing each who dared face her. Others from her army did the same. Still, inevitably, the enemy would breach the fort.

That was when the fighting became the toughest and bloodiest of the two days. The Gota leader, a towering man that stood almost seven feet tall, led the warriors down to the ground level of the fort. There he found Miralda, flanked by Arana and Marluna.

"Marluna see to the north palisade, Arana you go to the east. I'll handle the south." Miralda instructed before catching sight of the Gota leader. "Or I'll handle this bastard." She said, unsheathing her spatha.

The Gota leader nodded. He wore the sigil of Thorifsonn, painted on his breastplate.

"You must be Thorifsonn." Miralda yelled out. The man nodded. "I'm General Miralda Holt, Lady of the Holt lands, descendant of Jarl Ivar Haroldsonn. Do you know the name?"

"Of your ancestor but not of you." The man replied, stepping closer.

"Fitting, because no one will ever remember your name." Miralda responded right before rushing the man with her sword, ready to strike.

The Gota leader dodged the strike, but Miralda rolled out of the way of his counterstrike and then called out her order. Suddenly, five other warriors charged in with maces and war hammers. They dealt many hard blows to the man, dropping him to the ground. A pool of blood leaked out of his armor as he lay dying. Plate armor was good at stopping arrows and sword strikes, but blunt objects could still do enough damage to maim or even kill. In this case, the latter.

Miralda regarded her housecarls. "To the palisades and keep up the defense!" She ordered. The general then stood over her fallen opponent, piercing his now exposed neck with her blade for good measure.

With the Gota leader, Thorifsonn, dead, Miralda had thought that the invaders would fall into a power vacuum, yet she miscalculated. The Gota paid little attention to the lack of a leader and instead increased their attack. If anything, killing the leader did more harm to the Lotcalans than good.

Sigurd Hardstone and Manor Lord Strongmotte pushed back against the coming tide with their forces. Strong men from the Blue Mountains, they could match the Gota mercenaries. The Elysians stood little chance. These were the same warriors that they had always fought against and that gave an advantage to the Hardstone and Strongmotte armies.

Swords clanged against the steel plate armor and other sword with echoes across the valley. Miralda lunged at one warrior wearing the heavy plate and swiped upwards with her longsword. The blade scraped the right side of the man's armor and cut up into his arm at the shoulder joint. The warrior's right arm fell to the ground, removed from the body. Miralda looked at the man, writhing in pain on the ground. She delivered the killing blow before moving on to another duel.

The Thousand Man Battalion rushed to the flanks beneath the ramparts and fought harder than they had yet to fight. Without Gabriel, the group was not at full strength and Marluna could only do so much. Arana left the band to her, and she could not form a phalanx like they trained to do. The battalion broke down within minutes of the fierce and close fighting. Those that stayed sacrificed their lives to give the fort more time. It was brutal but necessary.

Arana, away from her unit, led others with honor of the eastern palisade. She matched many of the Gota in size and height, few had ever fought such a woman. The Hun woman was more than any had expected to find fighting against. Arana cursed the Gota that stormed the fort, ordering those around her into the thick of the fight. She was a fighter and one of the most skilled. The Hun woman gave out an ear piercing war cry, ushering her soldiers onward and down the rampart, into the mass of Gota mercenaries. Arana was a force that turned the fight back to the Gota, but in time she too fell, wounded from an arrow to her side. She picked herself up to fight on but just as she did, she was struck down by a Gota ax. Arana would be just one of the many heroes to fall during that fateful battle.

Miralda saw the ferocity of her own army begin to waver, but they were stuck. She knew the instinct was to retreat to Antei, but that wasn't possible with the fort built the way it was and the size of the invading army. There was nowhere for them to run, and they were surrounded. She called out and rallied another push to the earthen bulwark of the fort. Perhaps a last push.

"Here and now we push them back or we enter the afterlife heroes!" Miralda yelled, prompting cheers in return.

The general ran, followed by hundreds of warriors, into the mass of Gota that had breached the artificial hill, colliding in a violent crash. Swords swung, clanging against other swords or armor. Few found soft points to slash against. Others used axes and war hammers, battering the heavy armor of the Gota. A desperate, breathless fight was not what Miralda had wanted, but it was what she got, nonetheless.

Lightning flashed across the sky and thunder echoed just before another torrent of rain fell in sheets across the field. The ground, already saturated, became a sticky pit of mud. The ground felt like tar under the feet of all the warriors fighting to wade through the muck.

Miralda stepped back from the rampart, a place that she had rooted herself for the past couple of days. She looked around the battle and felt a shiver.

"This isn't right. The sky looks odd." Miralda said, looking up as a blue bolt of lightning shoot through the sky and down onto the Elysian force.

Along the northern palisade, Marluna kept her battalion fighting. The battle was beginning to turn, but the elf could not hold out along with her warriors. While their skills might not be as honed as the hardened warriors that they were facing, the fact remained that these Lotcalans were up against a wall, fighting for their lives.

The crafty elf was dazzling in her display of fighting prowess, dodging and maneuvering around the heavier warriors. Her blades swirled like fans within her hands, so fast and precise that the Gota were powerless to stop her. However, her battalion wasn't quite as skilled as her, and they had tougher times against the invaders. Some falling to ax strikes while others slipped on the wet ground, leaving themselves prey to the skilled Gota.

The clouds over the battlefield swirled, and the winds kicked up, raising dirt and smaller pieces of the battlefield into the air. A flash of light from the northern skies soared past the fort and blasted above the invading force, sending many men flying into the air and back to the earth, dead. The ground shook from the battle to a standstill, but a soft hint of a rumbling came into the ears of the warriors. The rumbling from the north grew louder until the ground around the fort cracked and fire erupted around the Gota. The fire burned the warriors with a flame hotter than a blacksmith's furnace.

"Mage fire?" Marluna asked herself from atop a hill on the northern palisade wall. She looked around and spotted a small group, just silhouettes, to the north.

Rain shrouded the group but when one of the shadowy figures stepped out, Marluna could make out the top of a corinth helm's plumage of horse hair, dyed white.

"Mestra?" Marluna smiled, thinking back to the mage's helm.

The silhouetted woman was indeed the mage Mestra, raised her hand and lifted into the air a few feet before forming a tornado above her. The others around her extended their arms out to the levitating mage, giving her more power.

Mestra leveled her arms with the battlefield, sending the tornado to the Elysian and Gota formations. The storm rapidly rushed through the warriors, killing many and sending others running.

Bodies flew throughout the field, landing prone in horrific positions and amongst the already dead or dying. Those that ran from the mage's storm were not so lucky.

The rumbling was not just from the mages' spell, but from hooves. Thousands of hooves descended from around the western edge of the fort, led by the king, parting the sea of invaders with a devastation that neither the Elysians nor Gota had thought possible. Lancers skewered many with steel points that, aided by the speed of the horses, pierced the heavily armed Gota. Those warriors, in their plate army, were trapped between the storm and the king's defense.

Miralda watched the king's army banner wave as it weaved through the deadly sea of warriors. Cheers erupted from the fort as they saw the king lead the heavy horsemen through the Gota and Elysians. Miralda called out for her own force to rally and storm down the hillside.

Sigurd and Manor Lord Strongmotte rushed down the hillside they guarded after seeing the general attacking. The king's army roared behind them as more magical bolts of lightning blasted through the sky. Both of the lords from the Barony of Hardstone were accustomed to the use of magic, and seeing it employed against the invading horde was a blessing for the grizzled lords. They attacked with a renewed vigor as they swung their swords and thrusted their spears at the confused Gota and Elysians.

King Gabriel led the lancers, heavily armed riders with large spears, in their charge deep into the heart of the invader's army. They toppled the men as they rode down their flanks and stampeded over those that fell in the confusion. A mass of horsemen tearing through the sea of steel.

Behind the heavy cavalry rode lighter armed horsemen, led by Minimoto. These riders ushered in the infantry. All yelled their battle cries as they rode or ran into the battle. Soon the tide had turned and the Lotcalans, having the superior numbers and bolstered by the Amazon contingent, fought the invaders off of the hillside fort. Soon, the Elysians rushed away from the fort, but the Gota stayed to fight. They relished the renewed attacks by the incoming fighters. The mayhem was what drove the Gota on and spurred the fight. This was a new battle with an ancient relative.

The Elysians finally broke free and sounded a retreat, but the Lotcalans never let up. Some broke from the main army and rode down the Elysians, killing the stragglers or taking some prisoner.

The Gota held strong, unhorsing many Lotcalans as they stalled in the crowd of soldiers. The sea of men became a sea of shields, with many of the infantry buckling up against the heavy wooden shields of the Gota. Shieldwalls on both sides of the conflict pushed the warriors tight against one another. This kept the mages from launching any more attacks, at least nothing effective that wouldn't hurt their own allies.

King Gabriel still sat upon his horse, swinging his sword down on any Gota warrior that approached too close. He was fighting as many as he could, pulling on his horse's reins to maneuver the steed, but the attacks from the Gota were just as fierce. The Gota on foot knocked the king from his horse, and Gabriel rolled from the falling beast. Gabriel retrieve a spear from the ground and swung it high, hitting a Gota mercenary in the head, staggering the warrior. He kicked at another, knocking them both back a few steps. Several Amazons close by joined in the fight and guarded the king by creating a phalanx around him. Two heavy horsemen from the Lotcalan cavalry joined in and used their heavy kite shields to protect the king.

"Move, dammit!" Gabriel shouted, but none of his warriors let him through into the fight.

Around them the battle was turning into chaos as the warriors from each side continued to hit and slash at each other with wild abandon. Miralda was leading another charge of Lotcalans to the west, focused on the exposed right flank of the Gota.

Gabriel found his sword on the ground and picked it up before pushing his way between two Amazons and back into the melee. He swung an overhead strike down onto a nearby Gota warrior, dropping the unlucky victim, before moving to another duel. The warriors that had been there to protect him followed the king into the battle and scored hits of their own, adding to the number of the dead.

Gabriel rushed over several bodies, not noticing Manor Lord Strongmotte laying prone on the ground. He only saw the fight, an effect of tunnel vision that overtook his eyes from within his nasal helm. He rushed about the battle, blocking and trading blows and sword strikes with the Gota enemy. He cut a few more down before he met up with Minimoto, in his own sort of bloodlust.

The Quarmi commander pulled his curved blade from the chest of a fallen Gota warrior. The grey skinned friend of the king had lost his helm. It lay not far away on the ground with one of its decorative elf antlers broken. The white hair of the Quarmi leader flowed down to his shoulders, his tied knot having come undone. Minimoto looked to Gabriel and grabbed the king close.

"You fool!" He shouted over the war cries. "Protect yourself! If you fall, then the kingdom falls along with you."

The warriors that protected the king caught up to him and encircled him and Minimoto in another defensive phalanx.

Another horn echoes across the valley. This time it sounded different, higher in pitch and longer in tone. A horn that Gabriel and a few others had heard of before in legends. A Gota war horn.

"A retreat or a call for another attack?" Minimoto asked.

Gabriel panted. "I don't know, but Gota rarely retreat."

"The Elysians did long ago." Minimoto said. "How long, I don't know, but the sun is past the midday and I know it was still morning when I saw the last Elysian banner run south."

Gabriel nodded. "Then pray that this is a retreat."

Soon the battlefield looked calm as the Gota that had been in the fight retreated south and east. Those few that stayed fought to the bloody end. Only a handful prisoners were taken that day from the Gota ranks. One of the captives, a warrior that ignored the horns of his retreating brethren, held some value.

As night fell and the battle weary soldiers took stock in the outcome, Miralda ran over to the king, kneeling before him.

"Sire." She said.

Gabriel motioned for her to rise. "General, you've held out."

Miralda smiled before removing her helm. "Aye, and we'll continue to if they attack again." She looked to the south, following the king's eyes. "I've sent five hundred warriors three miles south to act as the advance guard."

"Let them rest general." Minimoto responded.

"Forgive me, but this war rages on and we cannot afford the luxury of rest. Not now." Miralda replied. "We have learned more of our enemies."

Gabriel and Minimoto followed Miralda to a well-guarded Gota warrior, flanked by seven of Miralda's housecarls. He wore a red cloak over steel plate. It was not as fancy as the other Gota, more of a patch work. Still, it had served him well. His head was shaven and he had etched tattoos in his skin from his head to his hands.

Miralda grabbed the man by his chin and lifted his head up. "This one is called Garthar Red Skull. He is the Jarl of Kerik. They call themselves the 'horse breakers'." Miralda said.

The man looked up to Gabriel, spitting at him before saying something in his native tongue. *"Falsk konge af en tåbelig folk att dyrkan falsk guden! Min slægt vil slagte dit rige."*

"My old Gota is a bit rusty, but he thinks his people will destroy this kingdom?" Gabriel asked Miralda.

The general looked to her housecarl Sven. "I heard slaughter." The housecarl nodded. Miralda turned back to Gabriel. "He said his kin will slaughter this kingdom and we are foolish for believing in the Creator."

"Good thing that our languages still hold some similarities or I might have been insulted at something simply lost in translation." Gabriel smirked.

"Your grace, he's also been bragging about a thousand more ships sailing to our coast." Miralda continued.

Gabriel looked at the Gota warrior. The prisoner smiled with blood oozing down his chin.

"You and those whelps in Gotistan aren't Gota. Not anymore, not true Gota. We are the true Gota and we will show you what your ancestors forgot about their blood. Your kingdom will die. My people are coming." The warrior said in broken Lotcalan, chuckling.

Gabriel nodded. He looked to the crowd around them and then back to the warrior. He unsheathed his sword. *"La dem."* Gabriel said in the old Gota tongue before cutting the man's head off.

Gabriel looked back to Miralda. "We won't keep prisoners. Too much of a burden on an exhausted army." Miralda bowed. "However, before the sentence is to be carried out, get the names of those that are executed. They shouldn't die nameless if it can be helped. We'll offer prayers to the Creator for their souls." Miralda bowed again and then went off to relay the orders.

Gabriel and Minimoto walked to the tent that had been set up in the earthen fort.

"My lord, I know you are tired, but I have news. It's of Ter Nog and it isn't good."

"Bulwyf couldn't break the siege?"

Minimoto looked at his friend and lowered his head before answering. "Our dear friend has..."

Ter Nog was a bloodbath. Bulwyf ordered warriors to the walls, repelling a fourth attempt by the Elysians to take the western gate. This fourth attempt was looking and feeling to be the strongest and much more likely to turn the battle. However, Bulwyf and the other defenders resisted.

The Lotcalan leader, reviled by his own men but still followed, could feel his advantage slipping away. An advantage won by brutality.

"Bang the drums and storm the walls!" Isidore called out. "Purge these heathens from the city!"

Bulwyf waited atop the wall, as three siege towers inched closer. He waited another moment and then shouted out the orders his archers had waited on. Flaming arrows and ballista bolts, both covered in pitch and cloth, hurled to the towers and ignited the wood and leather structure ablaze.

Bulwyf grinned as one tower shook to a standstill.

"Chains!" He ordered.

Another ballista shot a bolt with a heavy chain attached. The bolt impaled the tower and hooked on the tower's own bracing.

"Now!" Bulwyf ordered as two of his soldiers cranked the chain on a wench and pull the tower off of its supports.

The siege tower toppled over in a pile of wood and rubble, Elysian soldiers falling to the ground within the rubble. The remaining two towers received bolts and chains of their own, piercing the structure and bringing the tall siege engines to the ground.

The Lotcalan commander looked down to the fallen artillery.

"Drop the pitch on the wood and light the pile to hell." Bulwyf ordered.

His men followed the order, dumping boiling tar and pitch down from the wall before throwing flaming torches on the rubble. Bulwyf looked down and grinned.

"That'll keep them back for a while so we can regroup. Reload the ballistas!" He ordered.

Bulwyf looked out to the field below him and spotted an enraged Isidore. The Elysian ordered another tower to be sent. Bulwyf hoped that his tactics had been enough to hold the general back. He looked back to his captain.

"They have thousands still out there." Bulwyf said. "I want to end this sooner than later. If they get reinforced from the south, then we're finished."

"You can challenge their general." The captain replied.

Bulwyf grinned at the joke. "I'm not General Miralda. That's only for the honorable." Bulwyf turned to walk down the stairs to the ground. "I want to load the mangonels. Send them a few barrels."

"Barrels of what my lord?"

Bulwyf turned back to his captain. "Load the mangonels with barrels full of rats, diseased if you can find them, and hurl them at their camp. It looks close enough."

The captain looked shocked.

Bulwyf noticed the confused look on his soldier. "It will drive them to push up their attack before they are actually ready, and it'll make them easier to defeat."

The captain nodded. Bulwyf saw him rush off with several other men.

"This will bring them in sooner, and then I'll have Isidore's head on a pike." Bulwyf said.

The plan was simple and Bulwyf watched as twenty three barrels of rats were loaded and launched over the city walls, in four waves, down onto the field. Bulwyf's estimate was correct that the rats fell close enough to the camp that they scurried close and sent the camp into shock and chaos. The simplicity of his idea was that the rats that lived would enter into the camp and cause confusion. The dead rats would fester or be eaten by the living, which would create more disease in the camp. Either way, Bulwyf was more than satisfied.

"Tonight, go out there and line the field with pitch. We'll torch them again." Bulwyf ordered. "I want their camp to be hell on earth."

Gabriel walked out of the tent. His knees were weak and his stomach turned. Gabriel gripped a post of the tent and bent over. He knew of war and the sacrifices it took to win battles. However, in Gabriel's mind that should never include killing innocents. The stories from Minimoto and the dozens of reports coming in of his cousin's ruthlessness filled Gabriel with sorrow. These were his people, and they suffered while he was away at the hands of his own blood. The king felt the weight of another's actions.

Minimoto stepped out of the tent and looked to his king.

"Sire, I will handle this, but we cannot delay. With the Amazonian reinforcements rushing to Ter Nog, we have to advance south towards Gib." The Quarmi leader said.

Gabriel looked back to his friend. His eyes were watering, but he understood. "Yes, we'll riding out in the morning. I need to know that Syrena has arrived safely."

Minimoto nodded. "Of course, your grace. We'll rest here for the night and by dawn the queen will have certainly arrived with the siege equipment."

From a few yards away Marluna limped up to the king carrying a helm, cupped in her hands. Gabriel saw her and strolled to her.

"Arana?" The king said. "She's hurt?"

Marluna sniffed back a sob and shock her head gently. "She fell, sire." Marluna lowered her head in a sob. "Several Amazons are carrying her for burial."

"No." Gabriel said. Tears were beginning to run down his cheek. "She would want to be placed on a pyre and have her ashes cast to a northern wind. She told me so once."

"My lord, that is against..." Minimoto began, but he stopped short and looked to several guards from Antei. "Run and bring her body here and prepare a pyre for her." The guards rushed off to follow the orders.

"Creator damn me if he must, but Arana earned such respect."

The king took the helm, a silver masterpiece with a wolf etched on sides. Gabriel knew the wolf design was to honor Ymir, the chief deity of the twenty-seven old gods. Marluna bowed and limped away.

"Marluna, where do you plan to go now?" Gabriel said.

The half elf turned back to Gabriel. "The battalion needs a leader. They've asked me to guide them and I plan to for as long as I can."

The king smiled. He then walked to Marluna and handed her the helm. "Take this then and make her proud."

"Yes, sire." Marluna said, taking the helm. She smiled to her former trainer before bowing and walking back to her warriors.

Gabriel walked back into the tent, patting Minimoto's left shoulder as he walked by him. The Quarmi leader lowered his head.

"This war has taken too much from us already." He looked up to the sky. "Creator, help us make it through this." He said to himself before walking back into the tent.

Hell and Agony

The battlefield outside of the western gate of Ter Nog roared with a flesh melting blaze. Bulwyf left the city, along with five hundred soldiers of the king's army. This would be his fight to finish. The commander knew the limitations of his gamble, and those limitations were coming fast.

Isidore lasted longer than Bulwyf ever expected, but this battle had to end. The initial tactics threw the Elysian general off his guard and even disturbed him enough to make him act too impulsively. However, Bulwyf noticed something that bothered him with each renewed attack. The Elysians were settling into the siege. That could prove disastrous. If Isidore could last any longer or crack the defenses, then the battle would be lost for Lotcala. Bulwyf could not take such chances.

That was what led to the decision to torch the outlying field and take the battle to the Elysians.

Draped by a starless night, Bulwyf rode out of the gate, followed by his soldiers. This was a quick attack and one meant to sow discord in the Elysian camp. The Elysians could see the Lotcalans coming from the gate, but why were they leaving the city?

That answer came soon after, when the Lotcalan soldiers ignited the pitch that had been covertly laid out the week prior. Flames erupted, trapping the Elysians inside a torrent of fire. The flames engulfed the siege towers that were being staged, leaving none functional. The fire soon spread to the trebuchets and the catapults. None of Isidore's siege engines or war machines were spared from destruction.

The soldiers within the camp, having already put on their armor or preparing to mount a defense, looked around for guidance. Isidore was, however, on the other side of the flames.

Bulwyf gave the order and a volley of arrows, tipped with bodkin points, soared through the air and rained down onto the confused Elysians. The crafty commander scanned the battlefield to find the Elysian general. It took more time than Bulwyf would have wanted to spy him through the constant barrage of arrows, but finally Bulwyf found Isidore.

The Lotcalan commander made his way over to the Elysians, crossing over bodies and vile substances on the battlefield.

"I hoped you would be left on this side of the battle." Bulwyf said. He held his nasal helm under his arm and gripped his war-axe. Bulwyf's chain mail was darkened from the soot and the grim of the previous days' of battle. "Your men are trapped and your siege engines are destroyed. This is the end for you, here at Ter Nog. Do you concede defeat?"

Isidore looked around and saw his men falling to more arrows. He saw the flames raging through the field and tearing through his encampment. In that moment he saw that his army was in tatters, scattering throughout the area, trying to run from the chaos but ultimately finding more chaos.

"This defeat... the siege, I've lost. A loss that will not haunt me for I will redeem myself by defeating you." Isidore responded, unsheathing his sword and rushing at Bulwyf.

The Lotcalan commander had expected, and hoped, for such a reaction. He threw his helm at Isidore. The Elysian slowed as the helm struck him on the shoulder. Bulwyf rushed towards Isidore and struck him in the right arm with his axe. The blade sunk deep into Isidore's arm. The padded gambeson was not enough to stop sharpened steel.

Isidore stumbled back from Bulwyf and looked at him in shock. His right arm hung limply. He tried to grip his sword in his left hand, but his strength was failing him.

"This world you've created for your king, is all of this worth it?" Isidore asked, shouting over the cries of his men being slaughtered.

"Is what worth it?"

Isidore looked back to the city and then to Bulwyf. "All of this death and destruction. You've murdered innocents all in some ploy to unnerve me, but all you've done is stop me for now. You've delayed the invasion of Elysia, but that's all. More will come. This city, your cousin's kingdom, all of this will have to fade into the tomes of history. Into the forgotten reaches of time." Isidore threw his sword down and then gripped his arm. His blood oozed down his hand and arm. "I'm beaten. I can't wield my sword, but you're not victorious. Not here, not today."

"You and I have very different ideas of victory then." Bulwyf scoffed, walking towards the wounded man.

"We do. I should have seen that from the beginning, but I was blinded with rage. Your plan worked well, and for that I salute you. However, you still have to go back into the city, without an enemy at the gate to take the attention off of you. Good luck with that." Isidore finished as Bulwyf reached him.

The Lotcalan commander sneered at his foe before burying his axe in Isidore's skull. Isidore fell to the ground, crumpling into a heap at Bulwyf's feet.

Bulwyf looked around to the battlefield and he saw his handiwork. The fields were aflame, his men were leading a massacre of the Elysians. Even the town's guard and a few brave townsfolk had come out to join in the savagery. He thought back to the fighting and lowered his head amongst the brutality. He saw his blooded mail and surcoat. His hands were caked in days' old blood. Still no tears or remorse.

"I am what I am and I do what needs to be done. If not me, then who?" Bulwyf said to himself.

The march south was uneventful, the queen arriving to rendezvous with Gabriel was the only source of fanfare to speak of. However, that all changed as the Lotcalan army saw the garrisoned fortifications outside of the walls of Gid, Elysia's fortified capital.

Atop a ridge that looked down on the city from two-and-a-half miles away, King Gabriel, Queen Syrena and several officers, barons and manor lords sat atop their mounts. They surveyed the field below them and the roads leading to the city.

All were dressed for war, chain mail with surcoats, many embroidered with the sigils of their respected homes or of the king's army. Syrena, however, kept her legionnaire muscled cuirass and battle skirt. None were cleaned after the previous battle. Time was too short, and upon looking at the city's outlying field, it seemed to prove that point well.

Minimoto looked to his lifelong friend, Gabriel. "Sire, those walls are the least of our worries if we can't get passed those garrisons. We have to mount our trebuchets within that field."

Gabriel nodded.

Syrena was a bit more vocal in confidence. "Those forts are not a problem for the Legion."

"Forgive me, your grace, but you only have half a cohort here." General Miralda said from the queen's left. "Will they be enough?"

Syrena grinned to the general. "With your army to make up the difference, yes." Syrena motioned for Ino to join her. "Ino, you and Miralda prepare the attack on the garrisons on the field."

Miralda nodded. "By your leave, your grace." She said before turning her horse back to the camp. Ino rode alongside her.

Syrena looked to her husband. "That Miralda will be an excellent leader for the years to come."

"Thank the Creator she's a loyal friend." Gabriel smiled.

Minimoto chuckled. "I'd hate to be her enemy. Of course, some have found out what that's like."

"She'd make a fine legionnaire." Syrena added.

The group turned back to the camp, ready to begin their preparations.

Those preparations would take place in the king's tent as the sun fell that evening. Within the king's tent, a small group of lords and officers talked of the coming siege. Many had taken the time, knowing that a long encampment loomed, to remove their armor and wear less formal attire. Mostly tunics and trousers for the men and gowns for the ladies, though Miralda opted for trousers and Syrena kept her chiton.

"The Elysians know that we can't siege them from this ridge. Our trebuchets cannot reach the nearly three mile distance." General Miralda said.

"I doubt there are any that could." King Gabriel replied. He offered her and the other lords each a cup of wine. "I've heard that Captain Constantine has been working on something that might help us." He finished before turning back to his map.

Miralda, sipping her cup of wine and sitting on a wooden stool nearby, grinned. "He has, Sire. Though, admittedly I'm not much for siege engines but I have to say that his designs are fascinating." She put the cup down on the ground and flattened her tunic and trousers. Though she was a general in the king's army, she wore the sigil of her family, a golden squirrel, on her tunic. "One trebuchet is larger than any other I've heard of. Nearly fifty feet tall."

"Fifty feet tall?" Baron Canton said, shocked. "Is that possible? What sort of range would a machine of that magnitude have?"

The other lords stood or sat around the tent, all murmuring their own surprise.

Miralda shook her head. "Hard to say, my lord." Miralda answered. "Our largest currently can send a fifty pound load nearly a thousand feet. That trebuchet stands thirty-five feet tall with four thousand pounds of counterweight. This one would be fifteen feet taller and adds another three thousand pounds of counterweight."

Manor Lord Silverstone looked to the general. "Three and a half tons is a mighty weight, general." He looked around. "The wood to make such an engine must be massive. How many working hours would this take to complete?"

Miralda looked to Silverstone and shrugged. "Forgive me, my lord." She had to keep to the formality. Though she was a general, she was still a gentry-knight's daughter. "This is an unfamiliar experience for us but I'd think that the good captain would tell us that to build it he'll need that field cleared first." She thought for a second as many of the lords looked to her. "At least fifteen hundred feet toward the wall should be cleared and secured for us."

The other lords nodded, whispered among themselves, and offered plans. King Gabriel, looking at maps, just pondered the best route. There was a strain in his face and a weariness upon his brow. Syrena noticed her husband's frustrated eyes.

"The night is winding down." Syrena said to the group. "Perhaps we can finish this conversation in the morning." She finished, taking her husband's full cup from in front of his hand.

The lords stood in response. King Gabriel looked up. "Yes, I'm sorry, my lords. I've thought of a plan." He looked around the tent and saw everyone looking back to him. "Given that our goal is to get close enough to attack the walls, then we have little option but to send warriors down onto the fields. That can be done from two flanks with an additional maneuver in the center."

The lords looked on as their king explained his plan. A simple yet concise idea.

"I'll lead the lancers down from the eastern slope and around the right flank. We'll lead the cavalry down and storm the garrisons there. Miralda will take the infantry down the western slope and storm the left flank. Archers will head down the center and soften their defenses before we get there. Once we make our attack, they will act as reinforcements to the flanks." King Gabriel finished.

"Leading a cavalry charge on an uneven field is an arduous task." Baron Lostwood responded. "A three-pronged attack is wise, sire, I just worry that the terrain will hamper the riders."

Others seemed to agree, but Gabriel was steadfast in his feelings.

"This is a tactic that will inflict the most damage to the garrisons." Gabriel replied. "A fast and hard strike."

"My lord, I agree with that, but I think the concern is with the possibility of retreating or falling back." Manor-lord Uffeson said. "That slope might prove to be a hindrance. Once there on the field there will be no retreating."

Gabriel nodded and the other lords agreed. Syrena moved to join her husband. She laid her hand on his left shoulder. "The king has given the plan." She said. "I volunteer to march with General Miralda."

The general smiled and bowed to the king and queen. "Thank you, your grace." She said to Syrena. "However, I think it wise for one of you to stay back. For the sake of the kingdom." She added, noting the look on the faces of the monarchs.

Syrena nodded, standing straighter. "I'll take that into consideration, general." She looked to the rest of the lords in the tent. "Thank you all for your time and advice. The hour has come that we retreat to our own tents, and that hour has grown late. I bid you all a good night, for it is time to rest. Tomorrow we will begin."

The lords bowed before exiting the tent, leaving Syrena alone with Gabriel. The queen looked to her husband and gently placed her hand on his. Gabriel clasped hers in return.

"Is it too wishful to want to be in Antei drinking mulled wine by the fire and listening to the logs crackling?" Gabriel said.

Syrena smiled. "No." She replied softly. "Is that why you journeyed north all those years ago?" She asked. "To be away from a life of war and holding court?"

Syrena heard a few stories of his experiences, but never the reason for leaving. Syrena would be lying to herself if she said she wasn't curious.

Gabriel smiled to his wife. "I never wanted to be king and for many years it seemed like I didn't have to worry about it." He lowered his head and chuckled. "Honestly, being a prince and a baron wasn't enjoyable. I wanted less for myself. I wanted a life of adventure and if possible to fight in some battles, but my father insisted I live a courtly life. Sure, we learned how to plan tactics, how to fight, but that wasn't the goal. We stayed back while others fought for us. I did not want that." Gabriel said. He looked into Syrena's eyes. "I'm sorry, but I did not see a future in Amazon being the placeholder for your sister. A courtly life less exciting than what I had here. It was my duty, but it scared me because it meant that I would be useless. That's why I left. I saw that I could help people in the north while using the skills I had learned here."

Syrena reached in to hug her husband. The two shared the warm embrace. The nights had grown longer and time was passing by faster than either had imagined it could. Here, however, locked together in this moment, the two could stop for at least a few hours and breathe together as one.

The dawn was yet again early. The sun has always had a reputation for such madness.

Gabriel left his tent, alone since Syrena had awoken earlier. He walked off to meet with the cohort of legionnaires she had brought. He dressed in his mail and kingly surcoat. Donned in the dark green of the kingdom and marked with a golden stag upon his chest, Gabriel strolled through the camp.

Walking past many of his fellow countrymen and women, all stood and bowed to his presence. Gabriel simply smiled and waved them to be at ease. His goal was to be seen in confident spirits and not appear so mysterious.

Even in the years prior to leaving to go north, Gabriel had been thought of as sociable but solitary as well. Upon his return, many had heard rumors of him they had yet to understand any truths about. Therefore, walks such as this one held special opportunities to see the king as a man just as the other men of the kingdom. He wasn't just any man of the kingdom, however. He was the king, and he carried that massive weight upon his shoulders and those that bowed to him would never know the weight that he felt as he walked passed.

Across the camp, Syrena walked with Honora. The veteran commander stuck around to see the battles play out. She knew of the current affairs within the Queendom so for her this was the best place, near her liege.

"With the jailors returning and the Queendom settling back in, I think that the winter will finally be a joyful time for Amazon." Honora said. "So many are ready for a restful season or two."

Syrena smiled to her friend. "I'm glad to have been able to help with that." She looked to her left, toward a nearby tent, and saw Megara with Domino sitting outside. "I thought the jailors returned."

Honora looked over and grinned. "The others have, but Domino refused to return by the Queendom and he's a bit shy to go north yet. So, he's staying around the army for now. Megara is watching him." Honora said, seeing Syrena's look of concern. "She'll make sure he behaves, though I'm not sure she has any plans on returning to the queendom. Not without him at least."

Syrena looked back to Honora. "She'll give up her post for a man?"

"You did." Honora responded with a smirk.

"That's different. My marriage was for an alliance."

Honora wasn't fooled. The elderly woman cocked an eyebrow up and faced her former pupil. "You came for love and that's the only reason. Just because you're a princess means nothing." She tapped her cane on the ground for added effect. "If I had fallen in love with a man worth it, I would have left too." Honora walked but stopped short and turned back to Syrena. "Actually, I did fall in love with such a man. He just didn't ask me to leave, so I didn't." She shrugged before turning back to walk away.

Syrena caught up to Honora a moment later. "You've never mentioned your husband."

"Nor have I ever needed to, but he wasn't my husband." Honora stopped and placed both her hands on the handle of her cane. She lifted her head and closed her eyes, thinking of a distant memory. "There was a time before the Treshan War. A good time, a time of peace and prosperity. Goddesses help me that sounds cliché but dammit it was." Honora smiled and looked to Syrena. "He was a general in the Treshan army. General Anders Stronglance. We spent seven good years, corresponding and meeting when we could. Official visits and envoys. All good and fun." She lowered her head and sniffed softly.

"The war came." Syrena said in a hushed voice.

Honora nodded. "That damn war. Your grandmother took offence to something the king of Tresha said. Something that no one knows, but damn if she didn't get her armor twisted for it. We marched on and fought a nearly twenty year war for it. In the end, Anders fell in battle, as did your grandmother. You know the war's history well enough, but that war destroyed my hopes for a future." Honora straightened herself. "I had a legion to command, however, and I couldn't just leave myself crying on the ground about him. He wouldn't want that, anyway. I mourned and moved on and here I am."

Syrena nodded, reflecting on the words. She knew of the many wars with Tresha over the past decades, she had fought in several of them, but she hadn't known of such a story.

"Thank you, Commander." Syrena said. "Thank you for your story."

That night, campfires and songs rose from the ridge. Looking down on the field below, Gabriel saw the same movement he had seen the day before. Syrena stood at his right and gazed over the field.

"This will not be a simple task. Even with Ino and Constantine working on the siege engines and Miralda leading the infantry." She said. Syrena was as pragmatic as anyone Gabriel had ever known.

"Do you want to stay back?" Gabriel foolishly asked his wife.

Syrena looked to her husband with a glare as icy as the hands of the god of death, itself.

"In what world would I ever stay behind from a battle?!" She shot back venomously. The guards standing by took a step back.

"I'm only saying because of..." Gabriel began but was cut off by his wife.

"You married a princess of the Amazonian Queendom! We do not stay behind!" She roared. "I have commanded more warriors than you've ever seen, and I will never shy away from battle. Through broken bones, scars and mourning for lost friends, I've fought with every inch of my being. Should I fall, then may it be a death so glorious that the gods add me amongst their numbers! Until that time I will fight and strike fear into those that stand against me as I've been taught since the first day I drew breath!" Syrena finished.

Gabriel stood in silence and Syrena took a breath to calm herself. Amazons were known for ferocity but also their ability to be diplomatic when needed.

"Besides, I'm a foreign queen and the people would not follow me as they would you. However, as the king and the last of your line, maybe you should defend the camp."

Gabriel looked to his wife and clasped her hand. "They won't follow me if I stay behind. These people still know their Gota roots and they won't allow a coward to lead them."

Syrena gave a knowing nod. "Then let the burning fires echo our arrival and victory. It is all or death."

"A glorious death." Gabriel added.

"A death that will ring across the world and let the spirits stand in fear of our arrival to the afterlife. Nothing less will do." Syrena smiled.

In three mornings, the army completed preparations for the first attack to begin. It was up to the archers and the infantry to begin the attack. They would hold little back and too much was at stake to consider holding back any ground in any case. This was the last push to Gob and one that would have to perfect. Rarely was any attack ever perfect, however.

Two hours before dawn, Miralda and Syrena stood side by side as their army massed behind them.

"No phalanxes or shield walls." Miralda said. She fastened her helm with a leather strap under her chin, but her words were clear enough. She held her longsword in her right hand. Ready to begin, clad in her chain mail and the king's army surcoat.

Syrena wore her standard muscle cuirass, steel greaves and gauntlets. Her corinth helm upon her head, its plumage wafting in the breeze.

"This will have to be completely brute force and shock." The queen replied. "It'll take about half an hour to reach the outskirts of the encampment. Then we hit hard and fast."

Miralda nodded. "A deep and violent push."

Both women stood watching the little movement on the field, campfires smoldering out. Neither woman took their eyes off the field below them.

Suddenly, a volley of flaming arrows flew high in the sky off in the distance. Syrena took a step forward and Miralda followed, along with their army. The battle was beginning.

The two women walked down the slightly angled slope. Behind them, thousands of soldiers followed. All ready to fight. As the Lotcalan army stepped closer to the camps, their pace quickened. After a steady walking pace for the first part of the slope, now they jogged. The time for conserving energy had passed. The enemy loomed close, just a couple hundred yards away. Close, yet the guards had not noticed them. The plow of the archers' arrows was working.

Their jog, with weapons and shield clutched tight close to the body to minimize noise, hastened. Now, just a hundred yards away, the Lotcalans broke out into a run. Queen Syrena, wearing a lighter weight armor, sped up with spear and shield in hand. This was what her training had led up to. The many battles, the years in the Herd and the weeks leading up to this ultimate battle had prepared her for this fight. Her arms didn't feel the weight of the shield, nor did her back feel the heft of the armor. All of it was as light as a feather for the Amazon. That was in part because of the training, but also the adrenalin that surged through her veins.

A horn blew from the west and the Elysian guards took notice of the rushing army, but it was too late to mount a defense. Syrena thrusted a spear into a nearby Elysian, sitting by a campfire. Such an old tactic, using the cover of darkness against the flames. Too hard to see the approach with eyes not accustomed to the night. More Elysians fell quickly, not ready for a fight.

The Lotcalan army fanned out into the night, Miralda leading many around to the northern side, kicking out campfires to dispel the light. It also gave the archers a sign of where their comrades were.

The skilled general found little resistance in the camps at first, but soon the Elysians pushed back. With nowhere to run they had little choice but to fight, alongside their new found Gota allies.

"Here they come!" Miralda yelled. "Spread out and give them hell!" She roared and then dashed into the fray, drawing her longsword and slashing down on the first Gota she faced.

More came, but so did her army. Close combat with swords, axes and spears. The crafty general was much more mobile than her opponents, diving beneath their attacks and striking from a lower position into exposed flesh. Miralda and her warriors used their previous experience in battles against the Gota to their advantage. The larger and heavier armed warriors couldn't keep up with the lighter armed Lotcalans. Lessons well learned turned into signs of victory for Miralda with each enemy killed or taken down. She moved closer to success.

Syrena initially saw similar success as well. Fighting closer to the city but out of archer range from the city walls, the queen led her smaller cohort and new subjects into the camps. Her reputation was well known, and Syrena showcased every bit of her skill as she fought deeper into the camps. Knocking swords and spears away with her shield and piercing armor and skin with her heavy spear. Mestra, beside her, fought just as hard and ferocious. Both women vowed to fight to the last breath and to make their ancestors proud.

This would be the test and the makings of true warriors. They must set the example!

Many of those fighting by their side were not professional soldiers. Miralda had led the King's Army, but Syrena led conscripts and baronial soldiers. These were men called during times of war. Skilled in some aspects of fighting but not as cohesive as the legion and here they had fought for months on end and many were weary. Syrena knew she had to encourage their fighting zeal.

Screams of war, agony and hatred echoed out of the field and up the ridge. The horrors as blood spilt on each side. The element of surprise won the first strikes and initial victories for the Lotcalan army. The fighting was just as they preferred; fast and light. Soon, it became apparent that the core of the Gota camps were not so easily defeated. What had kept the Gota outsiders so well employed through the centuries since their break from Gotistan was their skill in war, and now the jarls called up their warriors to defend their cause.

This was the true test, as Queen Syrena saw it. Warriors fighting with the last gasp of a glorious cause, no matter that it wasn't noble in the least.

Syrena rallied her soldiers around her. They all looked to her. Many had just run off the slope, their eyes wide with zeal for the fight and victory. The march had been long, but they knew Syrena would led them to victory and glory. First, they had to fight a wave of Gota and Elysians rushing their way. Not a tall task for most of the baronial men. A few gentry-lords had taken places in the front lines with their new queen.

Syrena plunged her spear into a Gota warrior, one without his plate armor. He jerked backwards, ripping the spear point from his flesh with a violent spasm of blood and entrails. Syrena stood over the warrior after he landed and sank the spear's tip into the man's chest for the death blow.

A mass of Gota warriors faced her, Mestra joined her side. She gripped her spear with two hands, having let go of her shield to better move in the close quarters of the camp.

"This is what we live for." Mestra smirked under her Corinth helm.

Syrena smiled under her own helm. "This is what they die for."

Both women looked at one another. "Honor and death!" They yelled in unison.

Their legionnaire sisters joining on command from Queen Saria ran up behind them joined in their battle chant.

"Alala, alala, alala!" All the legionnaires shouted in a loud, guttural voice.

The Lotcalan army among the two cheered at the words. They knew the war cry of the Legion, and it was time to show the might of a combined force.

These Gota, had never fought against Legionnaires. In ancient times, during the War of Conquest, the Gota that had sailed from Gotistan joined forces with the then nomadic Amazons. Then the bonds of the brother and sister nations were formed. In battle and sealed in blood. These were not those Gota, and Syrena was ready to prove that these outcasts were not worthy of the name Gota.

The legionnaires led the charge in a violent clash against the Gota warriors. Two walls that met with a force so great that the ground quaked and sound stopped for a second as if the world had stood still of a split second. The legionnaires formed a tight unit, protecting their princess with a wall of shields. Lotcalan warriors and back rows of legionnaires stabbed and shot arrows past the front line.

"Hold this line!" Mestra yelled out, thrusting her spear into the Gotas on the other side of the front row.

The mage took a place behind that line. Without her shield she would hinder the strength of the phalanx. However, it was her skills fighting with a spear where she'd provide a deadly offensive weapon against the push of the Gota warriors.

Syrena did the same, holding her sisters from behind and stabbing with her spear through the space between two warriors. While Miralda had guessed that shieldwalls and phalanxes would not be useful in the camps, and for her they weren't, Syrena made use of the Legion's best and oldest tactic. She knew, as did her sisters, that the goal would be to beat the Gota into a stalemate and trap them within the camp. It would be a war of attrition, however, and that was where the Legion excelled.

Looking around the field, Syrena saw the scattering of Elysians to the west. "It's time." She said to herself, thinking of the cavalry's coming charge.

King Gabriel rode at the head of the cavalry, into a swarm of lances and pikes carried by the Elysian infantry. They knew the attack was coming, or at least they had a damn good idea. Some Elysians might have been trying to escape the coming onslaught from the archers and the infantry attack on the left flank. Now, however, they were caught in the charge of thousands of horsemen, riding at a full gallop down yet another gentle slope.

The king, in the lancer standard steel scale mail armor and coif, rode down with the lance out. Just as he did in the previous battle, he rammed the point of his lance into the first adversary he could find. Not a hard task, as a line had poised themselves against the Lotcalan riders. However, the Elysians found that the Lotcalans were greater in number and better prepared.

What the Elysians thought would be a siege battle was breaking down into a full pitched fight. This was not what they were prepared for.

Gabriel and his fellow lancers tore through the first ranks of the Elysians. More riders, lighter armed, rode down the slope. These were baronial riders or other conscripts from the kingdom. Most had gambesons, chainmail or simple heavy cloth. The numbers gave an advantage, but soon the Elysians brought more effort into the battle.

Spear tips found marks in the steeds of many Lotcalan riders, sending men and horses tumbling to the ground. While the heavier armor of the lancer helped to protect them from harm from the fall, the weight held them down. This gave many Elysians a chance to fight back against the vulnerable Lotcalans. King Gabriel was one such vulnerable warrior.

The king landed with a thud onto the hard, frosty ground. He winced from the pain but pushed himself up as quickly as he could. Thank the Creator he could because no sooner had he lifted him up did an Elysian rush at him, spear aimed at the king's abdomen. Gabriel barely side stepped away in time, but he didn't have time to unsheathe his sword. Gabriel opted instead for a hard right handed punch to the Elysian's jaw.

Gabriel's hands were covered in mail over padded mittens. The blow to the Elysian's jaw, though the soldier was helmed, sent him back a step. Enough of a step for Gabriel to draw his sword, a one handed spatha, and plunge it into the Elysian's unprotected side. The king turned and faced an incoming horde of Elysians. Behind him and to his flanks came his own warriors. The fighting devolved to hand to hand combat on foot, while some still rode their mounts into the heat of battle. Those that rode did so with reckless abandon into the fray, leading to others being trampled. Such was the ways of battle, but Gabriel deftly moved around the field, his sword bloody from those that had dueled him. They had found his skill with a sword to be greater than expected.

This was not a time to show off one's skills, rather it was a time to survive with the best tactics. Gabriel saw more battles than he let on with a hardened foe in the Huns of the north, now he was fighting an ancient rival that more matched his own people.

Gabriel found a single-handed war axe and used it in his left hand to parry any chop at his opponents. His sword free to swing and stab in his right hand. Somewhere, however, he had lost his helm. Still, he had his steel scale to cover his upper body and thighs. This armor, though not impenetrable, kept him safe from most sword strikes. Lucky for the king, given he was fighting deeper into enemy territory.

Others joined him in his fight. Gabriel wasn't sure, but he thought he could make out familiar shouts. Voices carrying on the wind that he recognized as Miralda and lords that he knew. A few lords stood with him, Manor-lords Hafman, Blacktower and Overland had joined his side. All riders and expert warriors. Gentry-lords Alban and Longmane also stood with the king amongst the field outside of Gib.

Ancient rivals rushed to the fight, lords and commoners alike, tore through the field in a desperate ploy for victory. This was the final battle for one kingdom. That slope would see to that in one form or another.

Soon, the Elysians fell back toward the city. Gabriel and his army, swords and axes swinging, drove them further. Gabriel was right when he heard Miralda's voice. The general was commanding warriors. Her surcoat was bloody and covered in mud but she stood shouting orders for the king's army to fight. This was the success that Gabriel hoped for in his plan. Now he could see victory take shape. Still, he wanted to see his wife and hear of her victory.

Miralda saw the approach of the king and his riders, though the king was on foot along with several other lords and many warriors.

"To Elysia!" Miralda shouted.

Her soldiers gave a yell in response to the order.

The king turned toward the city. He saw the Elysians running that way but he didn't give chase. Instead, he walked over to Miralda.

"Is this enough distance?" Gabriel asked.

Miralda looked at to the city and then up to the ridge before answering.

"I think this should do it. Constantine said he needed just enough, and this looks to be the spot he pointed out." Miralda breathed a sigh. "Good thing too, because this push was much more difficult than I had imagined it would be."

"We're not finished yet." Gabriel said. He pointed to the outlying areas of the field. "Hafman, Longmane. Gather some men and clear out those other, smaller encampments." The king said. "We have to cover ourselves if we stage here."

"This city will be hell to take." Manor-lord Blacktower said.

Miralda nodded. "Yes, my lord, but we'll take her and then be done with those bastards."

"Any news of the queen?" Gabriel asked.

"She took to the south, and I lost sight of her force. I'd say the way things were going, she's been making it a fight. We had many running our way, but not to fight. Running from someone more like it." Miralda smiled under her helm.

Gabriel looked to the south, plumes of smoke rose from the field.

"Lord Blacktower, mount up some of our lancers and ride down to the south with me. We have seen little of our Gota cousins. I think that it's time for a proper reunion." King Gabriel said before walking back to find a horse.

Lord Blacktower nodded and shouted orders to riders nearby. Quickly, more riders appeared near the lord and his king, all willing to ride south toward the city and to find the queen.

As the king rode off, Miralda ordered the king's army into the clearing. She had to prepare the area for the siege. While they could still find areas of resistance, the Lotcalans had effectively driven the Elysian army either back into the city or to surrender. General

Miralda ordered a camp set up and for her soldiers to gather materials. The Lotcalans won the first stage of victory.

Gota warriors, famed for viciousness and skill, took the Amazon legionnaires to task in a grueling fight. This was not for the faint of heart. The eastern mercenaries, from a land they had been exiled to, knew that this was their last fight if they failed. The Elysians would not accept them into the city. They could not, nor would they attempt to join the Lotcalans. This could be their final hour, but what an hour it would be if it were.

The Gota leader, Jarl Rethel Skeldsson, was a mighty warrior. Feared and respected from around the world, he carried a large battle-axe, wielded in both hands. His long, breaded grey beard was stained in blood, some of his own and some from those around him.

Jarl Rethel roared orders at his men, pushing them on. The Gota shieldwall was damaging the Amazonian hold. Their numbers were greater than the Amazons on that side of the field, some legionnaires being left with Miralda. Jarl Rethel took advantage of the lacking fighting spirit of the conscripts and baronial soldiers from Lotcalan. With each Amazonian that fell, a Lotcalan had to step in. This was the danger of fighting with conscripts that were not trained to fight professionally.

The Gota warriors, many with axes, hacked at their opponents and cut limbs. The Gota used two handed pole-axes, five feet long, to chop down over the shields. Some Amazons had their skulls caved in with the dangerous blows of these war axes. The sharpened blades could break through the bronze helms of the Amazons. The few with iron or steel were not so lucky, being inflicted with heavy blunt force trauma enough to be killed.

That didn't stop the Amazons. They wouldn't run, they still had their honor to protect. There wasn't anywhere to run to, anyway. This was the battle to end all for the war. The Lotcalans had held in the north, though it took all that they had, and now they had to push in the south. The Gota mercenaries, however, were not about to let them win without a fight.

Syrena urged her sisters and her new soldiers on with shouts of encouragement. Victory, however, was looking less likely.

"Mestra!" Syrena called out. "Are there any spells that you can level at these bastards?"

Mestra, spear in one hand, a fallen sister's shield in her other hand, looked to the queen. "I don't have the room I need. Any spell I send could kill us all!"

Syrena nodded her understanding and returned to the fighting in front of her, thrusting her spear into a Gota opposing her.

"Then let's make this our stand to end all stands!" Syrena yelled.

The Amazons stood in defiance of the Gota warriors baring down on them. The mood turned to defense and to hold out for the king's army when suddenly a horn blew in the west. The horn blew twice more.

Jarl Rethel turned and looked toward the sound of the horn. Along the western horizon, he saw over a thousand horsemen. The king's banner waved above the center, with other banners mixed into the cavalry. A central rider pointed a lance to the Gota shieldwall, yelling a command that was muffled in Jarl Rethel's ears.

Another a horn blew, and the riders took off in a gallop. Lancers and spearmen took aim with their points at the Gota and in a moment, slammed into the Gota's line of warriors, just in front of what was left of the Amazonian phalanx. The ensuing chaos broke down the Gota shieldwall and allowed a moment for the conscripts and the Amazons to regroup and fan out an attack of their own. After the first wave of riders rode through the Gota, Syrena ordered a charge, sending her legionnaires into the violent fray.

King Gabriel, the central rider, had again been unhorsed. This time, however, he rolled out of the fall and landed in a crouch with his hand on his sword's hilt. Unsheathing it, he joined the fight amongst legionnaires and Lotcalans, dismantling the Gota army.

Syrena continued her fight, alongside her sisters Mestra and Nyx. Some Gota charged them, a final act of desperation of the battle. Nyx, fighting with a falchion, twirled on the balls of her feet, ducking an axe swing and plunging her short sword into the belly of a Gota warrior. Mestra leapt into the air, carried by a minor wind burst spell and landed with her spear point thrusting into the chest of another warrior.

The Gota saw the battle as lost, but they never would surrender.

Jarl Rethel sneered. "These Lotcalans are too much for us today." He looked around, spotting Syrena. "You!" He roared.

Syrena was close enough to hear him. She turned and squared up against him.

Rethel bellowed out a war cry and rushed at Syrena. He brought his two-handed axe down, clanging off her shield. Syrena pushed off and thrusted her spear at him. Rethel spun out of the way and swung his axe, but Syrena brought her shield up, blocking it. Syrena dropped to her knees and slammed her shield into Rethel's legs, knocking the large man down.

Syrena jumped on top of him and smashed her shield into his face before pushing the shaft of her spear against Rethel's throat. The Gota gulped for air, but he couldn't gasp any. Syrena pushed her spear shaft down further until she heard a crack. The jarl went limp under her. The surrounding fight was moving on as the Gota were running from the newly motivated Lotcalans. Syrena just rolled off of Rethel's lifeless body. Happy she had lived at least a few more hours.

The Final Wall

Within hours the Lotcalan warriors set up a new camp up amongst the rumble of the previous one. This camp, however, was made for the Lotcalans instead of the Elysians. The latter had been driven off or captured, leaving many prisoners.

They would be a task for later, however. Now the goal was to finish the siege and break through the wall of Gib.

"Captain Constantine, they tell me you can assemble a trebuchet big enough to take down these walls." King Gabriel said as he unfastened the chin strap of his nasal helm.

The young captain looked at the king and bowed. "Sire, it will be large enough, I'm sure, and with Lady Ino's help, we should finish it by the end of the week."

King Gabriel looked around the tent they stood in and focused his eyes on the other lords and officers.

"The other trebuchets? Are they being set up?" He asked.

One of the gentry-lords, Lord Roland Cullenhun, stepped up and bowed. "Aye sire, they are being set up and at this rate they should be able to be fired first thing in the morning.

The king nodded in reply. He looked to his wife, sitting on a chair and wrapping a bandage around her arm. She had some new scrapes and bruises, one rather grievous laceration, but nothing that Mestra couldn't heal. Gabriel smiled at his wife. She grinned back but it wasn't a look of love. Syrena's blood was still burning with warlike aggression, and that was shown plainly upon her face.

The king looked back to his lords and officers. "So be it." He said. "Let's get this field secure and the engines ready. I want to finish this as soon as possible." He turned to move closer to his wife but stopped. "Any word from Minimoto?"

General Miralda stepped closer. "The commander sent word that he was seeing to the trade roads to make sure we don't find any resistance at our backs." She said before bowing.

Gabriel grinned. "Good, then let's finish here and return as soon as we can. We have good news that in a few days we'll be able to assault the wall with our full strength. Let's make this time between now and then worth it."

The lords and officers bowed and left the tent, leaving Syrena and Gabriel alone. Syrena pulled Gabriel close and into her embracing kiss. This night, the fires burned too hot to ignore.

The days dragged on but finally the trebuchet was built. No special name, like those in years past. King Gabriel thought it poor taste. His reasoning was the purpose was not meant to be whimsical, but a machine to bring death. Death needed no other name.

King Gabriel stood next to Captain Constantine, the son of Manor-lord Jacob Pavia. He was a tall, lanky man with a thin blond beard. More of a scholar than a soldier, and Constantine had not gone to the War

Academy like the other officers had. Instead, he had apprenticed as an engineer with the dwarves in Panyakuta. As the third born son, no one had expected him to be a fighter, rather a builder. However, when offered a position in the king's army by Miralda, a woman with an eye for talent, he accepted the role. Newer and stronger forts were now dotting the landscape of the kingdom.

"At your command, sire." Constantine said as the two men overlooked the city.

"It will reach?" Gabriel asked. He was ready. Not only for the trebuchet to fire, but also for the following battle. His chain mail and surcoat ready for yet another battle. Gabriel tucked his nasal helm under his arm but he still wore a chainmail coif.

"Yes, sire. It will reach and it will be devastating." Constantine said. He was confident in the work. His calculation and calibrations had been double and triple checked. Everything was in place as it needed to be.

Constantine also knew the smaller trebuchets, had been operating for days. Some damaging from those machines was already being seen along the north wall. The captain sent battering and siege rams down to weaken the gate, with little effect.

Gabriel breathed a sigh. "Let it fly."

Constantine raised his left arm and then dropped it. An order behind the two was yelled and then the large, wooden apparatus creaked to life with knocks and springs sounding. A soldier knocked a heavy bolt out of the gear under the large beam, springing the mechanism to life and dropping the heavy counterweight at the end of the beam. The trebuchet's beam lifted up and brought a sling with the heavy payload along with it. The boulder flew out of the sling and towards the wall.

Constantine and the king watched it sail through the air for a moment before it crashed against the wall. He could see some rubble fall from the wall. Gabriel smiled and patted Constantine on the back.

"Well done." The king said before turning back to the camp. "A few more of those shots and we'll be in that city in no time." He said as he walked off.

Constantine watched as the king walked back to camp. He bowed, as was custom, though the king didn't see it. However, Constantine was happy to know that his machine worked and in the king's presence too.

Hours of trebuchets pounding the wall of the city turned into days. The walls were weakening, but not fast enough. Even with the new, large trebuchet, it wasn't enough. Not yet, at least. They still needed time. Now, if there were another four large trebuchets, then and only possible, the siege could end quicker. Another was being built, but that would take time and a massive amount of lumber. For now the siege was wearing on, and that meant that warriors who had been away from home for months were to be away for even longer. That hurt emotionally and camp life, for the Lotcalans, hurt physically.

The Amazons had perfected life in camps, almost to where they preferred such life. That was the image that Syrena had as she and Gabriel walked around the camp. She noticed the difference in how her legionnaires, what was left of them, sat and joked while the Lotcalans mostly kept silent and thoughtful.

"They should be happy to be here. It would be an honor to die in battle. My sisters, five thousand that joined me, number now around three hundred. But those that fell did so with great honor." Syrena said. "I'd die in battle if it were my choice." She said.

Gabriel shook his head. "I want to die in my sleep."

"That's boring." Syrena joked. She took Gabriel's hand and held onto it as they walked side by side.

"It might be boring, but it's peaceful." Gabriel grinned. "I've had enough of war for this lifetime."

Syrena nodded. She knew what he meant, and for her this war was worse than those that she had fought in before. It wasn't, however, though she knew that Gabriel had his own horror stories to speak of. If he ever felt the need to do so.

Later that night, Miralda was preparing for a morning raid along the wall. Scouts spotted troops riding out for provisions, and Miralda wanted to take advantage of the darkness.

Syrena asked that she take the baronial warriors with her. She agreed, but Miralda wasn't happy about it. The general did not fully trust many of the baronial warriors. She wanted trained soldiers, and these were not that. They were farmers, smiths and other craftsmen conscripted from the ranks of the baronies and tenants of the manors. Miralda respected their trades but not their martial skills. That was a deadly difference.

However, she was never one to disobey an order and her queen had given her one. Miralda rode at the head of the baronial forces. Several lords had joined her, including Baron Hardstone.

That the young baron had volunteered for the task was not lost on the general. To Miralda, Hardstone's involvement was to cement his reputation. Though he was following his father's orders, he retreated. That was something that Hardstone's were not known for, but the elder Hardstone was wise and knew that the barony would need him to continue on. Still, this tormented the young man.

Hardstone walked up to the general, but beside him was Lady Cwenwyth. Miralda sighed, knowing that the lady held a misplaced grudge over the general.

"My lord, my lady." Miralda said.

"No curtsy?" Cwenwyth said.

Miralda made a soft 'tsk' with her tongue, looking off to the side before answering. "I'm the ranking general of this army. As such, I bend only to the king and queen. In this role I am of the same level as the baron here." She finished, pointing to Hardstone.

Cwenwyth scoffed, but Hardstone stood steady. He knew the ranks, and he knew of the general's reputation. He wasn't about to risk her wrath.

"You are a lesser noble's daughter. A pawn for alliances." Cwenwyth said. "Your father has, what, six children, and you are the youngest?"

"That's right." Miralda replied. She tightened her gauntlet's strap on her right hand. Her housecarls stepped closer, but she waved them back. "Why are you here Cwenwyth?"

"I have a message from the queen." She smiled, pulling a sealed letter from her cloak.

Miralda accepted the letter, breaking the seal and reading the missive. She looked up to the two nobles.

"What are you playing at Cwenwyth?" Miralda said, and then she looked to Hardstone. "You too, what the hell are you trying to do? This is war! We don't have time for your games!" She finished looking to Cwenwyth.

The lady of the Manor of Highwind smiled. "When this is over Sigurd and I will wed and then we will petition for Gib to be added to our holdings."

It was Miralda's turn to scoff. "This isn't about lands. We are trying to settle this war and we might not even win with this final battle!"

"And that is why Sigurd will lead this army to the wall. I spoke to the queen and other barons and they agree that your lack of faith in our baronial army is detrimental."

"Lack of faith? I've been in each and every battle thus far, defeating rebellions so that this war can continue with us as victors, and you say I have a lack of faith?" Miralda crumpled up the letter. She approached Hardstone, matching him eye to eye. "This is a mistake. Don't expect me to come and save your ass!" She said to the larger man before walking off. "Let's go!" She said to her housecarls.

She could hear Baron Hardstone begin to move the baronial soldiers out of the camp. She kept her back to them as she walked to the king's tent. Several guards were there. They let her pass inside. There Miralda found the king sitting with Queen Syrena.

"Your graces." Miralda said with a bow once she was acknowledged. "May I ask why I was pulled from the attack for Baron Hardstone?"

Syrena stood up for her chair. "Of course you may. I pulled you when we determined that the king's army was needed elsewhere." Syrena replied. She took an empty goblet and poured some wine. "The king's army is maintaining the siege. We need your leadership here for that purpose." Syrena finished, handing the goblet to Miralda.

"The attack on the wall is part of the siege." Miralda responded, accepting the offered goblet. "I should have led that attack."

"Yes, you should have." Gabriel replied. "If we had another general here, or even a commander. They are away in other areas, fighting or maintaining peace." He sighed. "I haven't made the official announcement, but as you know because of the rumors, Lord Marshal Laoch fell in Fe." Gabriel stood. "I need a new Lord Marshal and that will not be General Argyle. Forgive me, I know he is your husband and a dear friend of mine, but he is too passive."

"He is." Miralda said. "But that's part of why I love him."

Syrena smirked at the comment, but Gabriel continued.

"You are the best soldier we have in the kingdom, skilled in strategy and physical prowess. Miralda, you are the only officer I can trust with this position. Will you accept?" Gabriel finished.

Miralda looked stunned. She heard that Laoch had been killed, and the loss grieved her privately. Lord Marshal Laoch had been her mentor, and many knew her as his best student. However, she never considered herself to be his successor.

"I can't, sire." Miralda replied.

"Why the hell not?" Syrena asked.

Miralda bowed and looked to the queen. "I'm a gentry-lord's daughter. Not a manor-lord and certainly not a baron. We are in a better position than most gentry-lord families, which is true. Many other knightly families are simple country knights with little lands or tenants. For the Holts, many forget that we are only a knightly family until times like this when we're made not to forget our place. Our standing, though much better than others, means little to this world. I'm a dame only if Baron Ironhand or the king deems it so."

"And I do." Gabriel said. He walked over to a table to the side of the tent and picked up a sword. It was an old sword meant to signify a noble rank. "All of this depends on our victory in many ways, but once that is assured, Elysia will be under our control. That will add nearly a third of our current lands to the kingdom. That is a lot of land to preside over. I would create three new baronies to help administer it like we do now. You and Argyle would hold one of those baronies but also rule over a larger portion of Elysia as a whole. You would be a duchess. Argyle a duke. The Duke and Duchess of Elysia." Gabriel presented the sword to Miralda.

Miralda looked at the king and then the sword. It was a one handed, double-edged blade with a fuller and a cruciform hilt. A brown leather grip and a jeweled pommel. She took the sword, tying it to her belt.

"Sire, I will honor you as your baroness. Creator willing, duchess." Miralda said with a bow. She lifted her head and then looked to the queen. "What of the letter and the baron's, your grace?"

Syrena lifted her finger, knowing the topic. "That was a ploy. Cwenwyth is not a friend of yours, and I see little use for her outside of her own lands. Honestly, she is little more than an afterthought for me. However, she wishes to wed Hardstone. The king might have words for that. I don't see the point in it except for her own greed. She has very transparent motivations."

"Lands and power." Miralda replied.

"Exactly. She will not be an easy one to deal with, I think." Syrena said, sitting back down. "My father and sister could handle things like this much better than I. Personally, I rather march an army there and subjugate them."

"That's been tried." Gabriel replied. "She's harmless for now. No one takes her seriously."

"Not yet, but she is vocal, and she disdains anyone who she feels is beneath her. She is an older minded noble with little appreciation for the modernization that you and your predecessors have started." Miralda answered.

Gabriel nodded knowingly. "It's true that the support from the Hardstone Barony was greater in the legends and tales of the past. They've grown inward as of the last couple centuries."

"They fear a centralized throne." Miralda replied. "We have to bring them to heel before they rebel."

"Let's finish this war before we start another." Gabriel said with a smirk.

Miralda bowed and left the tent. She knew she had to mobilize her standing army and then continue the siege. However, now she also knew she had to do as little damage as possible to the city. It would be her city soon!

Baron had pushed through what was left of the minimal defenses outside the wall and entrenched his forces. Rain saturated the ground from days of heavy downpours that had yet to let up. It weighed his men down by the extra load of water soaked clothing and the mud they had to shovel. Still, the army was hardened and ready. Many were from other baronies and they were not used to the same sort of treatment that the Hardstone soldiers were. Many were grumbling.

"It doesn't help that the wall is still standing and we have arrows raining down upon us!" Manor Lord Strongmotte said as he stood under a makeshift lean-to with Baron Hardstone and Manor Lord Greywood. "Our men can't break this wall down with rams and mangonels. We need something stronger."

"Don't you think I know that?!" Hardstone shouted in frustration. He looked around and saw his own equipment, some broken down and stuck in the muddy ground, try in vain to break through the wall. "This king is pushing us to attack a wall that has stood for centuries. It's a suicide venture."

"Speak lightly of your king, boy." A voice said from behind Hardstone.

The lords turned to see Baron Canton walking to join them.

"King Gabriel has powerful allies now." Canton continued. He wiped rain water off of his sleeves. "King Ahab did little to us lords while our king, the man who'd rather play ranger in the forests, comes and tries to treat with foreigners. A host of them showing up and just before the war began."

"What are you saying, Lord Canton?" Greywood asked.

"It's nothing, I'm sure." Canton said, waving off an invisible question. "Odd though to think about it." He replied. "The king returns home and shortly after a small contingent of Amazons arrive, one to marry. A fine choice for a wife of a nobody prince but then we hear a tale that an Amazon treats with the kings of Fe and Elysia, starting this war? That is an unfathomable coincidence. Then again, I've always been a worrier."

"You think he set all this up?" Hardstone asked.

Canton shook his head. "I think he used this as a chance to make us irrelevant." He turned away from the lords for a moment and then turned back. "Then again, more than one of his ancestors gained the throne through devious means."

"Like your ancestor, Queen Sirie." Strongmotte responded, reminding Canton of his and the king's shared ancestor.

Canton smirked and grimaced at the man. All knew the story of Sirie and the legend of how she became Lady of Estan and then Queen of Lotcala. Several people disappeared during her rise to the throne.

"So you see it runs in the family." Canton shot back in reply. "We have to win this war, we all agree on that and the king does as well. What we won't agree on is what happens after. I heard of a plan that he has to create three new baronies, installing minor lords to those positions. Strengthening his own personal army and loyalties with titles."

"Rumors." Hardstone said in response.

"Are they?" Canton countered, looking at the young baron. "The king gifted general Miralda the Sword of the Marshal. She is the new Lord Marshal, which means she can now lead baronial armies. A gentry-lord's daughter leading baronial men?" Canton shrugged when none of the men seemed to be too bothered. "I guess you all don't mind her and General Argyle, another gentry born, being named the Duke and Duchess of Elysia?"

"Duke?" Strongmotte questioned. "That's never been done."

"It will be now." Canton answered before he walked back to his tent. He turned back. "If we win, of course." He finished.

The men watched Canton return to his tent thirty or forty yards away. Strongmotte looked to Hardstone.

"We have to win. We've put ourselves here and there isn't much in the way of a retreat." Strongmotte remarked.

Hardstone solemnly nodded before kicking a stone at his foot. He couldn't help but feel slighted like other lords were sure to feel, but that would have to wait until after the war was over. Then, and only if they won, would it matter.

For their part, Elysia sent out regiments of warriors, armored for heavy fighting and with the goal of breaking the offensive push led by Baron Hardstone. It was difficult, and the muddy trenches dug into the field were becoming places worse than hell. The wall was still standing and now with the Elysian counter attack, the Lotcalans were pushed further back.

When they were just one hundred yards away originally, Hardstone's forces had been moved back to three hundred yards. Now he was within sight of the king's camp.

"Move out and strike at them!" Hardstone ordered.

The army had to push back and move during the night, trying to regain hard fought ground that wasn't bearing any real fruit. Instead, the baronial army was suffering heavy losses and their growing weariness was becoming apparent. A weariness that if left unchecked could grow into open rebellion. However, Hardstone and the other lords would not let up and push after push left more of the Lotcalans bloody and beaten. Some ground was gained, however, and the Elysians retreated back into the city. A few regiments remained on the field and they dug themselves in the open trenches that the Lotcalans had earlier abandoned.

The battle upon the field outside of the walled city of Gib was as furious as any that the war had yet seen. Fighting along the outer walls, stopping the push of siege equipment other than trebuchets, was bloody and slow going for the Lotcalans. Fire blazed atop broken down battering rams and portable palisades. Trees, once green with leaves and ripe with fruit, burned, dripping tar and ash in a sad display of humanity's worse actions. Beneath the trees were even worse signs of the evidence left by mortal kind's penchant for war. The dead sunk into the wet ground while soaring boulders flew over the bodies, crashing against the ancient wall.

Captain Constantine and Ino let fly every large payload of rocks and rubble they could find at the city's wall. The wall showed few signs of damage no matter the amount of stones and boulders hurled at it. The infantry on the ground kept the fight intense as the Lotcalans tried to charge at the garrison of the earthen fort that lay in front of Gib.

Ino and Constantine still had one trick, several casks of a black powder from the free cities in the east. It was explosive, and it could bring a stone wall down in a matter of seconds. The true drawback of the powder was its nature. It was a highly volatile material. It was stored in terra-cotta pots, wrapped in burlap and then tucked away in wooden casks. Much like the way they stored liquid fire.

"Send a load with a pot of the powder to the wall. Count it out and I'll cut the wicks." Ino said to

Constantine. "With your monster here, we can send these pots of fire soaring, burning anything they touch, but with the wicks we can make them explode at just the right moment."

Constantine pulled the level, cranking the beam back and the counterweight in position. He let the mechanism spring forward, the beam shooting up, dragging the heavy payload in the sling behind it. Once the beam reached its apex, the load flew out of the sling. The large pot of black powder flew for a moment before crashing into the wall.

"Twenty-five seconds." Constantine said, walking back to Ino.

Ino looked at the captain and then to the trebuchet. "From the apex to the wall?"

"Yes, another two from the time the lever springs to the apex."

Ino nodded. "Twenty-seven second wick then." She turned to her fellow artillery members. "Cut the wicks to burn for twenty-seven seconds."

Ino's soldiers went to work cutting cloth wicks and rubbing them in the black powder to make fuses for the pots.

"What is the powder made of anyway, Constantine?"

The Lotcalan captain smiled. "Simple concoction of coal, sulfur, and saltpeter. The sages in the chapter houses discovered it from the southern mages. This will help the liquid fire burn at a higher temperature and it should vitrify the stone."

"Melt the stone?" Ino asked.

Constantine nodded with a grin. "For a fire to burn so hot it has to reach temperatures far beyond a smith's forge. Twice as hot and for twice as long." Constantine looked to the stores of powder and liquid fire casks. "We have fifty wagons full of casks. We will need everyone to fire at a rate of a pot every ten minutes. This trebuchet will only fire every thirty minutes."

"Then why do so much if it won't work?" Ino questioned.

"The general is taking the rest of the army towards the city and will mount smaller trebuchets closer. She'll also take several wagons of each mixture and begin to bombard the walls." Constantine replied. "Add extra lime to the liquid fire pots. That will increase the chances of a high temperature and a longer burn time."

Ino nodded and walked off to ready the wagons.

General Miralda rode at the head of the army. Her artillery regiment had already rushed ahead to set up trebuchets. She was going to reinforce the soldiers and the provide relief for the baronial army. An army that she now had full control over.

Miralda arrived at the trebuchets and began unloading the wagons. She could hear the sounds of war from the south, the baronial army was still deep within the fight.

"Hardstone is having trouble." Manor-lord Hafmen commented.

Miralda turned back to the trebuchets. "We have a job to do, and Hardstone knew the risks. Begin the bombardment." She ordered.

Lord Hafmen hesitated, but then saluted and followed the order. Not long after, the first of the trebuchets cranked upward, sending deadly chemicals through the air on a collision course with the outer wall of Gib.

Constantine and Ino sent their own payloads high, crashing with the wall. Within an hour the wall was beginning to burn from the remnants of the explosive and flammable chemicals being shot at it.

"Not much longer now. I can see a flame spreading." Constantine said to Ino.

"Then let's not let up." The Amazon replied.

Beneath the flaming wall, Hardstones forces were struggling to keep the remaining Elysians at bay. Knowing they couldn't run back into a city beginning to be engulfed in flames, the Elysians fought with a greater ferocity. Hardstone couldn't keep up. Baron Canton was fighting to siege the western face of the city wall, but he was also having a harder time than he had anticipated.

Bruised and bloody Lotcalan warriors limped back to the trenches they had fought to win and found their comrades dead or dying. Above them, they watched as flaming pots of explosives soared and crashed into the wall. For four hours they watched and fought, watched and fought, until suddenly a great crash echoed across the field.

Miralda looked to the city and smiled. Constantine and Ino both grinned at their work. The city walls of Gib had finally fallen.

Once More for Glory!

The wall might have fallen, but the battle was not yet won. Miralda saw the wall break and a portion fall, but the army stayed in their place.

"Damn cowards!" The general cursed. She grabbed her helm. "We ride into the breach and bring the city to heel." She said to her housecarls.

At the king's camp, King Gabriel mounted his own steed. He looked to his wife, already wearing her armor and fastening her sword to her belt.

"I'll ride and meet Hardstone on the field. Miralda is riding to secure the breach. I'll meet her there after I arrive." Gabriel said to Syrena. "Canton is still sieging the wall and could breach the western face."

"Gods willing." Syrena replied as she mounted her horse. "I have some legionnaires left and we'll fight alongside Miralda."

Gabriel shook his head. "I don't want you to go out there." He said, looking to his wife with worry in his eyes.

"You wish to stop me from fighting?"

"Even if I could, I wouldn't. It is who you are." Gabriel replied. He snapped the reins of his horse and rode off with a hundred men at arms following him.

Syrena turned her own steed and rode out with her soldiers to meet with Miralda.

King Gabriel rode hard and fast to the Hardstone camp, but found the conditions in shambles when he finally reached it an hour later. The baron was sitting in the trench, but none of his own soldiers moved.

"My lord!" Hardstone said, standing up to greet the king.

"You've seen the wall fall?" Gabriel asked.

"Aye, my lord, we've been waiting for more men. We can't take it with what we have here." Hardstone replied. He motioned around him. "I've lost over half of my own force, and Strongmotte is further down with Lostwood's force. They've taken even heavier loses." Hardstone continued. "My lord, I'm afraid this siege is turning against us."

"We have to push on through." Gabriel replied. He clasped the shoulder of the young baron. "That breach is our chance. Baron Canton is on the western face trying to storm the ramparts. With his force..."

"Canton fell and the Elysians wiped his army out this morning. A rider just brought the news." Hardstone interrupted the king.

"What?" Gabriel gasped. "He had nearly two thousand warriors. Surely some made it to your camp?"

"A few stragglers, my lord. Fewer than seventy five." Hardstone answered. "Canton threw everything at that wall and was defeated each time. His rider said that the last they saw Canton, he had an arrow in his neck."

Gabriel stiffened. "Then we lead the charge from here. I have one hundred men, you have how many?"

"Seven hundred outstanding warriors left, my lord." Hardstone replied with pride.

"We charge the wall when Lord Marshal Miralda's force reaches us. We past them on the way and she is marching with five thousand strong."

Hardstone saluted his king with a bow. The two looked to the wall, the breach was still flaming, but the smoke clouded the field.

"We don't know how many are on the other side, my lord." Hardstone said.

"More than what I want to face, but face it we shall." Gabriel smiled to Hardstone.

The day wore on and soon Lord Marshal Miralda joined Hardstone and the king near the Hardstone camp.

"We've got to hit that breach now." Miralda remarked as she met with the two men.

"I agree, but it will be a bottleneck for certain." The king said in reply. "We need to have a plan."

"Those damn Elysians have been tough to defeat and now they are dug in and with each minute they have more time to mount a defense." Miralda countered. "Allow me to take our forces in. I have five thousand of the best trained warriors on the continent. Professional soldiers."

Hardstone scoffed. "Where were you these past few days?"

"Breaking that damn wall!" Miralda shot back.

"Throwing rocks while we died out here!" Hardstone responded angrily.

"I told you not to leave without me!" Miralda shouted.

Gabriel stepped in between the two. "Enough!" He said. "We have to go now. Hardstone ready your warriors and we'll make our charge."

The baron nodded and bowed before walking back through the trench, rounding up his men.

"Is it wise to take his men?" Miralda asked.

"Seven hundred more men and we'll need every single one." Gabriel answered.

Queen Syrena rode up to the battered and exhausted infantry. They all saw the ramparts fall from the successful barrage from Constantine and Ino's heavy artillery. However, there was little elation. These men, several hundred to almost a thousand, sat near the hill that the artillery camped on. There in Elysia, for almost two full weeks, the infantry fought outside the wall and the breach was just another battlefield waiting for them. At this moment they put the war on hold. They had little desire to continue on. For these infantry men fighting, marching and dying, this was a nobleman's war.

That was plainly etched upon the face of every man that Queen Syrena looked up, sitting atop her horse, her boar skin draped across her back. She too was bloody. The war had stained her once shiny muscle cuirass with blood and mud. Its sheen now gone. Some plumage of her helm was missing, ripped out or torn, and the helm feature two prominent scrapes along the side. She gripped her spear, covered in blood, blood that had run down her arm as she held her spear, now dry. Her arm was bandaged, wounded and in pain. Yet, she still held her spear aloft. The men, the infantry that had been ordered to fight in two countries in as many months, saw her and saw her current state. The nobles, the king and the queen, had marched those men to exhaustion by her husband and yet she was there now to implore them, to fight more, to die more?

For her there was no bow, no courtesy. Not in the trenches.

"Where is your leader?" Queen Syrena called out.

One man nearby pointed to a man lying on his back with blood dried on his face. She knew the face of Manor-lord Strongmotte. Another casualty of the war. Syrena ordered two of her legionnaires to move his body to the wagons before turning back to regard the soldiers in the trenches.

"Men, ready yourselves! We move into the breach!" Syrena yelled aloud.

More than a few groaned. Many ignored her. She was a foreign queen, after all and they were exhausted from the constant fighting. Syrena stiffened herself.

One man, a yeoman wearing a tattered tunic with the gentry-lord sigil of Longmane from the Lostwood Barony upon it, stood up and faced the queen. "Your grace, we are too few to face such a hoard that waits for us. In those walls there are trained warriors from Elysia, Gota and Fe waiting for us poor farmers and artisans." He motioned around himself. "We are not warriors from the King's Army. We are conscripts from the baronial lands just wanting to return to our families or what's left of them."

"Lotcalans! Brothers!" She called out from atop her horse. She removed her helm and tucked it under her arm. "I ask you to think not of your birth, for I do not think of mine. However, my thoughts are of your deeds now. I see and know your pain and your sacrifice!" She continued as a crowd gathered around her. "If I could but take away all of your pain and suffering of each moment before now I would gladly do so. For what can a queen do for her countrymen but be their mother. You men that have accepted me as your queen. I, your sister from Amazon, and that sisterhood dates back to the days of the conquest. For me there is no greater honor than to be your queen, your mother and your sister. Nay, the only greater honor I have is that today I am here amongst you, shedding blood with you. For our blood is bonded like no others can ever claim. For whosoever follows me into that hell beyond their broken wall will be my blood brother! We shall march into glory no others can claim! You tired, broken but never beaten men will be nobler than any of the barons, lords or gentry!" The men cheered at her words. By now many were standing.

Syrena continued on, looking upon each of their faces. "Today, I am not your queen. No, today I rank among you as protectors of the Kingdom of Lotcala. Today I ride not behind you, but with you as a blood sister, willing to take a sword through my heart for each of you. I seek only the brave to march with me today. For today." she pointed with her spear throughout the crowd. "For today, commoners, yeomen, and husbandmen, I seek you this day to show the world your stock. Would you return to your wives and children, fathers and mothers, showing them that you left the battlefield at the time of your king's greatest need? That you left your queen to ride beyond the wall alone? No! You will tell them that you joined your queen and saw glory this day! For this day, should we live, will be the day that will be spoken of for generations to come, and when they speak of this day, it will be you men that they cheer for! Our lives, our glory and our victory!" She yelled, thrusting her spear into the air.

The crowd around Syrena roared and cheered. They donned their armor and helms, picking up their swords, shields and axes to march alongside their queen. To march through the gates of hell and into glory!

They climbed out of the trenches and over the manmade earthen mounds and stormed toward the breach. Syrena dismounted and ran alongside the Lotcalan warriors. Her spear point glistening in the midday's sun. The first day in weeks without rain. What was left of her legionnaires, including Mestra, Ino and Nyx, followed their queen and new brethren. It was the final push, the last charge and the final battle.

Gabriel and Miralda watched as the queen led the charge of the combined Lostwood, Strongmotte and Greywood army. They had lost so many brothers, it was hard to muster the strength, but something in the queen's words encouraged them. That was the spark they needed, and after seeing the queen charge into battle, the king was encouraged as well.

Gabriel roared a battle cry, raising his sword high in the air, rallying his warriors. He stormed out of the trench, followed by Miralda and Hardstone. The dash to the breach wasn't as treacherous as the fighting on the field had been, but once atop the rubble, the Lotcalans saw their new battle. Waiting for them on the city side of the wall was the remainder of King Ahab's army. Thousands of angry, tired and near shell shocked warriors desperate to defend their homes to the death.

The siege had lasted for a month since the first Lotcalan troops arrived prior to the king. Though their food and water stores had sustained them and were continuing to sustain them, the fear of a larger army, when none had been expected to arrive, drove the populace to run or hide.

For the Lotcalans, climbing up the pile of rubble was much more grueling than they had expected. For the last month, they had waited for the walls to break.

The barons from Lotcala tried to storm over the walls with their siege towers, ram the gate down and knock it down with large boulders. Nothing had worked until Captain Constantine and Ino combined their potent chemicals to the payloads. That enabled the trebuchets to send the devastating force needed to enter the city, and enter it the Lotcalans did.

Syrena and her force of baronial conscripts reached the zenith of the wall's rubble first, tearing down in a violent clash. The Amazonian princess, who dismounted her horse at the beginning of the charge, led her new brothers, her spear already bloody with a fresh kill. She thrusted her spear into the flesh of another Elysian defender. Soon, however, the Elysian numbers grew near Syrena. More than ten warriors moved toward her, swords and cudgels drawn, ready to strike the warrior woman. The Lotcalans behind their queen rushed to her side, protecting her and fighting off any that got too close. Blood splattered over surcoats and mail, soaking cloth and staining the iron.

Gabriel crested the rubble with his force of warriors. By this point, however, he found it congested with men already engulfed in battle. He felt a punch from a mailed glove on his left cheek. Gabriel was staggered, and he stumbled to his right. He recovered and rushed with his shoulder to his attacker. Both men fell to the rubble beneath them. The force of the collision was enough for Gabriel to let go of his sword. He fumbled with the Elysian man underneath him, until he gripped a rock that he could grasp firmly enough. Gabriel pushed the chin of the man down, trying to pull away from him. The Elysian tried to claw at the king, doing his best to keep the king's hand with the rock away from him. Gabriel's position above the man was the advantage that he needed and he used it to attack with the rock, smashing it into the face of his attacker. Finally, the king returned his attention to the battle.

Trebuchets still slung payloads of rocks and burning bundles over the wall and down onto the city. General Miralda, pulling her sword from a lightly armed Elysian, groaned seeing the burning homes. She pulled a soldier close by.

"Run up to the trebuchets with a message!" She said to the soldier. "Tell them to stop firing those damned machines. They'll hit us or bring this down atop of us!" Miralda roared, letting go of the man.

The soldier rushed off to the camp. Miralda went back into the battle, slashing her swords down on an approaching warrior. It would be an hour before the artillery barrage would end, but the battle continued within the city.

King Gabriel's soldiers had taken the breached wall, but the city was not falling as easily. Though the wall was not an easy task. Numbers won that part of the battle, but the city's inner workings were from a smaller compound. Not heavily fortified, but the bulk of the Gota had remained near the city center, surrounding the king's palace.

King Ahab thought that an alliance and the treachery of a disloyal Amazon would help him win the war. He gambled that the Lotcalans and Amazons were tired of war. While that was the case for some conscripts of the baronial army from Lotcala, now they were encouraged and motivated but recent victories. The battle raging outside of his palace cemented their resolve. Ancient cousins were not enough to stop the Lotcalan push. Gabriel led the army against the remnants of the Gota mercenaries and their shieldwall. Defense mangonels were turned and used to pound the outer wall of the palace compound and the palace itself.

Hardstone fought at King Gabriel's side. Both men, young and full of vigor, took charge on the first line of their own wall. Hardstone, spear in hand, stabbed over the wall of heavy wooden shields. He struck several Gota, weakening the defenses.

Soon the fight was becoming one sided. Manor-lord Blacktower led warriors to the eastern side of the compound with ropes and hooks, tossing them to the top of the smaller wall. There they could climb to the ledge and assault the guards from the same level. Blacktower was a capable and experienced, leading hardened warriors, killing any Elysian that confronted them. His sword, a crucible steel sword named *Siren's Wail*, flashed in the setting sun light. He used it effectively, cutting down enemies, and piercing the leather and heavy cloth of the guards. The beautifully patterned blade showed little signs of blood from its victims.

"Move to the gatehouse!" Blacktower ordered before spying the Gota in charge of the guards.

He was a large man, taller than Blacktower and younger than the lord.

"You haven't won yet!" The Gota man yelled.

Blacktower smiled under his conical helm. "Haven't we?" He gripped his sword tightly. "My men will soon have the gate open and my king will kill yours."

The Gota warrior shook his head. "Maybe you'll win here, but this is war begun centuries ago." He pulled his axe from his baldric and pointed it to the palace. "He isn't our king. Our king is coming. He'll right the wrong that was done to us by your king's ancestor. First, however, he is taking back our homeland and then we'll take yours here."

The Gota warrior rushed toward Blacktower, who dodged and guarded a strike with his sword. Blacktower moved forward, side stepping the man. He slashed at the Gota warrior, cutting him along his back. He moved in a step and took another slash, severing the man's spine. The Gota fell forward and rolled on his back.

He grimaced as Blacktower stood over him. "What is your king planning for us?"

"Death." The Gota wheezed. "Death and fire. Vengeance."

Blacktower looked down at the battle. His men had successfully taken the gatehouse and the king's army, along with the baronial soldiers and Queen Syrena, were pouring into the palace compound.

"Godspeed to whatever afterlife you claim." Blacktower said before sinking his sword into the Gota man's heart.

Blacktower turned toward the palace and watched as the building burned. The surrounding city was aflame and in a fury of the battle. He knew it would be days if not weeks before the city would settle. Not a simple task.

The Uneasy Consequences of War

"They're children!"

"They're royal children with a very legitimate claim to the throne you just conquered."

King Gabriel put his head in his hand. He wasn't sitting on the throne. He refused. It was a king's throne, but not one he wanted. Instead, he named Miralda the Duchess of Elysia, telling her it was her throne. However, the pressing concern was Ahab's two young grandchildren.

The Lotcalan army executed Ahab after they won the battle. That deed was expected and with little ceremony. The older king refused to leave the palace during the war, and he kept his family close by. His three sons were dead. Two died during the battle, their bodies recovered and placed in the family crypt. The third had been executed along with King Ahab. However, Gabriel was torn on what to do with the youngest members of the family.

"I won't order the deaths of anyone that can't swing a sword." The Lotcalan king said, standing from the step he had been sitting on. "The sins of King Ahab shouldn't extend to them."

"No, we do not carry the sins of our fathers but we have to remember that these two are now a threat to anyone trying to establish a new Kingdom of Elysia." Miralda said. "I will not have your kingdom or your life threatened. I'll do it myself."

"Not if I don't order it." Gabriel countered.

Miralda sighed. "Sire, this is officially the Dukedom of Elysia now, under my jurisdiction, and this is a civil matter. Not something that the king should concern himself with."

"It involves royalty." Baron Hardstone interjected. "That would make the matter a kingly one."

Other nobles in the room agreed with him with nods and words of affirmation.

Miralda rolled her eyes. "So be it. Then what do we do with the Elysian lords that are still alive?"

"Where are they now?" Syrena asked as she entered the throne room.

Miralda, along with the other lords, bowed to the queen. The general stood and answered her queen. "In the cells beneath the barracks, guarded by several king's army warriors and a couple legionnaires that volunteered."

Syrena nodded. "And the children?"

"We're debating that. For now they are in the room back there." Gabriel answered, pointing to the royal quarters behind the throne.

Syrena smiled to her husband, seeing his distress over the debate. "Whatever happens to the lords needs to happen after you decide on the children. If it is discovered that we have spared them, we'll have no peace."

"Peace?" Gabriel remarked. "No, with them alive, I'll never win this war, will I?"

Lords and officers around the room solemnly shook their heads.

Mestra stepped closer to the king and Syrena. "My lord, if I may." She bowed and continued once Gabriel nodded to her. "If it helps, there are spells that will... ease them into slumber." She stepped back when Gabriel grimaced.

"We have to announce it. Whatever the decision. It has to be known throughout the land." Miralda spoke up.

"Exile." Gabriel said.

"Sire, I think..." Mestra began again. "I have to agree with Miralda. This war will continue so long as the Elysians hold out to the hope of the princes."

"Any spells that offer diversions?" Gabriel asked. "We provide an illusion of their deaths and instead they are sent away to the farthest reaches of the world."

"A skilled mage will be able to tell the difference." Mestra answered.

Gabriel nodded. "Then I've made my decision. Exile and we'll deal with whatever happens in the future." The king looked to those in the room. "That's it, return to your duties and start dismantling this siege. We have to help the people return to their lives."

The nobles and officers all bowed and left the throne room, except for Syrena and Miralda.

"Miralda." Gabriel said. He stood at a window that overlooked the city, a burning city. "I entrust you with their exile. Make sure they can never return."

"Sire?" Miralda questioned.

"Perhaps, while traveling along the road, they come across bandits that are less merciful than I or their ship sinks. Pirates. Anything can happen in the world." Gabriel commented, never looking to her.

"I see, my lord." Miralda said before turning to the royal rooms. She stopped before opening the door.

"My lord." She said turning to the king. "A week should be right to make the announcement."

Gabriel nodded and Miralda left the throne room. Syrena stepped up to her husband.

"War and the consequences it presents to us are never easy." She remarked.

"Nor should they be." Gabriel answered. "Now we have to travel north to Ter Nog. More to deal with."

Syrena put her head on Gabriel's shoulder. "These days will pass and one day we'll be at peace."

Gabriel kissed his wife. He loved her outlook on their future. He was less certain, but her optimism helped him see the possibilities.

Judgement and the Future

The smoldering fields of Ter Nog laid barren. The damage was done weeks prior, and only now was the king coming to see the horrors that his own bannerman had wrought on the people. Here Gabriel saw firsthand the remnants of the terrible battle it was to keep Ter Nog free. Gabriel heard rumors and tales but nothing that seemed believable, yet the story was the same from multiple sources and here he saw the leftovers of the slaughter.

Standing outside the gates of the city stood the bannerman in question. Bulwyf was unarmed and without his chainmail. Flanked by two guards, he looked like he was being held captive. Bulwyf wanted the king to see that he wasn't a threat and that he was still his loyal man.

The king approached the men.

"My lord Bulwyf, can you explain to me what happened here? You buried the dead?" King Gabriel asked of his cousin.

"Sire, there is nothing here to say that you haven't already heard, and every word I'm sure is true or with at least a thread of truth. I executed rebels and used them in the defense of this city. We have given the fallen, all the fallen, rights for the afterlife according to both the old gods and the Creator."

Gabriel dismounted and approached his cousin. "You quelled a rebellion, and that I heard, yet all the rumors point to a massacre in my name. Yet, the bodies are gone. I see only the remains of a battlefield."

"My goal was to defend this city from attack from Isidore of Elysia. We thought, I thought, it prudent to bury the dead and not risk anymore ill from the spirits."

Gabriel nodded. "And that was done well enough. Did it require such a show of inhumanity?"

"The goal was victory at any cost."

"This was barbaric even for our ancestors." Gabriel paused and sighed. "What you've done, what you admitted, I did not want to believe. I thought that maybe they were lies sent to discredit you and to sow dissention, but I see that they were true. You've said so yourself in so many words."

Bulwyf remained stone-faced. "What I did, I do not regret. They were rebels, and I could not fight a war against them and Elysia at the same time. They followed Harbor, and so I decided on the best course of action for the situation."

Gabriel stepped away from his cousin as others joined them. Barons, officers, and the queen approached Gabriel's side. "You ordered the bodies of the executed impaled on spikes to deter Isidore. Did it work as you planned?"

"It did. He felt little strength to fight as he was famed for." Bulwyf replied without emotion.

"And did you execute children?"

Bulwyf nodded solemnly. "Yes, sire."

"Children." Gabriel said. He looked to Bulwyf. "That is something that I cannot pardon."

Syrena from behind, Gabriel spoke. "My lord..." But Gabriel cut her off.

"Executing rebels and war prisoners in a time of war is one thing that can be justified, but the murder of their families and their children has no place in this kingdom!" Gabriel roared. His anger was palpable, yet he calmed himself. "What else do you have to say for yourself, Bulwyf?"

Bulwyf looked his cousin in the eye. "I understand entirely that my actions during the defense of this city were inexcusable, and no matter the outcome of the battle, I acted with dishonor. My only request of the crown is to not punish my men. These actions were my own. They were unwilling accomplices to my plan from the beginning." Bulwyf bowed to the king.

Gabriel sighed. "I will take that into consideration."

Gabriel looked around the field, seeing his barons, lords, and other officers watching him. He knew that the legitimacy of his reign, his legitimacy, depended on his response to this crime.

Gabriel looked back to his cousin. "Lord Bulwyf, as king, I thank you for your service in defending this great city and the people loyal to the crown. However, I cannot, nor should I ignore how you quelled the rebellion. Furthermore, the barbaric tactics you used to defeat the Elysians, were tied directly into the execution of the rebels. What I can't say is the exact number of rebels and those that were innocent. That is your saving grace." Gabriel paused. "Bulwyf, you are stripped of your titles, estate, and you are hereby exiled from Lotcala for the period of ten years. The crown will hold your estate and land until your exile is complete and I deem you fit to return to your previous glory."

Gabriel continued the sentencing. "Bulwyf, you will leave this place immediately and return to you manor, under escort, where you will have one day to retrieve any belongings that you can carry on horseback. You will then leave this kingdom from Gib."

Gabriel paused again. His words were strained and his voice was breaking. "You have won a significant victory here in Ter Nog, but you tarnished your name for it. Your exile from Lotcala will end in ten years, but you are never to set foot in Ter Nog for the remainder of your natural life on pain of death." Gabriel reached out and pulled his cousin into an embrace.

The two men hugged.

"Forgive me." Bulwyf said between his tears.

"Return to us, cousin." Gabriel said.

"Sire, we cannot let such things stand with only a sentencing of exile!" General Miralda protested once the king had convened his court in Jovag. Her anger was on full display as the king's decision to exile Bulwyf was laid out for all to bear witness to.

The court, every baron appointed, and all the lords, including the gentry, were in attendance for the first official court of King Gabriel and Queen Syrena. This, however, was becoming a stressful day on what should have been a celebration. A delegation from Ter Nog, made of the leading families, had come instead of a baron. They were there to seek what to do next since their home barony was without its baron.

"Your grace, my name is Gerald Foehammer. My fellow merchants and I have come with concerns for the great city of Ter Nog. Concerns that echo Lord Marshal Miralda's concerns." One delegate spoke up when called upon. Others around him nodded and sounds voices of affirmation. The man who had introduced himself as Gerald was an older, gray-haired man, and his tone was even. Clearly a true merchant with years of negotiating experience.

King Gabriel looked to the group and motioned for them to approach. "This is the time to speak on such matters." Gabriel reassured the merchants.

Gerald Foehammer, dressed in the finest merchant wares, looked up to the king and queen on their thrones. "Your grace, Bulwyf committed such heinous acts against the people of the city, even those that admitted to being insurrectionist did not deserve to be used in such a manner." Others from Gerald's group gave replies in agreement.

Gabriel held up his hand. "The question before me is of the exile of Bulwyf. His exile stands, and that is the final word on the matter." Gabriel said firmly.

The man bowed. "Your grace, the people of Ter Nog mourn their former baron and the entire Harbor family. Our history, it seems, is fraught with tragedy from the ruling class. Perhaps now is the time to seek alternative paths of leadership for our home." Gerald cleared his throat. "Maybe, Ter Nog could have elected leadership, sire. Still under your rule, of course." He stammered to finish seeing the king's eyes narrow.

Gabriel leaned back in his throne. Rubbing his chin, he pondered the question. "We've had several lords fall in this last war. A couple lords with no heirs, even. Harbor was marked as one such baron. However, I'm uncertain that leaving such a city without central rule is the wisest decision." Gabriel stood from his throne. "I have two baronies left to appoint." He announced. "Both as far as they could be from this throne room. Gib and Ter Nog. The way I see it, both are great cities that deserve the best of barons.

Therefore." Gabriel smiled to Syrena. "Our first child will take the mantle of Baron of Gib and our second will take the mantle of Baron of Ter Nog!"

Most of the nobles in the hall cheered the news. Miralda smiled and clapped, but Gerald Foehammer and his fellow merchants seemed to be less than thrilled.

Gabriel held his hand up to silence the room. "Until such time, I and Syrena will act as regents. However, I will need help. A king can't be everywhere at once and that was a mistake past kings made." He said, walking down from the dais that his throne sat upon. "For the Barony of Gib and its regency during my time away and until our first child reaches adulthood, I ask for Duchess Miralda to act as regent and steward." He smiled to his friend.

Miralda smiled and bowed to the king. "I would consider it my highest honor, sire."

Gabriel clasped her shoulder before turning back to the merchants. "Gerald Foehammer, you are a successful merchant as was your father? A loyal man to the crown?"

"Yes, sire, I am in both regards." Gerald replied.

"Your father was a knight, was he not? Fought in the war with Tresha?" Gabriel asked.

"Yes, sire." Gerald answered. His chest rose slightly from the pride in his voice. "My father, Sir Godfrey Foehammer, led men during the siege of the city and he fell against the Treshans, my lord."

"Would you be willing to act as steward and regent during my absence from Ter Nog until such time that our second child, Creator willing, comes of age?

Gerald looked shocked. His fellow merchants whispered from behind him.

"Yes, my lord. Of course." Gerald finally answered.

Gabriel took his sword from his scabbard. "Kneel." He said the Gerald. The man lowered himself to his knees. "Gerald Foehammer, in the presence of these nobles gathered here in my hall, I charge you with loyalty to your lord, your king and the Creator. Do you swear to protect the kingdom and its people?"

"I do." Gerald answered with a bowed head.

King Gabriel placed his sword on Gerald's shoulders, one at a time, starting with the left. "I name you Sir Gerald Foehammer of the Gentry House Foehammer. Furthermore, I name you steward of Ter Nog and its regent during my absence from the barony and until the next baron comes of age. Rise Sir Gerald."

Sir Gerald rose from his knees, his smile wide. He returned to his fellow merchants as the hall went back to the duties of the court.

Syrena smiled to Gabriel from her throne. Life was still hectic and news from Fe was that rebellions would be common, but for now peace was within their grasp. The future was theirs create... with a helping hand, of course.

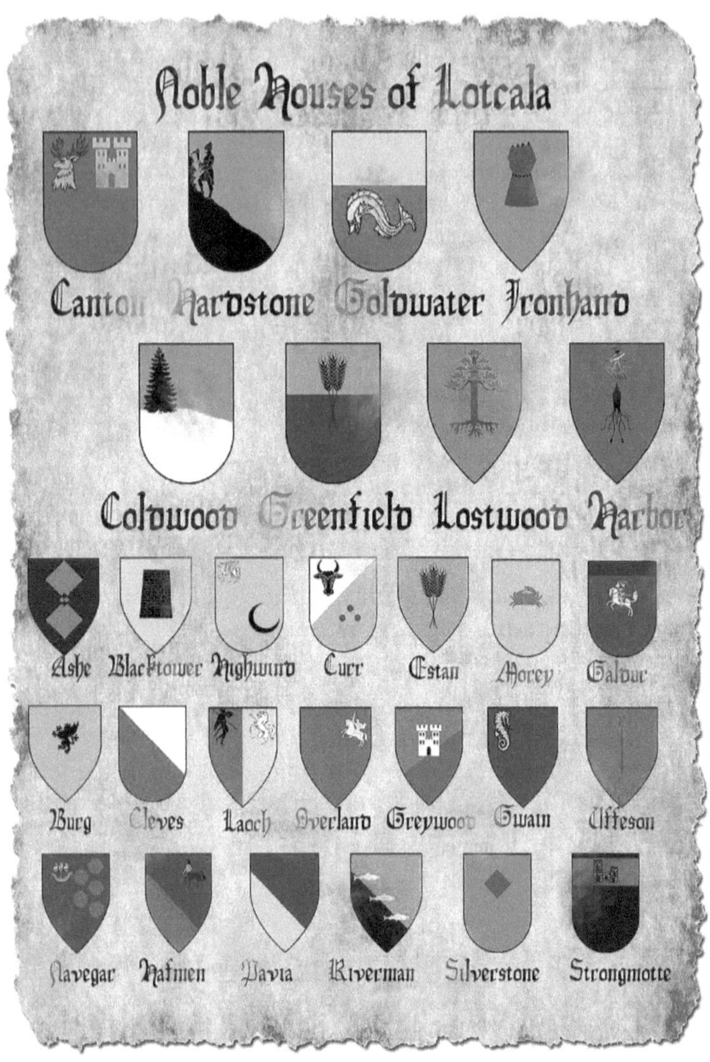
Noble Houses of Lotcala
Canton   Hardstone   Goldwater   Ironhand
Coldwood   Greenfield   Lostwood   Harbor
Ashe   Blacktower   Highwind   Curr   Estan   Morey   Galdur
Burg   Cleves   Laoch   Overland   Greywood   Swain   Ulfeson
Navegar   Hafmen   Pavia   Riverman   Silverstone   Strongmotte

River Docks
Moonstone River
Market Square
Motte and Bailey
Ruined Keep
Military Camp
Antei

About the Author

Joseph S. Samaniego is a historian from North Carolina specializing in medieval European History. He has a Master of Arts in History and has future plans to receive a PhD.

In his daily life, he is not only a Fantasy author with 5 titles to his credit, he also writes non-fiction and is a gifted fantasy cartographer.

When he is not spending time with his family, Joseph spends time reading, writing and playing video games.

www.ingramcontent.com/pod-product-compliance
Lightning Source LLC
Chambersburg PA
CBHW051553100726
47898CB00001B/79